MARY, MARY

ALSO BY ED McBAIN

The Matthew Hope Novels

Goldilocks (1978) Rumpelstiltskin (1981) Beauty and the Beast (1982) Jack and the Beanstalk (1984) Snow White and Rose Red (1985) Cinderella (1986) Puss in Boots (1987) The House That Jack Built (1988) Three Blind Mice (1990)

The 87th Precinct Novels

Cop Hater • The Mugger • The Pusher (1956) The Con Man • Killer's Choice (1957) Killer's Payoff • Killer's Wedge • Lady Killer (1958) 'Til Death • King's Ransom (1959) Give the Boys a Great Big Hand • The Heckler • See Them Die (1960) Lady, Lady, I Did It! (1961) The Empty Hours • Like Love (1962) Ten Plus One (1963) Ax (1964) He Who Hesitates • Doll (1965) Eighty Million Eyes (1966) Fuzz (1968) Shotgun (1969) Jigsaw (1970) Hail, Hail, the Gang's All Here (1971) Sadie When She Died • Let's Hear It for the Deaf Man (1972) Hail to the Chief (1973) Bread (1974) Blood Relatives (1975) So Long as You Both Shall Live (1976) Long Time No See (1977) Calypso (1979) Ghosts (1980) Heat (1981) Ice (1983) Lightning (1984) Eight Black Horses (1985) Poison • Tricks (1987) Lullaby (1989) Vespers (1990) Widows (1991) Kiss (1992)

Other Novels

The Sentries (1965) Where There's Smoke • Doors (1975) Guns (1976) Another Part of the City (1986) Downtown (1991)

ED McBAIN

MARY, MARY

WARNER BOOKS

A Time Warner Company

Warner Books, Inc., 1271 Avenue of the Americas, New York, NY 10020

W A Time Warner Company

Printed in the United States of America

ISBN 0-446-51738-0

Book design by Giorgetta Bell McRee

THIS IS FOR
Monaise and Angus MacDonald

MARY, MARY

1

She was in her late fifties, I guessed, a tall slender woman with gray hair and eyes the color of cobalt, wearing a pale blue smock stenciled above the breast pocket with the words CALUSA COUNTY JAIL. They had told me she wasn't quite all there, a sometimes foul-mouthed woman of eccentric habits and unpredictable ways, but she seemed very much with it on this sultry September afternoon at the beginning of autumn.

It was, in fact, difficult to imagine her in the role the local children had assigned, the "Mary, Mary, quite contrary" of the nursery rhyme, a bit of chanted doggerel that had become all too prophetic after the grisly discoveries three weeks ago. Sitting erect and attentive on the edge of her narrow cot, there was still a hint of rare beauty in Mary Barton's pale and faded face. There was, too, a persistent sense of elegance, strengthened by the lingering British accent in her voice.

The call from Melissa Lowndes had come at nine yesterday morning.

"I recognize the name, of course," Mary told me now. "But she was a child when last I saw her, and I can't understand her coming to my assistance so many years later."

"You knew her in London?"

The call had come from London.

"No, no," Mary said. "Well, not far from London, actually. I was teaching at a girls' public school in . . . it's the opposite in England, you know. Public is private. That is to say, a public school *is* a private school."

"Yes, I know."

"In any event, the school was in Lockbourne, St. Edward's Academy, a very fine girls' school. Melissa was one of my students. A delightful girl."

I was here because Melissa Lowndes had read about the murders in an international edition of one of the newsweeklies and had learned that her former teacher was to be represented by a public defender. She'd made some inquiries of friends in Palm Beach . . .

Actually, she'd said enquiries.

. . . and had learned that the two best criminal lawyers in southwest Florida were Benny Weiss and me. She'd called Benny first . . .

Everyone does.

. . . had discovered his plate was full at the moment . . .

It always is.

. . . and was calling me next to ask if I would agree to represent Mary Barton because she was certain the woman couldn't possibly be guilty of the heinous crimes attributed to her. Mary Barton had been charged with killing three young girls.

I told Miss Lowndes that I hoped Miss Barton was indeed innocent because it was my policy never to defend anyone I thought was guilty. She said she considered this rather odd since surely there was room in our criminal justice system for lawyers who defended people who merely *appeared* guilty—

"Yes," I said, "but I'm not one of them."

We'd never met in person, and had been talking on the phone for not quite three minutes, and we were already arguing. But by the end of the conversation, I agreed to visit Mary Barton in jail and to telephone Miss Lowndes with my decision.

I was here now.

And I asked the question I always ask in one form or another.

"Did you kill those girls?"

"No, I did not," she said.

"Do you have any idea how those corpses turned up in your garden?"

"No, I do not," she said.

"Three bodies buried in your backyard?" I said. "And you don't know how they got there?"

"And don't *give* a fuck," she said in her polite British voice.

Enter Mary, Mary, quite contrary.

"Why do you say that?" I asked.

"Because I really *don't* give a fuck," she said, in case I'd missed the point the first time around. "If someone planted those corpses in among my petunias, and if a telephone repairman dug up the yard and found those corpses, that has nothing to do with me. I had nothing to do with putting them there. And I don't give a flying fuck either way."

"Do you always use such language?" I asked her.

"Only when I'm irritated. This entire matter is irritating to me. I had nothing to do with killing those little girls. And I find positively disgusting the very idea of being incarcerated in a place where the toilet bowl doesn't even have a *seat* on it! If you plan to represent me, the first thing you should do is get me out of here."

"I'm afraid that's impossible," I said.

"Then go away," she said.

"The judge has denied bail . . ."

"The hell with him," Mary said.

"*Her,*" I said. "And besides, I haven't yet decided whether I *want* to represent you."

"Then don't waste my time, young man."

She was flattering me. I'm thirty-eight years old, which on my block is middle-aged; if you double thirty-eight, you get seventy-six.

"Tell me what happened," I said.

"When?"

"On the day they discovered the bodies."

"It wasn't *they*, it was *he*. Have you noticed that in our mad rush to construct a language that will accommodate ridiculous feminist demands, we've taken to using ungrammatical constructions? 'Everyone has their own favorite symphony,' a radio announcer will say. In an attempt to avoid the *correct* 'Everyone has *his* own favorite symphony,' which God forfend might be considered sexist. I used to teach English," she explained.

"I see," I said.

But she still hadn't explained the bodies in her backyard.

"A telephone repairman made the discovery, is that right?" I said.

The prompt.

I waited.

"Yes."

Briefly.

Hands folded primly in her lap, like one of the schoolgirls she'd taught years ago. Like one of the schoolgirls buried in her garden.

"Can you tell me the details?"

She sighed forlornly, rolling her eyes heavenward. She'd obviously been asked this question a hundred times already and was weary of reciting the answer. Virtually by rote, in a singsong voice smacking of British country lanes and revealing nothing but total boredom, she said, "Ten-thirty or thereabouts on Tuesday morning, the first day of September—what's today's date? One loses track of time in here."

"The twenty-first."

"Almost three weeks ago, then. I arrive home to find a telephone repairman in my garden, tearing up Jack, digging through flower beds and shell arrangements, searching for the cause of interminable static on the line, reported by dutiful neighbors. He comes upon something that should not be growing there. The something is the head of a young girl, later identified as seven-year-old Jenny Lou Williams of Somerset, Florida. The head is attached to the rest of the unfortunate girl's body. The telephone repairman comes screaming into the house asking if he can use the phone. Aren't they supposed to have portable things clipped to their belts? The police arrived ten minutes later. Two hours after that, my entire garden has been dug up, and they've uncovered two more bodies, and I'm placed in custody and dragged to what is euphemistically called the Public Safety Building, which lofty title cannot disguise what is a basic cop shop. End of recitation, give the student a generous A-plus."

"You seem somewhat callous about these young girls."

" 'Bitter' is the word you're seeking."

"Why?"

"I told you. I don't give a damn about them or the person who killed them. I've taken enough abuse since relocating in this Athens by the Sea . . ."

Sarcastically hurling back into Calusa's teeth its own promotional sobriquet.

". . . and I'm not overly thrilled by the ease with which the persecution of the innocent is now being extended. I did not kill those girls. You can take that or leave it, the choice is yours. You can also leave here if you don't believe me."

"Who were the responding officers?" I asked.

"Do you always avoid ultimatums?" Mary said.

"I'm trying to get at the facts."

"I'm trying to decide whether to call for the guard."

"I'll call him myself," I said, and rose and moved toward the thick bars that separated the cell from the corridor outside.

"Don't be so impetuous," she said. "Sit down."

Like the schoolmarm she once was.

I did not sit. I leaned instead against the gray wall upon which were scribbled the names of countless previous prisoners, a record of incarceration that went back months before Mary Barton's, and I looked her dead in those deep blue eyes, and I said, "I'm trying to be your friend."

"I have no friends," she said.

"Wrong," I said.

She blinked.

"Melissa Lowndes apparently feels otherwise."

"I hardly remember her."

"She remembers you."

"All the worse for her."

"Do you want to die?" I asked her. "The charges are three counts of first-degree murder. You're looking at the electric chair."

"I don't give a damn," she said.

"Did you use that kind of language when you were teaching school in England?"

"That was twenty years ago."

"Did you talk that way then?"

"I wasn't the same person then."

"Who were you?"

"I was Miss Barton."

"And who are you now?"

"Mary, Mary, quite contrary," she said.

"Tell me who responded. The names of the officers who responded."

"A fat fool in uniform was the first one, I don't know his name. All excited, he, too, uses the static-ridden telephone . . ."

Switching to the present tense again.

". . . to call his superiors downtown, they always have to call *downtown,* have you noticed that, though in Calusa there *is* no precise *downtown,* there is merely north and south and in between. The suits arrive some fifteen minutes later, a detective named Morris Bloom . . ."

"I know him."

". . . and his partner, Cooper Rawles."

"I know him, too."

"So do I. *Now.*"

"Did they question you?"

"Yes. Aren't they supposed to read me my rights?"

"Not until you're in custody. This was still a field investigation."

"Field is right."

"I'm sorry?"

"Well, not quite a *field,* but certainly a garden. The focus of all that attention, you see. Arms and legs sprouting like new plants among the blue sage and powder puffs, the bird of paradise, and . . . have you seen my garden?"

"No."

"A true wonder. The envy of townspeople for miles about."

I couldn't tell whether she was being sarcastic again. I let it go.

"What sort of questions did they ask?"

"Well, they are quite naturally all amazed," she said, shifting to the present tense again, and opening her arms and her eyes and her mouth wide to express wonder and awe; it suddenly occurred to me that she must have been a marvelous teacher. "And, quite naturally, they wish to know what I know about these moldering remains in my otherwise beautiful garden, a state of affairs for which I have no reasonable explanation. That's when they told me I had the right to remain silent and to . . ."

"Miranda," I said.

"Apparently," she said drily. "And clapped me in handcuffs and carted me off to the famous *downtown* we see in all the movies and television shows."

"Did they question you further there?"

"Only for an hour or so."

"Before formally charging you?"

"Yes."

"Just Bloom and Rawles?"

"I don't understand you."

"The interrogation."

"Oh. No. They called in an assistant state attorney."

"What was his name?"

"Hers. Patricia Demming."

"Mmm," I said.

This was not good news.

"What'd you tell them?"

"That I didn't know how those damn bodies had got in my backyard."

How to win friends and influence people.

"Why'd they charge you?"

"Because someone saw me burying one of the girls."

"What?"

"Or so she says *now*."

"Who?"

"A bimbo named Charlotte Carmody."

"Saw you *burying* . . ."

"Are you hard of hearing, young man?"

"When was this?"

"The night before the telephone repairman made his discovery."

"The last day of August?"

"Precisely."

"Saw you . . . ?"

"In the garden, baying at the moon while inhuming the body of Felicity Hammer, the youngest and most recent victim. The one at the end of the row, upon which geographical location the police premised their brilliant chronological deduction, the cocksuckers."

"But it wasn't you."

"It was not I."

"You did not bury that girl in your garden."

"I did not bury *any* of those girls in my garden."

"Do you know who did?"

She hesitated for the briefest tick of time.

Then she said, "No."

Our eyes met, held. Something in her eyes belied her outrageous manner. Her eyes said Help me. Please. Please help me.

"I want to look at your garden," I said.

"Are you taking the case?"

"Maybe."

The seasons come subtly in the state of Florida. The newspaper this morning had announced that tomorrow would mark the beginning of the autumnal equinox, but I was wearing the lightest-weight tropical suit I owned—and was sweltering nonetheless.

"Hey!" someone yelled. "You!"

A uniformed cop was coming around the corner of the cement-block house. Dark blue trousers, pale blue short-sleeved shirt, heavy piece holstered at his side, silver shield glittering on his shirtfront.

"What do you want here?" he shouted. "This is a crime scene!"

He came waddling toward me across the parched lawn, his black shoes dusty—we'd had no rain for the past three weeks, an unusual phenomenon for Calusa, where in September one could normally expect daily torrents at best and hurricanes at worst. He was a burly man with perspiration stains under his arms and across his chest, the irritated look of a redneck farmer on his face, all sweaty and flushed. Took his time, too, made his approach with all the smug assurance of an incumbent president, taking off his peaked hat and wiping his brow with a handkerchief he took from a back pocket.

"I'm an attorney," I said, and took a card from my wallet and extended it to him.

The cop put his hat back on, put his handkerchief back in his pocket, and only then looked at the card. Briefly.

"So?" he said.

"I've been asked to defend the accused."

"So?"

"I wanted to look the place over."

"I just told you it's a crime scene, didn't I?" the cop said, shaking his head in wonder at the stupidity of the citizenry he was forced to deal with day and night.

"That's why I'm here," I said calmly. "Because it's a crime scene."

The cop looked at the card again.

"Matthew Hope, huh?" he said.

"Matthew Hope, yes."

"Do I know you?"

"I don't think so."

"What makes you think I'm going to let you inside this house here?" he said, and jerked his head toward the building.

"I don't want to go inside the house," I said.

"No. Then what?"

"I want to see the garden."

"You and everybody else," the cop said.

"What do you say?" I asked, and resisted the urge to wink and nudge him with my elbow. "We're both on the same side."

"How do you figure that?"

"You're an officer of the peace, I'm an officer of the court."

"Then why you want to represent a crazy lady killed a half dozen kids?"

"I'm not representing her yet," I said.

"You just told me . . ."

"I said I've been asked to."

The cop looked at the card yet another time.

"You sure I don't know you?" he asked.

"You may have seen me around the Public Safety Building. I'm down there a lot."

"It's just you look familiar."

"In Morris Bloom's office," I said, finally dropping a name. "Detective Morris Bloom. He's a good friend of mine."

"Which don't mean shit to me," the cop said, but he was beginning to reconsider. "I guess you can take a look at the garden," he said at last. "Provided I stay with you."

"Sure," I said.

This was where Mary Barton had lived before they took her to jail.

A cement-block house painted white and sitting in a row of similar houses all up and down the street. From the front, you saw what must have been two bedroom windows, jutting with air conditioners that were silent now in the sultry September air. The entrance door between them was painted a blue as pale as the cloudless sky. Fences on either side of the house partially shielded it from the house next door. You walked around the side on a path fashioned of flagstones set too close together at regular intervals in the parched ground; I had to try hard to match my stride to the distances between them.

Mary, Mary, quite contrary, how does your garden grow?

This was what the children used to chant even before the bodies were discovered. It took but a moment to realize why. The garden came into view like some realized fantasy. There were flowers, yes, flowers in eye-dazzling abundance, angel's trumpet and bougainvillea, hibiscus and trailing lantana, coral plants and allamanda, and others I could not name, very few of them ever seen in such abundant display in the city of Calusa, where gardens were taken for granted and fishing was preferable to tilling the earth. Oh, yes, you could visit the newly refinanced, relandscaped, and renamed Luisa Cubero Memorial Gardens just off the South Tamiami Trail and witness there the ferns and ixora and candle cassia and queen's crape myrtle that grew in turbulent disarray here in Mary Barton's garden, but to find such an Eden anywhere else in the city was virtually impossible. So, yes, the flowers alone—the jungle of greens and reds and yellows and pale blues, the bursting radiance of blooms she had obviously tended and nourished through a drought that now seemed endless—these alone were reason enough for wonder and surprise. How, indeed, does your garden grow?

But rising out of this brilliant jungle was what appeared to be a magic kingdom to rival the one created by Disney across the state, except that this one had been painstakingly constructed from found pieces of flotsam and jetsam, tangled driftwood and spiraling shells, bottle caps and broken glass, pull-tabs from soda-pop cans, Christmas ornaments and lost earrings, all arranged in what looked like the turrets and minarets of a spectacular sand castle shining like a realized fantasy in the sun, around which and through which and over which the wonderful flowers and vines and leaves nodded and peeped and trailed along balustrades and arcades of wood and glass and shell and silver, yes, silver bells and cockleshells and . . .

Unfortunately.

. . . pretty maids all in a row.

The yellow crime-scene tapes were still up, stretching from live oak to coconut palm, defining the area where the graves had been found, the earth still open like an arid wound in the relentless sun.

"Something, huh?" the cop said.

"Something," I said, and decided in that instant to represent Mary Barton.

Because I could not believe that the woman who'd created this wonderland could also have murdered three young girls.

2

Melissa Lowndes came to my office directly from the airport. She'd arrived in Miami late the day before, had spent the night in the airport hotel there, and had taken an early commuter flight to Calusa this morning. A chauffeured rental limousine had driven her to my office, and she was sitting on the other side of my desk at ten o'clock that Wednesday morning, two days after I'd phoned to say I was taking the case.

She was obviously a woman of some means.

The dress she was wearing—fashionably short and revealing long slender legs, crossed now in a thoroughly businesslike manner—was a somewhat clingy blue wool jersey that might have served her better in a London swept by North Atlantic breezes. She was wearing more gold than I would have thought appropriate for a transatlantic plane ride, but she seemed thoroughly at ease with such a materialistic display. I particularly admired the gorgeous white-on-black cameo pinned to the front of the dress, and she explained that the piece was a Florentine work of art dating back to the twelfth century A.D., a gift from her former husband, a man named Elliott Rule whom she'd divorced last summer, reverting at the time to the use of her maiden name, which she much preferred.

All of this in a breathless British rush that was entirely enchanting.

Melissa Lowndes was in her late thirties, I guessed, a strikingly beautiful woman with cascading black hair that fell straight to her shoulders, almond-shaped brown eyes that gave her face a somewhat oriental cast, and a pouting lower lip that suggested a sulkiness entirely contradicted by her apparent openness and warmth.

"I caught the first flight I could," she said. "I'm afraid I didn't sleep well last night, but I wanted to talk to you before going to the hotel."

"Where are you stay—?"

"How is she?" she asked at once, and leaned toward me.

"Miss Barton? Fine. Well. Cranky. But fine otherwise."

"Cranky? Miss Barton?"

The brown eyes widened in surprise.

"I can't *imagine* her being anything but sunny and warm," she said.

"Well," I said.

The brown eyes searched my face.

"She may have changed a bit," I said.

Eyes still watching me intently.

"Since last you saw her," I said.

"That was a long time ago," she said.

"A long time," I said.

"I was just eighteen," she said.

Which confirmed my surmise about her age.

"St. Edward's Academy," I said, and nodded.

"Did she remember me?"

"Oh yes."

Well, not quite, I thought.

"She said you were a delightful girl."

Which was true. But she'd also said she wouldn't recognize her if she . . .

"I *was?*" Melissa said, sounding surprised. "I always thought I was a horrid little brat. She was so patient with me, you have no idea. But *cranky,* you say? Sunny Miss Barton?"

Sunny was hardly the word I would have used.

"Confinement often irritates people," I said.

"I can just imagine."

"Especially a free spirit like Miss Barton," I said, putting it as diplomatically as I could.

"Yes, she was always that. Sunny and warm and free and open, yes, a free spirit. A wonderful person to have known at that particular time of my life. I'm afraid my adolescence was an unusually stormy one," she said, and lowered her eyes as if in repentance, a gesture I found singularly false. I suddenly wondered just why she was willing to pay Mary Barton's legal expenses, and it occurred to me that I ought to explain what those expenses might come to; as the monkey said before urinating into the till, this could run into a lot of money. But a chauffeured limousine from the airport and a twelfth-century Florentine cameo seemed to negate such caution, so I decided to let money matters ride for the moment—thank you, I know all the lawyer jokes.

"You must be tired, I know," I said, "but when . . ."

"Still utterly exhausted," she said. "I find it impossible to sleep in airport hotels."

"But when you've had a chance to rest, I'd like to talk to you again. About Miss Barton. About what she was like when you knew her."

"All those years ago," she said, and her eyes seemed to go out of focus for a moment; she was either recalling the days of her youth or else falling asleep.

"Call me whenever you're ready," I said, rising and moving around the desk toward her, hoping to hasten her exit before she fell flat on her face. She rose as I approached, extended her hand, looked solemnly into my eyes, and said, "You won't fail me."

There was no question mark at the end of the sentence, no characteristically British rising inflection that often made *everything* sound like a question. This was a statement of fact. It may even have been a command.

I took her hand.

"I won't fail you," I said.

Ten minutes later, Patricia Demming called to offer me a deal.

I must explain that deals are common in American law; in fact, it is the rare case that ever makes it into a courtroom. But you must remember that most criminal lawyers are defending clients who are guilty as hell.

I am relatively new at this game and have been accused in some quarters of being somewhat starry-eyed where it comes to accepting a case. But as I'd told Melissa Lowndes on the telephone, and as I'm ready to tell any unsuspecting soul who is ready to listen, I will not defend anyone I believe is guilty of the crime as charged. There are enough lawyers out there who feel that copping a plea for a cold-blooded hatchet murderer is something of a triumph. I feel it's a travesty. So if you've killed your mother or your two innocent babes, don't come blab it to me. I will tell you to find another lawyer.

I wished with all my heart that someone hadn't allegedly seen Mary Barton burying a body in her backyard, but I believed nonetheless that she was innocent, and I was ready to do all I could to prove it. Patricia Demming felt she was guilty; the State Attorney's Office would not have taken the case to the grand jury if they'd felt otherwise. But this did not mean that Patricia—as she preferred being called, and God save the person who called her Pat—wasn't willing to cut a deal that might save the state a great deal of money. Trials, especially murder trials, consume an enormous amount of time. Time is money. Money is what most states in the United States do not have. Which was why Patricia Demming was on the telephone, congratulating me on having accepted the Barton case . . .

Did I detect a note of sarcasm in her voice?

. . . and then suggesting that we have dinner tonight to discuss a matter of mutual interest.

The only matter of mutual interest we shared at the moment was, in fact, the Barton case. Without putting it in so many words, she was telling me the state might be willing to offer a deal. We both understood the code. And since Calusa, Florida, is a friendly sort of town where legal adversaries can discuss even multiple murder over a few drinks and a sizzling steak, I agreed to meet her at Marina Lou's at seven-thirty that evening. Little did I know.

I had met Patricia a bit more than a year ago, when she'd joined the State Attorney's Office after an illustrious career that started in California and took her to New York. I'd crossed swords with her only once, however, while she was prosecuting what the newspapers down here had called the "Three Blind Mice" case. This was a witty reference to the fact that the victims had had their eyes gouged out and their penises surgically removed—ah, the creativity of our fine Calusa journalists. The case had never come to trial. Not because I'd accepted the deal Patricia offered me, which I had not, but because I finally uncovered certain facts that led . . .

Well, I'm normally modest and self-effacing, but I don't know any other way of saying I found the real killer. And, in the process, almost joined the list of his victims, which by that time had grown to five. In all fairness, Patricia was gracious in defeat. She may be a tough lawyer with a mind like a stiletto dipped in belladonna, but she is also an exceptionally beautiful woman who—when she chooses—can be utterly charming. That such occasions are rare is a fact more attributable, I'm sure, to the nature of her job than to her natural inclinations. A person can't prosecute three child abusers in a period of six months—which Patricia had just done—and still smile prettily for the television cameras.

She was smiling this evening when she walked into Marina Lou's.

Patricia is a tall and leggy blonde who enjoys a good deal of celebrity in this town where even a man belching on Main Street will get a standing ovation. Normally she appears on television news shows only infrequently, but she'd had greater exposure during her string of successful child-abuse prosecutions, and she walked now with the self-assurance even limited fame can bring. A sort of strut. No, not that. No. The cops in this town strutted, even the female ones. And most of your criminals strutted, as if they'd done something they should be proud of. Patricia's walk was more like the glide you saw on a high-fashion runway model, the confident . . . well, yes, *strut* that commanded attention, simultaneously accepted it as one's due, and at the same time denied having sought it. It was quite a trick, and she brought it off to perfection. Tonight, she was wearing a blue linen suit that matched the color of her eyes, causing them to seem aglow with icy fire—but that might have been due to the sun's position, low on the horizon and streaming sunshine through the long windows that overlooked Calusa Bay.

I rose as she approached.

"Hi," she said.

Every eye in the room was on her. The fearless prosecutor who'd just sent all those ugly sons of bitches to jail. The young star in the State Attorney's Office—well, thirty-six. Chosen by Skye Bannister himself to succeed him as the state attorney, provided the voters agreed, whenever he decided to make his expected run for the governor's mansion.

"Hi," I said.

We shook hands.

"Am I late?" she asked.

"No, no."

"Would a martini be too unprofessional?"

"Just what I was planning to have."

"Good," she said.

We both sat.

"Tanqueray," she said. "Up and very cold, a pair of olives."

The waiter sidled over. I gave him our drink orders—mine with Beefeater, and on the rocks, but with the same two olives—and we both turned to watch a forty-footer approaching the marina, her sails filled with wind and sunshine.

"I like this place better than anywhere else in Calusa," she said.

"It's where every real estate agent in town takes his prospects," I said.

"Or hers," she said.

"Or theirs," I said, remembering what Mary had told me about grammatical lapses.

"It's just beautiful," she said.

We watched in silence as the captain lowered his sails and began motoring in toward the dock. There's something very satisfying about watching a good sailor bringing his boat in. Or hers. Or theirs. Or the hell with it.

"Nice," I said.

"We should applaud," she said.

The drinks came. We raised our glasses.

"To justice," she said.

"Fair enough," I said.

We clinked the glasses together. We drank.

"Mmm," she said.

"Indeed," I said.

"Hard day," she said.

"You don't look it."

"I went home."

"So did I."

"Good. Otherwise we'd have frightened the horses."

I wondered about this. I let it go.

"So what's your deal?" I said.

"Oh, come on, Matthew," she said.

"Isn't that why you called me?"

"I called you because I wanted to sip a martini with you while we watched the sun set."

"Okay."

"But maybe we can discuss a little deal later on," she said, and grinned mischievously.

"The suspense is killing me," I said.

"Better you than your client," she said, and winked.

So that was her deal. She was ready to find a way that would allow us to sidestep the death penalty. Which wasn't bad if a person's client was guilty. Three times over, no less. But I did not think Mary Barton had done murder. Not even once.

The captain was throwing some lines ashore. Patricia turned to watch him again. She had a good profile and she knew it.

"You have a boat, don't you?" she said.

"Not a sailboat."

"What kind?"

"A nineteen-foot Grady-White."

"Ever use it?"

"Not so much these days."

"Too busy?" she said, and turned from where the sun was now staining the water a red so brilliant it looked like blood.

"My daughter used to enjoy it more than I did, actually. But she's away at school now."

"Joanna."

"Joanna, yes."

"I researched you."

"I remember."

"When I thought we'd be adversaries on the Leeds case."

She was referring to the Three Blind Mice case.

"I learned a lot about you. She's fourteen, right?"

"Going on fifteen."

"Very brainy."

"So they say."

"Like her father."

"Thanks."

"I met your wife last week. Your *former* wife. At a party on Whisper Key. Does your daughter look like her?"

"I guess. But she's blonde. Susan has dark hair. The last time I saw her, anyway."

"When was that?"

"Who remembers?"

"She's very beautiful."

"Thank you," I said, and wondered why. Susan was no longer my wife, why the hell was I acknowledging a compliment paid to her looks?

"She was with a very young man," Patricia said.

"Mm," I said.

"You disapprove," she said.

"It's none of my business," I said.

"Just checking," Patricia said, and grinned.

I wondered about this, too.

"Shall we order?" she said.

I figured I had to be mistaken.

Maybe this is a serious failing, but in a world of spectacularly handsome men, I think of my looks as only so-so, and I'm always somewhat surprised when a woman seems to be coming on to me. But wasn't it Queen Victoria who'd said that about the horses? And didn't it have a sexual connotation? Hadn't someone said something about some sort of alleged sexual misbehavior, and hadn't Her Majesty replied, "I don't care what they do, so long as they don't do it in the streets and frighten the horses"? Wasn't that Queen Victoria?

But, of course, Patricia hadn't been making a sexual reference. What she'd been talking about was the fact that we'd both gone home from work to shower and change before coming here. Otherwise, when one took into consideration Calusa's wilting September heat and humidity, we might each and separately have frightened not only the horses but the manatee. So how on earth could I have misinterpreted such an innocent statement?

And how could I have assumed further that Patricia had the slightest interest whatever in how I felt about my former wife, Susan, dating men younger than she, which was an understandable if slightly ridiculous thing for a divorced woman to do, and truly none of my business. But why had she said, "Just checking"? With that wide grin. Just checking *what*? If she was not checking on my attitude toward my former wife, in fact my *feelings* about my former wife, what, then, *had* she been checking? The condition of the U.S. dollar versus the Japanese yen? I was a lawyer, and she was a lawyer, and we both knew what a fishing expedition was, and her dropping that business about seeing Susan in the company of a younger man certainly smelled of a hook dangling in the water. So what *could* she have been checking if not my . . . well . . . my availability.

Well, maybe not.

And maybe later on in the evening, when she asked about the trip to Italy I'd made a year earlier . . .

How had she known about that, by the way, unless she'd been making discreet inquiries hither and yon?

. . . and specifically about the four days I'd spent in Venice, alone I might add, and asked me looking over the rim of her wine glass, the way women do on television commercials, asked me whether I had found Venice as romantic as she had . . .

Well, *everyone* finds Venice romantic.

But not everyone shoots a double-barreled blue laser beam over the edge of a glass containing amber-colored wine, not everyone lingers over the word *romantic,* "Did you find Venice as *romantic* as I did, Matthew?"

"Well, I was there alone," I said.

"So was I," she said. And added, "Pity."

I was imagining things.

Surely.

But no mention of a deal, no mention of the matter of mutual interest.

"Look how bright the moon is," she said.

Which I had already noticed.

We sipped cognac while the moon turned the water to silver. It was still a hot moist night, but the moonshine on the bay, aided and abetted by the air-conditioning inside Marina Lou's, made everything seem much cooler. Until she licked cognac from her lips and murmured "Mmm."

I was imagining things.

But then she said—and I couldn't possibly be imagining *this*, could I, Your Honor?—she said, "I have a bottle of twenty-year-old cognac at the house. A gift from one of my clients. When I was still practicing on the Coast. Never found the right occasion to open it."

I looked at her.

"Want to sample it?" she asked, and again that blue laser beam flashed out, touching my eyes, touching my mouth, and I thought Careful, Matthew, and I thought This can be very dangerous, Matthew, and I said, "Sure, why not?"

We drove in separate cars to her house on Fatback Key.

I was thinking of the way we'd met.

She'd been standing in the pouring rain—this was August a year ago—having smashed her shitty little Volkswagen into my brand-new Acura Legend parked at the curb outside my house. Rain pouring down. The car had cost me thirty thousand dollars two weeks earlier, and there she was apologizing for having swerved to miss hitting a goddamn cat, choosing instead to smash into the left rear fender of my brand-new, smoky-blue car. She'd been wearing red to match the color of the VW, red silk dress and red high-heeled shoes, soaking wet in the downpour, her long blonde hair getting wetter and wetter every second, her dress clinging to her skin. I remembered thinking that this was the scene where they're in Africa, and the gorgeous starlet falls into a pool near a waterfall, and when she gets out of the water you can see her nipples through her wet clothes. Which was exactly what I was doing, seeing her nipples through the wet red dress. So I looked away. I did not know at the time that she was a newly appointed assistant S.A., I did not know she was Patricia Demming. I knew that now, though, and I wondered now why I was remembering her standing virtually naked in the teeming rain, why in fact I was following her to her house on Fatback Key, because surely this was a foolish and dangerous thing to do, not to mention possibly unethical.

Fatback is in Calusa County, but it is not within the city limits of Calusa itself. Instead, it falls within the boundaries of Manakawa to the south. It is the wildest and narrowest of the county's several keys, flanked on east and west by the Gulf and the bay, two bodies of water that during the hurricane season sometimes join over Westview Road, the two-lane blacktop that skewers Fatback north to south. The bridge connecting Fatback to the mainland is a humpback that can accommodate only one car at a time. Directly over the bridge is a large wooden signpost with two dozen arrows pointing off either left or right, the names of the key's residents carved into the wooden arrows and then painted in with white. The moon was high as I followed Patricia over the bridge, the wooden planks rumbling under the wheels of my car. I caught a fleeting glimpse of the name DEMMING on one arrow in the bristling directional sheaf. This was really happening. This was where Patricia Demming—the assistant S.A. who'd be my opponent on the Barton case—actually lived.

The house itself was a stone and wood and glass architectural beauty on the bay side of the road, with a splendid view of both bay and Gulf from the upper stories, of which there appeared to be three at first glance but which Patricia informed me were only two, the illusion of another level created by a cathedral ceiling and attendant skylight in the second-floor master bedroom.

"I'll show you later," she said, and unlocked the front door.

The house was furnished in what Patricia described as "eclectic modern," a rambling mix of leather, steel, and wood softened by brightly colored, oversized throw pillows and abstract Syd Solomon paintings, a blend that seemed totally reflective of her personality. She went immediately to a bar unit with a drop-leaf front, searched though the bottles in it till she found one with a label done in green and gold, announcing the bottle's contents as twenty-year-old Prunier cognac, no liar she, this extremely beautiful woman with a matter of mutual interest to discuss.

She broke the seal, uncorked the bottle, poured into two brandy snifters.

We sniffed of the bouquet.

We touched glasses.

We sipped.

"Mmm," she murmured again.

"Mmm," I murmured.

We sipped some more.

Moonlight splashed silver on the waters of the Gulf. The night was still.

"So what's this matter of mutual interest?" I asked.

"Us," she said.

Your Honor, I take full responsibility for what happened next.

I am not one of the smug little lap doggets of this world, who—eager to broadcast publicly how irresistible they are to women, and how constantly alert they must be to thwart unwanted advances, and how terribly hard they must fight to protect their honor and integrity from predatory females who accuse them of "leading a girl on." I am not one of those self-serving self-satisfied trotting little doggets who boast of brilliant achievements while casually destroying someone else's reputation, I am not one of those, Your Honor, I pray with all my heart that I am not one of those.

It is true, Your Honor, that Patricia Demming made herself "comfortable"—as well she might have in her own home—after we'd each consumed two generous dollops of the smoothest cognac I'd ever tasted, taking off the blue linen jacket to reveal a long-sleeved paler blue silk blouse, fastened at the cuffs and down the front with tiny pearl buttons. It is also true that she unbuttoned the top three buttons of the blouse, even though a ceiling fan was whirling overhead . . .

"I hate air-conditioning," she said.

. . . but it is also true that by that time I had taken off my own jacket and rolled up my sleeves and loosened my tie and unbuttoned the top button of my shirt in defense against the September humidity and heat.

This is all true, Your Honor.

I am somewhat fuzzy about who kissed whom first.

It seemed to me that the moment was both spontaneous and simultaneous, our eyes meeting as she whispered the single word *Us*, our lips meeting not the tick of a heartbeat later.

My experience with women is limited at best, Your Honor; I do not claim to be an expert. But there was in Patricia Demming all the energy and drive and dedication and devotion she normally brought to the pursuit of her chosen profession, translated now into a fierce and unbridled passion that consumed us both and turned us each into abject slaves to each other's needs. There on her bed on the second story of her house, in a room with a cathedral ceiling and a huge slanting skylight that framed the silver sphere of the waxing moon, we found each other again and again and again and were surprised and delighted and grateful each and every time.

But there is always the next morning.

3

Skye Bannister, the elected state attorney for the Twelfth Judicial Circuit, was Patricia's boss, and the man she went to at ten o'clock that steamy Thursday morning. In truth, she would have preferred discussing the problem with almost anyone *but* Skye Bannister, who she suspected had hired her not because she was a damn good lawyer, but merely because she was a good-looking woman. It was an open secret that he would one day declare his candidacy for the governorship of the state. Patricia hoped he'd lose because he was such a sexist jackass; but she hoped he'd win because then he'd leave for Tallahassee, goodbye and good luck.

Meanwhile, she had to tell him she'd been to bed with Mary Barton's attorney.

This was not going to be easy.

Skye was a man who insisted on calling her *Pat,* even though she'd asked him at least a dozen times not to. Skye was a man who, despite the warning flags that should have gone up after the Clarence Thomas hearings, still insisted on friendly embraces, old Uncle Skye and his big happy family of little prosecutors, here's a nice avuncular pat on the ass, Pat. Skye was the man to whom she had to confess her little, ahh, indiscretion.

The State Attorney's Office had once been a motel, its rooms remodeled to accommodate the rambling structure's new function. Each of the offices sported a bathtub in its bathroom, rare for any office, completely exotic for offices engaged in the prosecution of criminals. Skye's personal office—the largest in the complex—had been fashioned by knocking down the walls between three of the erstwhile motel rooms. There were three bathtubs in his office. One pink, one blue, and one white. There was also a new corner window whose right angle embraced a desk that used to belong to his grandfather, William Bannister, a former state senator. Skye sat behind that desk now, golden sunlight touching his golden hair. To Patricia, he suddenly resembled a TV evangelical preacher; perhaps he knew she was here to confess.

"Come in, Pat," he said, and rose. "Sit down, please," he said, and smiled, and extended his open hand toward one of the two wing-back chairs in front of his desk.

She sat.

She had pulled her hair back into a tidy bun for this morning's meeting, and had chosen her severest outfit, a pinstripe suit the color of a wintry sky, black low-heeled librarian's shoes, opaque blue stockings; she was here to confess fornication with the enemy.

"Why'd you want to see me, Pat?" he asked.

Still smiling.

She wondered if he knew that while she was still an undergraduate at Brown, she'd decked the school's star quarterback for committing the same offense Skye now committed with regularity and immunity.

"I'd like to be taken off the Barton case," she said.

His eyebrows went up onto his forehead.

"Oh?"

"Yes."

"Why?"

"Personal reasons."

"Like what?"

"Just something personal," she said.

Come on, she thought, make this easy for me.

"What is it, Pat?" he said, leaning forward, elbows on the desk hands tented, voice low. "Tell me."

"I wish you wouldn't call me Pat," she said.

"I thought you liked being called Pat."

"As a matter of fact, I don't."

"But I've *always* called you . . ."

"As a matter of fact, I *despise* being called Pat."

"I think it's a nice name. Pat."

"I think it's a *lousy* name."

"Pat. A *very* nice name, in fact."

"But *Patricia* happens to be my name, and I don't enjoy bei called Pat. Which *isn't* my name."

"It *is* a nice name, though, you have to admit that."

"If you like it so much, I'll call *you* Pat, how's that?"

"Well, I certainly won't use the name if it offends you."

"What offends me is my having to ask you a hundred ti not to call me Pat, and you keep on doing it."

"I'm sorry."

"That's okay. But please don't call me Pat in the future."

"I won't."

"I'd appreciate it."

"Consider it done. Patricia."

"Thank you."

"Now . . . what's troubling you about the Barton case?"

"Nothing's troubling me about it. I'm having a personal p lem with it, and I think you ought to assign someone else t

"Is it the fact that the victims . . . ?"

"No, it has nothing to do with the victims."

"Because I didn't think you'd be squeamish . . ."

"I'm not squeamish . . ."

". . . after all those child-abuse cases you handled so brilliantly."

"Well, thank you, but it's not that."

"Then what is it?"

"Let's say it's conflict of interest."

"Oh?"

"Yes."

"Do you know Mary Barton personally?"

"No, I don't."

"Or any of the witnesses?"

"No, that's not . . ."

"Or the victims? Did you know one of the victims, is that it?"

"No. Skye, I think we'd be compromising the state attorney's position if I remained on this case. I think it'd be best all around for me to turn it over to someone else in the office. Immediately. This morning. Now."

"Why?"

"I told you why."

"No, you haven't. I thought this case was right up your alley, or I wouldn't have assigned it to you. So unless you've got a damn good reason . . ."

"I went to bed with Matthew Hope," she said.

"Pat," he said, "that was dumb."

That same morning, I explained to Mary Barton as delicately as I could that I had been . . . ahh . . . intimate with the woman who'd be prosecuting the case, a woman named Patricia Demming . . .

"Yes, I know her name," Mary said.

. . . and that whereas she planned to ask that another attorney be assigned to the case, something the state attorney would undoubtedly agree to since the dangers inherent in the situation . . .

"What dangers?" Mary asked.

I tried to explain that should we lose the case, should Mary be

found guilty as charged, any attorney cognizant of the situation would probably advise her to appeal, basing the claim on a conflict of interest that had led to a less than zealous representation. The state attorney wouldn't want to place himself in such a vulnerable position . . .

"Vulnerable how?" Mary asked.

The position of having a guilty verdict reversed because the opposing attorneys had been . . . ahh . . . intimately involved with each other. The question now was whether or not Mary wanted me to stay on as her attorney . . .

"Why wouldn't I?" she asked.

I explained that even if Patricia Demming was removed from the case, Mary might feel that because of our prior relationship, Patricia's and mine, I might not be able to pursue her cause with sufficient vigor . . .

"Well, would you?"

I told her that I thought I could, but that if we lost the case, for example . . .

"Do you plan to lose it?"

I told her that if she decided to keep me on as her attorney, I intended to defend her with every skill I possessed. But I also told her I would want a signed waiver from her, protecting me in the event she later decided I hadn't defended her vigorously enough.

"Protecting you from what?" she asked.

"Any later claim of conflict of interest. I'd have no objection, by the way, if you decided to ask another lawyer about this."

"Lawyers," she said.

"Lawyers," I agreed.

"You should've kept your zipper up."

"I guess I should have."

"Do you love her?"

"I think she's a very special person."

"Do you think she'll be removed from the case?"

"I think so, yes," I said. "I feel fairly certain that'll happen. And they'll undoubtedly make sure she stays far away from anything relating to the case . . . the new prosecutor, the files, the strategies the State Attorney's Office evolves . . ."

"How about you? Will she have to stay away from you as well?"

"I hope not," I said.

"Suppose the state attorney decides she *should*? Will you still want to defend me?"

"Yes."

"Then I'll sign your waiver," she said.

"Matthew?"

It was Patricia.

The digital calendar/clock on my desk read THU SEP 24 11:50 A.M.

"Hi," I said.

"When can I see you?" she asked.

"Right this minute," I said.

We met at a motel on the South Tamiami Trail. We sneaked into the room like burglars and fell into each other's arms as though we'd been apart for centuries rather than days, not even days, a day and a half, not even that, twenty-eight hours since we'd kissed goodbye yesterday morning, and I'd driven off in my smoky-blue Acura while she stood in the doorway of her house wearing a smokier black nightgown, her blonde hair blowing in the salty wind that wafted in over the Gulf.

She was dressed for work now, wearing a dark blue pinstripe tropical suit with wide lapels, "My gangster suit," she called it, an instant before she hurled the jacket onto the bed behind her. My hands had been on her from the moment the door clicked shut behind her, "Lock it," she whispered under my lips, but I was unbuttoning the front of the long-sleeved white blouse instead, "Oh, Jesus, lock it," she whispered, but I was sliding the tailored skirt up over her thighs, my hands reaching everywhere, my hands remembering her, my mouth remembering her, "Jesus," she kept murmuring under my lips, we were both crazy, kicking off the high-heeled shoes, a garter belt under the skirt, dark blue stockings, "For you," she whispered, "for you," lowering her panties, silken and electric, the skirt bunched up above her waist, her legs wide, entering her, "Oh, Jesus," she said, "Oh, Jesus," I said, clutching her to me, pulling her onto me, pulling me into her, enclosing, enclosed, "Oh, Jesus," she said, "I'm coming," she said, "this is crazy," she said, "this is crazy," I said, we were crazy, we were crazy, we were crazy.

Breathless and crazed, she told me how humiliating her meeting with Skye Bannister had been . . .

"You'd have thought I was on *trial*," she said.

. . . how he'd seemed to savor every moment of her discomfort . . .

"You didn't tell him what we . . ."

"Of *course* not!"

But now she wondered if her goddamn Catholic upbringing hadn't somehow lent a religious aura to the entire little scene being played out in the motel's papal chambers, His Holiness all but allowing her to kiss his ring after he'd agreed that her behavior had indeed tainted the state attorney's position. He'd wondered, in fact . . .

"Should I be telling you this?" she herself wondered, aloud.

"Yes," I said, "tell me."

Well, Skye had wondered if the Office *itself* hadn't been tainted, and if he should ask the governor to appoint a special prosecutor. Because suppose . . .

"No, you shouldn't be telling me this," I said.

"He wants a Chinese wall around me, Matthew."

"How high?"

"He's talking about sending me out of town to prosecute . . ."

"Oh, no. Jesus, no."

". . . a case coming to trial in Manasota County."

"Has he asked you to . . . ?"

"Not yet."

"You know what I . . . ?"

"Yes, stay away from you. Not yet."

"What if he does?"

"I'll die."

"Me, too."

"How'd we get into this?" she said, and sighed heavily.

"It was my fault," I said.

"No, mine," she said. "But I really *was* going to offer you a deal, you know."

"You offered me a better one."

"I don't know what happened to me. I don't usually behave that way. Everything just flew out of my head, the deal I'd prepared, everything. I think I must have been planning this for a long time, Matthew. I think I may have been planning it from the moment I ran into your car. I think it may have been *fated*, my running into your car . . . are you still seeing that girl?"

"What girl?"

"The Vietnamese translator."

"No."

"Swear."

"I swear."

"Do you believe in destiny?"

"No."

"You don't think this was fated?"

"Yes, I do."

"Then you do believe in destiny."

"No."

"I'm a very jealous person, you know, I'd rip out your eyes. This is crazy," she said, "I think I love you, Matthew."

"I think I love you, too."

"Yes, say it," she said.

"I love you, Patricia."

"Ahh, say it, say it."

"I love you," I said.

"I love you," she said.

"I love you," I said, "I love you, I love you, I love you."

We were crazy.

"I don't know why you're attracted to crazy people," Frank said. "And I also don't know why you left for lunch at twelve today and didn't get back to the office till . . . what time is it now? . . . two-*thirty*? A two-and-a-half-hour *lunch*, Matthew? What did you *eat*, Matthew? An entire steer?"

Frank Summerville is my partner.

Some people think we look alike. I don't know why. Some people think I also look like my former wife, Susan. Which would mean that *Frank* looks like Susan, which is a preposterous notion in that Susan is quite beautiful and Frank is not. I suppose I can understand why some people mistake us for each other, though— not me and Susan, me and Frank. I guess it's because we both have dark hair and dark eyes. But Frank has what he himself calls a "pig face," and I have what he calls a "fox face." And whereas I am an even six feet tall and weigh a hundred and eighty pounds (when I'm in shape), Frank is five-nine-and-a-half and weighs a hundred and sixty pounds *all* the time, year in and year out, summer, winter, spring, or fall. Moreover, he's originally from New York and I'm from Chicago; the cadences of our speech are different, the tonalities nowhere near alike.

But we are, after all, in the same profession, and we share offices in the same building on Heron Street in downtown (such as it is) Calusa, and we're often seen separately around town, representing the firm of Summerville and Hope, and there are those similar brown eyes and dark hair, so I guess, yes, it's perfectly understandable why *some* people—no, damn it, it is not understandable at all! We look no more alike than Laurel and Hardy, or Abbott and Costello, or Lewis and Martin, or, for that matter, Susan and me. And it was none of his damn business how long I took for lunch, which by the way I hadn't eaten. Or why I chose to represent people *he* thought were crazy.

"She's not crazy," I said.

"Then why did she kill three young girls and bury them in her backyard?"

"That is the state's contention," I said.

"It is also the contention of one Charlotte Carmody, who says she saw your nutty friend digging a grave for one of the bodies."

"Which doesn't necessarily make it true."

"The moon was full that night," Frank said. "Read the newspapers, Matthew. They can be very informative."

"There's only one newspaper down here, and it's a rag."

"*Time* magazine also mentioned the full moon, Matthew. So did *Newsweek*. And *USA Today*."

"There's no denying there was a full moon that night. That doesn't make Charlotte Carmody an unimpeachable witness."

"Tell me something, Matthew. Why do you think the neighborhood kids call her Mary, Mary, quite contrary?"

"Because she's eccentric."

"Ahh."

"But that doesn't make her *nuts*."

"No, it doesn't. It's killing three little girls that . . ."

"She didn't kill them, Frank."

"Matthew, that bitch in the State Attorney's Off—"

"She's not a bitch," I said.

Frank looked at me.

"She's a highly intelligent woman and an excellent lawyer."

"A highly intelligent *bitch*," Frank insisted, "who's going to . . ."

"I wish you wouldn't use that word to describe Patricia," I said. "Demming," I added.

Frank looked at me again.

"Patricia," he said, "Demming," he added, "is going to fry our fucking client and cost our fucking firm a great deal of future business."

"She isn't going to fry anyone," I said. "She's been taken off the case."

"Why?" Frank asked.

I told him why.

Warren Chambers didn't completely trust people who'd once been on drugs. Whenever they said, "I've been sober for three years now," or ten or two or four or eight, it seemed to indicate they were precariously perched for an imminent fall from grace. He had to admit that Toots Kiley looked terrific; he just wished she wouldn't keep telling him how goddamn sober she was.

Late that Thursday afternoon, they sat drinking coffee in a Leatherette booth in a pancake joint on Whisper Key. Toots had chosen the venue, which was close to the small condo she was renting with a girl—*her* word, not his—named Alison Perkins from Grove Park, Illinois. Alison's ambition, Toots was saying now, was to become a private investigator.

"Like you and me," she said, and rolled her eyes as if to say Spare me.

Toots had been named after the harmonica player Toots Thielemans. That was the name on her birth certificate. Toots. She didn't care what feminists thought. That was her name. Any feminist gave her static about her name, she'd knock her flat on her ass, teach her a little something about choice. Toots Kiley, that's me, take it or leave it, babe. A much better name than Alison. Or even Gloria. Or Betty, for that matter.

Toots was twenty-six years old, a tall, slender, suntanned blonde with frizzed hair and dark brown eyes. She was wearing a denim skirt, thong sandals, and a peach-colored, short-sleeved cotton blouse. Warren was ten years older, a tall, wiry black man who still looked like the college basketball player he'd once been. He was wearing eyeglasses, a seersucker suit, and a high-top fade. Sitting there in the red and black Leatherette booth, in a window streaming sunshine, they made a striking couple. They were here to discuss the Mary Barton case. Warren had been briefed on it yesterday; today he was telling Toots what Matthew Hope needed.

"She sounds totally nuts," Toots said. "Why doesn't he just move for a 916.2?"

"Public defender already did," Warren said. "Before Matthew took the case. Judge denied the motion."

"For a bona fide *fruitcake?*" Toots said, surprised.

"Psychiatrists found her competent."

"Strike one," Toots said, and rolled her eyes again.

"I've got the state attorney's witness list here," Warren said, and reached into the inside pocket of his jacket. "Matthew wants you to . . ."

"Who's prosecuting?" Toots asked.

"Patricia Demming."

"Holy terror."

"Tell me about it."

Toots accepted the single page he extended to her. Scanning it, she picked up her cup of coffee, sipped at it, nodded, and said, "What's he looking for? Background checks?"

"For his depositions, yeah," Warren said, nodding.

"Easy enough," Toots said. "How do we divide the list?"

"We don't. It's all yours."

"Can I keep this?"

"It's a copy."

"When does he need the information?"

"On Charlotte Carmody, immediately. The others by . . ."

"What do you mean immediately?"

"Early next week."

"Have a heart."

"Demming won't be wasting time."

"Today's Thursday already!"

"All day."

"What do you mean? Tuesday? Wednesday?"

"Wednesday latest."

"What's so special about Carmody?"

"She saw Mary burying one of the bodies."

"Terrific."

"If he can demolish her in deposition, he may move to dismiss."

"What grounds?"

"Insufficient evidence to sustain the charges in the indictment."

"Fat chance. What'd these other witnesses see?"

"Not much."

"But what?"

"Mary with each of the girls on separate occasions. Like that."

"Getting better and better."

"Being with them ain't killing them."

"Unless they end up buried in your backyard. Has Carmody been subpoenaed yet?"

"He's deposing her on the sixth."

"So what's his rush?"

"Wants to study it."

"When does he need the rest of this?"

"Soon as possible. He knows how good you are."

"Yeah, bullshit."

"He's offered you his staff, by the way. For typing up your reports."

"Is that cooze still working up there?"

"Which one?"

"The redhead."

"I don't know any redheads in his office."

"A blonde, then. Whatever."

"Only blonde there is Cynthia Huellen. And she's a nice person."

"I must be thinking of somebody else's office. Big redhead?"

"No," Warren said, and shook his head.

"Oh well," Toots said, and slid out of the booth. "What's my share come to?"

"I've got it," Warren said.

"Be easier if she *was* nuts, wouldn't it?" Toots said. "Save us all a lot of trouble."

4

On Tuesday morning, the sixth day of October, Charlotte Carmody came into my office to give her deposition.

Toots Kiley's background check, which had been typed up by Cynthia Huellen, was on my desk in a neat blue folder. Cynthia herself, in a neat yellow cotton dress, sand-colored panty hose, and yellow high-heeled shoes, was sitting beside the desk, ready to take backup notes. The court reporter, a dour-faced man in his late fifties, selected jointly by my office and the State Attorney's, sat with his pianist's hands poised over the stenotab in his lap. Miss Carmody was accompanied by two attorneys—a bright young whip Skye had sent over from the S.A.'s Office and her own personal attorney, both ready to leap to her defense should I ask anything objectionable.

I was there to hear her story.

Charlotte Carmody was the only witness who claimed actually to have *seen* Mary Barton burying a body in her backyard. If I could show that she was at worst lying or at best merely mistaken, then I would move to have the charges dismissed for insufficient evidence. Finding a body, or one or two or ten, in a person's backyard or basement or hall closet or upstairs attic was not in itself proof that the person had done murder.

Florida is one of only five or six states that allow depositions in criminal cases. A deposition is taken under oath and is part of the process known as "discovery," a legal requirement that makes it next to impossible for either a prosecutor or a defense attorney to come up with any surprises at a trial. Each knows beforehand which witnesses will be called on either side. Each knows what physical evidence will be introduced. Each has a chance to examine the witnesses and the evidence long before the case is tried. In the state of Florida, as in all of America, the statutes demand a speedy trial. I was hoping the case would come to court long before Christmas; jurors start getting itchy when the holidays get imminent.

Mary Barton had called Charlotte Carmody a "bimbo."

In truth, she did not resemble one.

I knew her to be twenty-seven years old. I knew she was employed as a teller at Calusa First National on Fourth and Marek. She was wearing this morning what she might have worn to work on any weekday, a simple gray suit of a lightweight, nubby fabric, darkish panty hose, low-heeled pumps. She was not wearing eyeglasses; I'd been hoping she might be. She was neither beautiful nor even pretty, but she was somehow attractive and her pale blue eyes seemed to mirror an intelligence within. Nothing flashy about her. Nothing even vaguely obtrusive in her manner. Even before I began questioning her, I knew she was going to be a tough witness.

"Miss Carmody," I said, "as I'm sure you know, I'm representing Mary Barton in this case . . ."

"Yes."

". . . and I'd like to ask you some questions regarding what you've previously told the police and the state attorney."

"Yes."

"I'd like to remind you that you should answer the questions verbally and not through any hand or head gestures . . ."

"All right."

"And I'd further like to advise you that if you don't understand any of my questions, please say so, and I'll rephrase them."

"Fine."

"All right, then, let's begin, shall we? First, can you please tell me where you live?"

"At 2714 Gideon Way. In Crescent Cove."

"Is your house adjacent to the house in which Mary Barton lives?"

"It is."

"Right next door to 2716 Gideon Way, isn't that correct?"

"That's correct."

"So that Mary Barton is your neighbor."

"She's my neighbor, yes."

"How long have you been living at 2714 Gideon Way?"

"Six months."

"Have you had much opportunity to talk to Miss Barton during that time?"

"I've talked to her, yes."

"Frequently?"

"I have to object to that."

This from her personal attorney, a man named Alderley Rudd, who looked and sounded as if he'd stepped out of Dickens, muttonchop whiskers, florid complexion, checked vest, potbelly and all.

"What's the problem?" I asked.

I should tell you that before a deposition, the lawyers agree on certain stipulations, one of them being that all objections will be reserved for trial. If anyone *does* object during a deposition, it's because the question is so blatantly leading or harassing or irrelevant or incomprehensible that it shouldn't have been asked in the first place. Rudd was objecting now because he knew where I was going and he wanted to be a pain in the ass.

"How do you define 'frequently'?" he asked reasonably. "Is frequently two times, or three times, or a hundred times? Is frequently . . . ?"

"If it bothers you, I'll rephrase it," I said. "Miss Carmody, during the six months in which you lived next door to Mary Barton, how many times would you say you'd spoken to her?"

Which was not at all what Alderley Rudd had expected me to hurl back into his muttonchops. In fact, I was silently congratulating myself on having nailed the question down so precisely when Charlotte Carmody said, "At least two dozen times," which was not at all what I'd expected her to hurl back at *me*.

"Would you say you knew her well?" I asked.

"No. She isn't an easy person to know. But I'd say we were neighborly."

"Friendly?"

"Neighborly."

"How would you describe her?"

"Now really, Matt."

This from Isadore Gold, the young attorney Skye Bannister had sent over. Twenty-seven years old and a graduate of Harvard Law, he resembled Abraham Lincoln so mightily that he had taken to wearing black suits and string bow ties even in the summer months. My hope was that no one would inadvertently assassinate him at the theater one night.

"Problem, Izzie?" I said.

"What difference will Miss Carmody's description make? We all *know* what Mary Barton looks like. Her picture's been all over the . . ."

"Well, I'd like to hear Miss Carmody describe her in her own words," I said.

Gold knew where I was going. And he didn't want to risk his witness telling me that Mary Barton had brown eyes when the whole world knew they were blue. He skewered me now with the exasperated look a person might give to a disobedient child. "Matt," he said—which, by the way, no one has called me since I was a kid—"Matt, can you be a bit more specific? I have no objection to your asking direct questions, but . . ."

"Certainly," I said. "Miss Carmody, how tall is Mary Barton?"

"About my height," she said.

"And how tall is that?"

"Five-seven."

"Would you be surprised if I told you she's five-nine?"

"I would."

"You insist she's five-seven."

"I feel certain she's about my height, which is five-seven."

"What color are her eyes?"

"Blue."

"Light blue? Dark blue?"

"A very dark blue."

"How much does she weigh?"

"I have no idea."

Cautious now. Burned once on Mary's height, unwilling to become a weight-guesser.

"Well," I said, "would you say she's about your weight?"

"No, she's heavier."

"How much do you weigh, Miss Carmody?"

"One-twenty."

"So you think Mary Barton weighs more than a hundred and twenty pounds, is that right?"

"Yes, I would say so."

"A hundred and fifty, would you say?"

"No, not that heavy."

"A hundred and forty?"

"No."

"Thirty? A hundred and thirty?"

"Somewhere between a hundred and twenty and a hundred and thirty."

In actuality, Mary Barton weighed a hundred and twenty-six pounds.

"Would you describe her as heavy?"

"No."

"Thin?"

"Slender."

"What color is her hair?"

"Gray."

"How does she wear it?"

"Short."

"On these twenty-four times you spoke to Mary Barton, where was she?"

"In her garden. And I said at least two dozen times. I didn't say twenty-four exactly."

"How many times, *exactly,* would you say now?"

"At least two dozen. Maybe twenty-five times. Maybe thirty."

Making it worse and worse for me.

"How long were these conversations?"

"They varied. Sometimes it was just a hello, sometimes we talked for two or three minutes."

"And you say all of these conversations took place in her garden?"

"I said she was in her garden. I was on my side of the hedge. Until later on, when the fence went up. Then we used to talk over the fence."

"How high is the fence?"

"Five feet high. Those are the development rules. We're not allowed to have fences higher than that."

"So you could barely see over it, isn't that right?"

"I could see over it."

"Well, the fence is five feet high, and you're five feet seven, so you could *barely* see over it, isn't that right?"

"I could see over it," she said again, more firmly this time.

"Could you see over it on the night of August thirty-first?"

"Yes, I could."

"Where were you that night when you claim to have seen Mary Barton in her garden? Is that the only place you've ever seen Miss Barton, by the way? In her garden?"

"One question at a time, please, Matt."

"Is that the only place?"

"Yes, I've never seen her anywhere else."

"Always in her garden."

"Yes."

"Never in front of the house . . ."

"I don't remember ever seeing her . . ."

"Or walking along the street . . ."

"Let her answer, please, Matt."

"No, I always saw her in the garden."

"All your memories of her are in that garden, is that right?"

"Well . . ."

"Well, if that's the only place you've ever seen her, then your memories of her are in that garden, isn't that right?"

"Yes, she was always working in the garden, the garden was her pride and . . ."

"What is she wearing in these memories of her in that garden?"

"Usually blue jeans."

"What else?"

"A smock with pockets."

"What color?"

"Green."

"Anything else? A hat? Gloves?"

"Gardening gloves."

"A hat?"

"A kerchief."

"Covering her hair?"

"Yes."

"Would you say this was her usual costume whenever you saw her in the garden?"

"Yes."

"A gardening costume, would you call it?"

"Don't put words in her mouth, please."

"Well, Miss Carmody, what *would* you call blue jeans and a green smock with pockets and gardening gloves and a kerchief? What would you call such a costume?"

"I would call it a gardening costume, yes."

"Because that's what she was *doing* on these occasions when you saw her, isn't that true? She was *gardening*, wasn't she?"

"Yes."

"And this was during the daytime, wasn't it?"

"Yes. Except for . . ."

"I'm talking about these specific times you had conversations with her. When you saw her wearing this specific costume . . ."

"Yes."

"This was always during the daytime, wasn't it?"

"Yes."

"All of these conversations took place during the daytime."

"Yes."

"Did you ever talk to Mary Barton in her garden at *night?*"

"No."

"Did you ever even *see* her in her garden at night?"

"I saw her in her garden on the night of August thirty-first."

"Yes, so you claim. But before then, did you ever see her gardening at night?"

"She wasn't gardening *that* night, either. She was . . ."

"I haven't yet asked you what she was doing, Miss Carmody. I asked if you had ever seen her gardening at night?"

"Never."

"Had you ever, in fact, seen her doing *anything* at all in her garden at night?"

"No."

"Ever talk to her at night?"

"No."

"Not in the garden or anyplace else, isn't that right?"

"Not anywhere."

"So the only conversations you ever had with Mary Barton, these twenty or thirty times, or whatever they were . . ."

"Really, Mr. Hope."

This from Alderley Rudd, shaking his head in reprimand.

"Isn't it true that the only conversations you ever had with Miss Barton were during the daytime, while she was gardening? You never spoke to her at night, you never saw her in her garden at night . . ."

"I saw her on August thirty-first. At *night*."

"All right, let's talk about that night. What time was it that you claim you saw her?"

"I *did* see her. I'm not just *claiming* I saw her, I *saw* her."

"At what time?"

"About ten o'clock."

"Before ten, after ten . . . ?"

"A little after ten."

"Five after ten?"

"A few minutes after ten."

"Two minutes, three minutes . . . ?"

"Come on, Matt."

"I don't remember how many minutes after ten. The ten o'clock news had just come on. It was a little after ten."

"Tell me exactly what you saw in the garden."

"I saw Mary Barton burying a little girl's body."

The room went silent. I could hear the court recorder's fingers tapping the words out on his machine. I could hear Cynthia Huellen's pencil scratching on her pad.

"Where were you at the time?" I asked.

"Upstairs. In my bedroom."

"Where in your bedroom?"

"At the window."

"At the window? I thought you were watching tele—"

"I heard something outside."

"While you were watching television?"

"Yes."

"Where were you when you were watching television?"

"In bed."

"So you thought you heard something outside . . ."

"I *did* hear something."

"What'd you do then?"

"I got out of bed."

"And went to the window?"

"Yes."

"Were there lights on in your bedroom?"

"Yes."

"Were there lights on in Mary Barton's backyard?"

"There was a full moon."

"That's not what I asked you. Were there lights on in . . . ?"

"I could see very clearly."

"That *still* isn't what I asked you. Miss Carmody, were there any lights on in Mary Barton's backyard that night?"

"No, there weren't."

"The yard was dark, is that right?"

"There was a full moon."

"Aside from the moon, was there any other light in that yard?"

"No."

"And the lights were on in your bedroom, you say."

"Yes."

"You didn't turn them off when you got out of bed, did you?"

"No."

"Black outside the window, light inside the bedroom."

"No, not black."

"Well, it was nighttime, wasn't it?"

"Yes, but . . ."

"So certainly there wasn't *sunshine* outside that window?"

"No, but . . ."

"It was *dark* outside that window, wasn't it?"

"Yes, but the moon . . ."

"*Despite* the moon. And in such circumstances—black outside, light inside—there would have been a mirror effect, wouldn't there?"

"I could see through the window."

"That isn't what I asked you."

"I had my face close to the glass, and my hands alongside my face. I could see everything happening outside."

"You could see over the fence, could you?"

"Yes."

"Five-foot-high fence, you could see over it?"

"Yes."

"Even though the grave you claim you saw being dug was only five feet on the other side of that fence?"

"I could see Mary digging a grave, yes."

"Your angle of vision was such . . ."

"I could see her, yes. Digging a grave and throwing a little girl's body into it."

"What was she wearing?"

"The little girl was naked."

"Yes, that was in all the newspapers. But what was Mary Barton wearing? You claim you saw her, tell me what she was wearing."

"A blue dress."

"Not jeans and a smock . . ."

"No."

"Or a kerchief and gardening gloves . . ."

"No."

"Which was what you *usually* saw her wearing in her garden . . ."

"Yes."

"Not that at all, but instead . . . a blue dress."

"Yes."

"What sort of blue dress?"

"A simple dress. A casual dress. Like a kind of denim."

"Well, was it denim?"

"It looked like denim."

"Couldn't you tell what it was?"

"Not from that distance."

"I thought you said you could see clearly."

"I could. But not what kind of material . . ."

"In spite of the full moon?"

"I don't understand your question."

"In spite of this full moon that was lighting up the entire backyard, you could not tell whether the blue dress . . . you could see it was blue, is that right?"

"Yes."

"But not what material it was."

"No, not what material. I couldn't *feel* the cloth, I could only see it."

"Are you aware that the police have been unable to find in Mary Barton's house the simple blue dress you described to them?"

"I don't know what she did with the dress."

"What else was she wearing?"

"White sneakers."

"Low-top, high-top?"

"Low. No socks."

"You *saw* that she wasn't wearing any socks?"

"I saw a blue dress and white sneakers."

"You know that the police couldn't find those sneakers, either, don't you?"

"I know what I saw her wearing."

"A blue dress and white sneakers."

"Yes."

"Which Mary Barton does not own."

"I told you, I don't know what she did with them. She could have done anything with those clothes."

"Tell me, Miss Carmody . . . why did you wait so long before coming forth?"

"What?"

"You said you saw her burying Felicity Hammer on the night of August thirty-first . . ."

"I didn't know it was Felicity Hammer at the time."

"Well, you saw her burying *someone*, didn't you?"

"Yes. A little girl."

"But you didn't tell this to the police until *after* someone else had discovered the bodies. Why didn't you come forward at once? Why'd you wait till the next day?"

"I was afraid to come forward."

"Why?"

"I was afraid of what she might do to me."

"But you weren't afraid the next day, huh? When you told the police . . ."

"I told them what I'd seen, that's all. I wasn't the one who called them in the first place, it was the telephone man. All I did was answer questions. So she can't blame me for starting it. She can't try to hurt me for starting anything."

"Why would she want to hurt you, Miss Carmody? Are you lying about her?"

"No, I'm telling the truth."

"Then why are you afraid?"

"Because she's crazy."

I kept going at her hammer and tongs. I tried every trick I knew, some of them less than noble, but she remained firm in her conviction that on the night of August 31, she had seen Mary Barton in her garden, wearing a blue dress and white sneakers—no socks—burying a naked young girl by the light of the moon.

I think it was the "no socks" that convinced me she was telling the truth as she'd seen it. There were uncertainties in her testimony, yes, but the clarity of this minor detail was overpowering, and I knew that any motion to dismiss on the merits would be flatly denied.

I was right back where I was when first I'd spoken to Melissa Lowndes on the telephone.

5

"I don't own and never have owned a fucking blue denim dress," Mary said.

She had taken to pacing her cell every time I visited her, somewhat like a caged lioness, which she resembled not in the slightest. Jailhouse pallor had begun to set in. The tan she'd acquired from working hours upon end in her precious garden had turned sallow, giving her face the appearance of aging parchment.

In response to my further demand for discovery, the State Attorney's Office had sent me a list of physical evidence it planned to present at the trial. Among the items listed were a blue denim dress, said to have belonged to Mary Barton and recovered at a dry-cleaning establishment in a Calusa mall. The dry cleaner's name had been added to the witness list as well. Skye Bannister had been busy. But he still hadn't told me who'd be prosecuting the case now that Patricia had been removed from it.

"The dry cleaner has identified you as the woman who left that dress with him," I said.

"I never heard of a place called Dri-Quik Cleaners," Mary said. "And why would I have gone to a mall all the way over on the other end of the fucking city?"

"The cleaner says there were blood spots on the dress."

"The cleaner is out of his mind."

"He identified you first from photographs and then from a lineup."

"Let him identify me face-to-*face,* the son of a bitch. Let him look me dead in the eye and tell me I'm the person who brought that dress in to be cleaned."

"Charlotte Carmody says you were wearing a blue denim dress the night she saw you."

"Charlotte Carmody is a bimbo and a busybody."

"She's the state's key witness."

"Fuck her *and* the state."

"Mary, will you please . . . ?"

"I don't know where they're dredging up these people! Why don't *you* find some witnesses who'll tell them I was asleep in bed when I was supposed to be burying that girl's body?"

"Are there such witnesses?"

"I sleep alone, thank you."

"Would you have *talked* to anyone that night? On the telephone? At around ten o'clock?"

"No."

"You're sure of that."

"I'm dead asleep by nine-thirty every night of the week."

"Is that what time you went to sleep that night?"

"Yes."

"You remember, do you?"

"I remember because my routine is unvaried. I go to sleep at nine-thirty, and I wake up at seven. I walk to the store to pick up a newspaper, read it while I have my breakfast, and then go to work in my garden. I'm usually there by eight-thirty, nine. Every day of the week except Sunday. The same routine."

"Are you familiar with the Templeton Mall?"

"I've been there."

"Were you there on the first of September?"

"No. Is that when he says I brought the dress in?"

"Yes."

"I was nowhere *near* Templeton that day."

"How do you know?"

"My car was in for service. A friend drove me to pick it up. Anyway, if I had a dress with blood on it, why wouldn't I just burn it?"

Good question.

"Who serviced your car?"

"The Toyota place on Meridian and Jackson."

"When?"

"I brought it in the Thursday before."

"Which would've been . . ."

"I don't know the date."

"The twenty-seventh?"

"I guess."

"Who'd you leave it with?"

"Joe."

"Joe who?"

"I don't know his last name. He's the service manager. He knows me. Ask him. Anyway, it's in his book."

"What kind of car?"

"A Camry."

"What time did you take it in?"

"Eight o'clock."

"You drove the car in at eight?"

"Yes."

"How'd you get back home?"

"They gave me a lift."

"Who drove you?"

"Some kid, I don't know his name. Blond kid."

"When did you pick the car up again?"

"I told you. The following Tuesday. They called me and said

I needed new brake linings and a new antenna, but they couldn't get the antenna till Monday."

"So the car was ready on Tuesday."

"Yes."

"The day the bodies were found."

"Yes."

"What time did you pick it up?"

"Around nine-thirty in the morning."

"How'd you get there?"

"Jimmy gave me a ride over."

"Who's Jimmy?"

"A man I know."

"Jimmy what?"

"Di Falco."

"What's his address and phone number?"

She gave me his address and phone number. I wrote them down. She also told me she'd known him ever since she began living in Calusa, and that he was a very good friend. She had minutes earlier told me she slept alone, thank you, but the way she now said the words "a very good friend" suggested that she might have known him intimately. It used to be difficult for me to believe that men and women in their fifties and sixties led active, sometimes hyperactive, sex lives. I changed my mind about this on a cruise I took to the Galápagos Islands, when people in their seventies—and older—were rocking the boat each night with their sexual gymnastics.

"How long ago would that have been?" I asked.

"How long ago would *what* have been?"

"Your coming to Calusa."

"I came back to America five years ago."

"What made you come back?"

"I was asked to tender my resignation."

"Why?"

"Personality differences."

"Between whom?"

"Me and the headmistress."

"What sort of personality differences?"

"We disagreed on curriculum."

"Tell me a little more about that."

"Why?"

"Because by the time this comes to trial, Skye Bannister will know all about you."

"I'm certain that what happened in England five years ago will be of little interest to anyone but me."

"And me. And the State Attorney's Office."

"It was all a matter of principle," Mary said, and sighed heavily. "I felt that twelve-year-olds were mature enough to read *Women in Love*. Mrs. Morden did not. I taught it, anyway. And was asked to resign."

"Did you?"

"No. I told her to sack me. Which required bringing me up on charges before the board of governors."

"What were the charges?"

"Insubordination. And . . ."

She hesitated.

"Yes?"

"Compromising the morals of minors."

"What did the board decide?"

"The morals charges were dismissed, of course, they were total nonsense. But the assorted J.P.s, knights, baronets, ladies, dames, dukes, earls, and lords did find me guilty of being insubordinate, which indeed I had been. And, just as Mrs. Morden had wished, I was asked to leave my position. By then, I didn't give a good goddamn. I'd had enough of all that snooty British shit and was glad to get out of there."

"Why'd you come here?"

"Florida sounded a nice place to retire."

"Where'd you come from originally?"

"Why do you want to know that?"

"I told you. Skye Bannister . . ."

Mary plunked herself down on the narrow cot. Sighing heavily, she said, "I don't know what my past has to do with these absurd charges. I did *not* kill those girls. Whatever I may have done . . ."

"Anything I should know about?"

"Nothing even remotely resembling murder, I can assure you."

"Then what?"

"Nothing."

"Ever been arrested for anything?"

"No."

"Speeding? Passing a traffic light? Parking in a . . . ?"

"I just told you. Nothing."

"Ever try any controlled substances?"

"Of course not!"

"How old were you when you went to England?"

"Thirty."

"Did you go directly to Lockbourne?"

"No, I spent a few years in London."

"Then what?"

"I read an advert for a teaching post at St. Edward's, and I applied for the position."

"When was that?"

"Oh, some twenty-five years ago."

"And you were hired, of course."

"Yes."

"To teach English."

"Yes."

"Had you taught English before?"

"Yes."

"Where?"

"In Purcell, New Mexico," she said, and rolled her eyes. "Must we rake up all this ancient history?"

"I'm afraid so," I said.

I'd asked only where she'd taught English before, but her recitation surprisingly began with her birth almost fifty-nine years ago, in a town called Renegade, in Lyman County, South Dakota. The only child of a doctor named Robert Barton and his wife, Judy, she remembered being pampered and fussed over . . .

"Spoiled rotten, I should say . . ."

. . . her every whim satisfied, her every wish granted, her room filled to bursting with cherished dolls, her silent playmates during the long Dakota winters.

"I was much loved," she said now, and lowered her eyes as if in reverent memory. I had the sudden feeling she was lying. Her recitation seemed delivered by rote. The memories sounded too pat . . .

. . . her doting parents submitting her photograph to a Beautiful Baby contest run by the local newspaper . . .

Her father teaching her how to ski on wooden slats he said had belonged to relatives in Norway . . .

Her sweet-sixteen party on November the fifth, forty-three years ago, the guests arriving in sleds on that crystalline cold Saturday . . .

I could not shake the feeling that she wasn't telling the truth.

In the September before her eighteenth birthday, she left for the University of Colorado at Denver and received her bachelor of arts degree four years later . . .

"Such a lovely graduation ceremony," she said now. "We stood in the summer sunshine . . . have you ever been to Denver? The air is so clear, so crystalline . . ."

That word again. As if rehearsed.

"We were so proud of ourselves. Ready to step out and conquer the world. How young. How foolish."

Both her parents were killed in an automobile crash two months later, while she was home visiting. She was not yet twenty-two years old. This was to be the last time she ever saw the town of Renegade. They buried her parents in the blistering August heat . . .

"We stood in the sunshine and wept bitter tears . . ."

Rehearsed, I thought. Theatrical.

"I was alone in the world," she said.

"No other relatives?"

"I told you. I was an only child."

"But no uncles or aunts? Cousins?"

"My parents came here from Norway."

Barton? I wondered. Norwegian?

"Was that the original name?"

"I think it was Borgen," she said. "Or Bargen, I'm not sure."

"Ever try to locate the family in Norway?"

"No. Why would I?"

"Just wondered."

"I knew my grandparents were already dead when Mother and Daddy came here."

Mother and Daddy. Fifty-nine years old and still calling them Mother and Daddy.

"So if I've got this right," I said, "you lived in Lockbourne . . ."

"Yes."

". . . and taught there for . . . well . . . twenty years, it would seem."

"Yes. A bit more than twenty years."

"And Melissa Lowndes was your student during some of that time."

"Yes."

"Tell me more about *Women in Love*."

"Absurd! In this day and age? Totally absurd."

"Yes, but what happened?"

"Mrs. Morden came in as the new headmistress. She was appalled to discover that I'd been teaching the Lawrence novel for God alone *knew* how many years. So she . . ."

"To twelve-year-old girls?"

"Yes. Why not?" she snapped, and her eyes blazed in challenge. I wondered if I would have wanted my daughter, Joanna, to be reading *Women in Love* when she was twelve. I decided she'd probably read it by the time she was ten.

"I'm only trying to think what the prosecution might make of it," I said.

"How will the prosecution even *know* about it?" she asked.

"You don't know Skye Bannister."

"I'm sure I don't. But of what possible relevance can a clash of values . . . five *years* ago, mind you . . . have to do with whether or not I committed murder? I find the very *word* repugnant! Those little girls at St. Edward's were precious to me. I loved teaching them because I loved watching them grow. Like the beautiful flowers in my garden. Reaching for sunlight, entering a castle of ideas. Growing in and around *ideas*. Nourishing themselves on a towering palace of thought. Those minds were my sacred trust. I would no more have injured those minds than I would have plucked out my own eyes."

She looked up at me.

Those eyes were moist now, the cobalt blue shimmering with tears.

"I never harmed any of my students in Lockbourne," she said. "I merely taught them to think for themselves."

A curt decisive nod.

"And I never harmed anyone here in Calusa, either."

Another nod.

"I did not kill those mutilated children in my garden," she said.

Despite the fact that an occasional murderer was incarcerated here in the Calusa County Jail, security in the visitors' room was remarkably lax—or so it seemed to Melissa Lowndes. She supposed she'd been expecting one of those maximum security setups she'd seen on television or in the movies, where there was a thick glass panel separating the prisoner from the visitor, and you spoke to each other through microphones, touched your hands to the glass to show undying love. Things were quite different here.

She was searched by a uniformed matron in a small anteroom—a thorough riffling of her handbag, a cursory pat of her clothing—and then led into yet another chamber where she was seated with several other women, three of them black, one white, and a fifth who looked Mexican; Melissa found it difficult to differentiate between the various nationalities roaming the streets of America. On Oxford Street in London, there was quite an exotic potpourri of nationalities, of course, but nowhere in Britain was there the profound racial mix one found in America, a melting pot, indeed! It quite unsettled her.

She wondered if she could smoke in here. There were no signs on the walls specifically forbidding it, but neither were any of the other women indulging. No one in America seemed to smoke anymore. She thought this rather odd. Were they really so terrified of cancer or heart disease or all the other dire ailments people everywhere else in the world took quite for granted? Or were they merely carrying their mania for health—oh, how they jogged and ran and *ex*ercised—to ridiculous extremes? She was dying for a cigarette.

Another uniformed person, a male this time, came into the room, holding a clipboard to which a sheet of paper was attached. He began calling off names. The other white woman and two of the black women rose and followed him out of the room. Melissa waited. He came back some five minutes later, read off two more names, and then led the remaining black woman and the woman who looked Mexican out of the room. Melissa wondered why he'd taken three of them on the first go-round, and only two the next time. Alone, she awaited his return, *still* dying for a cigarette.

The man came back in what seemed an eternity.

He looked at the clipboard, looked up as if surprised to discover her still sitting there, and then asked—superfluously, it seemed to her, since she was the only remaining person in the room—"Are you Melissa Lowndes?"

"Yes?"

"Follow me, please," he said.

She rose and followed him through the doorway into a narrow

passage rather like one of those little tunnels you walk through to board an airplane. There was a metal door at the end of the room. He unlocked the door with a key and led her into another chamber, this one furnished with a dozen small, narrow, steel-legged, Formica-topped tables. Each of the tables had a glass, or possibly plastic, panel some twelve inches high dividing it down its center. There was a chair on each long side of the table. The women who'd been led in earlier were now seated at the tables, talking to the prisoners they were visiting. All of the prisoners were female. All of them were wearing smocks with the words CALUSA COUNTY JAIL stenciled over the breast pockets.

A woman Melissa had never before seen in her life was sitting at the table closest to the entrance door.

"Your visitor's here," the uniformed guard told her, and Melissa realized with a shock that this was Mary Barton.

The woman seemed shorter than Melissa remembered her, but then again, Melissa had been smaller at the time, and she was seeing her now from a new perspective. Melissa remembered a *very* tall, slender, ruddy-faced woman with chestnut hair, dazzling blue eyes, and a magnificent smile. This woman appeared shrunken somehow, her blue eyes faded, her hair the color of sullied snow, a perplexed look on her face.

"Melissa?" she asked.

The voice was different, too. Huskier, almost parched. Melissa remembered a bright, chirpy voice, resonant and vital.

"Miss Barton?" she said, and thought Please don't let it be her.

"Oh my dear dear Melissa," the woman said, and her face brightened with a warm and quirky smile Melissa would have known anywhere. There was a sudden rush of memory so powerful it at once transformed that gray and dismal room to a windy knoll in England, and suddenly Melissa was an eleven-year-old girl again, sitting beneath a gnarled oak reading a trashy novel . . . and there was Miss Barton, tall and shining and caped, her chestnut hair blowing in the wind, a bit out of breath, *Hello, hello, are you an Eddie?* Yes, Melissa thought, I'm an Eddie, and opened her arms to embrace this magnificent woman who'd led her unscathed through adolescence into womanhood.

"None of that," the guard warned. "Read the sign."

The choice of good restaurants in Calusa is severely limited, a fact that many tourists discover only after they've made the long trek down from Illinois or Indiana. Once you've eliminated all the fast-food joints and the beef-and-beer chains serving two-for-one cocktails during Happy Hour, once you've gone through the multitude of Chinese restaurants, and pancake houses, and seafood chains serving last week's catch of the day, once you've eaten at the so-called Italian restaurants whose anything-but-Italian chefs serve canned tomato sauces over Ann Page pasta, once you've eaten at the only good Spanish restaurant in town (a branch of the famous one in Tampa) and the one good restaurant serving Continental food in elegant surroundings (with a branch in Palm Beach), then all you've got left is a handful of pseudo-French bistros serving vital organs sautéed in cheap wine, and two or three tiny and claustrophobic places serving what I call "designer" food, which invariably consists of exotic offerings like braised shallots, scallops, and shrimps served on a bed of wilted lettuce, grated shiitake mushrooms, and misted broccoli, with a lime and sun-dried tomato dressing, always arranged artistically on the plate. That's *during* the season.

There is no official beginning to the season down here, but it's generally conceded that the snowbirds don't start arriving till sometime shortly after Christmas. Before then, many of the restaurants, good and bad alike, are closed for the summer and/or the hurricane season, which sometimes overlap. So when Melissa Lowndes called to suggest that we have dinner together, rather than discussing the case in a "stuffy old office," I was hard put to think of anything that might impress a sophisticated visitor from London. Incidentally, I personally consider my office to be cheerful and bright.

In the state of Florida, there are restaurants named after more

Italianate marble tiles and flowing fountains and plush velvet booths, and replaced them with the standard furnishings of any restaurant with the word *Pirate* in its name. Varnished hatch covers served as tabletops, cargo nets hung from the ceiling, running lights in red and green decorated the portholed walls, and waitresses ran around in short, deliberately tattered black skirts, black high-heeled patent-leather pumps, black eye patches, and white silk blouses unbuttoned recklessly low over unfettered breasts. Melissa found it all utterly charming. One of the waitresses took our drink orders, asked Melissa if she was English, and then wisely said, "I thought you might be" in a southern accent Melissa, again, found utterly charming.

I was hoping parrot would not be on the menu.

The drinks were generous; never underestimate the culinary perceptions of a native New Yorker. Another plus—but this was true of any western exposure in Florida—was a breathtaking sunset that turned the quiet waters of the bayou to what resembled a carpet of fallen autumn leaves, all yellow and red and orange. We drank in silent gratitude; there are still places in America that inspire serenity.

"Do you miss autumn?" she asked, and I wondered if the fallen-leaves simile had occurred to her as well.

"Yes, I do," I said. "I miss *all* the seasons."

"Why do you stay?" she asked. "I mean . . . I should think it would eventually pale. The same wonderful weather day after day after day."

"Well, it isn't *always* wonderful," I said. "And some people find this kind of heat debilitating."

"I find it *glorious*," she said, and gave a delicious little shiver of appreciation.

"My partner Frank keeps threatening to leave," I said. "Day after day after day. But he never does."

"Why do you suppose not?" she asked.

"They say sand gets in your shoes," I told her. "They say the blood eventually thins."

pirates than ever sailed the bounding main, not to mention place
named after their various "coves" and "bays" and "treasures" an
"galleys" and "galleons" and even one, in Calusa, named Pirate
Pit, God knows why. There are also thousands of restaurant
named "Captain" something or other, the one in Calusa calle
Captain Jolly Roger, a creative wedding of the piratical and naut
cal themes, but then again not for nothing is Calusa known a
the Athens of the Sea.

I normally try to avoid any restaurant flying a skull and cross
bones or featuring a wheel and fishing nets in the entrance lobby
but a recent addition to Sabal Key was something called Pirate
Parrot (I know, beware, beware!) and it had been highly recom
mended by no less a connoisseur than native New Yorker Fran
Summerville, my chauvinist partner. So I booked a table fo
seven-thirty that night and picked up Melissa at the Hyatt som
twenty minutes earlier.

She had obviously learned very quickly that the weather in Calus
can still be insufferably hot at the beginning of October. The cling
red shift and open sandals she was wearing looked brand-new, an
were probably the result of a shopping expedition since her arriva
She wore a single strand of black pearls around her neck, earring
to match. Her black hair was pulled back and away from her face
fastened at the nape of her neck with a silver barrette. She looke
cool and comfortable and well rested, and confessed immediatel
that she'd slept virtually round the clock after our first meeting an
had been shamefully enjoying the Florida sunshine since—excep
for her visit this afternoon to the Calusa County Jail. Her reunior
with Mary had been a joyous one . . .

"We hugged, we kissed, we talked about old times . . ."

. . . and still shaken by it, she was eager now to hear all abou
whether or not I thought there was hope the case might be
dismissed, a notion I disabused her of at once.

Pirate's Parrot turned out to be a renovated Gianfranco's, one
of the worst restaurants ever to have opened and failed in Calusa,
if not the entire world. The new owners had ripped out all the

"It does seem Paradise," she said, and gazed out dreamily over the sun-stained water.

I didn't tell her we had drugs down here. I didn't tell her you could even buy drugs in prison down here. I didn't tell her that the redneck cops down here seemed to have nothing better to do than plant themselves in porn theaters so they could catch some poor bastard masturbating, never mind the boats full of cocaine off-loading on deserted beaches all up and down the Gulf Coast. I didn't tell her that the city of Calusa seemed to worry more about thong bathing suits on its beaches than it did about dope on them, despite the fact that George Bush's appointed drug czar had been the former governor of Florida. I didn't tell her that here in the Wild West of Calusa, Florida, you could legally wear a gun on your hip, but you couldn't legally wear a bathing suit *off* your hip. I didn't tell her that my partner Frank called Calusa a puritanical midwestern city located a few thousand miles south of its original bearings. I didn't tell her Calusa wasn't the Garden of Eden.

We began talking about Mary again when we were well into the main course. By then, we had each separately and enthusiastically remarked upon the quality of the food and the service and, incidentally, had consumed two glasses each of the chardonnay I'd ordered to complement our lobsters. Sitting with a plastic bib around her neck and attempting to dissect a lobster claw, Melissa told me what it was like to be studying at St. Edward's Academy all those years ago.

"You have to understand," she said, "that Lockbourne is in an extraordinarily beautiful part of England. There are these wonderful green rolling hills, and houses dating back centuries and centuries . . . well, *all* of England is filthy with them, of course, but none are quite so beautiful as those in the countryside around Lockbourne, at least to me. I'm biased, I know, I absolutely *adored* everything about the place. The town, the school, and of course . . . Miss Barton. Who, I suppose, was responsible for my deep appreciation of everything else. At that age, you know . . ."

She is eleven when first she makes the acquaintance of the woman who—she now tells me—made the most significant contribution to her development, the person who, in fact, she now deems responsible for the grown woman she's become. Picture, if you will, a grassy knoll under a cornflower-blue sky, rare in England at any time, rarer still in February. Picture, too, the long and lanky, somewhat ungainly creature who is Melissa Lowndes at the age of eleven, awkward and pimply, flat-chested, painfully shy, wrapped in a coarse woolen coat and muffler, wearing a long skirt to hide her long skinny legs, wearing brown oxfords as well, stained with mud, for the earlier climb to the top of the hill took her through some marshy ground. Her long black hair blowing in the wind, she is sitting beneath an ancient leafless oak reading, as it were, a paperback novel, when up the hill comes a tall slender woman in a long black cape, chestnut hair blowing all about her head, puffing from the climb, and startled to find Melissa sitting here.

"Hello, hello," she says. "Are you an Eddie?"

"I am, m-m-m-ma'am," Melissa says, for added to her prepubescent problems is a marked stutter.

"Oh, please, no ma'ams, I'm still a miss—more's the pity. I haven't met you before, have I?"

"No, m-m-ma'am, I'm a n-n-new student."

"What's your name, child?"

"M-M-M-Melissa Lowndes."

"I'm Mary Barton, how do you do? I teach English in the upper school, what are you reading? Are you a reader, Melissa?"

"I r-r-r-read all the time, M-M-M-Miss B-B-Barton."

"So do I. What are you reading now?"

Melissa offers her the book. Hesitantly. Mary takes it in her hands, turns it over and over as if it is a rare treasure, though it is merely a cheap romance of the sort the girls call "bodice-rippers."

"Well," she says at last, "I suppose we must read all sorts of trash, mustn't we, if we're finally to appreciate the better stuff," she adds, and hands the book back with a disdainful sniff. "Are you enjoying it, Melissa?"

"N-n-not very m-m-m-much."

"I should think you'd find it boring," Mary says. "A girl of your obvious intelligence."

The word *boring* throws Melissa. She does not yet know that Mary is American; she sounds so very British. She has not yet learned—Mary will later teach her this—that in America, boring has only one meaning, "uninteresting" or "dull," as in "The play was so *boring*, I left after the first act," or "His speech was so *boring*, it put me to sleep." In England, however—and this is what causes Melissa's momentary confusion—the word can also mean "bothersome" or "annoying," as in "I've got a run in my hose, how *boring!*" This is the meaning Melissa first understands, perhaps because the expression "How boring!" is the one most frequently used by girls her age. While she is pondering this, it also occurs to her that this tall chestnut-haired woman with the striking blue eyes has no reason to believe she really *is* intelligent, since, on the evidence, all she reads is trash. Is it possible that she's having her on? But no . . .

"Only an intelligent person could have found the most beautiful spot in all England," Mary says, and grins. "You're sitting under my favorite tree, do you realize, young lady?"

Young lady! Eleven years old! Melissa suddenly feels quite grown-up.

"Since you've usurped my place," Mary says, "I'm sure you won't mind if I join you. I'm still a bit winded from the climb."

They sit together, the young girl and the middle-aged woman, their backs against the leafless tree stark against the piercing blue sky, gazing out over the wooded valley and sandy heathland, across the weald to the distant downs.

Mary sighs.

"So peaceful," she says.

That was the first time they'd shared anything together. Melissa now told me that although they'd scarcely said a word to each other all the while they sat there on that blowy afternoon, and talked little on the walk down the hill and into the town and finally up the lane leading to the stone portals and iron gates of St. Edward's, she'd felt in her presence a closeness she'd never known before. In fact, it was with great disappointment that she learned she would not be in any of Miss Barton's classes until she entered the second form, still a year away. Young lady or not, Melissa was still only eleven, and Mary Barton only taught girls in the upper school—twelve years of age and older.

"How old are the victims?" Melissa asked me now, quite suddenly.

"The youngest was six. Felicity Hammer, the last of them."

"And the others?"

"One was eight, the other seven."

"Well . . . doesn't that strike you as odd?"

"How?"

"Mary taught adolescents. Even if by the furthest stretch of the imagination she could have done these terrible things . . ."

"Can you stretch your imagination that far?"

"No," Melissa said. "Absolutely not."

"Can you conceive of the crimes if adolescent girls were the victims?"

"No."

"Then what are you saying?"

"Mary was interested in passing on knowledge. It's quite impossible to believe she'd be attracted to a six-year-old mind."

"How about a six-year-old *body?*"

"Please. I find even the thought offensive."

"The girls were sexually mutilated."

"I know that."

"Let me ask you flat out, Melissa. In all the time you knew Mary Barton, did she ever do or say anything that could in any way have been taken as a sexual advance?"

"Nothing."

"For example . . . well, you said you hugged and kissed when you saw each other today. How about back then? Was there hugging and kissing with any of her students? Did she ever *touch* you?"

"Of *course* she did. She's a warm and loving person, she . . . listen, I truly find this conversation offensive."

"We'll move on then," I said.

She looked at me.

"Is the state attorney going to ask Miss Barton such questions?"

"Worse ones. If I put her on the stand."

"Will you?"

"It's a risk. But she's virtually all I've got."

"A risk how?"

"She may do herself more harm than good. I don't suppose she used any profanity when you were with her today . . ."

"I've never in my life heard Miss Barton use even the mildest obscenity."

"Well, she does now."

"I find that hard to believe. In fact, none of these characterizations fit her. They simply do not."

"Which characterizations do you mean?"

"Murderess. Child abuser. Child molester. Whatever they're calling her," she said, and shook her head in anger and disgust.

"The children were . . ."

"I *know* what was done to them. Or at least what was hinted at in *Time* magazine."

"I don't think you'd like to see the photographs," I said.

"I feel certain I wouldn't. But Miss Barton couldn't have done such heinous things, don't you see? She was the gentlest woman I've ever known. I remember once . . ."

There was a crushed butterfly. Someone had inadvertently stepped on it, and it lay fluttering, and unable to fly, on the path leading to chapel. This was a bright spring day in Lockbourne, ah to be in England. And the butterfly was all yellow and black, and fluttering feebly on the gravel path leading up the hill to where the old stone church stood in silhouette against an achingly blue sky. It was Miss Barton who first spotted the wounded butterfly. She cried out a single pained word, "Oh!" and knelt immediately and lifted the pitifully broken thing onto the palm of her hand. The girls crowded all round her in a flutter of pleated skirts. There was a mild wind that day, it keened in the overhead branches of the trees. And suddenly Miss Barton was weeping. And just as suddenly . . .

"She closed her fist on the butterfly."

I looked at Melissa.

"To put it out of its misery," she said.

I nodded.

"What else do you remember?" I asked.

"Everything," she said.

For the young girl who was Melissa Lowndes, this was a time of discovery.

Her parents had been divorced . . .

"It runs in the family," she told me now, with a wan smile.

. . . when she was nine years old, and the subsequent turmoil in her young life might have caused her to score poorly on her entrance exams to St. Edward's. But she was a clever child, and neither of her parents was surprised—nor particularly congratulatory—when she passed with very high scores indeed.

She was packed off to St. Edward's when she was barely eleven, and had met Mary Barton some ten days after she'd entered the school. But she did not come under her tutelage till she was twelve, at which time she entered the second form and was permitted to bask in her brilliant glow.

Melissa Lowndes had been through a divorce when she was nine years old. Her father had remarried almost at once . . .

She suspected that young Violetta—who was neither Italian nor Spanish, but merely as pretentious as her name—had been Daddy's little bimbo for years before the marriage ended . . .

. . . and by the time Melissa turned twelve, her mother was not only remarried as well, but pregnant with a child by her new husband, a listless clod named Peter who had nothing to recommend him but an anachronistic hippie's head of long blond hair.

Peter was a street musician. Melissa thought her mother had lost her mind.

She considered it significant now that the person to whom she reported her first menstrual flow was not her mother but Mary Barton, who by then had become her mentor, advisor, and role model.

Oh, the things that woman taught them! Oh, the innumerable joys she introduced, the golden doors she opened, the shining palaces they entered in her presence!

· Who but Miss Barton would take her class walking in the fall woods, pointing out to them the myriad late-blooming treasures unique to the season—blue elderberry shrubs festooned with fallen leaves, tufts of silvery grass, golden fronds of bracken, wild red guelder berries, seed capsules of rosebay, brownish red against dark green moss—teaching them to look for colors more subtle than those they might find in the summer or spring, and then taught them the Wordsworth poem . . .

> *A slumber did my spirit seal;*
> *I had no human fears;*
> *She seemed a thing that could not feel*
> *The touch of earthly years.*

> *No motion has she now, no force;*
> *She neither hears nor sees;*
> *Rolled round in earth's diurnal course,*
> *With rocks, and stones, and trees . . .*

. . . the last two lines of which she linked mysteriously to their woodsy expedition, and taught them besides that the word *diurnal* meant "daily," which Melissa was willing to bet not many people knew.

It was Miss Barton who took them to the sea one day in early spring, shortly after the Easter break . . .

As usual, Melissa had spent part of her holiday with her hugely imminent mother and Peter in the flat they were renting off Kensington High Street, and part of it with her father and his darling Violetta, who were then living in a three-story house overlooking Regent's Park, all the while longing to return to St. Edward's . . .

Which, of course, she did in mid-April when, despite the chill in the air, there were crocuses and daffodils blooming everywhere . . .

"The spring is always so lovely in England," she said now.

. . . oh, such a glorious spring, and Miss Barton, as usual, full of glorious ideas. This time she announced to the class that she had hired a big blue bus for an outing she had planned for the very next day. And when they all piled into the ramshackle vehicle the next morning, she herself got behind the wheel—which all the girls were certain was against the law or at least against St. Edward's regulations—and drove them to Lexton-on-Sea, where white cliffs fell away to a crashing gray sea below. And there, as they sat all about her in a semicircle facing the sea, their skirts bundled about them, their collars raised, their hair flying in the wind, she stood in her flapping cape and read to them aloud from *King Lear* . . .

> *Blow, winds, and crack your cheeks! rage! blow!*
> *You cataracts and hurricanes, spout*
> *Till you have drench'd our steeples, drown'd the cocks!*
> *You sulph'rous and thought-executing fires,*
> *Vaunt-couriers to oak-cleaving thunderbolts*
> *Singe my white head! And thou, all-shaking thunder,*
> *Strike flat the thick rotundity of the world . . .*

. . . and they learned that day the inseparable fierceness and beauty of Shakespeare's language and the sceptered isle that had inspired it.

She stormed into their biology class one day and railed against their instructor for allowing the girls to dissect *frogs* after she had only the day before taught them *Wind in the Willows,* which they had thought a mere children's fantasy until she pointed out the allegory at its very heart. When the instructor, a man named Peter Battington—why were there so many assholes named Peter in this world?

She surprised me when she used this word.

When Mr. *Peter* Battington demanded that Miss Barton leave his classroom at once or he would be forced to eject her bodily, she caught his hand in what she later described as a "thumb lock" (and still later taught them how to execute in the event they were attacked by muggers or worse) and forced him to his knees, and elicited from him a squealed promise that he would never again expose these impressionable young ladies to the horrors of dissection.

I was thinking of what someone with a knife had done to the little girls in Mary's garden.

But Melissa was saying now that their precious Miss Barton had taught John Lennon's lyrics with a reverence that made the girls view the Beatles in an entirely different light. "I Am the Walrus" must have been a good ten years old by then, but when she recited the words to them as poetry . . .

> *I am he*
> *as you are he*
> *as you are me*
> *and we are all together . . .*

. . . they listened anew and discovered fresh insights . . .

> *. . . pornographic priestess,*
> *boy you've been a naughty girl,*
> *you let your knickers down . . .*

. . . and learned how pallid were most rock lyrics when compared to the genius of Lennon's . . .

Yellow matter custard
dripping from a dead dog's eye . . .

"She was every teacher any young girl might have wished for," Melissa said, her eyes glowing. "A very special person who taught us to love the English language, and who taught us as well . . ."

She hesitated, staring off into space, searching for the words that would define for me this woman who'd been so very important to her.

"She taught us love," Melissa said at last, and nodded. "So when you ask, 'Did she ever touch you?' I say, yes, she touched me. She touched all of us. She reached into our hearts and found what needed to be nurtured there. And she caused us to grow. To become young ladies first, and then, by the time we went off to university, *women* who were ready to enter this larger world she'd taught us to understand.

"She touched us, yes. And she touched us physically as well, yes, if that's your question, yes. Kind reassuring touches of her hand . . . encouraging little pats when finally we understood something, warm . . . maternal embraces? Sisterly embraces? *Hugs.* Great crushing bear hugs that told us we were doing well, we were coming along, we were learning, we were growing, we were becoming the kind of women she'd visualized us to be. But to think of any of this as . . . no. We weren't children when we left her, you know, we would have known. We were eighteen by then, and sexually aware. There was *nothing* like that. We would have known. And neither was there anything that foreshadowed these terrible murders."

Melissa picked up her wine glass.

"There was never a more loved or respected teacher in all St. Edward's history. Ring them up. Ask them. They'll tell you."

I wondered if Mrs. Morden was still there.

"But surely," Melissa said, "you have people in this country who'll tell you the same thing, haven't you?"

"We're working on that now," I said. "Mary's background. Her past."

"I should expect so," Melissa said.

She'd been born in Renegade, South Dakota, on November 5, 1933. Her parents' names were Robert and Judy Barton. She'd attended elementary school in Renegade and then had gone on to secondary school and high school in the neighboring town of Lesterville. Her undergraduate studies were at the University of Colorado. She entered the college in 1951 and was graduated from it in June of 1955, two months before her parents died in a car crash. She entered N.Y.U. in September of that year and received her master's degree in June of 1957. She applied for the job at the Elizabeth Wagner School that summer and began working there in September of 1957, when the school term started. She left there in June of 1963 and spent several years in London before joining the staff at St. Edward's, from which prestigious girls' school she was dismissed after a brouhaha over curriculum. She had been living in Calusa for the past five years.

This much I had learned from Mary.

This much she had also told the two psychiatrists who'd examined her and declared her fit to stand trial.

One of them was named Dr. Milton Canfield. He had no question that under the meaning of Chapter 916.2, there'd been no question about her competence.

"There were only two criteria I needed to address," he told me. "First, did she have sufficient present ability to consult with her lawyer with a reasonable degree of rational understanding? The answer to that was yes."

I agreed that the answer to that was yes.

"Second, did she have a rational as well as factual understanding of the proceedings against her? The answer to that was also yes. I had no doubt that under the statute she was competent to stand trial."

Dr. Avery Haynes wasn't quite so sure.

"Well, yes," he said, "within the meaning of the act, she was competent, and I declared her so. But, you know . . . there were things that came up during our various discussions . . ."

"What sort of things?" I said.

"Well, for one, a definite ambiguity about self. For example, she sometimes made references to herself in the third person. *She* did this, *she* did that, rather than *I* did this, *I* did that. And I detected certain unconscious comparisons to an evil alter ego. Some *other* person, if you will, who is and—at the same time— is *not* a part of Miss Barton herself. A quite *other* person who sometimes commits violent acts. Although I must confess these acts were never clearly defined for me. I feel confident, however, that at some time in her past, she's heard voices . . . which, as I'm sure you know, is often a symptom of paranoia. And I was convinced as well that she feels persecuted, hounded, chased by demons she cannot control . . . another sign of paranoia. But is she competent under the meaning of the statute? She is competent under the meaning of the statute."

The trial was set to begin on November 23.

The State Attorney's Office had four witnesses who'd seen Mary in the presence of the murdered girls on the weekend preceding the discovery of the bodies. They also had a witness who'd seen Mary burying Felicity Hammer in her backyard. They had yet another witness who claimed Mary had brought her bloodstained dress to him to be dry-cleaned. As physical evidence, they had the dress itself, a bloodstained shovel found in Mary's potting shed, and a pair of white, low-top sneakers in Mary's size, which had been recovered in a sewer drain four blocks from the dry-cleaning shop. The sneakers, too, were bloodstained. And soil samples taken from their soles matched the chemical composition of the soil in Mary's garden. Skye Bannister felt he had an airtight case. As for myself, I had nothing to show that

Mary Barton had not committed the murders as charged. My entire case would be built on misidentification.

Toward the end of October, Skye Bannister came to me with a simple deal. It was, in fact, the deal I'd thought *Patricia* was going to offer the first night we went berserk. Skye was asking me to exchange the electric chair for three consecutive life sentences without parole; he was asking me to lock up my client forever.

"I'm trying to be perfectly fair with you, Matthew," he said. "We've been very lucky so far that your reputation in this town hasn't been sullied, not to mention Pat's or the State Attorney's Office. I consider it unfortunate that I have a hot-pantsed assistant . . ."

"Leave it right there," I said.

"I'm sorry you're so touchy about this, Matthew, but . . ."

"Just stop calling Patricia hot-pantsed, and while you're at it, stop calling her Pat."

Skye looked at me.

"Maybe I'll forget all about the deal," he said.

"Good, do it," I said. "I'll see you in court."

"I'd rather settle this now," he said. "Take the deal. I'd planned to send Pat . . . Patricia . . . to another county to sit this out. There's a murder I'm thinking of could take her through February. But if we can settle this now, I can always change my mind, yank her back from the boonies. After that, I don't care if the two of you screw your brains out on the dock at Marina . . ."

"Skye," I said, "I'm going to risk assault and punch you right in the fucking mouth."

"You've already committed assault," he said. "Chapter 784.011: An 'assault' is an intentional, unlawful threat by word or act to do violence to the person of another, coupled with an apparent ability . . ."

"You hear me, Skye?"

"All right, all right, all right, all right," he said, waving his hands in the air. "All I'm trying to say is that attorneys *have* had relationships with attorneys in the State Attorney's Office before, without putting the office in jeopardy. So long as you and Pat . . . I find it very hard to call her Patricia."

"Try," I said.

"So long as you and Patricia never lock horns, I see no reason why you can't continue enjoying each other's company."

"Gee, thanks so very goddamn much," I said.

"Matthew," he said at his pontifical best, "I wish you'd believe I'm trying to be your friend."

"I believe it," I said. "But tell me something. If you think you've got such an airtight case, why are you shopping a deal?"

"Because I feel sorry for that poor woman," Skye said.

"Why? If she's such a monster . . ."

"I think she is, yes."

"Then why not send her to the chair? Why not rid society of her?"

"Because I feel justice will be adequately served if she spends the rest of her life behind bars."

What he was saying was that he'd already announced to the press that he was in favor of repealing Florida's capital punishment laws. Old Uncle Skye was planning to ride into the governor's mansion on a platform that wasn't wired to the electric chair. A bad way to start would be to go for the death penalty in the Barton case.

"I'm trying to show a little mercy here," he said.

Bullshit, I thought.

"Well," I said, "I'll relay your offer to my . . ."

"Good."

". . . client, but I'll advise her to turn it down."

"Why?"

"Because she's innocent."

"I've assigned Max Atkins to the case," he said. "I think you know him."

Max "The Ax" Atkins.

A terror.

"I know him," I said.

"Tell your client she takes the deal or Max fries her."

"I'll tell her," I said.

I offered the deal to Mary.

She told me she could not in any good conscience go to prison for something someone else had done.

I wondered if this "someone else" was the evil alter ego Dr. Haynes had uncovered. Some *other* person who was and—at the same time—was *not* a part of Miss Barton herself. A quite *other* person who sometimes committed violent acts.

I told her I would relay her wishes to the state attorney.

And then, on the twenty-third of November, come what might, we would go to court.

There was always her and me. She was the bad one. They didn't know about her. About how bad she was.

She was the one who killed the cat.

They all said I did it. I told them it was her. They didn't know how bad she could be.

I kept saying, Daddy, I didn't do it, I swear, it was Mary Jean, I swear to God. I'll give you Mary Jean, he said, and took off his strap and whipped me on the backs of my thighs where it was tender, raised welts all up and down the backs of my thighs.

They'd found the cat under the front porch.

Throat slit, white fur all covered with blood.

Said I'd done it, whipped me on my thighs and locked me in the closet. Overcoats hanging above me, galoshes on the floor where I huddled, kept me in there all night where I whimpered in the dark. She had the bedroom all to herself that night, pretty dolls all over the bed, all over the bed, all to herself. She laughed when they finally let me back upstairs again. Only when we were alone would she tell me terrible things. Never when anyone else was around. Told me she was the one who'd killed the cat, so there! And she'd do it again, just try and stop her! Laughing. Lying on the bed with all the pretty dolls around her.

They always blamed me for the bad things Mary Jean did.

I never could convince them it was Mary Jean who was doing the bad things. I had nothing to do with all the bad things she did.

Thought I'd lost her once and for all when I moved to England.

Well, she couldn't follow me there, could she? All the way across the ocean? Couldn't do her bad things all the way over there, could she?

Mary Barton.

That's who I was in England.

Miss Mary Barton.

I was free. With no Mary Jean to get me in trouble anymore, I was free. No father to whip me anymore, he was dead. Mother was dead, too, couldn't shake her head whenever I told her Mary Jean had done it, shame on you. Always blame it on Mary Jean, don't you? Always blame the bad things on her, don't you? I'll give you Mary Jean. The strap burning the back of my thighs. No more of that. I was free. Free to teach whatever I wanted to, don't you tell *me* what to teach! I was free.

And then . . .

Ah, Jesus, why does everything have to end?

Why do the fucking Mordens of the world have to close in with their small minds and their mean thoughts, why do they have to come and steal the only thing that's keeping a person afloat . . .

The job I loved, the little girls I loved . . .

Why did they have to steal all that from me?

Why did they have to send me back to where Mary Jean was waiting to do bad things again?

Why?

6

Hear ye, hear ye, the Circuit Court of the Twelfth Judicial Circuit of the State of Florida, in and for Calusa County Criminal Division, is now in session, the Honorable Helen G. Rutherford presiding, all rise."

Judge Rutherford was in her late forties, I guessed, her prematurely white hair cut in a flying wedge that made it seem as if any wayward breeze might send her soaring up to the wood-paneled ceiling of the courtroom. She swept in from her chambers, black bat-wing robes swirling about her, took her seat behind the bench, smiled pleasantly, murmured, "Please be seated, everyone, please," and then looked out over the packed courtroom.

"Good morning, everyone," she said. "I see Miss Barton is present with counsel, and state is also present. The jury and all court personnel are present as well, so let's begin, shall we?"

Today was the seventh day of December, a Monday, Pearl Harbor Day all over America. It had taken us two full weeks to select the eight women and four men on the jury. The four men were all white. Of the eight women, four of them were white, three of them were black, and one was a Hispanic who'd migrated from Cuba fourteen years ago. She was the most intelligent woman on the jury. In fact, she was the most intelligent *person* on it. There's an old jury-selection rule of thumb that maintains, "One of anything is bad." Most prosecutors follow it scrupulously because they know that a lone ranger creates a potential for conflict and a possible later mistrial. I considered myself lucky that Atkins had let her slip by.

Six of the women had children of their own, one of them was pregnant, and the last one—my Mrs. Rodriguez from Cuba—was too old to bear. Two of the men were in favor of the death penalty in cases where the crime was particularly heinous—as Judge Rutherford had labeled this one when she'd denied bail—and two of them had said they were indifferent to it either way.

Rutherford turned to the jury now.

"Ladies and gentlemen," she said, "you've been selected and sworn as the jury to try the case of The State of Florida versus Mary Barton. This is a criminal case. The defendant, Mary Barton, has been charged with three counts of murder in the first degree. The definition of these crimes will be explained to you later, but before proceeding any further, I think it will be helpful if I explained certain other matters to you. To begin with, please understand that it is the *judge's* responsibility, *my* responsibility, to decide which *laws* apply to this case and to explain those laws to you. It is *your* responsibility to decide what the *facts* of the case may be and to apply the law to those facts. Thus, the province of the jury and the province of the court are well defined and do not overlap. This is one of the fundamental principles of our system of justice.

"It's important that you understand how a trial is conducted. At the beginning of the trial, each attorney will have an opportunity—if he so wishes—to make an opening statement. The opening statement gives each attorney a chance to tell you what evidence he believes will be presented during the trial. What the lawyers say is not—I repeat, *not*—evidence, and you are not to consider it as such. Your verdict must be based solely on the evidence or lack of evidence.

"Following the opening statements, witnesses will be called to testify under oath. They will be examined and cross-examined by the attorneys. Documents and other exhibits may also be produced as evidence. You should not form any definite or fixed opinion on the merits of the case until you've heard all the evidence, the opening and closing arguments of the lawyers, and the instructions on the law by the judge. Until then, you must not even discuss the case among yourselves. During any court recess, you will not discuss the case with *anyone,* nor permit anyone to say anything to you or in your presence about the case. If anyone attempts to say anything to you or in your presence about this case, tell him that you're on the jury trying the case and ask him to stop. If he persists, leave him at once and immediately report the matter to one of the bailiffs, who will advise me.

"In every criminal proceeding, a defendant has the absolute right to remain silent. At no time is it the duty of the defendant to prove his innocence. In fact, it is your solemn responsibility to determine if the state has proved beyond a reasonable doubt its accusation against the defendant. From the exercise of a defendant's right to remain silent, a jury is not permitted to draw any inference of guilt. And the fact that a defendant did not take the witness stand must not influence your verdict in any manner whatsoever.

"The attorneys are trained in the Rules of Evidence and Trial Procedure. And it is their duty to make all objections they feel are proper. When an objection is made, you should not speculate on the reason why it is made. Likewise, when an objection is sustained or upheld by me, you must not speculate on what might have occurred had the objection not been sustained, nor what a witness might have said had he been permitted to answer.

"Now I think I should explain something else to you. In any court of law, we have what we call 'bench conferences' or 'side bars' where the lawyers will come up and whisper to me and I'll whisper back to them. We're not trying to be rude or secretive, we're simply trying to clear up any matter of law on which there's a difference of opinion, so that we can decide fairly what should be allowed before the jury and what shouldn't.

"One last thing. There are two noise-making machines in the jury room. They blow a lot of wind and make a lot of noise. I've been told that without those noise-making machines, if the jury is sent to the jury room it can still hear what the judge and the opposing attorneys are talking about out here. Maybe a hundred years from now, we'll have a soundproof jury room, but meanwhile, I ask you please to put up with the noise-making machines. They're simply a way of making certain that the jury is presented only with the evidence and the facts, and not with arguments of law between the lawyers and the judge.

"So . . . I think that's everything. You may proceed with your opening statement, if you wish, Mr. Atkins."

"Thank you, Your Honor," Atkins said, and rose from the prosecutor's table and walked to the jury box. "Good morning," he said.

Atkins was in his sixties, a lean and handsome man who favored dark blue suits and ties, white shirts, and black highly polished shoes. He was now senior counsel on the state attorney's staff, but he had earned his reputation as a shark long before Skye Bannister tapped him for public service. I had never liked him because he treated me with a monumental lack of respect, rarely if ever greeting me in and around the courthouse or in the S.A.'s Offices, where I was a frequent visitor, exuding in my presence the air of an elder statesman too busy, too sophisticated, and too learned in the ways of the law to bother with a neophyte.

In his opening statement, he played the jury as if the verdict were already in. The fact that I was in the courtroom was of no interest to him. This was something he and the jury would work out together. He never once looked at me during his long opening statement. He never once looked at Mary, either. Neither of us existed. Max Atkins and the jury he was leading into complicity were getting ready to fry Mary, and the hell with anything else. What he did, in effect, was to provide a road map to the evidence. He summarized for them the allegations against Mary, explained how he intended to prove them, and then asked that they find the defendant guilty beyond reasonable doubt. He spoke for an hour and twenty minutes, and by the end of his persuasive discourse, I felt we'd already lost the case.

There was a brief recess before I started my opening statement. Seated at the defense table were Mary Barton and Andrew Holmes—newest addition to the firm of Summerville and Hope, and serving as my assistant during the trial. Dark curly hair, brown eyes, an aquiline nose, and a somewhat androgynous mouth with a thin upper lip and a pouting lower one. He was wearing a dark suit and eyeglasses that made him look scholarly. Beside him, Mary was dressed for court in a simple skirt, blouse, and jacket.

"Your Honor," I said . . .

A nod toward the judge.

"Ladies and gentlemen of the jury . . ."

Turning back to them.

"We're here in this courtroom today . . ."

. . . and I launched into what many defense attorneys call the "Let Freedom Ring" opening, explaining to the jury that we were here to seek truth and justice, and that it was important for them to listen very carefully to all of the testimony and to view with the same care any physical evidence presented to them. I gave them my own detailed guided tour of the evidence they would be hearing in the days to come, asked them to remember that Mary Barton was innocent until proven guilty, told them that it was the state attorney's obligation to prove her guilty *beyond* any reasonable doubt, and that if he failed in this, if there remained the *slightest* doubt whatever in their minds, they must bring back to this court a verdict of not guilty. I concluded with the sincere hope that after they had heard the evidence presented by both sides, this would indeed be their verdict.

I spoke for a bit more than an hour.

My partner Frank, who'd been sitting at the back of the court-room, told me during recess that I'd done a good job.

Mary Barton didn't say anything to me.

From the moment The Ax called his first witness, it became clear that his presentation would be modeled on what in law school we used to call the "Chronological Construct." This minute-by-minute approach made things simpler for the jury to follow, but it had several built-in dangers.

A jury at the start of any trial was traditionally more alert than it was three, four weeks into the trial; beginning at the very beginning—as Atkins now did—was considerably less dramatic than starting with, for example, the discovery of little Felicity Hammer's body while the telephone repairman was digging his trench. But Atkins's strategy was to make every man and woman on that jury feel privileged, an invited equal in his own living room, discussing matters as if they themselves had helped him prepare the case and had already reached the conclusion that the defendant was guilty as charged. Toward that end, a chronology made the law seem elementary and caused every juror to feel like a member of the Supreme Court.

"Miss Fowler," Atkins said, "can you tell me where you were living this past August? Do you recall where you were living at that time?"

"Same place I'm living now," she said.

Gertrude Fowler. Forty-seven years old, with short brown hair and a face wrinkled by too much smoking and too much exposure to the sun. Wearing a simple blue dress, sand-colored panty hose, and what my mother used to call "sensible shoes," she fastened her brown eyes intently on Atkins.

"And where is that?" he asked. "Can you tell us?"

"In Somerset, Florida."

"How far is that from Calusa, can you tell us?"

"About a hundred miles."

"Now, at that time, can you tell us what your occupation was?"

"I worked for the G&S Supermarket on Orange and South Tenth."

"In what capacity?"

"I was a checker."

"Can you explain that to us? What a checker does?"

His strategy was to personalize everything for the jury, include them in this exclusive collaboration of good guys versus subhumans beyond contempt. He never once looked at Mary or me. Everything was to the witness and to the jury. Tell us about it. Tell me and my learned colleagues all about what a checker does.

"I worked at one of the checkout counters," Gertrude said simply. "Tallying the purchases, sometimes packing when we didn't have a packer."

"I ask you to look at the defendant," Atkins said.

Old prosecuting attorney trick. Never refer to the accused by name. Depersonalize him or her completely, ever mindful that a jury doesn't want to bear any later guilt for having sent someone to prison or to death. The defendant. The accused. Certainly *not* a woman who had a name: Mary Barton.

Gertrude took a long, hard look at her. Atkins didn't even deign to turn from the witness chair.

"Have you ever seen this person before?" he asked.

The way he spoke the word *person* made it sound as if it were a synonym for *beast* or *creature* or *monster*. Have you ever seen this *person* before, a slight hesitation before the word, as if the word itself were unspeakable. Person. This *person*.

"Yes, I've seen her."

"Can you tell us where?"

"In the G&S Supermarket."

"When was this, Miss Fowler?"

"In August."

"This past August?"

"Yes."

"Do you recall the exact date?"

"August twenty-eighth."

"You saw the defendant on August twenty-eighth, at the G&S Supermarket in Somerset, Florida, is that correct?"

"That is correct."

"Do you recall what day of the week that might have been?"

"A Friday. We always have a busy day Friday."

"What time of the day was this?"

"A little past three."

"Five past three, ten past . . ."

"Ten or fifteen minutes past three, I'd say."

"Tell us what you remember about the occasion?"

"She came to the checkout counter with some candy she had purchased."

"Do you remember what kind of candy?"

"Not exactly. Some chocolate bars. A handful of chocolate bars."

"Did she say anything to you?"

"No, she was busy with the little girl who was with her."

"When you say 'busy' . . ."

"She was talking to her."

"To a little girl who was with her."

"Yes."

"Did you know who the defendant was at the time?"

"No, I did not."

"Did you know who the little girl was?"

"No, sir, I did not."

"Do you know who she is now? The little girl?"

"Yes, sir, I do."

"Your Honor, I ask that this photograph be marked for identification, please."

"May I see it, please?" I said.

Atkins, unwilling to be polluted by the stench of serial murder at the defense table, disdainfully handed the photograph to one of the bailiffs, who carried it over to me. I glanced at it briefly.

"No objection," I said.

"Mark it Exhibit One for the prosecution," Rutherford said.

"Miss Fowler," Atkins said, "I ask you to look at this photograph, please."

Gertrude took the glossy eight-by-ten, studied it, looked up.

"Do you recognize the little girl in this photograph?" Atkins asked.

"I do."

"Is she the same little girl you saw in the company of the defendant on August twenty-eighth?"

"She is."

"Your Honor, will the defense stipulate that this is a photograph of one of the murder victims, Jenny Lou Williams?"

"Mr. Hope?"

"So stipulated."

"Now, Miss Fowler, can you tell us whether or not the defendant said anything to you at the checkout counter?"

"Nothing."

"Did she say anything at all to *anybody?*"

"She was talking to the little girl."

"She was talking to Jenny Lou Williams, is that correct?"

"Well, I didn't know who the child was at the time . . ."

"But you know *now,* do you not, that she was Jenny Lou Williams?"

"Yes, I know that now."

"And you say the defendant was talking to her, is that correct?"

"That's correct."

"What did she say?"

"She asked her if she'd like to walk over to the park and eat all the nice candy there."

"Did she mention Jenny Lou's name?"

Personalizing the victim. Jenny Lou. No longer "the little girl." Jenny Lou now. The Defendant and Jenny Lou.

"No, she did not."

"Did Jenny Lou say anything to her?"

"Yes."

"What did she say? Please tell . . ."

"Objection," I said, rising at once. "That would be hearsay, Your Honor."

"Please approach," Rutherford said.

Atkins and I stepped up to the bench. He still would not look at me. His show was designed to indicate to the jury that I was somehow tainted by defending such a monstrous woman.

"Where are you going, Mr. Atkins?" Rutherford asked.

"To the events leading to the subsequent disappearance of Jenny Lou Williams on the twenty-eighth of August."

"Your Honor," I said, "whatever the witness says she *heard* the child say cannot be refuted in this court."

"Perhaps that's because Jenny Lou Williams is *dead*," Atkins said drily, still unwilling even to glance at me. "In any event, Your Honor, the deceased's conversation would be reflective of her state of mind and clearly excepted under the hearsay rule."

"I'll allow it," Rutherford said, "provided the child's conversation goes to her state of mind and not to the truth of the matter asserted."

"I promise it will, Your Honor."

"I'll cut you off if it doesn't," she said. "Let's proceed."

I went back to the defense table. Atkins went back to the witness chair.

"Miss Fowler," he said, "can you tell us what Jenny Lou said when the accused suggested they go to the park to eat all that nice candy?"

"She said that would be terrific."

"That was her exact word? 'Terrific?'"

"Terrific, yes."

"Did she seem excited by the prospect?"

"Leading, Your Honor."

"Rephrase it, Mr. Atkins."

"How'd she look when she said it would be terrific to go over to the park with the defendant?"

"Flushed. Happy. Eager to go."

"Did she ever once mention the defendant by name?"

"No."

"Did she seem to *know* the defendant?"

"Yes, she did. She took her hand as they were leaving the store."

"Jenny Lou took the defendant's hand?"

"Yes."

"And then what?"

"She went skipping out of the store, holding her hand."

"What time was this?"

"Three-twenty, I'd say. About then."

"Now, Miss Fowler, subsequent to that twenty-eighth day of August, did you ever see the defendant again?"

"I did."

"Where and under what circumstances?"

"In a lineup at the Public Safety Building in Calusa."

"When was this?"

"On the second of September."

"Did you at that time identify the defendant as the woman you'd seen in the supermarket on August twenty-eighth?"

"I did."

"Thank you, no further questions."

I took my time rising. I pretended to study some notes I'd already memorized, put them back on the defense table, and walked to where Gertrude Fowler stood waiting for what she was certain would be an attack, hands clutched over her pocketbook, eyes suspicious.

"Miss Fowler," I said in greeting, and nodded and smiled.

She said nothing.

"Miss Fowler, how old are you, please?"

"Forty-seven," she said.

"In good health?"

"Yes."

"Were you in good health last August?"

"Very good health."

"Eyes okay?"

"Eyes fine, thank you."

"You wear glasses, don't you?"

"Sometimes."

"While you were working at the G&S . . . by the way, do you still work there?"

"No, I don't."

"How long has it been since you've worked there?"

"I left in October."

"So you haven't worked there for . . . well, it'd be two months now, is that right?"

"Almost."

"Miss Fowler, when you did work there, did you wear eyeglasses?"

"I did."

"And you still wear them. Sometimes."

"For close work."

"Like what?"

"Reading."

"Like reading the figures on various supermarket items?"

"I was referring to reading a newspaper or a book. But yes, that, too."

"Were you wearing your glasses on the day you say you saw Mary Barton at the G&S?"

"I was."

"Your reading glasses?"

"Yes."

"How close were you standing to Mary Barton when you say you saw her?"

"No more than three feet away."

"Wearing your reading glasses. Your glasses for 'close work,' as you put it."

"Yes."

"Miss Fowler, when did you first learn that Jenny Lou Williams was missing and that foul play was suspected?"

"I don't remember."

"Well, she disappeared on that same day you say you saw her in the G&S, didn't she?"

"I don't remember when she disappeared."

"Didn't read anything about it in the newspapers?"

"No."

"Do you know it was all over the newspapers?"

"I suppose so, but I don't remember reading anything about it."

"See anything about it on television?"

"No, I don't recall seeing anything about it."

"I'm talking about the several days following her disappearance, you understand that, don't you?"

"Yes."

"When *did* you learn that Jenny Lou Williams had disappeared?"

"When I read about the bodies they dug up in that woman's yard," she said, and nodded toward Mary.

"I see. That was on the first of September, wasn't it?"

"Yes."

"Of this year."

"Yes."

"September the first was when those horribly mutilated bodies were discovered."

"Yes."

"And the news broke on television and in the papers the very next day. Well, television that *night*, in fact. Did you hear about the murders on television?"

"No, I read about them in the newspapers."

"So, as I understand this, between August twenty-eighth and September *second*, it would have been, you knew nothing further about Jenny Lou Williams or the woman you saw her with at the G&S checking counter."

"That's right."

"You heard about them again on the second of September?"

"I *read* about them."

"Did you see their pictures in the newspaper?"

"Yes."

"Mary Barton's picture?"

"Yes."

"And Jenny Lou Williams's picture?"

"Yes. There were pictures of all the victims."

"So that's when you remembered 'Gee, I saw these two at the G&S checkout four days ago!' "

"That's not the way I remembered it."

"How *did* you remember it?"

"I saw the pictures, and I thought they looked familiar."

"Yes, and then what?"

"I called the police."

"In Somerset?"

"Yes."

"And then what?"

"They questioned me. And then someone from the State Attorney's Office came up there to see me . . ."

"Do you remember who that was?"

"It was a woman named Patricia Demming."

"Did she help you remember Miss Barton?"

"She ran a lineup for me."

"At the Public Safety Building in Calusa, is that correct?"

"Yes."

"This was *after* you'd seen Mary Barton's picture in the newspaper, is that right?"

"Yes."

"*After* you knew she'd been arrested and charged with the murder of Jenny Lou Williams, is that right?"

"*And* the others."

"But it was Jenny Lou Williams you claim you saw with Miss Barton."

"Yes."

"And you identified Miss Barton in a lineup only *after* you'd seen her picture in the newspaper and knew she'd been charged with these crimes?"

"Yes."

"Were you wearing your glasses during that lineup?"

"The stage was . . ."

"Yes or no?"

"No."

"Thank you. No further questions."

Atkins unfolded the entire length of his long body from the chair behind the prosecution's table, sniffed the air in the space I'd recently occupied as though certain an animal had unexpectedly died in it, moved closer to the witness stand, leaned in to Gertrude, and said, "Miss Fowler, how far was the stage from the seats in the so-called Showup Room at the Public Safety Building?"

"I'd say twenty feet."

"Glass partition between you and the stage, is that right?"

"Yes."

"Could you see clearly at that distance?"

"I could."

"Without eyeglasses?"

"I don't wear distance glasses. I'm farsighted."

"So you could see and identify the defendant *without* the aid of eyeglasses, isn't that so?"

"Exactly."

"And you identified the woman in that lineup as the same woman you'd seen holding little Jenny Lou Williams's hand on the day she disappeared."

"Yes. The same woman."

"The accused."

"Yes."

"The person sitting right there."

"Yes. The very same person."

"Miss Fowler, let me ask you . . . why'd you wait five full days before coming forth?"

"Because I didn't know anything had happened to that little girl."

"And when you found out about it, you went directly to the police, did you not?"

"I did."

"Thank you very much."

"Mr. Hope?"

"Just a few more questions," I said, and walked over to the witness stand and leaned in tight, and said, "Tell me, Miss Fowler, who else was in the G&S on that August twenty-eighth?"

"What?"

"Who else was in the store that day? Do you remember any of the other customers?"

"Well . . . no, I don't."

"What kind of a day was it, do you remember that?"

"No."

"Sunny, cloudy, rainy, you don't remember, do you?"

"No, I don't."

"Because it was almost four months ago, wasn't it?"

"Well . . ."

"Well, that's what it was. Four long months ago, isn't that right?"

"Three months. Just a bit more than three months."

"Ah, only *three* long months ago. But you remembered Mary Barton and Jenny Lou Williams from that day, is that what you're saying?"

"Yes. Because the little girl was murdered."

"But when they were in that store, *if* they were in that store . . ."

"Objection."

"Overruled."

". . . *if* they were in that store, Jenny Lou Williams hadn't *yet* been murdered, had she?"

"Of course not!"

"Then what reason did you have to remember her? *Or* Mary

Barton? What reason did you have to remember a woman and a child checking out candy? What possible reason on earth?"

"I just remembered them, that's all."

"That's not a reason, Miss Fowler."

"I don't have a reason. I saw their pictures in the paper and I remembered them."

"Nothing further, Your Honor."

7

On Tuesday morning, the eighth day of December, Max the Ax called his second witness, confirming—if confirmation were needed—that he intended to build his chain of circumstantial evidence in chronological order. We were back again to the afternoon of August 28, picking up the sequence where Gertrude Fowler had left off . . .

The time is three thirty-seven P.M. Edward Farrow, sixty-nine years old, is sitting in a small park in the center of the town that is Somerset, Florida, basking in the sunshine, his straw hat on the bench beside him. It is his habit to go for his afternoon walk every day at two-thirty, walking for an hour, and then sitting in the park for fifteen minutes before ambling home leisurely. He's a fit-looking man, even though he suffered a heart attack three years earlier . . .

"Made me mad as hell," he tells the court in an aside. "I'd been going to Nautilus three times a week, exercising regularly, watching my diet, only thing wrong I did was smoke two packs of cigarettes a day . . ."

This last elicits laughter in the courtroom.

Edward Farrow was the worst kind of witness a defending attorney could hope for: a goddamn lovable old coot. Trying to impeach him would be like trying to stick a knife in George Burns's heart.

At three thirty-seven sharp . . .

He knows because he always sits on the bench for exactly fifteen minutes, cooling down, and he checks his watch frequently, a digital watch . . .

At three thirty-seven sharp on his digital watch, a woman walks into the park with a little girl. The woman has gray hair and piercing blue eyes that flash in the sunshine. The little girl is wearing a yellow dirndl . . .

"I know about different kinds of dresses," he says. "I used to be in the rag trade before I moved down to Florida . . ."

Eliciting another laugh, they just *love* this old bastard.

. . . skipping along in the sunshine, holding the woman's hand. He thinks at first it is her grandmother, but realizes almost at once that the two are not related . . .

"How did you come to realize that, Mr. Farrow?"

"I heard the little girl call her by name."

"What name did she use, can you tell us?"

"Mary."

"She called the woman Mary?"

"She did."

"Did the woman use the little girl's name?"

"Not that I heard."

"All right, what happened then?"

What happened then was that the woman and the little girl sat on the bench across from his, and the woman opened this little brown paper bag she had and reached into it and handed the little girl a candy bar, and then reached into it again and took out a candy bar for herself. And the two of them sat there in the sunshine, the woman chewing on one candy bar, and the little girl chewing on another one, the little girl chattering away, the woman nodding and smiling and occasionally patting her hand . . .

"Did the little girl seem at all frightened?"

"Oh no. She was having a dandy time."

"Did you hear anything else?"

"I did."

"What did you hear?"

"I heard the woman say, 'Let me drive you home now, darling.' "

"And did the little girl go with her?"

"She did."

"She went with the defendant?"

"Yes."

"Did they get up off the bench?"

"They did."

"Did they leave the park?"

"They did."

"Together?"

"Together."

"Mr. Farrow, I show you this photograph previously marked for identification," Atkins said, and handed it to him. "Can you tell me who that is in the picture?"

"That's the little girl I saw in the park that day."

"Did you know who she was at the time?"

"No."

"Do you know who she is now?"

"Jenny Lou Williams."

"How do you come by this knowledge?"

"I've since seen her picture in the paper and on television."

Atkins was adjusting his examination of Farrow to reflect the questions I'd asked his previous witness—cutting me off at the pass, so to speak.

"Mr. Farrow, if you saw the woman who was with Jenny Lou in the park that day . . . would you recognize her?"

"I would."

"I ask you to look around this courtroom. Do you see the woman you saw in the park with Jenny Lou Williams that day?"

"I do."

"Would you point her out to me, please?"

"She's sitting right there."

"Are you pointing to the defendant in this trial?"

"I am."

"Did you know at the time that this woman was Mary Barton?"

"I did not."

"When did you learn her name?"

"When I saw her picture on television."

"And is that when you came forward?"

"Yes, sir. That's when I called the police."

"Did the police subsequently run a lineup for you?"

"They did."

"And did you identify the defendant during this lineup?"

"I did."

"Identified her as the woman you'd seen in the park with Jenny Lou Williams on the afternoon of August twenty-eighth?"

"That's right."

"Your witness."

Toots Kiley had done a good job of research on Edward Farrow, and I'd surreptitiously tested the information when I'd deposed him. I was now ready to run it before the jury at full gallop. Farrow, old lovable grandpa that he was, sat all unsuspecting and smiling in welcome as I approached the bench. I didn't like what I was about to do to him, but he wasn't the one looking at the electric chair.

"Mr. Farrow," I said, "please tell me how old are you."

"Sixty-nine."

"In good health?"

"Thank God."

"Since the heart attack, I mean. No problems?"

"None at all, thank God."

"Eyesight okay?"

"A hundred percent."

"You could clearly see the woman and child when they entered the park, is that right?"

"Very clear."

Leading him down the garden path. Allowing him to believe I was about to challenge his eyesight.

"And when they sat down on the bench opposite you . . . could you still see them very clearly?"

"Very clear, yes."

"How far away would you say the other bench was?"

"It was just across the path."

"Six feet?"

"A little farther."

"Eight feet?"

"I think a bit farther yet."

"Ten feet?"

"Yes. I would say ten feet."

"Thank you. Do you remember the name of the park? The one you were sitting in that day?"

"Galin Memorial."

"On Galin Boulevard and South First?"

"Yes, sir."

"About ten, twelve blocks from the G&S Supermarket, isn't it?"

"Just about."

"Have you yourself ever walked from Orange to Galin and then down from South Tenth to South First?"

"I have."

"How long did it take you?"

"Fifteen, twenty minutes tops."

Leading him to believe I was challenging his accuracy about

the time the woman and the child had entered the park. Gertrude Fowler had testified that they'd left the G&S at about twenty past three, and Farrow had told the court that they'd walked into the park at three thirty-seven—so fifteen, twenty minutes tops was about right.

Farrow was smiling, knowing the time was about right.

So was Atkins.

The men and women on the jury were doing some arithmetic of their own, and they also knew Old Foxy Grandpa was right.

"And you're sure you were sitting in the Galin Memorial Park that afternoon?"

"Positive."

"It wasn't some other park."

"No, it was the Galin Park."

"Mr. Farrow, I show you this and ask you to look at it."

"What is it?"

"Well, that's what I'm about to ask you," I said.

The jury laughed. Everyone in the courtroom laughed. Oh, how they loved their favorite old grandpa.

"Okay, I'm looking at it," he said, and shrugged, and everyone laughed again.

"What is it, can you tell me?" I said.

"It says on top it's a survey of Galin Park."

"Is there a date on that survey?"

Farrow studied the drawing again.

"There's a date here in the lower right-hand corner," he said.

"Could you read that date out loud, please?"

"The date is December 17, 1990."

"Your Honor, I would like this marked, please."

"Mark it Exhibit A for the defense."

"We've previously stipulated, Your Honor, that this is an accurate survey of the property . . ."

"Yes, yes . . ."

". . . so I ask now that it be moved into evidence."

"So moved."

"Mr. Farrow, can you see the markings that give the width of the path that runs through the park?"

Farrow looked again.

"This figure here, do you mean?"

"Well, the width of the path is marked. Can you see where it's marked?"

"Yes?"

"Can you tell me what that figure is."

"Fifteen feet."

"So then the distance across the path, from your bench to where the woman and the child were sitting, was not ten feet as you say it was . . ."

"Well, when I said ten feet . . ."

"Yes?"

"I was estimating."

"But now you know the distance was fifteen feet, don't you?"

"Yes, that's what it says here."

"Well, you don't *doubt* the survey's accuracy, do you?"

"No, I'm sure it's correct."

"Then the distance across the path was fifteen feet, is that right?"

"Yes, it was fifteen feet."

"Mr. Farrow," I said, "do you wear a hearing aid?"

"I do."

"Are you wearing it now?"

"I am."

"Can you hear all right with it?"

"Perfectly."

"Were you wearing it on the day you saw that woman and child take the bench fifteen feet across the path from you?"

"I was."

Atkins looked suddenly alert. He knew where I was going now, but he was helpless to stop me. Toots Kiley had first come up with the knowledge that Farrow wore a hearing aid, and then had suggested that we test his hearing during the deposition. Getting the survey afterward was a simple task.

"Were they talking in conversational tones, Mr. Farrow?"

"They were."

"Just as we're talking in conversational tones, isn't that correct?"

"That's correct."

"And of course you can hear me, can't you?"

"Objection!" Atkins said, and jumped to his feet. "I really can't see what relevance the state of Mr. Farrow's *health* has to do with . . ."

"Your Honor, the witness has testified that he *heard* a conversation . . ."

"Overruled. You may proceed."

"Mr. Farrow, *can* you hear me?" I asked again.

"Of course I can hear you," he said, looking astonished. "How could I answer your questions if I couldn't hear you?"

"I'm standing right here, about three feet from the witness stand, and you say you can hear me, is that right?"

"Yes, yes, I can hear you."

"How about now?" I asked, and took several steps back. "Can you hear me now?"

"Yes, I can hear you."

"From about six feet away . . . would you say this is about six feet?"

"Yes, about that."

"And you can still hear me? Even though I'm speaking in a conversational tone."

"Yes, I can hear you."

"How about now?"

Another step back.

"Yes."

"And now? Same conversational tone, can you still hear me?"

Moving backward.

"Yes, I can hear you."

"How about now?" I said, and stepped quickly to the defense table, where Mary sat with her hands in her lap. "The bluebird flew over the hill and up to the moon," I said. "What did I just say, Mr. Farrow?"

"Yes, I can hear you," he said.

"What did I say? Repeat what I just said. Here, I'll say it again, in the same conversational tone. The bluebird flew over the hill and up to the moon. Repeat that, Mr. Farrow."

He looked at me blankly.

"Your Honor," I said, "with your permission, and in the presence of the jury, I would like to measure the distance from the defense table to the witness stand."

"Go ahead."

"Andrew?" I said, and took a tape measure from my jacket pocket. "My assistant and I measured the distance this afternoon, Your Honor . . . Andrew, would you hold this end, please? And discovered . . ."

Laying the tape on the floor, pulling it toward the witness stand, Andrew holding the other end . . .

". . . that the distance was . . ."

Moving closer and closer to where Farrow sat, watching . . .

". . . exactly fifteen feet."

I looked up into Farrow's face.

"Mr. Farrow," I said, "can you hear me now?"

"Of course I can hear you!" he said.

"Good. Then perhaps you'll read the marking on this tape for me."

Farrow leaned over.

"Fifteen feet," he said.

"Thank you," I said. "No further questions."

Atkins took his time coming toward the witness stand. He had nowhere to go in his redirect and he knew it. He was searching for a handle, but none came immediately to mind.

"Mr. Farrow," he said, "how do you like Mr. Hope's voice?"

"Objection!" I said.

"Sustained," Rutherford said.

"Would you say that his voice is similar to the defendant's?"

"Not at all."

"Or to little Jenny Lou's voice? Her voice that you heard when she was still alive. At all similar to either of those voices?"

"No, not at all."

"Incidentally, when you heard Jenny Lou calling the defendant by name . . . was she fifteen feet away from you at the time?"

"No, they were just crossing over to the other bench."

"Would you say they were . . . well, how far *would* you say they were from you? When you heard Jenny Lou call her by name?"

"Six feet, I would say."

"And you say she used the name 'Mary'?"

"Mary was what she said."

"No further questions."

I went immediately to the witness stand and said, "Mr. Farrow, when they were crossing over to the other bench, were their backs to you?"

"No. Well, partially."

"Mr. Farrow, I'm going to move to where I was when we were talking earlier," I said, "to right about here . . . which you said was about six feet away, didn't you?"

"Yes."

"And I'm going to turn my back partially to you, and I'm going to say three names in a conversational tone, and I want you to repeat those names to me. Would you do that for me?"

"Sure."

"First, tell me if this is the way they were turned partially from you," I said, and turned my back to him.

"About like that," he said.

"James, Alice, Frank," I said, and turned immediately to the witness stand. "What names did I just say?"

I had done this less dramatically in my own office while I was deposing him, not running him through the drill, but simply ascertaining that he could not hear me at all from certain distances and could not hear me correctly from other distances when I was turned away from him. I was not shooting blind. I knew his answer before he gave it.

"I'm sorry," he said. "I couldn't hear you."

"Witness is excused," I said.

Jenny Lou's mother was quite another matter.

It was one thing to risk losing sympathy by exposing an old man's hearing problem; it was something else to risk losing the whole ball game by attacking a still grieving mother.

Martha Williams was dressed in a simple gray dress that managed to convey a sense of mourning without being overtly black. A not unattractive woman in her mid-thirties, she took the stand, swore that she would tell the truth, and then sat looking somewhat bewildered. Big blue eyes, brown hair parted in the center and cascading on either side of her face to about the line of her chin. Hands folded in her lap now. Skirt demurely lowered over her knees.

"Mrs. Williams," Atkins said, "are you the mother of Jenny Lou Williams?"

"I am," she said. Voice firm. No anger in it. The anger was all gone. Only the grief was left. And the desire to see justice done. All this she transmitted to the jury through her bearing.

"Do you remember the afternoon of August twenty-eighth?"

"I will never forget it."

This was somewhat unresponsive. But there was imminent danger in objecting to anything this woman said.

"What were you doing at ten minutes past three that afternoon, do you remember?"

"I remember."

"Please tell us," Atkins said, and virtually bowed her in to the jury, his arm swinging toward them, the palm of his hand flat, stepping aside to give her center stage.

It is Martha's habit—her obligation, in fact, her maternal

duty—to meet the school bus every weekday when Jenny Lou comes home. Jenny Lou is only seven years old, and in the second grade. She leaves for school at eight-thirty in the morning and boards the bus for the return trip home at approximately a quarter to three. The Judy Cornier Elementary School is on South Third and Michel, not too distant from Galin Memorial Park and very close to the G&S Supermarket on Orange and South Tenth. The bus makes stops all along the way, of course—well, all school buses do . . .

She is a powerful witness. She sits looking dignified, grieved, but in total control of herself, narrating the events of that afternoon in a calm, well-modulated voice. The only clue to her distress is in her hands: she keeps wringing the handkerchief clutched in her long fingers. The jury alternates its attention from her face to her hands.

Their house, she tells them, is on Pineview and Logan, near the oval with the development marker on it, Suncrest Acres. The bus, though, doesn't come into the development itself, it stops outside near the entrance pillars on the main north-south road, Abbott Avenue. Abbott and Suncrest Drive. That's where the bus stops. Every weekday afternoon at ten minutes past three. And that's where Martha Williams is waiting for her seven-year-old daughter on the afternoon of August 28, a Friday, the end of the week, the beginning of a nightmare . . .

"Your Honor," I said, "may we approach, please?"

"Yes, come on up," Rutherford said.

This was delicate. The jury was already scowling at me, wondering why I'd stopped Martha Williams's engaging narrative the moment she'd uttered the word "nightmare." I could see some of the women leaning forward, frowning, as if hoping to overhear whatever we were about to whisper at the bench.

"What is it, Mr. Hope?"

"Your Honor, I don't understand the purpose of Mrs. Williams's testimony."

"It will become clear," Atkins said. He never said anything directly to me, the superior, supercilious son of a bitch. Everything to the judge, the jury, and the witness, nothing to me.

"When?"

"Your Honor?"

"*When* will it become clear?"

"In due course."

"Make it clear to me now. Where are you going?"

"Your Honor, the chronological order of events will irrefutably link the child's disappearance and subsequent murder to the defendant."

"I don't see how Mrs. Williams's testimony will contribute anything substantive to that premise, Your Honor."

"Perhaps the state can elucidate."

"The time of the child's disappearance is crucial," Atkins said. "I intend to show . . ."

"Your Honor," I said, "I think he's . . ."

"Let him finish, please, Mr. Hope."

"I intend to show that while Mrs. Williams was waiting for her child to get off the bus, the child was in fact with the defendant."

"Haven't you already established that?" Rutherford asked.

"Not to my satisfaction," Atkins said.

"Mr. Hope?"

"Your Honor, I think the state has called Mrs. Williams simply to play on the jury's sympathy. A woman waiting for her child to get off the bus . . . and I assume Mr. Atkins will wring from her that moment of panic when she realizes the child isn't on the bus . . ."

"Please ask Mr. Hope not to try my case for me, Your Honor."

"May I continue, Your Honor?"

"Please."

"I'm merely saying that the mother waiting for the bus, the child not being on the bus, the mother calling the police to report the disappearance . . . all this does nothing to confirm or deny that the child was with the defendant. All it does is tug at the jury's heartstrings, Your Honor. That's all it's designed to do, and that's all it does."

"Mr. Atkins?"

"I would like the jury to hear her story, Your Honor."

"Mr. Hope, do you intend to cross-examine?"

"Not if she's going to continue in the same vein. I consider all of her testimony irrelevant, immaterial, and inflammatory."

"I tend to disagree, Mr. Hope. If the state can show that the child was not where she was supposed to be at such and such a time and can demonstrate that the child was somewhere else at that time—as has already been established, by the way—then it seems to me the circumstantial link is not only clear but very strong as well. You may continue, Mr. Atkins. But don't milk it."

"Your Honor?"

"I *said* don't milk it."

"Thank you, Your Honor," Atkins said, and almost bowed to her. He went back to the witness stand. I went back to the defense table. Andrew looked at me hopefully. I shook my head.

"Mrs. Williams," Atkins said, "was your daughter, Jenny Lou, on that bus as you'd expected her to be?"

"She was not," Martha Williams said.

And now came the long heart-rending narrative I'd tried to circumvent, the tearful mother of a victim relating first the uneasiness she'd felt and then the panic after a call to the school had ascertained that the last time anyone had seen her daughter was while she was picking up her lunch pail in her classroom at approximately two-thirty that afternoon, the call to a classmate who informed Martha that her daughter had not boarded the bus at all, and then the call to the police and the whole missing-persons routine and the subsequent fear and desperation when she and her husband realized that their daughter had been abducted, their daughter might in fact be dead.

"Your Honor," Atkins said, "I would like this marked for identification, please."

"Let me see it, please," Rutherford said.

I knew what he was showing her. It was a photograph on his evidence list; I had already seen it.

"Show it to the defense, please," Rutherford said, and handed it down to the deputy clerk.

"I have no objections," I said, waving the photograph aside. This was calculated. If I objected to the jury seeing this picture, and if the objection was overruled—as I felt certain it would have been—the jury would wonder why I'd tried to suppress it.

"Mark it Exhibit Two for the state," Rutherford said.

Atkins retrieved the picture and carried it to the witness stand. His voice low, almost reverent, he said, "Would you please look at this, Mrs. Williams?"

She accepted the photo.

And burst into tears.

"Can you tell me what you're looking at, please?" Atkins said.

"A picture of my . . . my dead baby," Mrs. Williams said.

"When did you first see this photograph?"

"On the second of September this year."

"Where did you see it?"

"In the Medical Examiner's Office here in Calusa."

Sobbing uncontrollably now.

"Why was this photograph shown to you?"

"So I c-c-could identify my baby."

"Your Honor, I would like this photograph moved into evidence, please."

"Mark it in evidence."

"May I publish it to the jury?"

"Please."

The photograph had been taken in the morgue at Good Samaritan. It showed the mutilated body of seven-year-old Jenny Lou Williams. Atkins carried it to the first juror—one of the men—who looked at it briefly and then passed it on. I watched the jury reacting.

"Mrs. Williams," Atkins said, "I now show you this photograph previously marked for identification. Can you tell me what it is?"

She took the photograph. Her handkerchief was to her eyes. Tears were streaming down her face.

"That's Jenny Lou when she was alive."

"When was the picture taken?"

"Two weeks before she disappeared."

"Your Honor, I would like this moved into evidence, please."

"Mark it."

"May I publish it to the jury?"

"Go right ahead."

Atkins walked to the jury box, handed the photo in, and turned again to where Martha Williams sat waiting for his next question. As he walked toward her, he said, "Now, do you recall ever seeing anyone suspicious in your neighborhood?"

"Objection! Vague and unclear."

"Sustained."

"Did you ever spot any strangers going through? On foot . . . or in a car?"

"In cars, yes, there are always strangers going through. In Florida, as I'm sure you know, people drive into developments just to look at the houses. Or up canals, by boat. Suncrest Acres is a very pretty development. People are always coming through."

"In cars?"

"Yes. Mostly. We're not on any canals, and we don't get too many people wandering in on foot."

"Do you recall any strange cars going through during the month before Jenny Lou disappeared? By that, I mean cars you knew didn't belong in the development."

"Yes."

"Would you remember those cars by year and make?"

"I'm not sure I would."

"If I recalled a specific year and make for you, would that help you to remember it?"

"Maybe."

"In the month before Jenny Lou disappeared, do you recall having seen in the neighborhood a white, 1992 Chrysler Le-Baron?"

"I don't know what a Chrysler LeBaron looks like."

"If I showed you a picture of such a car, would that refresh your memory?"

"It might."

"Your Honor, do I need to have this marked?"

"What is it?" Rutherford asked.

"A brochure showing the Chrysler line for 1992, in which there's a photograph of a white Chrysler LeBaron."

"Mr. Hope? Any objection to him showing it to the witness without the court marking it?"

"No objection."

"Proceed."

"Mrs. Williams, I'm showing you a photograph in this brochure, would you look at it, please?"

She took the glossy brochure, looked at the page.

"Can you tell me what that automobile is called? It's printed there on the bottom of the . . ."

"A Chrysler LeBaron."

"And what color is the car?"

"White."

"Do you now know what a white, 1992 Chrysler LeBaron looks like?"

"I do."

"Very well then. Can you tell us, please, whether you ever saw such a car driving through Suncrest Acres at any time before the disappearance of Jenny Lou?"

"I believe so, yes."

"Do you remember when?"

"Sometime in July, I guess it was."

"How do you come to remember this car?"

"I believe it slowed down when it passed the house."

"Lessened its speed?"

"Yes."

"Did you see who was driving the car?"

"Not really."

"Could it have been a woman?"

"Objection, Your Honor. It could have been a woman, it could have been a man, it could have been an orangutan, it could have . . ."

"Sustained."

"Was a woman driving the car?"

"Objection. Leading, Your Honor."

"Sustained."

"Could you tell if it was a man or a woman driving the car?"

"Not from where I was standing, no."

"Where *were* you standing when you saw the car go by?"

"In my living room."

"You looked out into the street, did you?"

"Yes. Through the living room window."

"Do you remember what color hair the driver had?"

"I think it was gray."

"Same color as the defendant's hair?"

This was somewhat leading, but I let it pass.

"Yes," she answered. "Same color as the defendant's hair."

"Long or short?"

"Short."

"Like the defendant's hair?"

"Yes."

"But you can't say with certainty, can you, that it was the defendant driving by in that white car?"

"No, I can't."

"Because that would be misleading the court, wouldn't it?"

"Objection."

"Sustained."

"Do you remember what the driver was wearing?"

"No."

"Can you say with any certainty that the driver was a woman?"

"I really can't. I didn't get that good a look."

"Thank you for your honesty, Mrs. Williams."

Which little fillip might have been objectionable if the witness hadn't been the victim's mother. Rutherford nonetheless frowned in disapproval at Atkins, who walked back to his table seemingly unconcerned. He had managed to convey to the jury that even though the absolute truth might be injurious to his case, he had been unable to force his witness to testify that the person she'd seen driving that white car was Mary Barton. Such integrity would surely be rewarded in heaven. Or so the jury was expected to believe.

I knew where Atkins was going, of course, and Mrs. Williams probably knew, too. There is not an attorney on earth who won't prepare his own witness for the sort of testimony he or she will be asked to give. Atkins was setting the stage for his later witness, a man named Harold Dancy, who lived in Alietam, Florida, only forty miles distant from Calusa and Mary Barton's infamous garden. Meanwhile, I still had Martha Williams to contend with, purer than the driven snow and unwilling to tell a lie even if it meant her daughter's fiendish murderer would go free.

I had told Judge Rutherford in our side bar that I might not cross-examine, but with the jury still passing around two photographs—one showing a live and beautiful little girl, the other showing a corpse fresh from its grave in Mary Barton's backyard—I felt I had no choice. Reluctantly, I approached the witness stand. Her eyes were dry now. She looked into my face defiantly.

"This must be terrible for you, I know," I said.

She said nothing.

"But if you'll bear with me," I said, "there are several questions I'd like to ask you."

Still nothing. I was the man defending the woman she believed had brutally slain her daughter.

"Let's talk a bit about that car, shall we? Before the state attorney . . ."

Big Bad State Attorney. Not Mr. Atkins. Either the State Attorney or the Prosecuting Attorney or the Prosecutor, all of which conjured images of someone trying to send someone else to the electric chair.

"Before the state attorney showed you that picture of the white Chrysler LeBaron, had you ever seen one?"

"I may have. But I'm not good on car names. There are so many car names nowadays."

"Used to be easier when there were just Fords or Chevys or Buicks and so on, hmm?"

"Yes."

"So . . . when you saw this white car driving past your house, you didn't know it was a 1992 Chrysler LeBaron, did you?"

"I did not know at the time, no."

"Before the prosecutor showed you that picture today, had he ever shown it to you before?"

"Well . . ."

She hesitated, glanced at Atkins, and then seemed suddenly confused.

"Yes or no, please," I said.

"Yes."

"When did he show you that photograph in the brochure?"

"In his office."

"*When*, please, Mrs. Williams?"

"Last month."

"Showed you that same photo?"

"Yes."

"Identified it for you as a 1992 Chrysler LeBaron?"

"Yes."

"Did he go over any other testimony you might be expected to give?"

"Yes, we discussed it."

"Prepared you for your testimony, did he?"

"Yes."

"Said he'd be asking you about this white car?"

"Yes."

"Asked if you remembered such a car?"

"Yes."

"Showed you a picture of one."

"Yes."

"So when you testified earlier . . . I believe I have this exactly, I'm sure the record will verify it . . . when you said, 'I don't know what a Chrysler LeBaron looks like,' you weren't telling the exact truth, were you?"

"What I meant was I didn't know at the time what a Chrysler LeBaron looked like."

"But that's not what you said."

"No, it isn't."

"I'm not suggesting that you were trying to mislead the court . . ."

"I wasn't."

". . . but I did want it clear on the record that the prosecutor had earlier shown you this photo. And that you knew full well what a 1992 Chrysler LeBaron looked like when you said you *didn't* know what it looked like."

"At the *time* was what I meant."

"Yes, that's clear now, thank you. But Mrs. Williams, when you say—as you did earlier—that you *believe* you saw such a car driving through Suncrest Acres, and you *guess* it was in July, and you *believe* it slowed down when it passed the house, and you *think* the car was white . . . well, did you or did you not see the car, and was it in July, and did it slow down, and was it white?"

"It's difficult to remember that far back. I was trying to tell the truth as I remembered it."

"But you qualified it, did you not?"

"No, I told the truth as I remembered it."

"But you just said it's difficult to remember that far back."

"It is."

"Was it difficult to remember that the driver's hair was gray?"

"I remember that it was gray."

"Mrs. Williams, I know this is difficult for you, but I'd appreciate it if you answere   Vas it *difficult* to remember
that the driver's hai

"No. I remember

"Didn't you earli   /as gray'?"

"Yes, I think that

"You *think* you s   gray'?"

"Yes."

"Does that mean   was gray?"

"No, I'm sure it

"Then why did y   *bought* it was gray?"

"Because it was   nd it's hard to remember.
My daughter was *k

Oh boy, I thoug   Right up the chimney.

"Your Honor," A   ; to his feet, "I ask that the
court excuse Mrs. W   . But I would like to object
at this time to the w   adgering and harassing the
witness. By my cou   ed some five times that the
person she saw driv   ray hair. The defense attorney insisting that s   r over and over again isn't
going to *change* the   stified that . . ."

"Is this your clos   r. Atkins?"

"No, Your Hono   . ."

"Your objection   not believe that Mr. Hope
was harassing the   ignore all of Mr. Atkins's
comments followin   Vitness will confine herself
to answering the q   make no further comments
on the merits of th   Mr. Hope."

"Just a few more questions," I said. "Mrs. Williams, when is
the first time you saw the defendant, Mary Barton?"

"I saw her on television the day she was arrested."

"I mean in person. When did you first see her in person?"

"Today."

"In this courtroom?"

"Yes."

"Had you ever seen her before today?"

"No."

"Never saw her on your street, did you? Pineview and Logan, isn't that what you said?"

"Pineview. The corner of Logan."

"Never saw her on Pineview Street, did you?"

"No."

"Lurking about? Or walking past the house?"

"No."

"Did you ever see her at the bus stop?"

"No."

"Abbott Avenue and Suncrest Drive, isn't that where you said the bus stop is?"

"Yes."

"Just outside the entrance road to the development."

"Yes."

"You never saw Mary Barton waiting there at the bus stop, did you?"

"No."

"Or walking past it?"

"No."

"Never saw her anywhere in the vicinity of your home, isn't that true?"

"I never saw her."

"Or in the vicinity of Suncrest Acres?"

"I never saw her anywhere near there. But . . ."

"Did you ever see her in the vicinity of the Judy Cornier Elementary School?"

"No."

"That's the school your daughter attended, isn't it?"

"Yes."

"And you never saw Mary Barton there, waiting in the area where the children load onto the buses, did you?"

"No."

"Or anywhere in the neighborhood surrounding the school?"

"I never saw her near the school, no."

"Are you familiar with Galin Memorial Park?"

"I know where it is."

"Have you ever been there?"

"Once or twice."

"Ever see Mary Barton in that park?"

"No."

"How about the G&S Supermarket? Do you know it?"

"No."

"Never been there?"

"Never."

"Then you couldn't possibly have seen Mary Barton there, isn't that so?"

"I never saw her there."

"Mrs. Williams . . . did your daughter ever mention having been approached by a woman answering the description of Mary Barton?"

"No."

"Did your daughter give you any reason to believe that she was being stalked by a woman answering Mary Barton's description?"

"No, she didn't. But . . ."

"Yes, please tell me," I said.

This was a risk. I didn't know what she might say, and a lawyer should never ask a question to which he does not already know the answer. But at the same time, I didn't want the jury to think I was cutting her off. Tell me, I'd said, inviting her to elaborate. But now I was holding my breath.

"I had the feeling someone was watching her."

"Your Honor?" I said.

"I'll allow that," she said, and turned to the jury. "I want to explain to you," she said, "that this is admissible only as to the witness's state of mind and not as to the truth of whether or not someone was *actually* watching. Go ahead, Mr. Hope."

"I'm sure you worried a great deal about your daughter," I said.

"I did."

"The way any mother would worry about her seven-year-old daughter going off into the world alone."

"Yes."

"But you didn't have any *real* reason to expect she was in imminent danger, did you?"

"No."

"That is, you didn't actually *see* anyone who might pose a threat to her."

"No, I just had this feeling."

"Well, feelings aside, you certainly never saw Mary Barton near any of the places your daughter frequented, did you?"

"No."

"Your home . . . her school . . . the bus stop . . . ?"

"No."

"In fact, did you ever see Mary Barton *anywhere* near your daughter?"

"No."

"Thank you, no further questions," I said.

"No further questions," Atkins said.

"Let's adjourn till tomorrow at nine," Rutherford said.

8

The distances troubled Toots most.

"What I don't understand," she told Warren, "is why she would've started her rampage . . ."

"Well, *if* she did it," Warren said.

"Well, we have to believe she *didn't* do it."

"Amen," Warren said.

"But for the sake of argument, *if* she did it, why would she've started her rampage . . ."

"If you can call it that," Warren said.

"Call it whatever you want to call it, okay? An extended adventure, okay? Why would she've started it so far from home?"

"Why indeed?"

"Take a look at this map," she said.

They were in a diner on the South Tamiami Trail, sitting in the booth closest to the door. All day long, they'd been trying to come up with something on Charlotte Carmody. So far, they had nothing. But nothing looked better over dinner. Warren had ordered a couple of hamburgers and a glass of beer. Toots had ordered turkey breast and Swiss on rye, no mayo, but lots of mustard. She was drinking a glass of milk. The day she'd kicked cocaine, she also stopped drinking anything alcoholic. Substance abuse was substance abuse. That's what she'd learned and that's what she believed.

The diner was decorated with Santa Clauses and red and green bells hanging from red and green tinsel stretched from corner to corner. A sickly-looking, artificial, miniature white Christmas tree was on the counter near the cash register. Nothing down here ever looked Christmasy. Warren wondered why they even bothered. He took a look at the map.

Somerset, where little Jenny Lou Williams had lived before her disappearance, was some ninety-eight miles from Calusa. Toots had marked the town with the numeral 1 in a circle. It was close enough to Eagle Lake to make it an attractive inland location, but its real advantage was its proximity to all the lakes in Osceola County, one of the loveliest areas in all Florida. Moreover, Route 17 was a major north-south artery, providing easy access to other parts of the state.

"The next one was snatched in Alietam," Toots said, and put her finger on the circled numeral 2. "Kimberly Holt. About forty miles outside Calusa."

For the most part, the towns dotting this inland part of the state were featureless and unattractive; even the landscape looked dry and dusty, dotted with scruffy palmettos and cabbage palms, gnarled scrub oaks twisting mossy branches against a brassy sky.

"And finally," Toots said, poking her forefinger at the circled numeral 3, "little Felicity Hammer was grabbed right here in Calusa. Now, it's entirely possible that Mary Barton drove the ninety-some-odd miles from Calusa to Somerset in search of her first victim . . ."

"That would've meant almost a two-hundred-mile round trip," Warren said.

"Exactly my point. That's a lot of traveling, Warren."

"It is."

"Mary isn't stupid . . ."

"Far from it."

"So why'd she range so far afield? Didn't she realize a stranger in any of these dinky little towns would be noticed? And remarked upon? And remembered later? Do you see my point, Warren? If she planned to bury her victims in her own backyard, why not *choose* them in Calusa, *kill* them in Calusa, the way she finally did with Felicity?"

"You're making Matthew's closing argument."

"I'm making the only argument he's *got*," Toots said, and shook her head. "I'll tell you something, Warren, if we don't come up with something to impeach Carmody when she takes the stand . . ."

"I know," Warren said.

"*She's* the one we really have to worry about. *She's* the one who saw Mary burying that kid."

"Yeah," Warren said glumly.

Toots was silent for a moment.

Then she said, "You think she's innocent?"

"I *hope* she is," Warren said.

The voter registration list from which they were working named the residents of 603 Palmetto Court as Bradley Morse and Nettie Morse, presumably his wife. The Morses lived in the same sort of cinder-block and stucco house that Mary lived in. In fact, all of the houses here in Crescent Cove, as the development was called, were of the same inexpensive construction, creating the look of a hastily constructed 1930s shantytown. Actually, the houses had been built in the late fifties, when Calusa was experiencing a boom that would transform it from a sleepy fishing village to a city of fifty-thousand-plus people.

Despite its name, Crescent Cove wasn't on water. If it had been, the homes here would have become treasures to be purchased, bulldozed, and replaced with houses costing half a million bucks or more. In the state of Florida, the only thing more precious than cocaine was water. The *Cove* in the development's name came from pure whimsy. The *Crescent* was somewhat architecturally founded in that the layout of the development was in fact semicircular, the outermost rim containing more houses than the innermost, which was called a *court* because of its comparative coziness. The only mildly interesting house in Crescent Cove belonged to Mary Barton. And the only thing that made it special was the garden in which the dead little girls had been found on a sunny September morn. There were five houses in the semicircle that formed Crescent Court. Lights were burning in all five of them.

They'd started their canvass of Mary's neighborhood on her own block and had worked inward over the past several days until they were now at the development's hub. There weren't many more houses to go, and so far they'd been unable to turn up anything Matthew could use against Charlotte Carmody when the state attorney called her. Given Atkins's chronological approach, they hoped that wouldn't be for some time yet. But if he changed his mind and decided to put her on tomorrow—

"Watching television," Toots said, and nodded toward the house ahead. She'd based her conclusion on the fact that the light showing in one of the front rooms, presumably the living room, had a bluish cast to it. Warren didn't ask her how come she knew the people in there were watching television. He himself knew that if you wanted to fool a burglar into thinking you were home watching the TV, you screwed a blue light into one of your lamps, drew the blinds, and felt at least partially safe when you went out on the town.

This was a Tuesday night, not a big night out in Calusa, though nowadays not too many people were going out to eat, anyway. More often than not, even on Saturday nights, people were staying home. Renting a video, sending out for pizza, that was about all they could afford for an evening's entertainment. In most cities and towns, you didn't go out because you couldn't afford it. In

other cities and towns, you didn't go out because you were afraid
you'd get killed on the streets. A thousand points of light were
shining in living rooms all over America, a real legacy. But most
of them were blue.

Warren rang the doorbell. He was hoping they weren't watching television or a video in there because people tended to get
pissed-off if you interrupted their viewing habits. He knew cases
where people had killed their spouses for changing a television
channel without first opening the matter for debate. People were
touchy about the TV they watched. Toots was thinking the same
thing. Also, it was getting close on seven-thirty, and people didn't
like their homes invaded after dinnertime, what the rednecks
down here called suppertime.

The voice behind the door said, "Who is it?"

Forty years ago, when this development was first built, people
used to go to sleep here with the doors unlocked, sometimes
standing wide open for cross ventilation, with just a screen door
for protection. Nowadays, you didn't unlock the door, no less
open it, till you knew damn well who was standing outside there.
It didn't help that Warren was black. This was one of the reasons
he and Toots were working this particular job in tandem. Not
too many people in America were eager to open a door for a
black man. You see him standing with a blonde out there, it took
off the curse. Sometimes.

"Sir," Warren said, "we're gathering information for a trial
now in progress. Could we talk to you for a moment, sir?"

Silence inside there.

Guy looking out the peephole, seeing Warren standing there,
wondering if this was legit or not.

"Got some identification?" he asked.

"Yes, sir," Warren said, and dug out a plastic-encased card
identifying him as the recipient of a Class A license to operate a
private detective agency in the state of Florida, seal and all. He
held it up to the peephole in the door.

More silence inside there.

"How about your lady friend?" the man said.

"She works for me," Warren said.

"Let me see that again."

Warren held it up to the peephole again. It had cost him a hundred bucks, renewable annually on the thirtieth day of June. Which, together with the five-thousand-dollar bond he'd posted, might open the door for him. He hoped.

"This about the crazy lady lives here in the Cove?" the man asked.

Door still closed. Voice coming from behind the wood. Muffled.

"It's about the woman accused of murder, yes, sir," Warren said.

"I ain't interested," the man said.

"Sir, we . . ."

"Go away," he said.

They got the same response, or variations of it, in the next two houses on the street. Warren had let Toots do the talking at the last house, but that hadn't helped. No one wanted to get involved with the crazy lady, and the doors had stayed locked and closed. Two houses to go now, blue flickering lights behind the windows of each, TV Time in the good old U.S. of A.

The voter registration list gave the occupant as Euphemia Loupe. Warren guessed she might be black. In fact, he was *wishing* she'd be black, stand a better chance of having the door opened. Hopefully, he rang the bell. The door opened at once, and she was white.

"Been watching you come up the street," she said. "You Jehovah's Witnesses giving away that magazine of yours?"

"No, ma'am, we're not," Toots admitted.

"Then what you selling?" Euphemia asked.

"We're . . ."

"Never mind, I don't want it or need it," she said, and started closing the door.

"Ma'am, we're working for Mary Barton," Toots said, figuring *Fuck it, get it over and done with.*

A suspicious look crossed Euphemia's face. She was a woman in her early sixties, Warren guessed, with stringy gray hair and a snaggle-toothed mouth, dressed in a belted blue robe and house slippers, a pinkish nightgown visible in the V neck of the robe, little floppy collar, little frayed pinkish bow. Her brown eyes darted in the light of the fixture to the left of the door, searching first Toots's face and then Warren's.

"Thought you was gonna give me a free magazine," she said. Eyes darting.

"No," Toots said, trying to sound sorrowful. She was thinking that Euphemia Loupe was nuttier than Mary Barton was supposed to be. Warren was thinking the same thing. He was ready to move on to the last house on the semicircle.

"You going to help Mary or harm her?" Euphemia asked.

"We're trying to help her, ma'am," Warren said.

"Then come on in," she said.

Skye Bannister had spoken to the state attorney for the Twentieth Judicial Circuit, telling him he had to isolate one of his assistants from a case his office was prosecuting, and asking if the Twentieth could accept her on temporary assignment until the trial was over. Lamont Spencer, the S.A. down there, asked no questions; he and Skye had done favors for each other before. He told him to send Patricia on down, one of his people was just beginning jury selection in a murder case in Pine Crossing and might could use a good right arm.

The Twentieth embraced Hendry, Charlotte, Collier, Glades, and Lee counties. Hendry and Collier were largely underwater, since the two counties shared between them much of the Big Cypress Swamp. Pine Crossing wasn't far from the county seat, on dry land some fifty or so miles from Lake Okeechobee. When Patricia called me that Tuesday night, she said the town was pretty quiet as compared to Calusa, but she'd found a good Mom-and-Pop restaurant that served humongous steaks and big breakfasts. She said she planned to go cross-county to Clewiston this coming weekend, take a boat out on the lake, see if she could catch some bigmouth bass. She said she missed me. I told her I missed her, too.

I knew hardly anything about her.

When first we'd locked horns, back on the Leeds case last year, I'd asked Andrew to run a background check on her, and he'd come up with some interesting facts. Her full name, for example, was Patricia Lowell Demming, the middle name apparently bestowed upon her in honor of her paternal grandfather, Lowell Turner Demming, who'd been a superior court judge in New Haven, Connecticut, where Patricia was born. But . . .

"I've been wondering about something," I said.

"Yes, what?"

"When you were telling me about your little confessional encounter with Skye the Pontifical, you said something about a Catholic upbringing."

"Yes?"

"But Patricia Lowell Demming sounds as WASP as . . ."

"Ah, but me mother was Catholic, don't you know?" she said, suddenly affecting an Irish lilt as fresh and as green as clover. "Catherine McConnell, if you please, as Irish as county Kilkenny. I was raised by the nuns till I was sixteen and went off to Yale. M'dear mother rued the day forevermore."

"What were the nuns like?" I asked.

"Holy," she said.

"Did they rap you on your knuckles with a ruler?"

"I'd have rapped them on their heads with a garden hoe."

"That bad, huh?"

"Oh no, sir, I was good and pure and innocent, sir."

"Until Yale."

"Yes, sir, Yale corrupted me, sir."

I remembered Andrew reporting that she'd been kicked out of

Yale for smoking dope in class, went from there to Brown, where she'd graduated Phi Bete, and then . . .

Well, there was a small incident at Brown, too.

Apparently a football player—unaware of her peculiar idiosyncrasy of wanting to be called by her own name and not some other person's idea of what her name might be—came up to her and said, "Hi, Pat, my name's . . ." and she'd hit him on the nose and broken it in three places. She later told a reporter from the school paper, the *Brown Daily Herald,* that pat was what you did to the head of a child or a dog, or Pat was a drunk sitting at the bar with his pal Mike, but Pat was not what you called someone you didn't know when her name was Patricia. She also reported that even the nickname Trish offended her.

Listening to Andrew telling me all this, I decided back then that I liked what I was hearing, even if she was my adversary. I've always felt that people should be called what they wish to be called, don't you? If Salvatore wants to be called Evan, I owe him the dignity and respect of free choice, which isn't always so easy to come by in this land of the free and home of the brave.

"Is it true they called you the Wicked Witch of the West?" I asked her.

"Bitch," she said. "Not Witch. *Bitch.*"

"Why?"

"Oh, guess," she said.

Andrew had reported it as "Witch." The Wicked Witch of the West. This was after she'd graduated from N.Y.U. Law and was working for a Los Angeles firm named Dolman, Ruggiero, Peters, and Dern. She'd really made her rep, though . . .

"How'd you like New York?"

"It wasn't Pine Crossing, believe me."

"Is anything?"

In New York, she'd worked for Carter, Rifkin, Lieber, and Loeb, legal bombers if ever the breed existed. Even there, where nobody's nice who doesn't have to be—don't let my partner Frank hear that—Patricia became known as truly ruthless, a criminal lawyer who successfully defended a wide variety of criminal cases, including three murder cases, in one of which a woman had been charged with strangling her six-month-old baby in his crib. Even on that one, she refused to cut a deal, going for an acquittal and getting it. With all this criminal experience under her belt, she kissed off Carter, Rifkin, crossed to the other side of the street, and joined the D.A.'s Office, where she worked for three years before moving down here to Florida. When Skye Bannister learned a S*T*A*R had arrived in Calusa, he snapped her up in a minute.

Her courtroom style had been described as flamboyant, seductive, aggressive, and unrelenting—somewhat like her style in bed. But she had also been described as unforgiving; you made one slip and she went straight for the jugular.

That was what I knew about her.

"What's your favorite color?" I asked.

"I can't believe you said that."

"I said it. What is it?"

"You know what it is."

"No, I don't."

"I was wearing it the night we met. Do you remember what I was . . . ?"

"Red."

"Yes. What color are my eyes, smartie?"

"Mauve."

"No, puce."

"What are you wearing now?"

"Why do you want to know?"

"Just curious."

"Ho-ho-ho, just curious. I'm wearing a long flannel nightgown with a little bluebell design on it. And my hair is up in curlers."

"You are not, and it is not."

"You're right. It's loose and fanned out all over the pillow."

"Oh? Are you in bed?"

"No, I'm standing outside on the back porch. Under the little yellow light here. With mosquitoes flying all around it. It's insufferably hot here. Is it hot in Calusa?"

"Yes."

"Do you realize it'll be Christmas in a little more than three weeks?"

"I know. My daughter gets home on the fifteenth."

"Are you looking forward to it?"

"My daughter or Christmas?"

"Your daughter."

"Yes. I want you to meet her."

"I will," she said, and hesitated, and said, "I miss never having had children."

"Were you ever married?" I asked.

"Didn't your report give you that?"

"No, just the essentials."

"Marriage is nonessential, huh?"

"Were you?"

"Never."

"Any serious involvements?"

"How could I get to be thirty-six without having had at least a few serious involvements?"

"How many?"

"None of your business."

"When was the last one?"

"In New York."

There was a sudden silence on the line. I had the feeling I was treading dangerous ground. What until now had been all fun and games had turned serious all at once. The silence lengthened; I'd lost her. She was no longer in Pine Crossing with mosquitoes swarming around a yellow light outside, but was instead up there on the frozen tundra with the snow and the wind and the bitter cold.

"Next question," she said.

There was an ineffable sadness in her voice. I had never been envious of another man in my life, but I found myself wondering now what he had been like and how it had ended and why he was still capable of causing such sorrow.

"We ought to have dinner with Frank and his wife some night," I said. "He's a native New Yorker, you'll have lots to talk about."

"I hate New York," she said.

And the line went dead again.

"Patricia," I said, "I'm sorry if I . . ."

"No, no," she said.

I heard her take a deep breath. When she spoke again, it was as if she'd snapped a switch, clicking off whatever memories had saddened her. The voice on the line became airy and light again, the manner playful.

"Ask me what I'm really wearing," she said.

"What are you really wearing?"

"Oh, just something down-homey."

"Like what?"

"Black garter belt, fishnet stockings, no panties, no bra. Just your ordinary grits-and-gravy outfit. What are *you* really wearing?"

"Pajama bottoms."

"Silk?"

"No."

"How disappointing. I'll have to buy you some silk pajamas."

"Were you a real pothead or just an occasional one?"

"Yale, you mean? I was framed."

"Sure."

"A good mouthpiece coulda got me off with a suspended."

And again, there was a silence. As if her forced playfulness was really too difficult to maintain. I waited.

"Do you have real mood swings?" she asked.

"Yes," I said. "Do you?"

"Yes. Sometimes I just want to be alone."

"Do you want to be alone now?" I asked.

"No, I want to be with you," she said.

"Yes," I said.

"I love you, Matthew," she said.

"I love you, too."

"Mmm," she said, and there was another silence. And then she said, "I'm wearing nothing but white bikini panties, good night, Matthew," and there was a click on the line.

I didn't know why I was smiling, but I was.

I was looking over the report Toots Kiley had made on the next state's witness certain to be called, when she and Warren showed up at my office unannounced. This was at seven-thirty on Wednesday morning. I was due in court at nine and I still wanted to look over the deposition I'd taken from Harold Dancy. I was not happy to see them—until they played a tape they'd made the night before at the home of a woman named Euphemia Loupe.

They assured me first that Mrs. Loupe had agreed to be taped and had told them that she'd cooperate in any way possible in the future; Mary Barton was her friend and she knew she'd been falsely accused. She'd told them . . .

"Well, it's all here on the tape," Warren said, and snapped on the recorder. There were three voices on the tape. I recognized Toots's and Warren's. I assumed the third voice belonged to Euphemia Loupe. Warren jumped in with both big feet:

WARREN:	Mrs. Loupe, we'll get right to the point, if that's all right with you.
EUPHEMIA:	Yes, that's fine. I told you, Mary is my friend.
WARREN:	A woman named Charlotte Carmody.
EUPHEMIA:	Bitch of the world.
TOOTS:	Why do you say that?
EUPHEMIA:	Lying, no-good, scheming, meddling bitch.
TOOTS:	Yes, why?
EUPHEMIA:	She never saw nothin' in that backyard.

TOOTS: How do you know?
EUPHEMIA: 'Cause she's a lying scheming bitch.

"You call this a reliable witness?" I said.
"Give it time, Matthew."

WARREN: . . . Barton were neighborly.

"Run it back, please," I said.
Warren hit the rewind button. And then the stop button. And then the play button again. The tape picked up several speeches back.

EUPHEMIA: . . . saw nothin' in that backyard.
TOOTS: How do you know?
EUPHEMIA: 'Cause she's a lying scheming bitch.
WARREN: She claims that she and Miss Barton were neighborly.
EUPHEMIA: Neighborly, ha!
WARREN: Weren't they?
EUPHEMIA: Didn't get along at all.
TOOTS: How do you know?
EUPHEMIA: Mary told me.

"Worthless," I said.
"Hang in there," Warren said.

WARREN: . . . tell you this?

"Want me to run it back?"
"I've got the gist."

EUPHEMIA: . . . tea every week. Either my house or
              hers. Have you seen her garden? It's a
              lovely garden.

WARREN:	Lovely. And you say she told you this over tea?
EUPHEMIA:	Over tea, yes.
WARREN:	Her house or yours, would you remember?
EUPHEMIA:	Hers. We were sitting outside, looking at the garden.
TOOTS:	And she said that she and Charlotte Carmody didn't get along?
EUPHEMIA:	Lowered her voice when she told me. Almost a whisper. Didn't want that bitch next door to hear us talking about her.
TOOTS:	When was this, do you remember?
EUPHEMIA:	Just before the fence went up. That's why she was talking so low, Mary. There wasn't no fence up at that time. Just a low hedge. We weren't allowed to have fences in the development, you see. There was a rule no fences. And voices carry, you know. Now there's fences all over the place. Everybody's got a fence now, you'd think there was something to hide, this shitty development. When my husband was alive, we lived in Tampa. In a house cost a hundred thousand dollars. Wasn't no fences in *that* development, you can bet on that.
WARREN:	And this was when?
EUPHEMIA:	Freddie died it'll be five years come February. Had to sell the house in Tampa, couldn't afford to keep it up. Only good thing in this development is Mary, and now they're trying to send her to the electric chair.
WARREN:	I meant . . . excuse me, Mrs. Loupe . . .

but when did you have this conversation with Mary?

EUPHEMIA: Oh, it must've been in the summer some-time.

WARREN: This past summer?

EUPHEMIA: Yes.

WARREN: When? Would you remember?

EUPHEMIA: July sometime? August?

WARREN: Which?

EUPHEMIA: Sometime during the summer. Her garden is just lovely in the summertime.

TOOTS: Was it in August, would you remember?

EUPHEMIA: I'm not good on dates.

TOOTS: Was it sometime in August?

EUPHEMIA: Maybe so.

TOOTS: The beginning of August? The middle?

EUPHEMIA: More toward the end, I think.

WARREN: Would it have been the twenty-eighth of August?

EUPHEMIA: I really don't remember.

WARREN: Do you remember if it was a weekend?

EUPHEMIA: I don't know.

TOOTS: Did you sometimes have tea on the weekend?

EUPHEMIA: Well, yes, of course. There's no set time for having tea, is there? It was Mary who introduced me to the custom, you know. She used to live in England. My husband and I went to England once. He was trying to trace his Norman ancestors. We spent . . .

WARREN: Mrs. Loupe, the twenty-eighth was a Friday. Would you remember if you had tea with Mary that Friday?

EUPHEMIA: I'm sorry, I can't recall.

TOOTS:	Did you *ever* have tea together on a Friday?
EUPHEMIA:	Oh yes. But on other days as well. It depended on how we were feeling. Good friends simply pick up the phone, isn't that the way?
TOOTS:	Do you think Mary might remember?
EUPHEMIA:	Mary remembers everything important.

That was the end of the tape.

Warren snapped off the recorder.

"What do you think?" he said.

"I think if Mary was having tea with this Loupe woman, then she couldn't have been in Somerset, Florida, abducting Jenny Lou Williams. But . . ."

They both looked at me.

"Mary read the depositions, she *knew* there'd be witnesses who'd testify where she was that day. Why didn't she tell me where she *really* was? If, in fact, she was in her own garden, sipping tea?"

"Ask her," Warren said simply.

I got to the women's section of the county jail at twenty minutes to nine. Mary had already had breakfast, and was dressed in the simple blue she would wear to court this morning. The courthouse was only five minutes away from the detention facilities. We had about ten, fifteen minutes to talk.

She asked me how I thought the trial was going.

I said I thought it was going well, that we had made some dents in the testimony.

She said, "Dancy will be damaging, won't he?"

"Nothing we can't handle," I said.

"I wish this were over," she said.

"It will be," I said. "Mary, tell me something. Do you remember where you were on the day they say you were in Somerset?"

"I've already told you. I was home. Working in my garden."

"No special plans for the weekend?"

"None."

"Do you know a woman named Euphemia Loupe?"

"Yes, I do."

"She claims she's a friend of yours."

"She is."

"She remembers having tea with you sometime in August. Sometime toward the end of August."

"That's entirely possible. We often enjoyed tea together."

"She can't remember the exact date. Can you?"

"No."

"Would it have been the twenty-eighth? When they say you were in Somerset? Or anytime that weekend? When they say you were roaming the countryside abduct—"

"It could have been, I don't know. I won't lie under oath, Mr. Hope."

"No one's asking you to."

"In fact, I'm not even sure I want to testify."

"Why not?"

"I don't see as it'll do any good."

"You're innocent, aren't you?"

"I'm innocent."

"Then you've got to get up there and let them know it."

Mary shook her head.

"It won't do any good," she said. "They've already made up their minds about me. They already think I'm bad."

9

Overnight, the elves had put up a Christmas tree in the courthouse rotunda. When I arrived there that Wednesday morning at five minutes to nine, it was aglow with lights and gleaming with ornaments and tinsel. This was still only the ninth of December, but in America nowadays they start decorating for Christmas before Thanksgiving. Actually, the courthouse elves were a little late this year, but they weren't selling anything.

I walked down the hall from the rotunda to the elevators leading to the upstairs courtrooms, said hello to a few attorneys I recognized, went up to the second floor and down the corridor to where the state attorney in and for the Twelfth Judicial Circuit was hoping to put Mary Barton in the electric chair. Mary was already seated at the defense table with Andrew, a uniformed officer standing discreetly by. Sunshine flooded the courtroom, burnishing the walnut paneling, giving the lie to the Christmas tree downstairs.

Where I came from, Christmas was snow and sleighs and ropes tied around the downtown buildings to keep you from getting blown off the sidewalks by the fierce winds that came in over the lake. Christmas was woodsmoke and pine, blazing fireplaces and long underwear. Christmas was kissing eighteen-year-old Susan Fitch under the holly. This Christmas, I would have to pick up my daughter at Susan's house. The thought did not offer much joy. And yet, there'd been Christmases together, too many to count, many of them good ones. Divorce is a kind of killing, but it cannot kill the memories.

Judge Rutherford came in at ten minutes past nine, apologized for being late—probably got caught in a snowstorm out there—and immediately asked Atkins to call his first witness. Mary sat with her hands folded on the table. No handbag looped over the ear of a chairback. You could always tell a female defendant in a criminal trial: unlike women anywhere else, she would not be carrying a bag.

"Call Harold Dancy, please," Atkins said, and then turned toward the back of the court, directing the jury to where Dancy would be making his entrance. I knew what to expect and so did Atkins; the jury didn't.

Harold Dancy was the most sympathetic sort of witness any lawyer could pray for. To begin with, he was black, and in Florida—and perhaps anywhere else in America—this meant that he was innocently handicapped by his color. But Dancy's handicap went more than skin-deep. He was a wounded veteran of World War II, and he came into that courtroom on crutches, the left leg of his trousers pinned up above the knee. There was an audible gasp from the jury—I think it came from Carmen Rodriguez. Every eye in that courtroom was on him as he made his slow way down the center aisle, and took the stand, and leaned into his crutches as he raised his right hand and placed his left upon the Bible to take the oath.

"Please be seated," Atkins said.

Dancy sat. And leaned his crutches against the side of the

witness stand. And one of them fell over. And he bent to pick it up. I was thinking that all I needed now was for him to fall off his chair. He rested the righted crutch upon the other one; they both seemed solidly planted now. He adjusted his eyeglasses on the bridge of his nose. Round, gold-rimmed glasses. Round chubby face. If he'd had a white beard, he would have resembled a one-legged black Santa Claus.

"May I have your full name, please?" Atkins asked.

"Harold Michael Dancy."

"Where do you live, Mr. Dancy?"

"704 Bell Road, Alietam, Florida."

"Were you living there on August twenty-ninth?"

"I was."

"Same address?"

"Lived there since I got out of the Army."

"When was that, Mr. Dancy?"

"Nineteen forty-six."

"How old are you, can you tell us?"

"Sixty-eight."

"When were you in the Army?"

"From March of 1942 to June of 1946."

"Where did you serve?"

"In Italy."

"Is that where you were wounded?"

"Yes, sir. Taking a German machine-gun nest."

"Did you receive a Purple Heart for this action?"

"I did, yes, sir."

I dared not object. Technically, Atkins was leading his witness, but the heroes of certain wars are sacrosanct. I kept my mouth shut.

"Now, Mr. Dancy, do you remember what you were doing on the twenty-ninth day of August this year?"

"I do."

"How come you to remember this date?"

I raised my eyebrows slightly at the archaic usage. *How come you* indeed? Would Atkins wear a powdered wig and a black robe to court tomorrow? How come you to be so attired, milord?

"The thirtieth is my wife's birthday," Dancy said. "This was the day before. I was shopping downtown for a present."

"What do you mean by 'downtown,' sir?"

"Downtown Alietam."

Downtown Alietam. From the description provided by Warren and Toots, I knew that the main street of the town ran for two blocks on either side of the highway and then became an instant memory. Lining the main drag on either side of the road were shops overhung with wooden balconies so that, rain or shine, the citizens—all eight hundred and six of them—could run their chores without fear of sunstroke or drowning. On the twenty-ninth of August . . .

"I remember it was raining," Dancy said. "The rain . . ."

. . . was coming down in sheets, water running off the black asphalt into the gutters lining the road and then channeling off onto the now-muddy dirt roads that led to the groves and houses that collectively formed the town. This is orange country, for the most part, and the rain is welcome here. Dancy stands under the portico to the town's hardware store, looking glumly out at the teeming rain, waiting for a break so that he can cross the street to the Miramar Boutique, where he plans to buy his wife a lacy nightgown for her birthday.

This last elicits a warm chuckle from the spectators in the courtroom; they are in love with this cuddly, one-legged war hero, and the women in particular adore the idea of a sixty-eight-year-old man still thinking of his wife in terms of a lacy nightgown.

The rain keeps coming down. Up the street, a block from where the shopping district ends, the bell on the First Baptist Church begins tolling the noon hour, each sonorous bong melting into the heavy rain. It is twelve noon in Alietam, Florida. Dancy looks at his watch. He's a minute fast. From the corner of his eye, he sees a woman coming up the sidewalk toward him.

She's wearing a plastic raincoat and one of these plastic things women put on over their heads, like a scarf, only plastic, and she's holding a little girl by the hand. Well, not holding the girl's hand, actually, she's instead dragging her through the rain by the wrist, more like. The little girl is struggling to get away from her. She is wearing one of those cute yellow rain slickers, the child, and one of those hats you call a sou'wester, also yellow, and she is wearing black galoshes, and she's digging her heels in on the wet sidewalk, trying to keep from being dragged by the woman.

Well, the woman looks a little embarrassed by all the fuss this child is making. Dancy figures her for a grandma who has the little girl on her hands for a Saturday, trying to treat her to a good lunch up the street, there's a ribs joint up the street, but the child is struggling like she wants an ice cream cone instead. The woman's very patient with her, tells her as they come abreast of him, Now come along, Kimberly, the car's right up the street, but the child keeps yelling No, I don't want to, no, leave me alone, and the woman just keeps shaking her head as they go past him, tsk-tsking and saying Now now, Kimberly, is that a way to behave?

When she finally gets the child to the car—it's parked just in front of Thimble 'n' Thread, which is a yarn shop—there really is a fuss, the child yanking her hand away when the woman bends over to unlock the door on the passenger side, and starting to run off but not getting very far because the woman scoops her up and swings her around and tosses her onto the front seat of the car. The child is really screaming now, Help me, somebody please help me, but the woman slams the door shut on her words. The rain and the wind are fierce now. The woman's raincoat—it's one of these plastic things you can see through—flaps around her as she unlocks the door on the driver's side of the car. Her hair is blowing all over her head. She gets in and starts the car. As the car drives off, the little girl is banging her fists on the side window.

Dancy is watching all this.

He sees all this.

"Now then, Mr. Dancy, can you tell us what kind of car it was?"

"Yes, sir. It was a white, 1992 Chrysler LeBaron."

"You're sure of that, are you?"

"Positive. I was a forward observer in the war, sir. I know what I'm seeing."

"Did you happen to notice the license plate on the car?"

"No, sir, I did not. It was raining too hard."

"Now tell us, please, Mr. Dancy, have you previously identified this woman you saw that day?"

"Yes, I have."

"How was identification made?"

"First from photographs and later from a police lineup."

"Would you recognize that woman if you saw her again?"

"I would."

"Is she here in this courtroom?"

"She is."

"Would you point her out to us, please?"

"She's the woman sitting right there," Dancy said, and pointed directly at Mary.

"Let the record show that the witness is indicating the defendant, Mary Barton. Now tell us, sir, what did you do after the defendant drove off with that little girl?"

"Kept waiting for the rain to let up."

"What time was it when they drove off?"

"Must've been five past twelve."

"Did you look at your watch?"

"No. I'm just estimating. I figure it must've been around that time."

"What did you do then?"

"Rain finally let up, I went across the street to the Miramar and bought my wife her nightgown."

Another chuckle from the spectators.

"And then what?"

"Went up the street, had me some ribs for dinner."

"And then?"

"Went over to the Sheriff's Office."

"Where is that, sir?"

"On Main Street, across from First Florida Federal."

"Why did you go there?"

"Because over dinner I got to thinking about that little girl, and I figured maybe something was wrong there."

"To whom did you speak, would you remember?"

"Deputy Sheriff Martin Spaeth."

"Would you know . . . ?"

"Hardee County Sheriff's Department, yes, sir. Right there on Main Street."

"Thank you. What did you tell Sheriff Spaeth?"

"I told him I saw a little girl being dragged inside a car and I suspected it was against her will."

"Did you describe this little girl to him?"

"I did."

"How did you describe her?"

"I said she was maybe seven or eight years old, with long brown hair and brown eyes . . ."

"Excuse me, you noticed the color of her eyes, did you?"

"Yes, sir, her and the woman went right on past on their way to the car."

"Please go on."

"Like I said, she was seven or eight years old, with long brown hair and brown eyes, and she was wearing a yellow rain slicker and sou'wester tied under her chin, and black galoshes, or boots I guess you'd call them, short black boots."

"Did you notice anything else about her?"

"She was wearing braces on her teeth."

"Anything else?"

"Nothing special."

"Did she mention the woman's name?"

"No, sir, she did not."

"Did she seem to . . . ?"

"Objection."

"Sustained."

"How would you describe her behavior that day?"

"Angry."

"Anything else?"

"Scared, I guess."

"Did you tell all this to Sheriff Spaeth?"

"I did."

"Described the woman for him, too? The defendant there?"

"Yes, sir."

"And the car she was driving?"

"Yes, everything."

"When did you next hear from Sheriff Spaeth?"

"That same afternoon. Must've been around three, four o'clock. Flora was baking a cake for her own birthday the next day . . . Flora, that's my wife . . ."

Another friendly chuckle from the spectators.

". . . we were fixin' to celebrate her birthday, as I told you . . ."

"Yes . . ."

". . . and the phone rang, it must've been three, four o'clock that Saturday afternoon, she was just putting the cake in the oven. It was Sheriff Spaeth, he asked me would I mind running down to his office again, there was a picture he wanted to show me."

"Did you go down there?"

"I did."

"And did he show you a photograph?"

"He did."

"Your Honor, we've previously stipulated that this is a photograph of Kimberly Holt taken this past July. May I have it moved into evidence at this time?"

"Mark it Exhibit Three for the state."

"Mr. Dancy, is this the photograph Sheriff Spaeth showed you on August twenty-ninth this year?"

"It is."

"Did you recognize the little girl in this picture?"

"I did. She was the child I saw getting in that car with Mary Barton."

"May I have this published to the jury, please?"

"You may show it to them."

"Now Mr. Dancy," Atkins said, walking toward the jury box and handing the photo to the foreman, "was there anyone else present when Sheriff Spaeth showed you this picture?"

"Yes, the child's parents were there in his office."

"Did you know at the time why they were there?"

"Yes, I did. They had reported their little girl missing that afternoon, and I was there to see if it was the same child."

"Was it?"

"It was."

Crossing back to the witness stand now.

"The girl you saw being dragged to that car by the defendant . . ."

"Yes."

". . . was Kimberly Holt?"

"She was."

"The girl you saw the defendant lift into that car was Kimberly Holt?"

"Objection! Asked and answered."

"Overruled."

"She's the girl I saw, yes."

"Scooped her up, you said . . ."

"Yes."

". . . and swung her around . . ."

"Yes."

"Your Honor, this has all been asked and . . ."

"I'm allowing it, Mr. Hope."

"Tossed her onto the front seat of the car, you said . . ."

"Yes."

"That child was Kimberly Holt . . ."

"Yes."

". . . and the woman who did those things to her and drove off with her was the defendant, Mary Barton?"

"That's who it was."

"Thank you, Mr. Dancy."

I can tell you I would rather have faced a regiment of mounted Mongolian cavalry troops than this one-legged hero of the Italian campaign. For the past month now, I had tried to work out an approach that might be more effective than the one I'd used in my deposition of the man, but I still had no real strategy that would impeach him or even damage his testimony. I approached the stand hoping I was exuding a confidence I definitely did not feel. Sitting as still as cold celery soup, he awaited my first question.

"Mr. Dancy," I said, "were there many people in downtown Alietam that Saturday afternoon? We're talking about August twenty-ninth. Many people in town?"

"Fair amount."

"You said you were standing in front of the hardware store, is that right?"

"That's right."

"Waiting for the rain to let up?"

"Yes."

"Roof over your head?"

"The sidewalks are roofed over, yes, both sides of Main Street. That's a nice thing about Alietam."

"So you were protected from the rain, is that right?"

"Yes."

"Anyone else standing with you there on the sidewalk?"

"Oh yes."

"Also waiting for the rain to . . . ?"

"Objection."

"Sustained."

"How many people were standing out there on that covered sidewalk with you? Outside the hardware store."

"I don't remember."

"Would you say there were *ten* people?"

"I don't remem—"

"Your Honor, he's answered the question."

"Sustained. Let's move on, Mr. Hope."

"But there were *some* people out there with you, isn't that right?"

"Yes."

"You don't remember the exact number . . ."

"I don't."

"But you weren't out there *alone,* were you?"

"I was not alone."

"Were there people elsewhere in the town as well?"

"Well, yes."

Cautiously. Not knowing where I was going.

"I mean, you could see other people moving about, could you?"

"Yes."

Still cautiously. Waiting for me to spring some kind of trap. I hated to tell him I had no trap. All I had was an honest confusion about what the main thoroughfare of a small town might have looked like on a rainy Saturday in August.

"Would you say the town was crowded that day?"

"I'd say it was about usual for a Saturday."

"Please understand, I'm not asking you to tell me how *many* people were in town that day, Mr. Dancy . . ."

"Couldn't tell you if you *did* ask me."

"I realize that. But would you say Saturday is *normally* a busy shopping day in Alietam?"

"It is normally, yes."

"People in the stores?"

"Yes."

"People walking on the streets?"

"Yes."

"Crowded as compared to a weekday, isn't that so?"

"Yes. Normally."

"So then, it *was* crowded that Saturday, wasn't it?"

"Well . . . crowded as it'd be on any Saturday."

"For example . . . could you see people moving about on the other side of the street?"

"Yes, I could see people all *over* town that day. I've already told you there were . . ."

"But were there people on the other side of the street?"

"Yes, there were."

"And, of course, there were people on your side of the street."

"Yes."

"This woman you saw, and the child with her? Were *they* on your side of the street?"

"Yes."

"Walking toward you at first?"

"Yes."

"And then coming abreast of you?"

"Yes."

"And then walking past you toward a car parked in front of the yarn shop, isn't that what you said?"

"Yes, that's what I said."

"And were there other people walking toward you, and coming abreast of you, and then past you at the very same time?"

"There were. But I saw the woman and child, if that's what you . . ."

"I'm not asking whether or not you saw them, Mr. Dancy. I'm asking if there were other people moving on that sidewalk at the same time?"

"He's answered the question, Your Honor."

"He qualified his answer, Your Honor, and I'd like a straight yes or no. Were there other people moving around you on that sidewalk at the same time?"

"Yes."

"At the same time that the woman and the child were moving

toward you, and coming abreast of you, and finally moving past you, there were *other* people doing the same thing?"

"Yes."

"Now you said this child was raising a fuss."

"Yes."

"Tugging and pulling and yelling and trying to get away from this woman in the plastic raincoat . . . you're sure it was plastic, hm?"

"It was plastic."

"A see-through sort of coat, you said."

"Yes."

"What was she wearing under it?"

"I don't know."

"You could see through it, couldn't you?"

"Yes, but . . ."

"Well, what was she wearing under it?"

"I told you, I don't know."

"How close did she pass by you?"

"About three, four feet."

"But you didn't see what she had on under this transparent coat."

"It was raining."

"But not under the portico, was it?"

"No, but . . ."

"No rain to obscure your vision under the portico, was there?"

"No . . ."

"But you can't tell me what she was wearing under this transparent coat."

"No, sir, I can't."

"And you say this child was making quite a scene, is that right?"

"Yes."

"Did anyone else react to the way she was behaving?"

"Objection, Your Honor. Witness has no way of knowing what anyone else . . ."

"Sustained."

"Mr. Dancy, did you *see* anyone else reacting to the way this child was behaving?"

"I don't remember."

"All these people going by on the sidewalk, did you see any of them raising an eyebrow over this child trying to get away from this woman?"

"I wasn't looking at anyone else. I was looking at the woman and child."

"Did you hear any of these people *commenting* on what was happening?"

"No, I didn't."

"Did you hear anyone say, 'Look at what that woman is doing to that child!' Anything like that?"

"No. Nothing like that."

"Nothing at all? You didn't hear *anyone* at *all* say anything at all about this tug-of-war going on between a woman in her late fifties and a six-year-old child?"

"I didn't hear anyone saying anything, no."

"No one commented to you about it?"

"No."

"Yet the child was yelling loud enough to have attracted your attention, wasn't she?"

"She was."

"But not anyone else's attention?"

"Your Honor . . ."

"Sustained."

"Did you notice anyone else reacting to the child's yelling?"

"Well . . ."

"Yes or no, please."

"No."

"How about when the child was yelling, 'Help me, somebody please help me!' Did you see anyone reacting to that?"

"No, but . . ."

"Did you *yourself* react to that?"

"I certainly did."

"How?"

"I was amazed by it. And shocked."

"Amazed and shocked, I see. But did you *do* anything about it?"

"Not right then."

"This was at five past twelve, you said. When the woman and the child drove off. Around that time, isn't that right?"

"Around then."

"And shortly thereafter—although you were shocked and amazed by what you'd just seen and heard—you went across the street to buy your wife a nightgown."

No laughter this time.

"Is that what you did, Mr. Dancy?"

"Yes."

"How long did that take, would you suppose?"

"About half an hour."

"So at twelve-thirty, twelve-forty, thereabouts, you went up the street to have lunch."

"Around then."

"How long did it take you to eat lunch, Mr. Dancy?"

"About forty minutes."

"And during lunch, you started thinking about that little girl again, isn't that what you said . . . ?"

"Yes."

". . . and decided to go to the Sheriff's Office."

"Yes."

"What time did you get to the Sheriff's Office?"

"It must've been around one-thirty."

"In other words, an hour and a half after you were so shocked and amazed by what you'd seen and heard . . ."

"Objection, Your Honor. Defense is characterizing . . ."

"Your Honor, the witness has *testified* that he was shocked and amazed. I'm merely . . ."

"My opponent is mocking Mr. Dancy's words, Your Honor."

"Overruled. Proceed, Mr. Hope."

"An hour and a half after you were so shocked and amazed by this incident no one else seems even to have *noticed* . . ."

"Objection, Your Honor."

"Sustained. Don't press your luck, Mr. Hope."

"My question, Mr. Dancy: *did* it take you an hour and a half to report this incident to the Sheriff's Office?"

"It did."

"What took you so long?"

"I'm black, sir."

I had stepped right into it. In that single instant, I thought *There it is*, the single answer that'll cost me the trial. In any other business you can make mistakes that are damaging only to yourself; in defending someone accused of murder, your mistake can cost that person her life.

I'm black, sir.

The jury turned its attention to me.

Waiting.

Four men and eight women.

Max Atkins had made certain that all of the men were white and I guessed that right about then he might've been feeling a faint twinge of regret. Certainly, none of the rednecks he'd handpicked gave a good goddamn *how* Dancy had felt about going to the sheriff that August afternoon. Most of them probably believed he *should've* stayed out of business that was none of his black-assed concern. But there were eight women on that jury, and four of them weren't white. It seemed to me—

None of this was conscious, all of it was intuitive, I was desperately thinking on my feet while the courtroom clock ticked, and Judge Rutherford watched me with a quizzical gaze that said *Yes, Mr. Hope, are* there any further questions, and Atkins watched me with his hands folded over his vest, not daring to smile at my predicament, and Mary watched me, her face impassive, realizing I'd made a terrible mistake and perhaps wondering just how costly it would prove—

It seemed to me in those next fleeting thirty seconds that an apology was owed Mr. Dancy, not because I was a bully who'd picked on a cripple, and not because I was a racist who'd attacked a black war hero, but because I should have understood that this was the Deep South, and the fact that it had taken him *only* an hour and a half to make up his mind was not merely admirable, it was courageous.

So whereas the better part of valor might have been to excuse him at this point—No further questions, thank you, Mr. Dancy—I nodded in acknowledgment instead: Yes, my nod said, I know how difficult it must have been for you. But the nod wasn't enough, I knew the nod wasn't enough, the apology was still necessary. An apology to Dancy and to those several people on the jury who, like him, were not lily-white in this land of Ivory soap and Wonder bread. An apology for years of casual injustice, an apology from all those whites on the jury who might just possibly understand how difficult it really *had* been for Dancy that afternoon, and an apology from Atkins's four rednecks as well, who didn't give a damn and would never give a damn about a black man's problems. *And* an apology from me, personally, yes.

"Mr. Dancy," I said, "I apologize."

He blinked. I didn't know how the jury was reacting to what I'd just said, and I didn't give a damn. This was to Dancy, one-on-one.

"I should have realized why you were reluctant to go to the authorities."

He blinked again.

Atkins said nothing. He was undoubtedly calculating whether this would be to his advantage or not.

"You were reluctant, weren't you, Mr. Dancy?"

"Yes, I was."

"Can you tell me why?"

"I think you know why."

"Was it because the incident you'd witnessed was between two white people?"

"Yes."

"A white woman and a white child."

"Yes."

"Were you afraid you'd be told this was 'white business'?"

"That crossed my mind, yes."

"Were you afraid you'd be told to stay out of it?"

"Yes."

"Or that you'd somehow become involved in it?"

"Yes."

"But you went anyway."

"I went anyway."

I'd apologized. I'd paid my debt to him. But I had a further debt to Mary Barton, and it was a greater one.

"Mr. Dancy," I said, "I have a few more questions, if you don't mind."

He was immediately suspicious. Had Mr. Charlie led him down the garden path once again, patting him on the back like a Good Ole Boy, while all the while planning to string him up from the nearest oak? His eyes narrowed, his fists clenched. I visualized him in combat all those years ago.

"This woman you saw," I said, and hesitated. "What color were her eyes?"

"I don't know."

"Didn't you see her eyes?"

"I didn't pay much attention to her eyes."

"How about the child's eyes? Did you notice them?"

"She had brown eyes, yes."

"But you didn't notice the color of the woman's eyes."

"No, I didn't."

"You noticed that the child had long brown hair, didn't you?"

"Yes, I did."

"What color hair did the woman have?"

"Gray."

"You saw the color of her hair?"

"Yes."

"Even though she was wearing . . . what did you call it? 'One of these plastic things women put on over their heads,' isn't that what you said? 'Like a scarf, only plastic?' Aren't those your words, Mr. Dancy?"

"Yes, but . . ."

"But you said later, didn't you, that her hair was blowing all over her head. When she got in the car. Isn't that how you described her hair? As 'blowing all over her head'? Aren't those your exact words?"

"Yes, but . . ."

"Was she wearing a plastic scarf or wasn't she, Mr. Dancy?"

"She was wearing one."

"Then how could her hair be blowing all over her head?"

"I don't *know* how. But I'm sure she was wearing the scarf."

"The same way you're sure her hair was gray?"

"I'm sure her hair was gray, yes."

"The same way you're sure the woman you saw that day was Mary Barton, hm?"

"I'm sure it was her, yes."

"But you don't know how her hair could've been blowing all over her head when she was wearing a scarf."

"Maybe she'd taken it off by then."

"Ah. Maybe. Yes. Was her hair long or short, Mr. Dancy?"

"Just like the defendant's."

"Short, then, is that right?"

"Short, yes."

"If it was so short, Mr. Dancy, how could it be blowing all over her head?"

"It was very windy."

"Even if she'd taken off the scarf, how could such short hair be blowing all over her head?"

"I don't know how, but it was."

"Mr. Dancy, when and where did you first make positive identification of Mary Barton as the woman you'd seen that day?"

"In the State Attorney's Office in Calusa, Florida, on the third of September."

"Five days after you'd witnessed the incident in Alietam."

"Yes."

"When did you telephone the state attorney in Calusa?"

"The day before."

"September second?"

"Yes."

"Why did you call him?"

"Because I recognized Mary Barton's picture on television."

"When did you see her on television?"

"That same day I called the state attorney."

"September second."

"Yes."

"Tell me . . . between August twenty-ninth and September third, did you ever again see the woman you saw on that rainy Saturday in Alietam?"

"Never. But . . ."

"Had you even seen a *photograph* of her?"

"No. But . . ."

"Never saw her picture on television before September *second*, had you?"

"No."

"But on September *third*, when you looked at this woman who'd been arrested for murder, you jumped right up and said, 'By golly . . .'"

"Objection, Your Honor."

"Sustained. Cool it, Mr. Hope."

"You immediately recognized her as the woman you'd seen five days earlier, is that right?"

"Yes, that's right."

"Ever see her *before* that day?"

"No."

"First time you ever saw her in your life was on August twenty-ninth . . ."

"Yes."

"This woman who may or may not have been wearing a plastic rain scarf . . ."

"She *was* wearing the scarf!"

"This woman whose *eyes* you didn't notice . . ."

"I was watching the little girl. She was dragging . . ."

"This woman whose *hair* you're sure was gray, even . . ."

"Yes, it was."

". . . even though she was wearing a rain scarf over it. Now, Mr. Dancy, when you went to the S.A.'s Office, did they show you photographs of Mary Barton?"

"They did."

"What photographs?"

"Pictures taken at the time of her arrest."

"Mug shots?"

"Yes."

"These?" I asked, and immediately turned to Rutherford. "Your Honor, I'd like these marked for identification, please."

"Mark them Exhibit B for the defense."

"Mr. Dancy," I said, handing him the pictures, "are these what they showed you?"

"Yes."

"These pictures with the numbers across the bottom?"

"Yes."

"And the date behind the prisoner, and the words 'Calusa Police Department' on the wall, are these the pictures they showed you?"

"Yes."

"Would you say they're good likenesses of Mary Barton?"

"Objection, Your Honor."

"Sustained."

"If you had not previously seen Mary Barton on television . . ."

"Objection, Your Honor."

"Sustained."

"Mr. Dancy, please look at the photographs again."

He looked.

"Do those pictures even *remotely* resemble Mary . . . ?"

"Objection, Your Honor."

"Sustained."

"Your Honor, the jury will be seeing these pictures, they'll . . ."

"Approach, please."

We went up. She looked mad as hell, I couldn't imagine why.

"What is it, Mr. Hope?" she asked.

"Your Honor, these photographs were taken after hours of questioning and considerable stress. They are *not* good pictures—no mug shots are—and I'm sure the jury will recognize that fact when they look at them. In addition, Mary Barton had already been charged with the crime and Harold Dancy knew this. That he made positive identification from bad photographs of someone he knew had been arrested for murder and charged with murder goes directly to his ability to perceive, Your Honor. As does the matter of the plastic scarf and the hair blowing and the color of the woman's eyes and the fact that no one on that crowded street seems to have witnessed or cared about what Mr. Dancy claims he witnessed and cared about. He saw my client's picture on television and then he was shown bad photographs of her and *only* her, no other suspects, and I submit that this was so suggestive that it tainted his identification. If I'm not allowed this line of questioning . . ."

"Do you propose to show that identification was made *solely* through these photographs? It's my understanding there was a subsequent lineup as well."

"There was, Your Honor. But . . ."

"Exactly the point, Your Honor," Atkins said. "Even if the witness *were* an expert on photography, which admittedly he is not, his opinion of the photographs would be irrelevant in light of the subsequent lineup identifi—"

"Your Honor, I submit that the earlier photo ID *influenced* the later lineup ID. Moreover . . ."

"Moreover, you're interrupting me, Mr. Hope," Atkins said

drily and without looking at me. "I was about to say, Your Honor, that although photo identification may be viewed skeptically by the courts, lineup identification is commonly accepted as valid evidence. Questioning its use would have been proper only at a pretrial hearing."

"Mr. Hope?"

"Identification is *the* single key issue in this trial, Your Honor. If I'm not allowed to question before the jury what appears to be misidentification . . ."

"Well," Judge Rutherford said, "as you pointed out earlier, the jury has eyes of its own, so why don't we let *them* decide whether showing the pictures influenced the later lineup ID. As to eliciting from the witness any testimony as to the quality of the photographs or whether or not they faithfully resemble the defendant, I will not allow it. So that's that as regards whether the pictures are wonderful or mediocre or just plain rotten. If you wish to bring out anything else about the pictures—anything that doesn't relate to whether or not they actually resemble the defendant— that's fine with me. Okay? May we proceed now?"

"Thank you, Your Honor."

"Thank you," Atkins said.

I walked back to the witness stand. Dancy had a puzzled look on his face, as if he was wondering what the hell *that* had been all about.

"Mr. Dancy," I said, "when you went to the S.A.'s Office that day, did he ask you to identify Mary Barton from anything other than these photographs?"

"I don't understand the question."

"Did the state attorney show you any *other* photographs? Pictures of any *other* women?"

"No."

"Did he run the television footage you'd seen the day before?"

"No. But I'd seen that for myself."

"Of course you had. Did he run a lineup with Mary Barton in it?"

"Yes, he did."

"Other women in that lineup?"

"Yes."

"How many?"

"Four."

"Four other women in the lineup. Did any of them have gray hair?"

"Not to my knowledge."

"You picked the only gray-haired woman out of that lineup, isn't that right?"

"Yes."

"And you picked her out of that lineup only *after* you'd been shown mug shots of Mary Barton, isn't that so?"

"Yes."

"You knew while you were looking at the lineup, didn't you, that Mary Barton had already been charged with murder?"

"Well, I knew *one* of those women in the lineup had been charged with murder."

"Had you seen those other women on television?"

"No, but . . ."

"Had you been shown mug shots of those other women?"

"No."

"When the state attorney showed you the mug shots of Mary Barton, did he ask if the woman in them was the woman you'd seen abducting Kimberly Holt five days earlier?"

"Yes."

"And how did you answer him?"

"I said yes, she was the woman I'd seen."

"When he showed you these photographs, you said, 'Yes, that's the woman I saw in Alietam five days ago.' Is that essentially what you said?"

"Yes. Maybe not exactly in those words . . ."

"But essentially."

"Yes."

"In other words, you looked at these photographs and made positive identification from them."

"Yes."

"These photographs and these photographs alone."

"Yes."

"And only *afterward* were you asked to pick Mary Barton out of a lineup, is that also correct?"

"Yes."

"No further questions. Your Honor, I move that the pictures be marked as evidence and published to the men and women of the jury."

"So moved. Mr. Atkins?"

"No further questions."

"Let's recess for lunch," Rutherford said. "This court will reconvene at two P.M."

"All rise!" the bailiff shouted.

10

There is something unnerving about British candor; I suspect it was responsible for both the rise *and* the fall of the empire. Suntanned and looking very American in a simple yellow frock, Melissa Lowndes told me over lunch that she'd been reading the newspaper coverage of the trial, and watching the nightly television reports, and she thought I was doing a lousy job. *Lousy* was the exact word she used. It did not sound very British on her lips, but the message could have been coming from Queen Victoria herself.

She had not personally seen me in action. She was not permitted in the courtroom because I planned to call her as a character witness—something not without its own inherent risks. I told her I was sorry she felt that way, and then went on to explain that the case was an extremely difficult one in that so *many* witnesses were able to identify Mary and to place her in proximity to the victims. All a defense attorney *could* do, really, was attempt to fault the identification. But in the light of . . .

"How many more will there be?"

"Only one more who saw her with a victim. Then there's . . ."

"Only one!"

"They've also got the guy who runs the dry-cleaning shop."

"How do you know all this?"

"The other side has to supply its list of witnesses. I've already deposed both of them. The one who claims she saw Mary with Felicity Hammer is a weak witness. I'm not even sure why Atkins is putting her on."

"Maybe he's planning a surprise."

"There are very few surprises in a Florida courtroom. Not since the disclosure rules went into effect, anyway. I know what she's going to say, and I'm ready for her."

"How about the dry cleaner?"

"He may be the toughest of them all."

"Why?"

"He claims he was with Mary for a good ten minutes. Talked to her, asked her about the dress, gave her a receipt for it, saw her driving off in that same white LeBaron. We're trying to zero in on the car now, but . . ."

"You told me Mary drives a Cam—"

"I know that."

"Then what difference does it make *how* many people saw her in that damn white car? It isn't her car, they're obviously mistaken."

"Well, that's for the jury to decide, you see. I plan to put on witnesses who'll testify that Mary's car is a red Camry and that she wasn't anywhere near Callahan's place of business . . . that's the dry cleaner's name, Jerry Callahan . . . on the day somebody brought that dress in. But you see, it's for the *jury* to weigh all this evidence and then decide what they want to bel—"

"Yes, I think I understand how it works," she said drily. "Do you normally find your courtroom manner effective?"

"Well, I . . ."

"Because from what the newspaper says . . ."

"The *Calusa Herald-Tribune* is the worst newspaper in the entire world."

"Be that as it may, they find your style extremely unpleasant."

Right between the eyes.

"In fact, they think you're not a very attractive advocate."

Twice, for good measure.

"I'm sorry they feel that way," I said.

"Mm, yes," she said, and smeared green peas onto her fork with her knife, the way they do. "Mr. Atkins is far more stylish, they seem to think. In his television interviews, he looks rather donnish, in fact, which I consider a decided plus. Most of the television commentators, by the way, felt you were far too aggressive with the first child's mother . . ."

"That was a calculated risk."

"And the way you treated the black man was abominable."

"I thought I made the best of a difficult situation."

"Which you yourself created."

"No, *he* created it. I was going for a specific answer. In fact, when I deposed him, he gave me *exactly* the answer I wanted, and I was expecting him to repeat it in court."

"And what was that?"

"He told me the reason he'd waited so long was that he wasn't *sure* about what he'd seen. Well, he played the black card instead. It's always difficult to combat that, Miss Knowles. Contradict it, you sound prejudiced. Go along with it, you seem . . . well, look how well Clarence Thomas used it."

"Clarence who?"

"Well . . . it doesn't matter anymore. I figured the best way out was to apologize for having been so insensitive to the special conditions of the black man here in Florida. I thought I'd rescued it. Maybe I did, maybe I didn't. That's for the jury to decide."

"I have no faith in juries," she said flatly, and lifted the pea-laden fork to her mouth. With her left hand, of course. The way they do.

"I wouldn't be practicing law if I didn't have faith in juries," I said.

"Then perhaps it's *you* in whom I have such little faith," she said.

"Yes, you've made that abundantly clear. What would you like to do, Miss Knowles? Replace me?"

"I think that would be a mistake at this juncture. Sink or swim, Mary's stuck with you."

"Thanks a lot," I said, "you really bolster my confidence."

"I'm merely being frank."

" 'Blunt' is the word. I'm looking at an army of witnesses who saw Mary with the three dead kids, and another witness who'll swear she brought a bloodstained dress to his shop, and yet another one who saw her burying at least one of the victims, and all *I've* got is Mary's goddamn car, and whatever character witnesses I can round up in addition to you, and Mary herself— *if* she agrees to take the stand. And you say I'm not doing the job, huh?"

"Yes," she said in that same irritatingly flat voice. She put down her fork, picked up her napkin, dabbed at her mouth with it. "I'm paying you very good money to keep Mary Barton out of the electric chair," she said. She raised her eyebrows slightly, the way some judges do when they're about to throw the book at you. She put down the napkin. Folded it. Smoothed it on the table with an air of finality. Lifted her eyes to meet mine again. Raised the eyebrows again. "I don't want her to die because of your ineffectualness," she said.

I said nothing.

"Have I made myself clear, Mr. Hope?"

"As clear as are the skies of England," I said.

The woman's name was Sarah Santangelo.

She was fifty-two years old, a plump, attractive little woman wearing a black dress and carrying a huge black handbag that made her look like a doctor on a house call. She told the court that she lived right here in Calusa, in a development called Ben-Avi Shores, corner of Avrum Way and Rachel Street. Lived there for seventeen years, in fact, from when she and her husband came down from Pittsburgh one winter and decided to stay. Pittsburgh was a lovely city now, she told the court, but back then it was all steel mills and smoke, they were happy to get out of it. Three minutes on the stand and she had the jury eating from the palm of her hand.

"Now, please tell us, Mrs. Santangelo," Atkins said, "do you remember where you were and what you were doing on August thirtieth at three o'clock in the afternoon?"

"I was at the Republican Club picnic on Palm Island."

"You remember this precisely, do you?"

"Oh, yes. Vice President Quayle was supposed to be there."

His name still got a laugh, even here in Calusa.

"But he didn't show up," Mrs. Santangelo said.

Another laugh.

"That's how I remember the time. He was supposed to get there at three, but he was delayed in Tampa or something, I never did get it straight. It was a good picnic, anyway, even without him."

Another laugh. They loved her even more than they had Harold Dancy. Maybe the two of them could go on the road together after the trial was over. Dancy and Santangelo. Songs, banjo playing, and snappy patter, available for hayrides, bar mitzvahs, and strawberry festivals.

"Now, Mrs. Santangelo, can you describe the layout of Palm Island for us? Where the picnic took place? So that we'll be able to understand how you happened to see what you saw that day."

"Well . . . what you do," Sarah said, "is you drive over the Causeway to Lucy's Circle and then over the little bridge to Palm Island. Palm's between the Circle and Stone Crab Key. Sort of parallel to the Causeway. It's hard to explain. What it is, though, is this sort of little park at the end of the island—it's just this one end of the island that's called Palm, the other end is Sabal Shores. Which isn't a development, by the way, it's just part of the island. I don't know why the whole island isn't called Palm. What it is . . ."

There're these picnic tables, and a concession stand, and good water to bring in boats and anchor them. This Sunday afternoon at the end of August, there are a good many boats bobbing on the water close to shore, and the picnic tables are packed with people who've driven over from the mainland or even from Stone Crab Key nearby. It's a beautiful day compared to the terrible rain they had yesterday in Calusa, well, all over Florida for that matter, and the Republican Party has hired a band to play, and there are giveaway balloons and sandwiches and beer, this is a presidential election year, and the party is going for broke. Well, look, they planned to send Quayle down, didn't they?

There are hundreds of kids here.

Kids all over the place.

In the water, swimming in and around the anchored boats, and frolicking on the beach that wraps around this end of the island like a boomerang, the younger kids building sand castles and stomping in puddles of water, the older kids tossing Frisbees or playing volleyball at one of the two nets set up at either end of the beach, or softball on the small grassy field near the crowded parking lot. The Republican Club has set up tables brimming with ham and cheese sandwiches wrapped in sandwich bags, and there are several kegs of beer, and tubs full of canned soft drinks floating with chunks of ice, and they've also arranged for the concessionaire to dispense free ice cream pops and cones and sandwiches, and so there are lines of kids at the food tables and the concession truck. On yet another line, there are kids waiting to have their free balloons filled with air by a man running a compressor and wearing a Bush-Quayle button in his lapel and a straw boater with a red, white, and blue hatband. The band is playing all the old summertime favorites and some of the older couples are dancing on a makeshift platform, where still more kids are running around between their legs, playing tag or just racing around for the hell of it. There are more kids here today than there are grown-ups.

So Sarah might not have noticed this particular kid if she wasn't bleeding.

The Santangelos are sitting at a picnic table close to the parking lot. That's because Sarah's husband, Mike, wanted to finish mowing the lawn and cleaning the pool before they set out for the picnic, telling Sarah there was plenty of time, Quayle wouldn't be getting there till three, which of course he didn't show at all. But they'd got there around one, and naturally the parking lot was full except for an illegal spot Mike found marked with diagonal white lines on the black asphalt. And it was a good thing there were only the two of them because all they could find was a small space at the end of one of the picnic tables. She had made sausage and pepper sandwiches to take to the picnic, the sweet kind Mike liked so much, never mind the ham and cheese they were giving away, and she and Mike were sitting there cramped at the end of the table with a family of people so blond they looked like they'd just come from Sweden, the mother, the father, and two little boys, all of them blond as sunshine. Sarah sits eating the sandwiches she herself made and drinking the beer Mike carried over from where they were pumping it out of a big metal keg.

The little girl was bleeding from the mouth.

Six or seven years old, Sarah guessed, bleeding from the mouth and crying.

In a white car pulling out of the parking lot.

Woman at the wheel. Little girl wearing a bathing suit, little bikini top over no breasts at all, blood spilling from her mouth.

"I got to my feet," Sarah said now, "just as the car went by."

"And was the child, in fact, bleeding?"

"Oh yes, she was bleeding, all right. And screaming her head off, though you couldn't hear her 'cause the windows were closed."

And now came the routine of identification, the same story I'd heard from Sarah Santangelo at the deposition, Atkins running her through the drill once again, asking her to describe the little girl and then ascertaining from a photograph he first had marked for identification and later had moved into evidence that the little girl bleeding from the mouth was indeed little six-year-old Felicity Hammer, whose mother at that very moment was having her paged over the park's lost-and-found speaker system. And then Atkins took it the necessary step further, having Sarah identify the woman driving the car as none other than Guess Who, the defendant, Mary Barton, sitting right there across the courtroom, sir. And, of course, he went on to nail the coffin shut by eliciting from her the information that the car was—lo and behold—a 1992 white Chrysler LeBaron, the very same vehicle that had been spotted in Somerset on Friday and in Alietam on Saturday.

I was ready to destroy all this testimony in ten seconds flat because after I'd taken Sarah Santangelo's deposition, Toots Kiley had gone to Palm Island to map the location of the picnic table and its proximity to the parking lot, and had discovered (a) that a stand of pines would have partially obstructed any clear view of the lot and (b) that the sun at three that afternoon would have been shining directly into Sarah's eyes while any car went by.

So I was waiting patiently for Atkins to finish his now tired routine of positive identification of victim and bloodthirsty beast when something unexpected came up. I had explained to Melissa at lunch not forty minutes ago that each side in an opposing suit must present witness lists to the other side, and the contending lawyers are allowed the opportunity to question these witnesses before trial. But there is nothing on God's green earth that states a lawyer must tell the other side what questions he is going to ask when the case comes to trial. I had also told Melissa there were very few surprises in a courtroom nowadays. Well, this was one of them; I was totally unprepared for what came next.

"Now Mrs. Santangelo," Atkins said, "as this automobile went past you . . ."

"Yes?"

". . . out of the parking lot, as you said . . ."

"Yes?"

"Did you happen to notice the license plate?"

"I did."

"And can you tell me what the letters or numerals on that plate were?"

"Only the first three letters."

"What were those letters?"

"Y-A-M. I remembered them because they spelled out yam, you know? Like a sweet potato? Yam. Y-A-M."

"Did you see the other letters or numerals on the plate?"

"No, I'm sorry, I didn't. The car was moving, and also, as it turned to go out of the lot, the sun was in my eyes."

"Did this affect your ability to see the plate?"

"Yes, the car moving and the sun blinding me."

"Was there any other obstacle to your vision?"

"Yes, there are pine trees lining the parking lot there. I could only see the car on and off. I saw the little girl bleeding, and then the car was behind the pines, and then I caught a glimpse of the woman driving, and then the plate, and then the car was hidden by the pines, and when it came out again I was looking straight into the sun."

"But you did get a good look at the little girl . . ."

"Oh, yes."

". . . and the woman . . ."

"Yes."

". . . and the letters Y-A-M on the plate."

"Yes, I did."

"Were these letters on the left-hand side of the plate or on the right?"

"On the left. They were the first three letters. Y-A-M."

"Now, aside from the association you made with sweet potatoes . . ."

"Well, that's the first thing that came to mind."

"I'm sure it did. But aside from *that* association, did those three letters, Y-A-M, mean anything else to you?"

Oh, Jesus, I thought.

"Not all three of them," she said.

"Well, did *any* of them mean anything to you?"

"Just the first letter."

He's about to blow the red Camry, I thought. He's about to ask her . . .

"The letter Y?"

"Yes. The letter Y."

"What did the letter Y mean to you?"

"It meant the car was rented."

"How do you happen to know this, Mrs. Santangelo?"

"My husband Mike works for Hertz. Every rental car in the state of Florida has a license plate starting either with the letter Y or the letter Z."

"And the letter you saw was a Y."

"Yes."

"And that's how you knew it was a rental car."

"Yes. That's how I knew."

Me, too, I thought. This was not information one normally carries around in the baggage of his mind, but a license plate number had weighed heavily in the Leeds case, and I happened to know that what Sarah Santangelo had just told the jury was true. Nor had there been any clue that it was coming. Atkins's witness list did not include anyone from a car rental company. He'd wanted to surprise me, and he had. If what he'd got from Sarah was a fact—and it was—there was no sense challenging it. He had me.

"Your witness," he said.

The smug little bastard had just established that the white

Chrysler LeBaron everyone had been talking about since the trial began was a rental car. I could have Mary testify six ways from Sunday that the car she'd been driving for the past year was a red Camry that happened to be in the shop for repairs on the weekend in question, but it wouldn't matter a damn. The woman who'd abducted those children, the woman who'd now been positively identified under oath by three separate witnesses, had been driving a rental car—if Sarah Santangelo was to be believed. And who could doubt the sworn testimony of this plump, jolly little woman who'd made sausage and pepper sandwiches to take to the picnic? The sweet kind Mike liked so *much,* don't forget.

"Was it a Hertz car?" I asked her.

"What?"

"The car you saw. Was it a Hertz?"

"Oh. No. Hertz rents Sables, Tauruses, and Volvos. You can't get a Chrysler from Hertz. Not in Calusa, anyway."

"And you're sure this was a Chrysler?"

"Yes."

"Even though the sun was in your eyes?"

"Only part of the time."

"Even though the car was flashing in and out of the trees?"

"I didn't say it was flashing in and out. I said it was hidden by the pines every now and then."

"Mm-huh," I said, and walked back to the defense table, and took from it a large chart I'd had prepared. "Your Honor," I said, "the state attorney has previously stipulated to this chart's accuracy. I would like to have it moved into evidence, please."

"Exhibit C," Rutherford said, and nodded to the clerk.

I went to where Andrew was setting up an easel where it could be seen by both the witness and the jury. The chart had been mounted on a stiff board. I put the board on the easel's rack . . .

"Can you see this all right, Mrs. Santangelo?"

"Yes."

"Your Honor, is this visible to the jury?"

"I believe it is."

"Thank you. Now, Mrs. Santangelo," I said, "would you take a close look at this chart . . ."

"I'd better put on my glasses," she said.

"Yes, please do."

She dug around in her purse, finally came up with an eyeglass case, extricated her glasses from it, perched them on her nose—all to the delight of the courtroom spectators—put the eyeglass case back into her purse, snapped the purse shut, and leaned forward to peer at the chart.

"Would it help you if you came up here?" I asked.

"Yes, I think it would."

"Your Honor?"

"Go ahead."

Sarah came off the witness stand, walked around it and down to where the chart rested on the easel.

"Can you see it clearly now?" I asked.

"Oh, yes," she said cheerfully, and someone in the courtroom laughed.

Rutherford scowled out over the rows of spectator benches.

"Mrs. Santangelo," I said, "can you tell me what this is?"

"Well . . . it looks like a . . . I don't know . . . some kind of landscape plan."

"Do you see a label there in the lower right-hand corner?"

"Yes, I do."

"Outlined in red there? The little label?"

"Yes."

"Can you tell me what's printed on that label?"

"It says Palm Island Park, Calusa, Florida."

"Thank you. Now, Mrs. Santangelo, do you see the area lettered with the words 'Parking Lot'?"

"I do."

"And do you see another area lettered with the words 'Picnic Tables'?"

"Yes?"

"Now, there's a red arrow affixed to that area, pointing to one of the outlined tables. Do you see the arrow?"

"I see it."

"Mrs. Santangelo, is this where you and your husband were sitting on August thirtieth when you saw the white Chrysler LeBaron with the Y-A-M plate on it?"

"Well, I really don't know," she said, shrugging, and turning from the chart to look directly at the jury box. Spreading her arms wide, opening her hands in supplication to the jury, she said, "There are all these little rectangles drawn on it, how am I supposed to know which one . . . ?"

"Mrs. Santangelo, during your pretrial deposition, didn't you tell me that you and your husband were sitting at a table adjacent to the parking lot?"

"Yes, but there are a lot of tables near the . . ."

"Didn't you say it was the third table from the telephone booth?"

"Who can remember how many tables it was from a phone booth? Who even remembers a phone booth?"

She shrugged again and gave me a totally bewildered look. Somewhere in the courtroom, someone else laughed. Rutherford scowled again.

"Mrs. Santangelo," I said, "didn't you testify under oath that when your husband, Mike, went for the beer, you told him he could remember the table because it was the third one from the telephone booth? So he could find his way back. Do you remember saying that?"

"It was so long ago, who can re—?"

"If you looked at the transcript of your sworn deposition, do you think that might refresh your memory?"

"It might. I really can't remember whether we were sitting six tables, or four tables, or two tables . . ." A shrug each time, and spectator laughter accompanying each shrug. ". . . or a hundred tables from the phone booth."

I ignored the laughter. I was thumbing through the deposition Andrew had just handed me. I found what I wanted on page 46.

"Would you please read this?" I said, and handed it to her. "Take your time, read it carefully."

I waited.

She read it slowly and carefully and then looked up at me.

"Do you now recall telling me that the park was very crowded that day, and you were afraid your husband might get lost. So you told him . . ."

"Well, that's what's typed here."

"Well, isn't that what you said? Under oath?"

"I suppose it's what I said."

"Mrs. Santangelo . . ."

"Yes, it's what I said."

"And did you also tell your husband to use the phone booth as a marker? The exact language, I believe . . . well, you look at it . . . the exact language was, 'We're three tables down from the phone booth, right on the edge of the parking lot.' Isn't that what's in your deposition, Mrs. Santangelo?"

"Yes."

"Now do you remember saying it?"

"Well, if it's here . . ."

"Yes, it's there, all right."

"Then I guess I said it. But I don't see what difference it makes where we were sit—"

"Your Honor?"

"Just answer the questions, please, Mrs. Santangelo."

She shrugged again and looked to the spectators for sympathy. This time, no one laughed.

"Mrs. Santangelo," I said, "can you locate on that plan of the park an area marked 'Pine Trees'? Can you do that for me?"

And now I put her through the drill, getting her to admit that from where she was sitting, the glimpses she'd had of the car would have been intermittent and fleeting, painstakingly reconstructing for the jury the barrier of pines that most certainly had limited her vision, showing her as well meteorological charts that showed the angle of the sun in relation to the picnic table at three P.M. that August thirtieth, when Sarah Santangelo claimed to have seen the last of the three victims bleeding from the mouth, in a white rental car driven by a gray-haired woman.

But I knew the damage had already been done.

The information Atkins had drawn from her still sizzled on the jury's forehead as if it had been emblazoned there with a branding iron.

YAM: sweet potato.

Y: rental car.

The jury had been told . . .

Whether they believed it or not was another matter . . .

But they'd certainly been told that Mary Barton had rented a white Chrysler LeBaron on the twenty-eighth of August and had begun a three-day killing spree that ended with the burial of those little girls in her garden on the last day of August.

That was what I was dealing with.

That was what would not go away.

From a pay phone off the courthouse rotunda, I dialed Warren's office number and got a recording saying he was in the field. I left a message for him to call me at the office when he was free, and then I tried him at home. I got no answer there, so I called Toots Kiley. She picked up on the third ring.

"Toots," I said, "this is Matthew, they just pulled a surprise on me. Here's what I'm going to need."

She listened.

Then she said, "That's all, huh?"

"I know," I said.

"When do you need it?"

"As soon as you can get it. If we can find who rented that car . . ."

"Suppose it turns out to be Mary?"

"Then I'll advise her to change her plea."

"Y-A-M, huh?"

"That's all."

"White Chrysler LeBaron."

"Yes."

"Okay, let me get cracking. Where will you be?"

"We've recessed till tomorrow morning, I'm heading back to the office now. Where's Warren, do you know?"

"Sure," she said. "Crescent Cove again."

The man Warren was talking to at four o'clock that Wednesday afternoon was sitting by his backyard pool drinking a gin and tonic. He had offered Warren a drink as well . . .

"Yardarm's high, young man," he'd said with a wink.

. . . but Warren had declined on the basis that he was here on business. The drink in Chester Lawson's hand sure looked inviting, though. So did the swimming pool. Lawson had just taken a dip. His reddish-blond hair was plastered to his forehead and his floral-patterned swimming trunks were hanging low over a belly that testified to high living and saturated fats. Warren was wearing a seersucker suit, white shirt, narrow blue tie. He was sweltering. Christmas right around the corner—he could see a tree already up inside Lawson's lanai—and he was sweating bullets out here in the sunshine.

He was here because he was still bothered by something Euphemia Loupe had told them.

The part about a fence going up.

Just before the fence went up, Euphemia had said.

Charlotte Carmody had testified in her deposition that a fence most definitely separated her property from Mary's on the night of August thirty-first, when she'd viewed Mary digging a grave in her backyard. It seemed unlikely to Warren that on the thirty-first Charlotte had stood at her window looking down over a five-foot-high fence that hadn't been there three days earlier, but anything was worth a try.

There wasn't no fence up at that time, Euphemia had said. *Just a low hedge. We weren't allowed to have fences in the development, you see. There was a rule no fences.*

In her deposition, Charlotte Carmody had mentioned the hedge, too.

I was on my side of the hedge. Until later on, when the fence went up. Then we used to talk over the fence.

If Matthew could use the *absence* of a fence to establish a fixed point in time—and Euphemia was certain the conversation had taken place *before* the fence went up, *just* before the fence went up—then maybe he could show that Mary had been in her own garden on the weekend of the abductions and murders.

It was a long shot.

But long shots sometimes won horse races.

"How long have you been president of the association?" he asked Lawson.

"Crescent Cove has its elections in June," Lawson said. "Sure I can't get you something?"

"Positive, thank you," Warren said.

"Man who was president before me sold his house and moved to another development. He'd be president still, you want the truth. Bob was a very popular fellow. Some say he had to move 'cause his wife caught him sneakin' into their neighbor's bed, but that's just talk, you ask me. Though when you think of it, the neighbor's gone, too, who knows? Anyway, I'm the new president. For two years, anyway. We have our elections every two years, in June."

"Bob what?" Warren asked.

He was writing. Write it all down. Easier to keep the facts straight that way. Names, dates, all of it. Make up your report from what you'd written down, not from what you remembered. He'd learned that when he was a police officer in St. Louis. Write it all down, son.

"Bob Giannino. That's Robert. Robert Giannino."

"How do you spell that?"

"Search me, these Eye-talian names," Lawson said, and shrugged.

"How long have you been living in the development?" Warren asked.

"Six years. Me and the wife came down from Cleveland."

"Do you know Mary Barton?"

"Figured this was about her. Never met the lady."

"You were here when the 'No Fences' rule was in effect, weren't you?"

"Oh, sure. That only changed recently."

"How recently?"

"Though you see all these fences every place you look, you'd think they were *always* here, wouldn't you?"

"When *did* the rule . . . ?"

"You want my opinion, good fences make good neighbors. Fewer rules there are about the way people live, the better off everyone is. We used to have a rule about the kind of *shingles* you could put on your roof, can you believe it? That changed, too. Even before the fence rule changed. What happens, you see, is somebody decides he just isn't going to *live* by the rule, and he challenges it. That's what happened with the fence rule. Well, figure it out for yourself. Is it my neighbor's business I want to sit here by my pool at four in the afternoon, enjoying a swim and a drink? What business is that of his? None. But if there was still only the hedge separating our property—well, you can still see the hedge there inside the fence, that's all there used to be, that little low hedge. Three feet high, that was the development rule. You couldn't have nothing over three feet high. You planted a hibiscus, you had to keep trimming it back to three feet 'cause that was the rule. Your neighbor could look over the hibiscus, see you swimming bare-assed in your pool, whatever. What kind of rule is that, limiting a person's privacy? Rules like that don't serve no purpose, do they? You get rules like that, people are gonna break 'em.

Either break 'em or challenge 'em, which is what somebody did with the fence rule."

"When was it changed? The rule?"

"Voted on it during the general election. That was in June."

June, Warren thought. A hell of a long way before August.

"June *when?*" he asked.

"We have our elections the fifteenth of June, every two years. Something like this, a rule change, it can be proposed and voted on *anytime,* you understand. It just happened to coincide this year with the general election."

"On the fifteenth of June."

"Yes. Fell on a Monday this year. Sometimes, if the fifteenth falls on a weekend, we'll have the election the Monday after. But this year it happened to fall on a Monday itself. Owners voted overwhelmingly to change the rule."

"From a three-foot hedge . . ."

"Well, it didn't have to be a hedge. It could've been any kind of planting."

"But no higher than three feet."

"That's right."

"To a five-foot-high fence."

"Which is a sensible height for a fence, don't you think? You go much higher than that, it begins to look like a prison stockade."

"When did these fences start going up?"

"Oh, pretty much right after the rule changed."

"Any of them go up in August?"

"Some people put 'em up *immediately.* I mean, some people couldn't *wait* to get those fences up, some of them went up that very same month, June. Others went up in July, still others in August, like you said. Some people, of course, *still* don't have no fences, they couldn't care less anybody sees them running around starkers. You ask me, some women *like* to be spied in the nude. Gives them some sort of thrill, you know? Well, it takes all kinds, don't it?"

"When did Mary Barton put up her fence, would you know?"

"Like I said, I don't know the lady. Didn't know her before the rule changed, don't know her to this day. Saw her garden, though, before the fences went up. Have you seen her garden?"

"Yes."

"Used to be able to see it from all over. You'd turn into the street, first thing you saw was the garden. People used to come for miles around, just to see the garden. Created a lot of traffic here in the development, I'm not surprised there were complaints."

"Oh?" Warren said. "Were there complaints?"

"About the traffic, yes. Cars coming in and looking for the street the garden was on, slowing down, asking directions, got to be a pain. I understand some people complained."

"Which people, would you know?"

"No, I wouldn't," Lawson said. "I try to mind my own business. Sit here in my own backyard, mind my own business, hope others'll do the exact same thing."

"When you say there were complaints . . . do you mean to the association?"

"To the police, I think. About the traffic. The other complaints, I'm not sure about."

"What other complaints?"

"Well, you know, not everybody agrees that garden is such a masterpiece."

"Uh-huh."

"Some kind of 'en*chanted* creation,' the newspaper called it. Not everybody agrees with that."

"Uh-huh."

"Some people think it's an *eyesore,* in fact."

"Uh-huh."

"So there were complaints, is all I'm saying. This was before the fence rule got changed. Now, with all the fences around it, you can't see the whole garden. You can still see the *towers,* whatever they are, the spires, whatever you want to call them, stickin' up above the fences, but you can't see all the wire and string and broken shells and whatnot. Which, of course, some people think is a work of art, but not everybody."

"Uh-huh."

"Is all I'm saying."

"But these complaints," Warren said. "The eyesore complaints. Were they made to the association or to the police?"

"I think there's a law against creating an eyesore, isn't there? Isn't there something called an eyesore law?"

"I don't know," Warren said. "I'll have to ask the man I'm working for."

"Think he'll get her off?" Lawson said.

"It's not a matter of getting her off," Warren said, with more conviction than he felt. "It's that she's innocent, sir."

"Well, maybe so. Like I said, I don't know the lady."

"But would you know if anyone complained to Mr. . . . Giannini, is it?" He looked at his notes. "Giannino, excuse me, would anyone have complained to him about the eyesore Miss Barton's garden was creating?"

"You'll have to ask Bob himself about that," Lawson said.

"Can you tell me where he's living now?"

"Got himself a condo on Whisper Key."

"Would you know the address?"

"Got it someplace inside," Lawson said, and lumbered to his feet, and hiked up his flowered trunks, and then lifted his empty glass from where it was sitting on a round plastic-topped table alongside the chaise. "Time to freshen this, anyway," he said, and held up the glass appraisingly to the sun. Half a lime looked back at him like the sliced eye of a dragon.

Warren pulled to the curb at the first phone booth he spotted. He could never understand why there were hardly any public telephones on Calusa's streets or highways. You wanted to call somebody, you had to go into a restaurant or a supermarket, make a pest of yourself. He pitied any married man having an affair in this town. Anybody who'd ever done the double on his wife knew that a pay phone was an absolute essential. But in this town, you could be prepared with all the loose change in the world, and you'd still have to drive for miles before you found a phone you could use. Midwesterners—even transplanted ones— didn't cheat, he guessed. Too busy milking their cows or mowing their wheat, or gleaning it, or whatever the hell they did to it.

Nick Alston picked up on the first ring.

It was four thirty-seven by Warren's digital watch.

"I thought you were the guy supposed to relieve," Alston said. "He's got a habit calling in sick every fuckin' Wednesday. I think he's got a girl he goes see on Wednesday, when her husband's away. How you been?"

"Fine," Warren said. "How about you?"

Alston had lost his partner a while back—a euphemism for the fact that Charlie Macklin had been shot dead while sitting a crime-scene house on the beach. The last time Warren had seen him, Alston was drinking heavily. Never a handsome man, his brown eyes had been shot with red, his craggy face puffed and bloated, his straw-colored hair stringy. Warren kept meaning to call him, see how he was doing.

"I almost called you a coupla times," Alston said.

"Oh. How come?"

"Thought we'd have a few drinks together. Maybe go bowling."

"We can skip the drinks," Warren said, "but I wouldn't mind bowling."

"I'll give you a ring," Alston said, "next time I get the night off."

Down here, it was not an easy thing for a redneck cop to offer a hand of friendship to a black man. Warren appreciated the gesture, but it made him feel shittier than he was already feeling about not having called Alston.

Compounding the felony, Alston said, "Meanwhile, what's on your mind? I know you wouldn't be calling if you didn't need a favor."

Warren thought of saying Hey, no, Nick, what kind of thing is that to say? And he thought of saying, You're right, Nick, I should've stayed in touch, but somehow time rushes by, you know, and all at once it's weeks and then months and . . .

"Can you run something by your computer for me?" he said.

Toots was licensed to carry but she wasn't strapped tonight because this was a routine milk run and she wasn't expecting any trouble. What she'd figured was a trip to the airport was the fastest way to get all the rental car information she needed. There were some wildcat rental companies operating outside the airport, but the bigger ones were all concentrated here. Roving from counter to counter would be quicker than calling all of them on the telephone.

The airport serving the tri-city area that was Calusa, Sarasota, and Bradenton had until as short a time as five years ago been a cinder-block warren of dinky little one-story buildings housing the half dozen airlines flying in and out of here. The area's growth, coupled with deregulation, had trebled the number of flights coming in and going out, making a new airport mandatory. The planes came in from all over the United States these days, even though officials at the nearby university complained on an average of once a month that noise from the jets was disrupting classes.

Toots kind of liked the old airport better.

Then again, she liked the old Calusa better than the thriving tourist mecca it had become.

The first time she'd come down here was in a camper with her parents, when she was just six years old. Calusa was on the cusp of discovery then, but there were still pristine deserted beaches where they could spend lazy days sunning and swimming and fishing for their evening meal. No hotels at all back then. Well, one. Built by the same man who'd built the Ca D'Ped Museum back in 1927, but only to lodge his friends—not the museum, the hotel. Not many motels back then, either, all of them spread few and far between on the South Trail.

Toots would play with her sand bucket and her shovel, watching her father standing in the surf, casting over and over again, gulls wheeling overhead every time he pulled a fish out of the water. Her mother used to wear a yellow bonnet that matched the color of her hair. People back in Rockford used to tell Toots she was the spitting image of her mother. It was her father, though, who'd named her Toots, after the man he considered the best harmonica player in the world. Her father had been an E-flat piano player, picking out tunes by ear in just that one key. He stopped playing piano altogether when her mother died of cancer. Toots was fourteen then, a bad time for a girl to lose her mother—well, was any time a good time? At the funeral, she remembered her father banging out tunes for his wife on the upright piano in their lace-curtained living room—

"This is for you, Lucy."

—and began crying so hard she thought she'd never stop.

She left Illinois when she turned eighteen, took a bus across the border into Wisconsin, spent a few months in Milwaukee, anything to get away from the town where her mother had died and her father was still alive, yes, but as still as any stone, sitting in the living room with curtains gone gray, staring at the old upright as if in accusation. Six months later, she drifted down to Chicago, where she got a job as a waitress in a saloon that had a piano player who smoked pot and who introduced her to it. She was nineteen, a late starter when one considered the average age most kids in America started experimenting with dope.

A year later, she thought it might be nice to visit Calusa again. She'd had some happy times in Calusa.

She could still remember sitting on the beach, building dream castles of sand. Could remember her mother calling to her father in her lilting voice, "James, don't go out too far!" Her father laughing it off. How they loved each other. She wrote to her father from Calusa. Called him from there. His voice was dead. She could not bear the grief in his voice.

Two months after she'd arrived in Calusa, two months after a variety of waitressing jobs, she answered a blind Help Wanted ad in the only newspaper down here, a rag called the *Calusa Herald-Tribune*. She went for the interview cautiously; the headline read FEMALE TRAINEE FOR INTERESTING, EXCITING WORK, and she thought at first that somebody might be trolling for topless dancers or party girls, there'd been plenty such ads in Chicago. But it turned out that a guy who ran a detective agency was looking for a woman he could train in investigative techniques, to lend him a hand with a caseload that was becoming burdensome. Starting salary wasn't bad, either. She figured Why the hell not?

Otto Samalson reminded her a lot of her father. Didn't look anything at all like a private detective, which he told her was a plus. If you looked like a cop, you'd be made in a minute. He always referred to himself as a cop. A private cop, to be sure, but nonetheless a cop. Otto was a good ten years older than her father—though since her mother's death, Daddy looked a lot older than he was—little bald man, just like Daddy, she thought he should be making ice cream sundaes behind a soda fountain someplace. Same color eyes as her father's, too, same hint of mysterious sadness in them, maybe 'cause Otto was Jewish. Taught her everything she knew, made her one of the best damn private cops in this town. Toots Kiley. Where'd you get that dumb name? he used to ask her.

Then, all at once, on a case she was working for him, all the shining dream castles crumbled, all the sand rushed out into the ocean.

Ironically, it was a cop who got her started. A *real* cop, never mind a private one. A Calusa P.D. redneck son of a bitch cop who was helping Otto for a slight fee sometimes known as a bribe. As with so many private investigations, this one involved tailing a wayward spouse. In this instance—and that was why Toots was on the case, instead of Otto himself—the person under surveillance was a woman. Their client was a well-respected and quite wealthy proctologist—if you're going to start looking up men's assholes for cancer of the colon, a good place to start your practice is not in a college town but in a geriatric community. Dr. Eugene Milsen was in his forties, with a gorgeous wife and two darling little girls and a house on what passed for Calusa's Gold Coast, overlooking the wide expanse of bay that faced Lucy's Key and the Cortez Causeway. Milsen had everything a man could wish for, except perhaps a faithful wife. Which is why he hired Samalson Investigations to put a tail on Sonia.

Well, one thing led to another . . .

There *were* mysterious and unexplained absences, usually at night . . .

There *were* charges to stores like Victoria's Secret and Frederick's of Hollywood, apparently for lingerie Milsen himself never saw . . .

There *was* the matter of a secret bank account under Sonia's name into which large sums of money were being deposited each and every month, leading to the suspicion that there was, in fact, a sugar daddy in the picture . . .

And there *was,* lastly but most importantly, the redneck son of a bitch cop named Rob Higgins, who had information vital to the investigation the firm was conducting.

Which led to him sitting with Toots in a nondescript faded green Ford . . .

Otto had taught her the more nondescript the better.

. . . at a little after midnight on a September morning some three years ago, outside a New Town whorehouse Higgins had been investigating for the past month and a half.

New Town was what they called Calusa's black section.

Every city in America has its black section, never mind the South.

So here was a nice girl from Milwaukee, sitting in New Town in the empty hours of the night, in a faded green automobile with a redneck cop who claimed that Sonia Milsen was working as a hooker in the two-story wooden house across the street, where the shades were drawn and the lights were dim.

"Your lady ain't fuckin' *around*," Higgins told her, "she's just plain *fuckin'*."

Toots thought Well, stranger things have happened, that's for sure.

She wondered what Eugene Milsen would do when he found out his wife wasn't having an affair, after all.

If this turned out to be true.

"Best time to go in is after the next wave gets here," Higgins said. "You get a surge of business around eleven, your guys who got to get up early in the morning. Then it's quiet again till around one, guys hurryin' to get in there before closing time, which is two o'clock."

Toots said nothing.

It was going to be a long night.

"We'll see 'em when they start marchin' up the stairs to the second floor there. You 'member the Sinatra song?"

"No," Toots said.

"'Bout girls who live up the stair?"

"No," she said.

"Course, he didn't mean *these* kind of girls, do you snort?"

She turned to look at him.

"We got an hour or so 'fore the action starts, you feel like doin' a few lines?"

She kept looking at him. She knew what he meant, of course. She was just surprised that a cop was making the offer. Live and learn, she thought.

"What do you say?" he said.

Just say no, she thought.

"Why the hell not?" she said.

That was how it started. Just like that. An hour later, higher than a fucking kite, she'd gone up the stairs with Higgins, who'd knocked on the door and shoved it in the moment it opened a crack, and stuck a gun under the nose of a frightened seventeen-year-old girl who spoke no English, and led Toots down the hall where, lo and behold, there was Sonia Milsen wearing nothing but black open-crotch panties from Frederick's of Hollywood and black boots with four-inch spiked heels and incidentally blowing a black guy who was at least six feet four inches tall all over.

Toots got some good pictures.

She also got a cocaine habit she didn't even try to kick until after Otto fired her.

Took her two years to finally sober up.

She was about to ask Otto for her old job back when he got killed tailing yet another wayward spouse. The way Toots looked at it, if there weren't husbands and wives cheating on each other, there'd be very few reasons for private eyes in this world. You come home and find your husband or wife slaughtered in your bed, you don't call a private eye. Neither do you call the little old lady who's secretary of the garden club and who solves murders in her spare time. You might call your lawyer, but the first thing he'd ask you is "Did you do it?" If you answered yes, he'd say, "Don't touch anything, I'll be right there." If you answered no, he'd say, "Call the police." Toots sometimes felt that the private eyes she read about in novels or saw on television or in the movies were entirely figments of the American imagination. Male or female, none of them seemed *real* to her, their involvement with murder. She ever stumbled across a dead body, she'd wet her pants, never mind sisters in crime. Or brothers in crime, for that matter. The first job she'd had offered to her after she was clean again was trailing a wayward spouse, big surprise.

It was Warren who'd offered her the job.

He'd had his doubts, but he was willing to take a chance. She wouldn't forget that, ever. First person she called was her father, long-distance in Rockford, Illinois.

"Daddy," she said, "I'm clean again, I've got a job."

"That's good, Toots," he said in that same hollow voice.

He died in his sleep a month later.

She went up for the funeral.

No tears this time. She realized he'd been dead for a long time, she'd really lost both her parents when she was fourteen.

She wondered why this was coming back to her now. Maybe it was walking through the airport parking lot again. The middle-of-the-night call from her Aunt Sylvie, the hurried packing, the long walk through this same lot, carrying a small suitcase, rushing to catch a six-thirty A.M. flight to . . .

"Right there, sister," the voice said.

She did not like being called sister, even by sisters. But this was not a sister talking to her. This was a deep-voiced kid some six feet tall who stepped out from behind a parked black Cadillac Seville, his muscles bulging in a white tank-top shirt, his jeans tight around a weight lifter's thighs, short black boots on his feet, a knife in his right hand.

"And shut it," he said.

He was white. This didn't surprise her. Crack was color-blind, its users came in every stripe and persuasion.

He was no older than sixteen. This didn't surprise her, either. Some users started when they were ten.

And he was desperate.

She saw this in his eyes.

She'd been there.

"The bag," he said, and held out his hand palm-upward.

The bag was hanging from a strap on her left shoulder. Big leather tote with all her stuff in it. Money, credit cards, comb, hairbrush, chewing gum, loose change, compact—everything but a piece, which was what she needed most just now. The knife was nervous. The tip kept describing tiny circles on the air, like radar scanning the night for a target. Off on the airport's access road, a car's headlights swept past. There was the sound of a jet warming up on the distant tarmac.

"Sonny," she said, "why don't . . . ?"

"Don't give me no Sonny shit," he said. "The bag! Now!"

"Sure," she said, and lifted the strap off her shoulder with her right hand, and then clutched the strap in both hands, right shoulder angled toward him, left shoulder back, and then she swung around and stepped out onto her right foot, shifting her weight, remembering what Otto had taught her about a bad situation only getting worse, going for it *now*. She used the bag like a sling without a stone in it, whipping it directly at his head, catching him on the right side of his face, just above the cheekbone. He let out a startled little yelp, recovered immediately, and came at her with the knife.

Her knee came up.

She caught him in the groin, a little bit off the money, but close enough to cause him to arch away from her, head coming forward, ass pulling back, tucking in his balls in defense against further attack. She smashed him across the bridge of his nose with the edge of her hand, hearing something splintering in there, ready to drive the fucking bones back into his brain if she had to, the knife flailing the air wildly now, the blade snicking altogether too close to her, the tip catching her sleeve, a bright line of blood suddenly strident against the pale green fabric.

She went for the knife hand because that was the only hand that could hurt her. Sidestepping as he lunged again, the knife coming at her, a plane rushing into the air in the distance, she caught for his wrist, got cut again, felt the burning shriek of open flesh on the palm of her hand, thought This is it, sister, and made another desperate grab for him. She got behind the knife this time, catching his wrist and yanking wrist and arm up behind his back until she heard something crack, kept pulling up on it, anyway, ready to break the fucking thing off at the shoulder if she had to. His arm all crooked, the knife still in his twisted hand, he was turning toward her again in screaming rage when she clobbered him on the back of the neck, both hands clenched together, hitting him as if she were wielding a mallet. He went stumbling forward to the asphalt, tried to brace his fall with his one good arm, lurched onto his face when she stepped on his spine, and then lost it completely when she kicked him in the head with the point of her high-heeled shoe.

She stood over him, breathing hard.

She picked up her bag and walked to the terminal.

In the ladies' room, she rinsed the blood from her hand and then made a makeshift bandage from three Kotexes she bought from the machine on the wall. She was still breathing hard when she approached the airport cop and showed him her laminated ticket.

"There's an unconscious kid in lot number five," she said. "He's got a broken nose and a broken arm. You may want to call an ambulance."

The cop looked at her.

"Thanks," she said, and walked over to the Hertz counter.

At a few minutes past eleven that night, Patricia called me at home. I was lying in bed reading the deposition I'd taken three weeks ago from the man who owned Dri-Quik Cleaners. She apologized for calling so late . . .

"No, no, I'm still awake," I said.

"I know you have to be in court early . . ."

"So do you."

". . . but our strategy meeting broke up just a few minutes ago."

"How's it going?" I asked.

"That's right, we can talk about *my* case, can't we? Matthew, the guy's going to walk. You wouldn't *believe* what's happening down here. We've got his prints all over the murder weapon and three people who witnessed him pulling the trigger, and he's going to walk. Do you know a man named Avery Sloat?"

"No. Who is he?"

"The assistant S.A. assigned to the case. I'm supposed to be helping him out. He thinks that means handing him papers in court, like a paralegal just out of junior college. He calls me Pat, is it catching or something? Do you know the S.A. for the Twentieth Judicial Circuit?"

"Not personally."

"Man named Lamont Spencer, good ole boy smokes a fat cigar, keeps telling us we're doing a fine job. Doesn't he see the case going down the drain?"

"I don't understand. What happened to . . . ?"

"We put a witness on today who swore up and down that he saw the defendant . . . who, by the way, has a prior for armed robbery and two priors for rape, God knows why he's still on the street . . . saw the defendant . . . whose name is Brian Asquith, where do they *get* these names, Matthew? . . . saw him pointing a gun at the girl behind the bar in the Caffrey Bar & Grill, which is a saloon in lovely downtown Marble Hill, Florida, where the shooting took place . . . saw him pointing the gun, and firing the gun, and putting three beautifully placed shots in the poor girl's forehead . . . saw all this, and swore to all this in a deposition and swore to it again all over again today during our direct, and on comes the defense attorney . . ."

"What's his name?"

"Don't ask."

"Tell me."

"Have I told you I loved you?"

"Not tonight."

"Okay, then, I love you."

"Okay, then, tell me his name."

"William Spires, a sly old codger who wears a white suit and a watch on a chain."

"Go hide the silver."

"Tell me about it. Anyway, the Codger gets on, as he is known in the trade, and puts Asquith through the paces . . . are you *sure* the defendant sitting there is the man you saw . . . are you *sure* this is the gun you saw . . . we'd already moved it into evidence . . . are you *sure* the woman you saw getting plugged three times between the eyes is the same woman whose photographs you were shown . . . are you sure this, are you sure that . . . all the mis-ID jazz . . . and of course Asquith is sure, he was sitting at the bar not three feet from where the action took place, he got the lady's *blood* all over him, in fact, he's not only *sure*, he's *positive*, he's dead *cert*. So he remains unshaken throughout, the Codger can't put a *dent* in his testimony, and finally it's our turn again.

I tug at Sloat's sleeve, he turns to me and says, 'Yes, Pat?' I tell him to excuse the witness, we've proved our point. He says, 'Just one thing I forgot to ask him.' And he goes up to the stand. Well, Matthew, the first thing he says in the redirect is . . ."

"Don't tell me."

"I'm telling you. The first thing he says is, 'Mr. Asquith, I meant to ask you . . . you hadn't been *drinking* that evening, had you?' "

"Oh God."

"The guy's sitting there at the bar, he's already testified he'd been sitting there for an hour and a half before the shooting occurred, what the hell did Sloat *think* he was doing there, making fudge? So Asquith admits well, yes, he *was* drinking a little, but of course this didn't in any way affect his ability to determine what was happening. Oh, *no?* The Codger steps up for the recross, and he looks Asquith straight in the eye, and now that the can of worms has been opened, he gets from him that not only had he been drinking a little, he had been drinking a *lot,* he had in fact consumed five drinks in the hour and a half he'd been sitting there, he was in fact cockeyed *drunk* when the shooter blew open the bargirl's forehead. So our key witness went right out the window, and tonight we had a meeting to determine what our *future* strategy should be, other than slashing our wrists or jumping out the window. I didn't hear you say you loved *me,* by the way."

"By the way, I love you," I said.

"Want to talk dirty?" she asked.

"Yes," I said.

"Let's," she said.

11

Jerome Callahan . . .

"Most people call me Jerry," he advised Atkins.

. . . was a man in his mid-forties, sporting the sort of mustache Tom Selleck wore, but otherwise resembling him not in the slightest. Putting himself immediately on a familiar first-name basis seemed to startle the staid and proper Max the Ax, but it sat well with the jury, who visibly settled back on its collective haunches ready to enjoy a morning's visit with a man who'd just extended a symbolic hand in friendship. Call me Jerry. Nice Uncle Jerry mustache, ill-fitting beige tropical suit that made him seem all dressed up for a special occasion, striped tan and lavender rep tie, pleasant toothy smile, shock of brown hair hanging on his forehead, bright sparkly blue eyes—How do you do, folks, I'm here to help in any way I can.

"Mr. Callahan," Atkins said—subtly upholding the dignity of these proceedings, not for nothing had he graduated from Harvard Law, lo those many years ago—"I wonder if you can tell us what sort of business you're in."

"I run a dry-cleaning establishment," Callahan said, with a solemn dignity of his own.

"What is your place of business called?"

"Dri-Quik Cleaners."

"And where is it located?"

"At 2411 Templeton Court. That's in the Templeton Mall."

"Here in Calusa?"

"Yes, sir. On Seaway and Benning."

"Now, Mr. Callahan, can you tell us where you were on the first of September? To refresh your memory, that would have been the Tuesday before the Labor Day weekend."

"Yes, I was in my store on that day."

"All day?"

"From eight in the morning to six at night."

"Was anyone else working with you?"

"No, I was alone that day. The girl who works for me was out sick. I was alone."

"Your Honor, I would like this marked for identification, please."

"Exhibit Five, the state," Rutherford said.

"Now, Mr. Callahan, do you recognize this dress I'm showing you?"

"I do."

"Can you describe it for us, please?"

"It's a blue cotton denim dress."

"Is there any way of telling what size the dress is?"

"Yes, there's a label here that gives the size."

"And what is that size, Mr. Callahan?"

"Eight. It's a size eight."

"Have you ever seen this dress before?"

"I have."

"When did you first see this dress?"

"On the morning of September first."

"What was the occasion, do you remember?"

"A woman brought it into my store for cleaning."

"What time was this?"

"I had just opened the store. It was around eight-thirty in the morning."

"And you say a woman brought this dress into the store."

"Yes."

"Was it in this condition when you first saw it?"

"No, it was badly stained."

"Stained with what, Mr. Callahan?"

"With what appeared to be . . ."

"Objection, Your Honor."

"Sustained."

"Mr. Callahan, did you have any conversation with the woman who brought the dress in?"

"I did."

"What did you say to her?"

"I told her the dress was badly stained, and I wasn't sure if I could get all the stains out."

"Did she make any reply?"

"Objection, Your Honor. The woman's reply would be . . ."

"Your Honor . . ."

"Let's come up, shall we?"

We went up to the bench. As usual, Atkins did not look at me. I felt like kicking him in the shin to get his attention.

"Yes, Mr. Hope, let's hear it," Rutherford said.

"I think Mr. Atkins knows that . . ."

"Never mind what I know," Atkins said, looking straight at the judge.

"Well, then, perhaps he *doesn't* know that whatever his witness says about this woman's reply would be clearly inadmissible under the hearsay rule. In fact, I haven't yet heard anyone identified as the woman in that store."

"Well, Mr. Hope," Rutherford said, "surely *you* know he's going to have the woman identified, don't you? Because if he *doesn't* have her identified, you can ask me to throw out the dress *and* anything the witness has already said about it. Or her. Or *anything,* for that matter."

"Your Honor, such testimony put in improperly could be grounds for a mistrial."

"Well, let's be sensible here, shall we? An identification is inevitable."

"Moreover, Your Honor . . ." Atkins said.

He always seemed to have a *moreover* up his sleeve.

". . . taking the dress to a dry cleaner to have stains removed from it is a demonstration of guilty conduct and whatever the woman *said* about the action would be excluded from the hearsay ru—"

"Your Honor," I said, "I don't see how the simple act of taking a dress to a . . ."

"Attempting to have stains removed from it would constitute an attempt to obliterate evidence, Your Honor," Atkins said.

"Are you planning to show that the woman's conversation pertained to these stains?"

"I am."

"Then I'll allow it, Mr. Hope," Rutherford said. "Let's proceed, please."

Atkins walked back to the witness stand. Andrew's eyes met mine as I returned to the defense table; he knew we'd lost another one.

"Mr. Callahan," Atkins said, "what did this woman say to you when you told her you might not be able to get those stains out?"

"She said it was her favorite dress, and I should try."

"Was there any further conversation?"

"Yes. I asked her if she knew what kind of stains they were."

"What did she say to that?"

"She said they were berry stains."

"Did they look like berry stains to you?"

"Objection, Your Honor."

"Sustained."

"Mr. Callahan, how many years have you been in the dry-cleaning business?"

"Twelve. Ever since I came down to Calusa."

"Have you seen very many different types of stains on garments during those twelve years?"

"I guess I've seen every type of stain there is."

"Have you seen bloodstains?"

"I have."

"Can you tell us how a dry cleaner recognizes a bloodstain?"

"Well, you have to understand that without conducting extensive tests, a dry cleaner can't know for sure what any stain is."

"Is it usual for a dry cleaner to conduct such tests?"

"No, sir. Not unless there's some sort of lawsuit going on."

"What do you mean?"

"Well, a person may bring in a sweater, for example, and later claim that the sweater came back with stains on it that weren't there when he brought it in for cleaning. And the customer may bring suit, let's say, in small-claims court to recover for damages. In which case, the cleaner may send the sweater out for testing to determine the nature of the stains. To prove that they couldn't possibly be stains that had occurred during the dry-cleaning process. Like that."

"Who does these tests?"

"Well, there's a place in New York called the Neighborhood Cleaners' Association, the N.C.A., and there's another one in Washington, the I.F.I.—that's Washington, D.C., not the state of Washington . . ."

"Yes, go on, please."

". . . called the I.F.I., the International Fabric Institute. They've got a school that teaches dry cleaning in Silver Spring, Maryland. Either one of these places can analyze any kind of stain for you."

"Did you send this dress out for analysis?"

"No, sir, I did not. There was no need to do that."

"Without testing, then, how *would* a dry cleaner determine whether a stain was a bloodstain?"

"Experience, that's all."

"How would experience help you in making your determination?"

"Well, for one thing, a bloodstain will have a distinctive color and consistency. You can tell . . ."

"Objection, Your Honor. Witness is a dry cleaner and not a serologist."

"In light of his experience, I'll allow his opinion—albeit nonscientific—for whatever it's worth to the jury. Please proceed."

"I was saying," Callahan said, "that you can tell from the color of the stain that it's blood and not ketchup or chocolate or gravy. It just *looks* like blood."

"And how does blood look?" Atkins asked.

"That depends on the fabric, and it depends how long it's been on the fabric."

"Let's say the fabric is a cotton denim like this dress."

"Well, a fresh stain would be red at first. Then it'll begin turning darker, a sort of maroon. And after five or six days, it'll turn black."

"When you say black . . ."

"I mean *black*. Like ink. To the naked eye, a spot of blood looks exactly like an ink spot. In fact, if you were to take one of those old-fashioned fountain pens, if you flipped the nib at a piece of fabric, the drops that would spatter on it would look like blood. The shape of the drops and the color. That's what a bloodstain five, six days old looks like. Exactly like a black ink stain. There's a very sharp outer edge, a definite line between the stain and the end of the stain. Especially with a fabric like the one we're talking about, the stain'll sink in and it'll be extremely defined and very dark. And the stain'll feel like blood, too. It'll feel thick or stiff, the fabric has a definite *feel* to it when the stain is a bloodstain, when it's *blood* clotted in the weave there. So you look at the stain, and you touch it, and you know it's blood, that's all. It's like seeing a stop sign and knowing immediately what it is by its shape and its color. Any dry cleaner in the world can look at a bloodstain and tell you right off what it is. Experience tells him exactly what it is."

"What did your experience tell you the stains on that dress were?"

"My experience told me they were blood."

"Did you mention this to the woman?"

"I asked her if they were bloodstains."

"And what did she say?"

"She said they were berry stains."

"Did you reply to that?"

"I told her if they were berry stains, we'd know the minute we began working on them because they have a tannic base and they'd be soluble in acid. But I knew they weren't berry stains. They were blood, all right. I told her we'd probably have difficulty removing them, and that there was a good chance our working on them might even make them worse."

"*Were* you, in fact, able to remove them?"

"Not entirely. As you can see, the stains are still visible."

"What attempts did you make to remove them?"

"Well, first we immersed the dress in water, tried to dissolve the blood that way, or as much of it as we could, but that wasn't much help. Then we applied ammonia to the stain itself, because any stain of animal origin—like blood—is soluble in ammonia. When that didn't work, we tried ammonia with a soap lubricant. Most cleaners would've stopped right there, but the lady had told me it was her favorite dress, so I kept trying."

"What did you do next?"

"I put the dress in a digestion solution."

"A what?"

"A digestion solution. It's this enzyme that comes in a powdered form, you dissolve it in warm water and you soak the garment in it for about forty-five minutes. A hundred and ten degrees, the water. What the enzyme does, it literally eats whatever's causing the stain to adhere. Then after that, you go back to steps one and two again. That's about all anyone can do."

"But you say you were not, in the final analysis, entirely success-ful in removing the stains?"

"Well, the edges aren't as defined, but they're still black. Blood is very difficult to get out."

"Your Honor, I would like the dress moved into evidence, please."

"Mark it."

"Now, Mr. Callahan, this woman who brought the dress into your store on the first of September . . . do you see her anywhere in this courtroom?"

"Yes, I do."

"Where is she? Would you please point her out to us?"

"She's sitting right there."

"Your Honor, let the record reflect that the witness is pointing to the defendant, Mary Barton."

"The record will so reflect."

"Now, Mr. Callahan, when someone brings a garment in for cleaning, do you normally fill out a receipt for the garment?"

"I do."

"What does the receipt look like?"

"The top part is pink. That goes to the customer. Then there's a sheet of carbon paper . . . well, you know what a dry cleaner's receipt looks like, don't you?"

"If you could help the jury . . ."

"Well, there's the top part, the pink part, and then the sheet of carbon paper, and then the bottom part, the yellow part. I fill out the receipt and give the customer the pink part, and I keep the yellow part for my files."

"When you say you fill out the receipt . . . what do you write on it?"

"The customer's name and address."

"Did you ask this woman for her name?"

"I did."

"What name did she give you?"

"Mary Jones."

"Did you ask her address?"

"I did."

"What address did she give you?"

"2716 Gideon Way."

"Here in Calusa?"

"Here in Calusa."

"Did you ask this woman who called herself Mary Jones for her telephone number?"

"That's not my usual practice."

"You do not normally ask a customer for his or her telephone number?"

"No, I don't. If somebody doesn't pick up a garment by a certain time, we drop them a postcard."

"Was this garment ever picked up?"

"Not by her," Callahan said, and nodded toward where Mary was sitting.

"Did someone *other* than the defendant pick up the garment?"

"The police did. After I called them."

"Why did you call them?"

"To tell them about the dress."

"Please explain, Mr. Atkins."

"I saw this woman on television, and they were saying she'd been arrested for the murder of three children, and she was the same woman who'd brought in the dress. But they didn't say she was Mary Jones, they said she was Mary Barton. So I put two and two together and figured bloodstains on the dress, phony name . . ."

"Objection, Your Honor. Witness is drawing conclusions."

"Sustained. Strike that last."

"As a result of your seeing Mary Barton on television, what did you do?"

"I called the police."

"Was Mary Barton the woman you'd seen on television?"

"She was."

"Was she the same woman who'd earlier identified herself to you as Mary Jones?"

"Yes. The same woman."

"Did you write the name 'Mary Jones' on the receipt you gave her?"

"I did."

"And '2716 Gideon Way' for her address?"

"I did."

"Your Honor, I would like this marked for identification, please."

"Mark it Exhibit Six for the state."

"Mr. Callahan, I ask you to look at this, please."

Callahan accepted a yellow slip of paper some three inches wide by four inches long. I knew what it was; I'd seen Atkins's evidence list.

"Can you tell us what it is you're looking at, please?"

"It's the bottom half of one of my receipts. The yellow half I keep in the store."

"Can you read the name lettered at the top of the receipt?"

"Yes. The name is Mary Jones."

"Did you letter that name onto the receipt?"

"I did."

"Can you read the address below that?"

"2716 Gideon Way."

"Did you also letter that address?"

"I did."

"Your Honor, I would like the receipt moved into evidence and published to the jury."

"Yes, fine."

Atkins carried the receipt to the jury box and handed it in. He took his time turning back to his witness. I was getting used to his style. He had just established that a woman who'd given Callahan a false name was the woman he'd later seen identified on television as Mary Barton. But Atkins was also setting the stage for several of his future witnesses, all of whom I'd already deposed. Like an industrious spider weaving an intricate web, he was leading each of his witnesses toward a single shining truth: Mary Barton had rented a car one weekend, had roamed the countryside in search of victims, had abducted them, killed them, buried them in her backyard, and had then tried to destroy all evidence of her crime. If Atkins could later show . . .

". . . when you called the police?"

"On the fifth of September. That's the first time I saw her picture on television."

"And when did the police pick up the dress?"

"That very same day."

"From the moment they picked it up till the moment you saw it in court today, have you seen that dress again?"

"I have not."

"Your witness."

I knew that Atkins would be calling the police officer who'd picked up the suspect dress, and I knew he'd be calling the young kid who'd found a bloody pair of size seven sneakers in a sewage drain four blocks from the Templeton Mall, and I knew he'd be calling the laboratory technician who'd conducted a battery of tests on the dress and the sneakers, and I knew there was no sense trying to refute Callahan's testimony that the stains on that dress were, in fact, bloodstains. When he'd told the court that any dry cleaner in the world could look at a bloodstain and tell right off what it was, he was speaking the absolute truth; we'd tried for weeks to find an expert who might contradict this testimony and we'd failed dismally. I was left with the same tired approach: misidentification.

"She said 'Mary Jones,' did she?"

"What?" Callahan said.

"This woman who came into your store with a bloodstained dress . . . by the way, are you sure that's the same dress? The one the prosecutor . . ."

Making it sound like *executioner*.

". . . showed you, are you sure it's the same dress this woman Mary Jones brought into your store?"

Planting the name Mary Jones. The woman who'd brought that dress in was named Mary *Jones,* get it, jury?

"Yes, I'm positive," Callahan said.

"Even though you haven't seen it since . . . when was it that the police picked it up?"

"September fifth."

"And today is the tenth of December . . . almost three months since you've seen that dress."

"I remember it quite well, though."

Getting nervous. Whenever people who don't ordinarily use the word "quite" in their everyday speech suddenly start putting on airs, you know they're uncomfortable.

"Anything distinctive about that dress, other than the stains?"

"No, but . . ."

"Just an ordinary blue denim dress, isn't it?"

"Yes."

"Kind you could pick up at Penney's or . . ."

"Objection, Your Honor."

"Overruled."

". . . or any department store, any clothing store, just an ordinary dress, isn't it?"

"Yes."

"Any tears or rips on it?"

"No."

"No monogram on it, is there?"

"No."

"No letters 'M.J.,' for example."

"No."

"And certainly no letters 'M.B.' "

"No."

"So—aside from the stains—there's nothing really remarkable about this simple blue denim dress, is there?"

"No, but . . ."

"Then what makes you think it's the same dress you saw almost three months ago?"

"The stains are distinctive."

"Ah. These stains that you said look exactly like ink stains . . ."

"No, I said they were *blood*stains."

"Well, excuse me, sir, but didn't you say . . . well, let me look at my notes here . . . I can have this read back to you if you like . . . didn't you say that if we were to take one of those old-fashioned fountain pens . . . well, here are your exact words, please correct me if I'm wrong . . . 'if you flipped the nib at a piece of fabric,' is what you said, 'the drops that would spatter on it would look like blood. The shape of the drops and the color. That's what a bloodstain five, six days old looks like. Exactly like a black ink stain.' Isn't that what you said?"

"Yes."

"Then these stains *did* look like ink stains?"

"Yes. But they were unmistakably bloodstains."

"So you've said. And it was these stains that caused you to recognize the dress almost three months later."

"Yes."

"Don't all bloodstains look pretty much alike, Mr. Callahan?"

"Not all of them."

"Well, bloodstains spattered on a dress, like ink from a pen . . . wouldn't these look pretty much alike?"

"More or less."

"Yet you say these *particular* bloodstains, or ink stains, or whatever they . . ."

"Objection, Your Honor."

"Sustained. Cut it out, Mr. Hope."

"These stains were sufficiently distinctive for you to know that the dress you were shown in court today is the very same dress Mary Jones brought into your shop on the first of September."

"Yes."

"Okay," I said.

With a totally incredulous lilt of the voice and a look of disbelief to the jury, both of which Atkins caught, but decided to let pass without objection. He knew that Callahan was not only sympathetic but very strong as well and probably felt that reining me in might lead the jury to believe he was overprotecting a witness who needed no help.

"Mary Jones," I said, and paused. "Is that the name she gave you?"

"Yes."

"Positive about that, are you?"

"Yes."

"Well, you wrote it down yourself, didn't you?"

"Yes."

"So you must've been certain the name she gave you was Mary Jones. No mistake about that, was there?"

"She told me she was Mary Jones."

"You asked her for her name . . ."

"Yes."

"So you could write it on the receipt . . ."

"Yes."

"And she said 'Mary Jones.' "

"Yes."

"Any hesitation when she gave you her name?"

"No."

"Just Mary Jones flat out."

"Well . . . no. Not flat out."

"What I'm asking, Mr. Callahan . . . did you have any reason to believe, at the time, that this might not be the woman's name?"

"Well . . . Jones," Callahan said, and grimaced, and rolled his eyes at the jury.

"Jones, yes. Is there anything wrong with that name?"

"No. But when people are using a false name, they'll use the name Jones, you know," he said, directly to the jury again.

"I see. Then you thought she was using a false name, is that it?"

"No."

"You thought it was her real name?"

"I don't know what I thought at the time. I asked her what her name was and she stood there looking at me, kind of puzzled, as if she hadn't heard what I . . ."

"But you didn't think the name was a false name, did you?"

"No. What happened was . . ."

"You've answered the question, thank you."

"May he finish, Your Honor?"

"You may conclude what you were saying."

"I was only going to say that I had to ask her again what her name was. 'Cause she didn't seem to understand. I said, 'Your name, your *name*,' and she just kept staring at me, so finally I said, 'Whose *dress* is this, ma'am?' and that's when she gave me her name, Mary Jones, and that's when I wrote Mary Jones on the receipt."

"When she gave you her name, you didn't say, 'Gee, that sounds like a phony name,' anything like that, did you?"

"No."

"You accepted it as her name, didn't you?"

"Yes."

"But today, here in court, you identified the woman as Mary Barton."

"Yes."

"No doubt in your mind, is there, that Mary Jones and Mary Barton are one and the same person?"

"No doubt at all."

"They look alike, do they?"

"Exactly alike."

"As much alike as blood spots and ink spots?"

"Well . . . laboratory tests would show that blood spots aren't ink spots."

"But you said earlier, didn't you, that to the naked eye, a blood spot looks exactly like an ink spot?"

"Yes, I said that."

"Just as to the naked eye, Mary Barton looks exactly like Mary Jones."

"I never said that."

"Well, *does* Mary Barton look exactly like Mary Jones, or doesn't she?"

"Mary Barton *is* Mary Jones."

"Ah. You know that for a fact, do you?"

"No, but I saw the woman who called herself Mary Jones and I can see Mary Barton . . ."

"What was Mary Jones wearing when she came into your shop?"

"A long dress."

"*What* kind of long dress?"

"Sort of a long granny dress. The kind you can find at Laura Ashley's. With a flower design on it."

"Was she wearing shoes?"

"I think so."

"What kind?"

"I didn't look at her feet."

"Then how do you know she was wearing shoes?"

"I don't know for sure."

"Any stockings or panty hose?"

"I don't know."

"Were her fingernails painted?"

"I didn't look at them."

"What color was her hair?"

"Gray."

"Light gray, dark gray . . . ?"

"Same gray as the woman sitting there."

"And her eyes?"

"I don't remember."

"Was she wearing lipstick?"

"I don't know."

"Any jewelry?"

"I didn't notice."

"Well, now, take a look at Mary *Barton*. What's *she* wearing, can you tell me?"

"A blue suit. I can't tell the fabric from here, but it looks like linen."

"A blue linen suit, okay. Is she wearing a blouse?"

"Yes."

"What color is the blouse?"

"White. With a stock tie."

"Stockings? Panty hose?"

"I don't know what they are. Blue leg coverings, anyway."

"Shoes?"

"Yes. Black with French heels."

"Is she wearing lipstick?"

"No."

"Can you see what color her eyes are?"

"Blue."

"Is she wearing jewelry?"

"There's a ring on her right hand."

"Can you see what kind of ring it is from where you're sitting?"

"No."

"Was Mary Jones wearing such a ring?"

"No."

"So, in many respects Mary Jones did not on that day in September look *exactly* like Mary Barton, did she?"

"You know what I mean," Callahan said, and narrowed his eyes.

"No, I don't know what you mean," I said. "Please tell the court what you mean."

"Their *faces* look exactly the same."

"But not their bodies?"

"I didn't study her body. Or Mary Barton's either."

"Or their manner?"

"Same answer. I didn't make a point of . . ."

"Or their bearing?"

"I can only keep saying the same thing," he said, and then hammered out each word. "They look exactly the *same*."

"How about their voices? Have you ever heard Mary Barton's voice?"

"On television."

"Well, did she sound like Mary Jones?"

"I can't remember what Mary Jones sounded like."

"So—you don't know if their *bodies* are exactly the same, or their *manner*, or their *bearing*, or their *eyes*, or their *voices*, or the way they *dress*, but you can only keep saying the same thing, as you pointed out, you can keep saying over and over again that they *look* exactly the same."

"They do."

"*Who* does, Mr. Callahan?"

"Mary Jones and Mary Barton."

"You sound as if you're talking about two different people."

"No, they're one and the same person."

"So you keep telling us. But isn't it true, Mr. Callahan, that you don't *really* remember a great many details about the woman you saw in your store that day?"

"I remember her quite well. And she's sitting right there," he said, and pointed at Mary again.

"Yes, so you keep saying, over and over again. But you've testified that you *think* she was wearing shoes even though you didn't look at her feet, and you don't know if she was wearing panty hose or stockings, and you don't know if her fingernails were painted, or whether or not she was wearing lipstick or jewelry, isn't that so? Didn't you say all those things?"

"Yes."

"In fact, Mr. Callahan, isn't it true that the only *real* similarity you can point out between Mary Jones and Mary Barton is the color of their *hair*?"

"They look exactly the same," Callahan insisted.

"Thank you," I said, "no further questions."

"I have nothing more," Atkins said.

"We'll recess till two this afternoon," Rutherford said.

We had sent out for sandwiches and coffee and we were sitting around the desk in Frank's corner office, trying to work our way past our misidentification dead end. Toots was talking around a Swiss and ham on rye. Warren was eating a hamburger he'd drenched with ketchup. Frank had his back to the window fronting Heron Street, where a huge Santa Claus on a sleigh was strung on cables and flying over the oblivious traffic below. He was eating a bacon, lettuce, and tomato on toast; Frank, not Santa Claus. I was eating a sausage and pepper wedge, the sweet kind that Mike Santangelo liked so much.

Toots's right hand was bandaged. She was holding the sandwich in her left hand, biting into it, chewing and talking at the same time.

"I hit every car rental place at the airport," she said. "Sixteen of them in all, including a few you had to take a five-minute bus ride to get to. Hertz, Avis, Budget, Thrifty, Enterprise, Alamo, National . . . you name it, I talked to them. What I could gather, they rent different cars all the time, depending on the deals they get from the manufacturers. Right now, for example, Hertz is renting Sables, Tauruses, and Volvos, don't ask me how the Swede sneaked in. Enterprise is renting only GM cars, same with Avis, same with Alamo, must've been a fire sale. Budget is renting Fords, Mercurys, and Lincolns, and so on down the line, no luck with a Chrysler LeBaron by ten o'clock last night. But perseverance is its own reward," she said, and bit into the sandwich again. Chewing, she said, "Oh, I forgot, an outfit named Used Car Rentals rents everything under the sun, but the cars are all three, four years old."

I was wondering when she'd get to it. I hated masters of suspense or even mistresses. I was also wondering how she'd hurt her hand.

"Make a long story short," she said, "there were three compa-nies renting Chrysler products this past August . . . Dynastys, Spirits, Fifth Avenues, New Yorkers, and—bingo!—Chrysler LeBarons. I talked to the people at General, Dollar, and Thrifty, their rates are all about the same, around a hundred and ten for the week, twenty-seven for the day. The sedan comes with power seats and windows, cruise control, AM/FM radio, air-condition-ing, and so on, when would I like the car? In each place, I asked to speak to the manager . . ."

"What'd you get?" Warren asked impatiently. I noticed *he* was noticing the hand, too, and didn't like what he was seeing. Too many dope users were accident-prone. He was scowling; I guessed he was wondering if Toots had fallen off the wagon and onto her hand.

"I asked them to check their records for the weekend of August twenty-eighth, see if they'd rented a white Chrysler LeBaron sedan to anyone. Only one of them asked me why should he, so I introduced him to Mr. Green."

"How much?" Warren asked.

"A C-note," Toots said.

"What'd it buy?"

"Something wrong with you?" she snapped.

"How'd you hurt your hand?" he said.

"On the job," she said.

Warren nodded.

"Okay?" she said.

"Sure, fine."

"Also, it's none of your business."

"I said fine, didn't I?"

Toots nodded, too. Curtly, sharply. She glared at him a mo-ment and then pointedly turned her attention to me. "Thrifty had six LeBarons for rent that weekend, two of them out-of-state drop-offs . . ."

"This was a Florida plate," Frank said.

"Y-A-M, I know," she said. "The other four were from their

own franchise. One was a coupe, two were convertibles—their most popular model, by the way—and one of them was a white sedan, with Y-A-M plates."

"Did you get a name?" Warren asked.

"I got a name. *And* an address."

"Please," I said, "don't let it be Mary."

"No, it wasn't Mary."

We waited.

"The Thrifty car was rented to a man named Charles Ruggiero from New York City, he was staying at the Hyatt that weekend. I called him early this morning, and he told me he was the only person who drove that car all the while he was down here—which was for a week, by the way."

"How about Dollar and General?" Frank said.

"Cut to the chase," Warren said impatiently.

"Okay. White LeBaron sedan, Y-A-M plate. The only other one that went out that weekend was from Dollar, to a man named Oliver Diaz, who rented it on the twenty-seventh, and reported it stolen . . ."

"Uh-oh."

"There's more," Toots said.

"Please, not Mary," I said.

"Who knows?" Toots said. "The car disappeared from outside his motel sometime that same night."

"The twenty-seventh."

"Well, technically the twenty-eighth. He got back from a movie around midnight. When he woke up in the morning, the car was gone."

"Has it been recovered yet?"

"Yes."

"Where?"

"Here in Calusa. Abandoned behind the Rhodes Stadium."

"When?"

"September second. But it's been rented a hundred times since, you won't get anything from it."

"Did you actually *see* the car?"

"I did. Clean as a whistle."

"Any bloodstains when it was recovered? Did you ask?"

"I asked. Nothing they could see."

"Forensics can squeeze blood from a stone," Frank said, apropos of nothing.

"Point is, the cops weren't looking for anything," Toots said.

"You talked to the police? Or just the car rent—?"

"The police, too. This morning. Officer David Links. Fremont Substation."

"We can always apply for a court order to have the car examined," Frank said. "Get our own forensic team in there . . ."

"Why?" I said.

"Why? Look for bloodstains, hair samples, fiber samples . . ."

"Yeah? And suppose we find a gray hair that matches Mary's?"

"Discovery cuts both ways, Frank."

"I know, Warren, but . . ."

"Suppose we find her fingerprints all over the goddamn steering wheel?"

"I doubt there'll be prints," Toots said. "They clean these cars pretty good."

"I just don't see what we can find that'll *help* us."

"Find bloodstains that match any of the dead girls'," Frank said, "we've at least got the car the murderer used."

"How will that prove *Mary* didn't steal it?"

"Well, it won't. But . . ."

"What motel was this guy staying at?"

"The Star-Way. On the South Trail," Toots said.

"Anybody see anything?"

"Nothing. Total dead end."

"What'd you learn at Crescent Cove?"

Warren told us what he'd learned. He told us he had Nick Alston working right this minute to see if any complaints had been filed about Mary's . . .

"Who's Nick Alston?" Frank asked.

"Calusa P.D. dick, worked with us on the Parrish case."

"Oh, yeah, right."

"What statute are we dealing with, anyway?" Warren asked.

"I don't know what you mean."

"If there'd been complaints about her garden. Is there such a thing as an eyesore law?"

"We'd probably be dealing with Chapter 823, huh?" Frank said, and looked at me.

"What's that?" Warren asked.

"Public Nuisance," I said.

"All nuisances which tend to annoy the community or injure the health of the citizens in general, or to corrupt . . ."

"It's a second-degree misdemeanor."

"Can you get an indictment for something like that?"

"Sure."

"Take a court order to have the nuisance removed, though."

"Well, let me see what Nick comes up with."

"What are you going for?"

"I'm trying to find out when that fence went up."

"Lot of good that'll do," Frank said. "You want my advice?"

"No," I said.

"Change your plea."

"Not a chance."

"Then get back to court. You've got ten minutes."

There comes a time in every murder trial when the parade of experts begins. It's safe to say that there are experts in this world who will convincingly testify to any side of any question. If the state puts on an expert who claims without question that the moon is made of green cheese, the defense will put on its own expert to demonstrate without question that the moon is really made of Gruyère. The usual procedure is to first elicit from the expert his claims to expertise—his degrees from whichever universities, the honors he's received, the number of years he's been in this line of work, the number of times he's been called to testify in courts of law—and then to elicit from him how he was able to determine, for example, that the chemical composition of the Atlantic Ocean is similar to that of Pepsi-Cola rather than Coca-Cola. It's for the jury to decide what it will swallow.

For the most part, expert testimony is difficult to understand because it deals in subjects on which only the expert is the expert. A juror who's an automobile mechanic can't be expected to know anything about anyone's semen but his own. So when he sits on a rape-case jury and listens to testimony about a five percent solution of 2,4-dinitro-1-naphthol-7-sulfonic acid, flavianic acid, and a resultant yellowish precipitate of spermine flavianate, he can be forgiven a certain amount of bewilderment. The trick is to make expert testimony seem crystal clear to everyone. The further trick is to present it as what law school professors are fond of calling "facts invincible."

That afternoon, Max the Ax was attempting to do just that.

Technically, only one of his witnesses was an expert. The others were there to testify on how the object or objects for examination had come into the expert's hands. If Atkins were a playwright, this conglomerate testimony would have been his *scène à faire,* the scene that is absolutely essential to a play's progression but which can often become blatantly expository and downright boring. Atkins was too skilled ever to confuse or bore his jurors. Working them like the old-colleagues-of-his he hoped they'd already become, he introduced them to his people one by one and in the ensuing three and a half hours—interrupted only by cross-examinations he hoped would appear futile in the face of cold, irrefutable facts—actually made arcane matters seem elementary, my dear Watson.

The person who'd found the bloody sneakers was a fifteen-year-old girl. Black, attractive, well-spoken, she testified that she'd been walking home from school—in Calusa, kids inexplicably return to school in August, the hottest month of the year—when she spotted at the bottom of one of these "concrete drainage ditches or culverts or whatever you call them" what at first she thought was a pair of jogging shoes with red trim, but which upon closer inspection turned out to be a pair of bloodstained sneakers. She didn't touch them, she'd been afraid to touch them. When she got home and told her mother about them, her mother called the police. A uniformed cop came around to talk to the girl and then asked her to lead him to where she'd seen the sneakers. Atkins brought out that this was on the first day of September, the very same day the woman who'd called herself Mary Jones had dropped off a bloodstained dress for dry cleaning. He also brought out that the drainage ditch or culvert or whatever it was called was only four blocks from the Templeton Mall.

Step One.

Step Two was swearing in the police officer who'd recovered the bloodstained sneakers and bagged and tagged them for transportation to the Templeton Substation. In a sort of expert testimony, Atkins had him patiently explain what a Chain-of-Custody tag was, and then first introduced for identification and then had moved into evidence the very custody tag the officer had attached to the bagged sneakers and had him read out loud to the jury the signatures on that tag—his own signature, and then his lieutenant's, and then the signature of the police laboratory technician to whom the sneakers were eventually delivered for forensic analysis.

Step Three in Atkins's evidentiary chain was to put on the stand the lab technician himself, who testified not only to the tests he had made on the sneakers but also to those he had made on the blue denim dress with its residual stains. To no one's great surprise, least of all mine, the bloodstains on the sneakers and dress were of the same blood group as the last of the victims, young Felicity Hammer, whom Sarah Santangelo had seen bleeding from the mouth. He also testified that a shovel delivered to him by the State Attorney's Office—Chain-of-Custody tag attached—had when examined revealed bloodstains of the same AB group, and that soil residues on the shovel matched soil samples taken from Mary Barton's garden.

Not content to leave it there, Atkins brought on a detective from the State Attorney's Office who, armed with a search warrant, had gone through the clothing in Mary Barton's house on the day after her arrest. Through this witness, Atkins introduced a list of garments found in Mary's closet, and elicited that her dress size was an eight, the same size as the bloodstained denim dress, and her shoe size was a seven, the same size as the bloodstained sneakers. While he was at it, the detective testified that he had recovered from Mary's potting shed a shovel that appeared to have bloodstains on it, which he had subsequently caused to be delivered to the Forensic Unit, and he had collected samples of earth from the garden, for delivery to that same unit.

Now there wasn't much I could do with the young black girl who'd first spotted the sneakers and reported them to the police. She had undoubtedly done her duty as a citizen and she was there only to establish the proximity of the sneakers to the location of Jerry Callahan's Dri-Quik establishment. It would have been pointless to seek a contradiction of where she'd first seen the sneakers, since her testimony was backed up by the police officer who'd recovered them in that very same spot, and with whom I couldn't do very much, either. The best I could manage was to get both of them to admit that there hadn't been anything about the sneakers that might identify their owner, and get the girl to say further that she hadn't actually *seen* the police officer attach a Chain-of-Custody tag to the bagged sneakers because all she'd done was point them out to him and then go home to do her homework. But all I was doing was whistling in the wind till I could get to the forensic expert himself, which opportunity Atkins allowed me the moment he had finished questioning him.

Some defense attorneys will attack an expert witness in ways that are sometimes effective. For example, you can try to make it appear that the witness has entered into some sort of guilty conspiracy with the prosecutor. Toward that end, you'll ask if he's discussed the case with anyone before it came to trial, hoping he'll fall into the trap and say, "No, sir, I did not," in which case you'll get him to reveal he'd most certainly discussed the case with the prosecutor, and this would make it appear they'd been in collusion regarding the testimony. But Phillip Dunnigan, the state's forensic expert, was too skilled for such elementary maneuvering—he'd earlier testified that he'd been called as an expert witness in a total of two hundred and twelve trials—and though I took an obligatory shot at it, he readily countered with a "Yes, sir, I spoke to Mr. Atkins about it and told him what my conclusions were." All open and aboveboard. Nothing the jury could condemn.

So I tried the next approach, I said, "Mr. Dunnigan, how long would you say you've been examining clothing or shovels or other objects for evidence of bloodstains?" and he repeated essentially what he'd told Atkins, flaunting his education and his years of experience and his honors and medals and trophies and awards and stopping just short of showing me his clean handkerchief and underwear.

I led him farther down the garden path (although he was already ahead of me) getting him to tell me approximately how many tests he'd made in all those years, and seeming to marvel at his industry and dedication, and then I said, "Just yes or no, please, Mr. Dunnigan, have you ever made a mistake in all those years?" But he was wise to the ways of the wily highwayman; he had testified often enough to know that no one could force him to give a simple yes or no answer if he chose not to.

"Your Honor," he said, "I can answer that with a yes or no, but I would prefer qualifying it."

"Answer it any way you wish," Rutherford said.

"I've made mistakes in my lifetime, yes," Dunnigan said with attractive modesty, "but the testimony I've given in court has always been accurate."

So I used this as a springboard, getting him to tell me that he was *sure* the blood on the sneakers was of the AB group and that this was Felicity Hammer's blood group, as was the blood on the dress, as was the blood on the shovel, but then asking him if he'd found any evidence of any blood *other* than that in the AB group—I knew Mary's blood was of the A group—and he said he had not and I said, "Are you sure about that?" and he said he was positive, and I said, "No mistake about that, right?" and he said there was no mistake. But there was really nothing I could do to seriously damage his testimony, except plant in the jury's mind the possibility that whereas the blood on the sneakers and dress might very well be Felicity Hammer's, this did not necessarily mean that the dress and the sneakers had belonged to Mary Barton. The shovel was another thing again. It had been found in Mary's potting shed and the initials "M.B." were burned into the handle.

When it came time for me to cross-examine the detective who'd searched Mary's house, I got him to admit that he had not found in her closets or dresser drawers any sneakers similar to the ones offered in evidence, nor any dresses of the same style, color, or fabric as the blue denim someone had dropped off at Callahan's dry-cleaning store. I got him to admit further that some of the sizes he'd listed were inaccurate and that in fact Mary had among her clothing some dresses that were a size seven and others that were a size nine.

"Isn't it true," I said, "that you went there *looking* for size eight dresses?"

"No, I was looking for evidence."

"Of what?"

"Of murder."

"How would a size eight dress constitute evidence of murder?"

"Well, there might have been bloodstains, you know."

"Well, did you *find* any bloodstains on any of the clothing you listed?"

"No, but my search warrant empowered me to look for evidence in the crime of murder."

"Isn't it true that you were instructed to look for clothing that might link Mary Barton to the clothing the state attorney already had in hand?"

"No, sir."

"That isn't true?"

"No, sir, it is not."

"Who asked you to apply for that search warrant?"

"Mr. Bannister, sir, the state attorney."

"Did he tell you what he wanted you to look for?"

"We had some discussion about it, yes."

"What did he say he wanted you to look for?"

"Evidence in the crime of murder."

"Were those his words? Or are they the words you used on your application for a search warrant?"

"One and the same, sir."

"His words and your words?"

"Yes, sir. One and the same."

"So that was all the explicit instruction he gave you, is that right? 'Bring me some evidence in the crime of murder.' "

"More or less, that's what he said, yes, sir."

"Well, did he say more or did he say less?"

"He told me to find whatever might be incriminating to the defendant, yes, sir."

"Like what?"

"Like whatever I could find."

"Like any size eight dresses?"

"I don't recall him asking me to look for a size eight dress."

"Did you know that the state attorney's list of physical evidence included a blue denim, size eight, cotton dress?"

"I believe I saw that on the list, yes, sir."

"And a pair of size seven sneakers."

"Yes, sir, they were on the list, too."

"So you knew this."

"Yes."

"Yet you didn't go to that house looking for any size eight dresses or any size seven sneakers."

"Not specifically, no, sir."

"You just *happened* to eliminate from your list the size *seven* dresses and the size *nine* dresses, is that right?"

"I didn't think they constituted evidence in the crime of murder, yes, sir."

"How about that shovel? Were you asked to look for a shovel?"

"I knew the state attorney might be able to use a shovel, yes, sir, if I could find one."

"How did you know that?"

"I knew he had a witness who'd seen the defendant burying one of those children."

"Did Mr. Bannister tell you he had such a witness?"

"I believe I knew it."

"Did he tell you?"

"It was common knowledge in the office. That he had an eyewitness who saw the burial and that the case was a lock."

"Your Honor!" I shouted.

"Strike that. Jury will disregard witness's editorial comments on the case."

"Did Mr. Bannister ask you to look for a shovel?"

"I'm an experienced detective, sir . . ."

"I'm sure you are, but that's not an answer to my question."

"What I'm trying to say . . ."

"*Did* the state attorney ask you to look for a shovel or did he not?"

"He didn't have to. He knew I'd look for any evidence in the crime of murder."

"Thank you," I said, "no further questions."

Max the Ax was ready to play his trump card.

The moment I dreaded most was at hand.

Atkins's next witness was a Calusa P.D. sergeant named Thomas Wilkes, a tall, slender, suntanned, graying man of some fifty-three years, who took the stand in uniform and sat poised and ready for any questions put to him. Resting on the floor not six feet away from me, on edge, angled against the prosecution's table, their backs for the moment hiding their content, were what appeared to be three board-backed posters some three feet long by two feet wide.

"Sergeant Wilkes, were you among the first of the police officers to arrive at 2716 Gideon Way on the morning of September first?" Atkins asked.

"I was."

Gravelly voice. Either a heavy smoker or a heavy drinker, or both.

"What occasioned your presence at the scene?" Atkins asked, his ornate language transporting all of us back to Victorian England again.

"I was called by the officer on radio patrol, who reported that the body of a dead child had been unearthed in the garden at that address."

"What time did you receive this call?"

"I clocked it in at ten forty-five A.M."

"And what time did you arrive at the house?"

"Some ten minutes later."

"So that you arrived at the scene at five minutes to eleven."

"Give or take a few minutes, yes, sir."

"Did you aid in a search of the garden at 2716 Gideon Way?"

"I *supervised* the search."

"How did you and your fellow officers conduct this search?"

"We dug up the garden adjacent to the area where the telephone repairman had unearthed the body."

"And what did you discover?"

"We found two other bodies."

"Where were these bodies discovered?"

"In the same row as the first body. The garden is set up in rows. This was the last row, where the tallest of the towers is. The bodies were buried in between the towers."

"Now, Sergeant Wilkes, were photographs taken of these bodies?"

"Yes, sir."

"At the scene?"

"Yes, sir."

"As the bodies appeared when they were exhumed, is that correct?"

"That is correct."

Atkins walked over to his table. He picked up his large, board-backed photographs from where they were angled against one leg of the table, and carried them to where three easels had already been set up at the front of the courtroom. Only a juror of sub-intelligence would have failed to recognize why those easels were there. The jury was already leaning forward in anticipation.

"Your Honor, I would like these marked for identification, please."

"Separately, Mr. Atkins?"

"Please."

"Objection," I said. "May we approach, Your Honor?"

Rutherford nodded us up to the bench.

"Your Honor," I said, "the photographs the state plans to introduce in this enlarged form—how big *are* those pictures, Mr. Atkins?"

"Their size is irrelevant," Atkins said.

"No, their size is exactly the *point*," I said. "This isn't a slasher film, Your Honor, this is a *trial*. Photos blown up to this size can serve no purpose other than to inflame and prejudice the jury."

"Your Honor," Atkins said, "the photos are accurate representations of what those little girls looked like when they were unearthed. The size is necessary to illustrate the extent of the wounds."

"He can show that by passing around eight-by-tens, Your Honor. There's no need to produce a horror show here. Showing these gory . . ."

"It would appear to me that a photograph is a photograph, Mr. Hope, and whether the jury passes around an eight-by-ten or views a larger picture from a distance, the effect will be much the same. If the state attorney feels he can better illustrate the nature of the wounds by showing these larger . . ."

"I do, Your Honor."

". . . photographs, then I'll allow it. Your objection is overruled," she said, and turned to the court clerk, dismissing us. "Mark them Exhibits Ten, Eleven, and Twelve for the prosecution," she said.

I went back to the defense table. Andrew looked up at me. I shook my head. Atkins was already at the witness stand again.

"Sergeant Wilkes," he said, "I show you Exhibit Ten, and ask if you know what it is."

"It's a photograph of the first body discovered. Felicity Hammer. The first little girl."

Atkins put it down beside the witness stand, so that its back was still to the jury. He wanted the full shock effect. He wanted to show all three photos virtually simultaneously.

"Sergeant Wilkes," he said, "I show you Exhibit Eleven, and ask if you know what it is."

"It's a photograph of the second little girl we found, Jenny Lou Williams."

"I show you Exhibit Twelve, and ask if you know what it is."

"It's a photograph of the third little girl, Kimberly Holt."

"Now, Sergeant Wilkes, can you describe the condition of these bodies when they were exhumed?"

"The bodies seemed to have been freshly buried; that is to say, they were not in an advanced state of decomposition. Their throats had been slit . . ."

A collective gasp from everyone in the courtroom.

". . . and their genital areas had been mutilated."

"In what fashion?"

"Cross-hatching, sir."

"Can you describe this for us?"

"A series of tiny little X-marks, sir, crosshatched onto the genital area. Around the vagina, sir. What would be called the mons veneris."

"When you say crosshatched . . ."

"With a sharp instrument, it appeared."

"Did you know what that sharp instrument was, at the time?"

"I did not."

"Was there blood on the bodies?"

"Dried blood. Caked blood."

"Were the bodies warm?"

"Cold, sir."

"Were you present when the photographs were taken?"

"I was present."

"And these are those photographs?"

"Yes, sir. Enlargements of them."

"Your Honor, I would like these photographs moved into evidence."

"Mr. Hope?"

"No objection."

"Mark them."

"May I publish them to the jury?"

"Go ahead," Rutherford said.

Atkins took his time. Carried each of the pictures to an easel, set them up so that the judge and jury had a full view, the spectators only a partial one—but he wasn't trying this case for the mob. He was trying it for the eight women and four men who now looked at the horrible enlargements of three naked, earth-smeared, blood-caked children with their slit throats and their mutilated genitals. They looked at the pictures long and hard. There was revulsion on their faces, as there was on mine. One or two of them glanced from the photographs to Mary, making an almost positive link.

"No further questions," Atkins said.

I walked to the witness stand.

"Were you shocked that day?" I asked.

"Sir?"

"When you discovered those slain and mutilated children, were you shocked?"

"I was, sir."

"Experienced police officer, but the sight of these children nonetheless shocked you."

"Yes, sir, they did."

"But, Sergeant Wilkes, was there anything about these bodies that would indicate Mary Barton had killed them and buried them in that garden?"

"Well . . ."

"Well, yes or no. As shocking as these bodies appeared to you, was there anything about them to connect them to Miss Barton?"

"Not that I could see."

"Was Miss Barton's blood discovered on the bodies?"

"Not by me."

"Well, by *anyone*? You're familiar with this case, was Mary Barton's blood found anywhere on these children?"

"I don't believe so."

"Were traces of Mary Barton's *hair* found on any of these bodies?"

"I don't believe so."

"Or fingerprints? It *is* possible to lift fingerprints from a dead body, isn't it?"

"Yes, sir, it is."

"But Mary Barton's fingerprints weren't found on any of these bodies, were they?"

"Not to my knowledge."

"So there was nothing that linked or connected these bodies to Mary Barton, was there?"

"They were found in her garden, sir."

"Ah. And you consider this a connection, do you?"

"Yes, sir, I do."

"But the garden's easily accessible to the public, isn't it?"

"Well . . . yes, sir."

"Nothing to stop anyone from marching right in there, is there?"

"There's a fence around it, sir."

"Is there a locked gate?"

"No, sir."

"So anyone can walk in there, isn't that so?"

"Yes, sir."

"So that the mere fact that these bodies were found in Miss Barton's garden makes no more connection to her than if they were found in *your* garden . . ."

"Objection, Your Honor."

"I'll allow it."

". . . or *anyone's* garden . . ."

"Objection!"

"You're pressing it, Mr. Hope."

"I withdraw the question. I have nothing further."

"Mr. Atkins?"

"Witness may be excused."

As a police escort came to the defense table for Mary, I could feel her steady gaze upon me. Tomorrow morning, Atkins would call Charlotte Carmody, whose testimony I'd been unable to shake during deposition. Mary's eyes followed me all the way out of the courtroom.

The evening air was hot and sultry.

I stood on the courthouse steps for a moment, looking at the lighted Christmas tree in the square, listening to the sound of carols pealing from somewhere up the street.

I could not shake the ominous feeling that the case was sliding rapidly downhill and there was nothing I could do to stop its dizzying descent.

Wall speakers in the motel lobby were blaring Christmas carols when Patricia got back after dinner that night. She asked the clerk for her key . . .

"Miss Demming, is it?"

"Yes, please."

Only been here a week already, the jackass.

. . . accepted the key attached to a large oval green plastic tag stamped with the number 411, and went down the hall to wait for the elevators. The music was being piped into the elevators, too. Christmas on a stick. She hated Christmas.

Alone in the room, she began crying.

She cried a lot this time of year. Not on the phone to Calusa, no, although she'd come close to it the other night when he'd begun probing a bit too deeply, poor dear man, having to put up with such stuff.

Do you have real mood swings?

Yes. Do you?

Yes. Sometimes I just want to be alone.

Do you want to be alone now?

Well, yes, if the truth be known, she did want to be alone just now, did not want to feel obliged to call Matthew Hope or any other man on earth, for that matter. What she wanted to do was order a Tanqueray martini, up and very cold, with a pair of olives, please, though she'd had two of those at dinner and they hadn't seemed to help the depressing mood that had come over her the moment she'd stepped out of the courthouse and seen the main drag alive with Christmas lights. She yanked a tissue from the dressertop box, dried her eyes, sat on the edge of the bed, crossed her legs, picked up the phone, and dialed room service.

"Moment, please," a woman's voice said, and there was a click, and then dead air.

She hated when they did that. She much preferred it when they just let the damn phone ring, instead of picking up and saying "Moment, please," or "Please hold," or any one of a dozen variations designed to let you think you'd been connected to the White House.

She kept waiting.

"Yes, please, how may I help you?"

Southern accent as deep as a wagonload of buttered grits.

"I'd like a Tanqueray martini, please," Patricia said, "up and very cold, with a . . ."

"A *what?*" the woman said.

"A Tanqueray martini . . ."

"A *what* martini?"

"Tanqueray," she said, and broke it down syllable by syllable. "Tank-uh-ray. Tanqueray gin."

"Tank of *what* kind of gin?"

"Is this room service?" Patricia asked.

"Yes, this is room service, ma'am."

"Do you ever take drink orders?"

"Yes, ma'am, we take drink orders all the time."

"Do you know what a martini is?"

"I surely do, ma'am."

"Do you know what a Tanqueray gin martini is?"

"That's what's throwin' me, ma'am."

"Ask your bartender if he knows what a Tanqueray gin martini is."

"Well, I'm back here in the kitchen, ma'am. What I do is I have to call this in to the bartender, a drink order."

"Yes, call it in and ask him what a . . . better yet, why don't you just connect me directly to the bar?"

"Drink'd have to come in here from the bar, anyways. So's I can send someone up with it. It's just the tank part's throwin' me, ma'am. Makes it sound like you want a *tank* of gin."

"Yes, I'm beginning to feel that way," Patricia said.

"Ma'am?"

"Do you know what a *Beefeater* gin martini is?"

"I surely don't, ma'am."

"What kind of gins *are* you familiar with?" Patricia asked sweetly. "The brand names. Do you know any gin brand names?"

"Well . . . Heineken?"

"Heineken, I see," Patricia said. "How long have you been taking room service orders?"

"I started last week, ma'am."

"I see. Do you have a pencil?"

"Yes, ma'am."

"I'm going to spell this out for you, and I want you to give it to the bartender exactly the way I spell it for you, all right?"

"Yes, ma'am."

"Are you ready?"

"Yes, ma'am."

"Then here we go. Tanqueray. That's T-A . . ."

"That's just what's throwin' . . ."

"Please let me finish!" Patricia said sharply.

Courtroom tactic.

There was a silence on the line.

"Just *listen,*" Patricia said. "And *write*. The name of the gin is Tanqueray. That's the brand name. This is how it's spelled. T-A-N, Q-U-E, R-A-Y. Have you got that?"

"Yes, ma'am. I just didn't understand it was a brand of whiskey, you see. Is it French? It sure does sound French."

"I don't know what it is. Do you think you have it now?"

"Oh, yes, ma'am."

"Good. So call the bartender . . ."

"Oh, I will, ma'am, now that I got it straight."

". . . and tell him I want a Tanqueray martini . . ."

One more time, she thought, and they'll send me a case every Christmas for the rest of my life . . .

". . . up, and very cold, with two olives."

"Two olives, yes, ma'am."

"Call him now, would you, please?"

"Yes, ma'am."

"And tell him to please hurry because I'm very thirsty."

"I will, ma'am."

"Thank you, Gloria."

"That's not my name, ma'am."

"It should be," Patricia said, and hung up, and wondered why she'd said that, and suddenly began crying again. She didn't know a single person named Gloria in the entire world. She hoped Matthew wouldn't call before her tank of martinis arrived. She hoped he wouldn't call her at all, in fact. She didn't want to make bright meaningless chatter tonight, and she didn't want a phone phuck tonight, and she didn't want to tell someone she loved him when tonight she wasn't at all sure that she could ever again love anyone at all. What she wanted to do tonight was put on her granny nightgown with the bluebell design, and drink her martini if it ever got here, and cry her eyes out for a Christmas Present that could never possibly equal that glorious Christmas Past a hundred years . . .

Shit, she thought, I forgot to give her the room number.

She picked up the receiver again, dialed the numeral 5 for room service.

"Moment, please."

Same voice.

She waited.

And waited.

And waited.

"Yes, please, how may I help you?"

"This is the Tanqueray martini again," Patricia said.

"Yes, ma'am, I already called that in to the bartender. But, ma'am . . ."

"I know, I didn't give you the room number."

"That's right, you didn't. Could I have that now, please?"

"It's four-eleven."

"Yes, ma'am, thank you. I would've called you back, but I didn't have the number, you see."

"Well, now you have it," Patricia said gently. "Did he say how long it would be?"

"That's why I wanted to call you back, ma'am. He doesn't have any of that Tanka whatever. All's he has is Gordon's, ma'am, that's a gin he has, would you like him to make a martini out of that?"

"Yes, Gordon's will be fine."

"Also, ma'am, the olives he's got is with these almonds in them, would that be all right, too?"

"Yes, fine."

"Plus the ice machine's broke at the bar, he's waitin' for one of the boys to bring him some ice from the big machine just outside the office, so it'll be a while, ma'am."

"How long a while?"

"Maybe twenty minutes, ma'am."

"Fine, just tell him to make it as soon as possible."

"Thank you, ma'am. My name's Margaret, by the way, not Gloria. We don't have any Glorias here."

"I'm glad to know that," Patricia said. "Ask him to hurry, would you please, Margaret?"

"Yes, ma'am, I surely will. Good night, ma'am."

"Good night," Patricia said, and replaced the receiver on its cradle and sat on the edge of the bed, and stared at a framed print on the wall across the room, an Indian wearing a buffalo robe and standing beside the dying embers of a fire, a wisp of smoke trailing up on the air, and suddenly she was laughing, her shoulders heaving, and just as suddenly, the way it did all too often in these weeks before Christmas, the laughter turned to tears.

She was still crying a half hour later when the bellboy brought her drink.

"Gordon's on the rocks," he said, "lemon twist."

She nodded bleakly.

"Will there be anything else, miss?" he asked.

Faint innuendo in his voice. Hopeful look in his eyes. Pimply-faced kid, maybe seventeen, eighteen years old, figuring the tearful lady might need some late night consolation.

"No, thank you," she said, "there'll be nothing else."

"Well, good night, then," he said, sounding miffed rather than disappointed.

She locked the door behind him. Called the hotel operator and told her no more calls tonight, please. The operator asked if that meant emergencies, too, and she said, "Yes, emergencies, too."

She turned on the television set.

There was news of the murder trial in Calusa.

She snapped it off again.

Staring at the Indian standing by his dying fire, she sipped at her gin.

The telephone rang just as the eleven o'clock news was going off. There'd been an extended segment on the witnesses Atkins had put on today. The weather for tomorrow was expected to be warm and breezy, with a high in the lower seventies. In sports, the Tampa Bay . . .

I grabbed for the receiver at once because I thought it might be Patricia.

"Hello?" I said.

"Matthew?"

Warren's voice.

"I just got through talking to Alston," he said. "I think you'll be happy."

12

Max the Ax's star witness was the woman who'd allegedly seen Mary Barton burying the body of a child in her backyard on the night of August 31. Dressed for court in a tailored green suit with subtle red piping—Christmas was very much on everyone's mind, this eleventh day of December—Charlotte Carmody took the stand, crossed her legs, looked first at the jury and then Atkins, and took a deep breath in preparation for sending my client straight to the electric chair.

Confident in the facts his witness would relate, satisfied that her pleasant manner and quiet good looks would favorably impress the jury, Atkins patiently and deliberately elicited from her the information that she lived right next door to the defendant, that she was on neighborly terms with her, that she certainly knew what she looked like . . .

Everything I'd asked her during the deposition.

. . . and that she'd talked to her several dozen times during the six months she'd lived next door to her, at first over the low hedge dividing their properties and later over the slightly higher fence that went up after the development rules changed. He got her to point out the woman she knew to be Mary Barton and then led his witness inexorably to the night of August 31 and asked her to tell the court what she had seen that night.

Charlotte calmly related having been in bed watching television when she heard something outside, and got out of bed, and went to the window . . .

Everything she'd already told me under oath.

. . . and by the light of a full moon saw Mary Barton . . .

The jury was silent.

Listening. Watching. Scarcely daring to breathe.

. . . saw Mary Barton wearing a blue denim dress and white sneakers . . .

Wheels turning, gears clicking, the jury remembering all those other witnesses describing the selfsame dress and sneakers.

. . . saw Mary Barton with a shovel in her hands . . .

"Digging a grave and throwing a little girl's body in it."

The exact words she'd used during the deposition.

But no one to challenge her this time. Not yet. Not until my turn came around. Meanwhile, Atkins went over it again and again, anticipating what my line of attack would be, getting his witness to tell "us" how frightened she'd been and why she hadn't come forward at once for fear of retaliation from a woman she frankly suspected was . . .

"Objection, Your Honor."

"Your Honor," Atkins protested, "she hasn't even finished her . . ."

"Witness's suspicions are inadmissible," Rutherford said, "*whatever* they're about. Objection is sustained."

"Miss Carmody, you have previously identified for us the woman you know as your neighbor, Mary Barton," Atkins said. "I would now like you to look around this courtroom and tell me if the woman you saw burying that little girl on the night of August thirty-first is here with us today."

Conveying to the jury the impression that a beast was loose among us.

"Yes, she is," Charlotte said.

"Would you point her out to us, please?"

"She's sitting there at the defense table," Charlotte said, and pointed to Mary.

"Are you pointing to the defendant in this case?"

"I am."

"Are you pointing to Mary Barton?"

"I am."

"Is Mary Barton the woman you saw burying the naked child that night?"

"She is."

"Thank you, your witness," Atkins said.

I took my time getting up. Looked again at the typewritten report Warren had delivered to my office early this morning, shuffled around some incidental and unimportant papers, leaned over to whisper absolutely nothing to Andrew, and then rose and approached the stand, and said, "Nice seeing you again, Miss Carmody."

She said nothing.

Nodded.

"You do remember me, don't you?"

"I remember you, yes."

"I took your sworn deposition, do you remember that?"

"Yes."

"On the sixth of October, do you remember?"

"Yes."

"In my office on Heron Street, wasn't it?"

"Yes, that's where it was."

"And I assume you also remember what you told me under oath, is that right?"

"Not word for word."

"Well, we have the actual deposition here," I said, "in case we need to refresh your memory as to actual words. Do you remember telling me, for example, that you were neighborly with Miss Barton? I believe that's the exact word you used, 'neighborly,' but we can look it up if you . . .".

"That's the word I used."

"Neighborly."

"Yes."

"Would you still describe your past relationship with Miss Barton as 'neighborly'?"

"Well, I don't know how neighborly she might think my testimony . . ."

"I said *past* relationship. When you and Miss Barton used to chat over the hedges and the fences, would you still describe that relationship as 'neighborly'?"

"Yes, I would."

"Not friendly, but neighborly."

"Neighborly, yes."

"Sometimes just said hello to her . . ."

"Yes."

"But other times you chatted for, oh, two, three minutes at a time, isn't that what you told me in your deposition?"

"Yes."

"And during these conversations, she was always in her garden."

"Yes."

"Did you *like* her garden?"

"What?"

"I said, 'Did you like her garden?' "

"It was a garden. I'm not particularly a garden person."

"That's interesting, but please answer my question."

"I neither liked it nor disliked it."

"You didn't, for example, talk to a man named Robert Giannino about that garden, did you?"

"No, I didn't."

"Robert Giannino?"

"No."

"Former president of the Crescent Cove Association? Until last June, anyway."

"Yes, I know who he is, but I don't recall talking to him about Mary's garden."

"You called her Mary, did you? In your various conversations?"

"Yes."

"Did she call you Charlotte?"

"I don't remember what she called me."

"Well, you had these two dozen or so neighborly conversations between April and September, when she was arrested, don't you remember what she called you?"

"She may have called me Charlotte, I don't know."

"What'd you call Robert Giannino when you went to see him?"

"I called him Mr. Giannino."

"You do remember going to see him, don't you?"

"Yes."

"This was shortly after you moved in, wasn't it?"

"Yes."

"When *did* you move in, Miss Carmody?"

"In April."

"Of this year?"

"Yes."

"Was it in April that you went to see Mr. Giannino?"

"I think it was, yes."

"Well, in fact, it was on April twenty-fourth, wasn't it? Exactly two weeks after you'd moved into the house next door to Mary Barton."

"I don't remember the exact date."

"Would you agree that it was very soon after you'd moved in?"

"It was relatively soon, yes."

"Why did you go to see the association president so soon after you'd moved in?"

"I had some questions about the association rules."

"What questions did you have?"

"I don't remember now. It was a long time ago."

"Well, it was in April, and this is only December. Surely you can remember why you thought it was so urgent to . . ."

"Objection, Your Honor. Counsel is characterizing . . ."

"Sustained."

"You don't remember why you went to see Mr. Giannino, is that correct?"

"I remember it was about some association rules. I don't remember what exact *questions* I had about the rules."

"Did you mention Miss Barton's garden to him?"

"Why would I mention her garden?"

"Do you want me to answer that, Miss Carmody? Or would you prefer answering it yourself?"

"I did not mention her garden."

"When you say you did not *mention* it, do you mean you didn't *speak* about it?"

"I don't know what Mr. Giannino told you, but . . ."

"Please answer the question."

"I did not speak about her garden, that's right."

"Did you make reference to her garden in some *other* way?"

"I don't understand the question."

"Would you remember having made reference to Mary Barton's garden in some way other than speech?"

"No, I don't remember."

"Well, perhaps this will refresh your memory," I said, and went to the defense table and accepted the sheet of paper Andrew handed me. Carrying it to the witness stand, I said, "Would you please look . . . ?"

"May I see that?" Atkins said.

"Certainly," I said. "Excuse me."

I went to where he was sitting and handed him the sheet of paper. He managed to accept it without looking at me. I should explain that an attorney is required to submit for discovery before trial only a list of those documents or other physical evidence he plans to use in his own case. He does not have to let anyone know beforehand what he'll introduce into evidence during his cross-examination of the other side's witnesses. Moreover, the opposing sides will usually append to their list of witnesses a boilerplate statement to the effect that they may *also* be calling any additional witnesses as are required to impeach anyone's testimony. I was prepared to call Giannino if I had to. Plus a few other people down the line if I didn't get from Charlotte exactly what I wanted. Meanwhile, Atkins was reading the document in his hand. He didn't like what he was reading.

Nodding, he handed it back to me. I assumed his nod meant he had no objections to my showing this piece of paper to his witness. Good thing, too. He'd have been shot down in a minute.

"Miss Carmody," I said, "would you please read this carefully and tell me if you recognize it?"

Charlotte took the document. She must have known what it was even before she looked at it, but she studied it carefully nonetheless. I gave her all the rope she needed.

"Recognize it?" I said at last.

"Yes."

"It's a petition, isn't it?"

"I wouldn't call it a petition."

"What would you call it?"

"A request."

"For what?"

"For an exception to the association rules."

"Well, doesn't the document begin with the words 'We the undersigned, hereby *petition* the Crescent Cove Association . . .'? Aren't those the opening words of that document?"

"Yes, they are."

"The document refers to itself as a *petition,* then, doesn't it?"

"Yes."

"Then do you agree it's a petition?"

"I would still call it a request."

"All right, then, you say this is a *request* for an exception to the association rules, is that right?"

"Yes."

"Actually, though, it's a request for an exception to a *specific* rule, isn't it?"

"Well . . ."

"Doesn't it say that the undersigned are petitioning for a *waiver* . . . that's the exact language used, isn't it? Not 'exception' but 'waiver.' Do you see the language there?"

"Yes."

". . . 'a waiver to rule number seventeen of the Crescent Cove Association Rules and Regulations, commonly known as the No Fences Rule.' That is the exact language in this petition, is it not?"

"Yes, it is."

"Do you now remember showing this petition to Mr. Giannino?"

"I may have shown it to him."

"Well, didn't you in fact *go* there to show it to him?"

"I may have gone there with that in mind."

"Didn't you, in fact, *leave* this petition with him when you left his home that day?"

"I don't know if this is the exact request that I left with him."

"Are you saying you don't know if this is the petition you and twenty-five other people in the neighborhood signed?"

"I don't know if this is the *physical* document."

"Well, isn't this your signature?"

"It looks like my signature."

"Charlotte Louise Carmody, that's your signature, isn't it?"

"As I said, it *looks* like my signature."

"In ink, isn't it?"

"Yes, but . . ."

"You're not suggesting it's a forgery, are you?"

"I just don't know if this is the *actual* request I took to Mr. Giannino's house."

"Do you think it's a *copy* of the petition?"

"No, I'm just saying . . ."

"Miss Carmody, do you agree that this document is either the original of the petition, or a copy of it, or a forgery of it? There's nothing in between that I know of. Now, which is it?"

"I guess it's the original."

"Thank you. And is this what you took to Mr. Giannino's house on the evening of April twenty-fourth?"

"Yes."

"And do you now remember discussing this document as it related to Mary Barton's garden?"

"I don't recall discussing the garden. Mr. Giannino and I talked about fences. About putting up fences. Being allowed to put them up. This had nothing to do with Mary's garden."

"These other people who signed the petition . . . do they all live in the vicinity of Mary's house?"

"I really don't know where they live."

"Miss Carmody, didn't you personally circulate this petition for signatures?"

"I did."

"Didn't you go *personally* to these people who signed it?"

"Yes, but . . ."

"Didn't you go to their *homes*?"

"Yes, but . . ."

"Knock on their doors? Ask them to sign this petition?"

"Yes, but . . ."

"Well then, don't you *know* where they live? If you went to their houses . . ."

"I'm saying I don't know where they live *now*. They might have moved. The way Mr. Giannino moved."

"Ahhhh, thank you for explaining that. I'll rephrase my question. At the time you were circulating this petition, did all the people who signed it live in the vicinity of Mary Barton's house, yes or no, please?"

"Yes, they did."

"So wasn't the purpose of this petition to allow Mary Barton's neighbors to put up fences that would hide her garden?"

"No. Her garden had nothing to do with it."

"The first three signatures on this petition are yours and those of the people who live immediately adjacent to Mary Barton's house, isn't that so?"

"I don't recall the order of the signatures."

"Then *look* at them. Your signature is the first one, isn't it?"

"Yes."

"And the second signature is for the man who owns the house on the left of Miss Barton's, isn't it?"

"I can hardly read the signature."

"Then look at the name lettered to the right of it, just above the address. The name is James Healy, isn't it?"

"Yes."

"And the address is 2718 Gideon Way, isn't it? Can you read that? It's clearly lettered in Mr. Healy's hand, I'm sure you can read it."

"Yes."

"And isn't 2718 Gideon Way the house immediately to the left of Mary Barton's?"

"Yes."

"Just as *your* house is immediately to the right."

"Yes."

"And just as the *third* house is immediately *behind* Mary Barton's house. The house belonging to Ralph Costanza, do you see his signature there?"

"Yes, I do."

"So these first three signatures are, in fact, the signatures of people who live on the properties immediately surrounding Mary Barton's garden, isn't that so?"

"Yes. But that has nothing to do with why we wanted an exception to the No Fences Rule."

"Did Mr. Giannino give you the waiver you were seeking?"

"He was not personally empowered to do so. He told me he had to bring the matter up before the board."

"Do you know if he subsequently did so?"

"I don't think he had to. The rule was changed by general vote in June."

"Do you feel your visit to Mr. Giannino was influential in having that particular proposal put on the ballot? Your handing him a petition signed by twenty-five people? Do you feel this influenced his . . . ?"

"Objection, Your Honor. Witness has no way of . . ."

"I can't rule on your objection because there are now *three* questions waiting for the witness's response. Mr. Hope, please ask one question at a time and please allow the witness an opportunity to reply before posing another one."

"Were you satisfied that your visit to Mr. Giannino had obtained results?"

"I saw no direct correlation between my visit and the later ballot proposal to amend rule seventeen."

"The No Fences Rule."

"Yes."

"No direct correlation."

"None."

"The proposal just magically appeared on the ballot . . ."

"Objection."

"Sustained."

"Did you ever mention to Mary Barton that you'd gone to see Mr. Giannino?"

"No, I did not."

"After that visit, did you still maintain your *neighborly* relations with her?"

"Yes."

"How about after you went to the police?"

There was a slight hesitation. She knew I knew. Whether or not she'd try to bluff it through . . .

"My relationship with Mary Barton was always a cordial and neighborly one."

"I asked you if your relationship was still neighborly *after* you went to the police?"

"If you're referring to my telling the police what I'd seen in her garden on the night of August thirty-first . . ."

"No, I'm referring to your visit to the police on the first day of May, a week after you presented your petition to Mr. Giannino."

There was a longer silence. She was weighing whether she wished to go the document route again. She had to've known I wasn't just pulling this out of thin air. If I had the petition she'd taken to Giannino, then I also had . . .

"Miss Carmody?" I said. "Would you please answer my question?"

"I believe our relationship remained the same," she said calmly.

"Then you do remember going to the Public Safety Building on the first day of May?"

"Yes."

"Can you tell me why you went there?"

"I was trying to get some information."

"About what?"

"A situation that existed."

"What situation was that?"

"A public nuisance."

"What information were you looking for?"

"Someone told me there was such a thing as a public nuisance. So I . . ."

"Objection! Hearsay!"

"State-of-mind exception, Your Honor."

"I'll allow it."

"I went to the police to ask about it. They told me there *was* a law about such things, and if it was found that such a nuisance existed, it could be abated or enjoined."

"What did you take that to mean?"

"Removed."

"The nuisance could be removed?"

"Yes, that's what I understood it to mean."

"Were you told anything about Chapter 823.01 of the Florida Statutes?"

"I don't remember the number. But they showed me a book with the pertinent law in it."

"Big tan book with orange, black, and gold trim?"

"Yes."

"Do you remember reading the words 'All nuisances which tend to annoy the community'? Do those words ring a bell?"

"Yes, they sound familiar."

"Is that the chapter you were shown?"

"It sounds like it, yes."

"Were you advised what to do if you wanted this public nuisance removed?"

"They said I would have to file a complaint, and if there was an indictment . . . if it could be determined that a public nuisance existed . . . well, it was all very complicated. I wasn't sure whether there'd be an indictment *before* or *after* a trial, or whether this would be a regular trial with a jury, it just sounded *very* complicated."

"Well, no one expects you to be a lawyer," I said.

"Thank God," she said, and we all burst out laughing, me, Atkins, the judge, the jury, everyone in the courtroom. Rutherford rapped her gavel, once and without real conviction. I waited for everything to calm down again.

"Miss Carmody," I said, "when you went to the police to inquire about public nuisance laws . . . did you have any *particular* nuisance in mind?"

"No, I just went there to inquire about the law."

"Do you recall talking to a Calusa P.D. detective named Wilbur Sholes?"

"I don't remember who I talked to. I was just there making an inquiry. I think there were two detectives I talked to."

"Didn't you talk primarily to a man named Wilbur Sholes?"

"I don't remember their names. One of them was black and the other one was white."

"Mr. Sholes is black, yes."

"I still don't remember his name."

"If I showed you his report on your conversation that day, do you think it might refresh your memory?"

"I didn't know there *was* a report. If a person goes to ask about the law, why would the police write a report?"

"Shall I answer that, Miss Carmody?"

"I just don't know why there was a report. How do I even know there *was* a report?"

"I have the report here, would you like to look at it? To refresh your memory?"

"You keep showing me these documents . . ."

"Miss Carmody, would it help your memory if you looked at this?"

"My memory doesn't need any help. My memory is fine, thanks."

"Good. Then answer this question. Did you go to the Public Safety Building to file a complaint against Mary Barton for . . ."

"I went there to ask about the law."

"*Let* me finish, please. File a complaint against Mary Barton for erecting, establishing, continuing, and maintaining a structure which tends to annoy the community, did you or did you not?"

"I did *not.*"

"Do you remember asking Wilbur Sholes if it was possible to bring charges against Mary Barton?"

"I asked him no such thing!"

"I'd like you to look at this report, Miss Carmody," I said, and handed it to her. "Can you tell me what's printed across the top of it?"

"Detective Division, Calusa Police Department."

"And under that?"

"Complaint Form."

"Thank you. Is there a date on that form?"

"May first."

"Is your name anywhere on that form?"

"Yes."

"Is it typed into the blank following the printed word 'Complainant.'"

"Yes."

"Can you look down to the bottom of that form and tell me who signed it?"

"Detective Wilbur R. Sholes."

"Now do you see the words 'Nature of Complaint'?"

"Yes."

"And do you see Detective Sholes's lengthy comments typed on the lines under those words?"

"Yes, I do."

"I'd like you to read his comments, please."

She read them silently. I waited. Atkins had his hands laced on his vest; he looked bored. Mary was staring at the witness, her neighborly next-door neighbor. All of this seemed news to her. She had described Charlotte Carmody as a bimbo and a busybody, but apparently she'd never known just how deep the woman's animosity ran.

Charlotte looked up.

"Have you now read Detective Sholes's comments?"

"I have."

"Do you now remember telling him that you wanted to file a complaint against Mary Barton because her garden was a public nuisance?"

"No, I don't remember saying that."

"Your Honor, may we approach, please?"

"Yes, come up."

"Your Honor," I said, "if Mr. Atkins will stipulate that this is a bona fide police report, I would like to move it into evidence without having to call an authenticating witness. I can always have Mr. Sholes brought in, but that would take a detective away from his normal duties and would cause the court unnecessary delay. I think Mr. Atkins will agree there can be no doubt as to the document's authenticity."

"Mr. Atkins?"

"Well, let me see it," he said. He glanced at it cursorily, nodded, and then said, "I have no objection."

"Thank you." Turning to the jury, I said, "In light of our bench conference, Your Honor, may we now have this police report marked and moved into evidence?"

"Exhibit D, the defense," Rutherford said.

"Miss Carmody, please read to the court, out loud, line three of Detective Sholes's comments, the paragraph beginning with the words 'Miss Carmody said an attorney friend had told her . . .' Do you see those words?"

"Yes."

"Please read them."

She cleared her throat, looked at the jury plaintively, as if she were being forced against her will to do something that might somehow incriminate her, and then began reading from the report:

" 'Miss Carmody said an attorney friend had told her there was a public nuisance law in Calusa, and if she went to the police with a complaint, they would tear down the nuisance. I explained that it wasn't that simple. I told her if she provided us with the information, we would turn it over to the state attorney, and he would then decide whether or not a crime was being committed. She seemed surprised that this would be considered a *crime* as such, stating that all she was talking about was an eyesore in her neighbor's yard. When I explained . . .' "

"You can stop right there, Miss Carmody."

She looked up at me.

"Do you now remember this conversation with Detective Sholes?"

"No, I don't remember saying any of this. I merely went there to ask about the law."

"Didn't Detective Sholes explain to you that maintaining a public nuisance was a second-degree misdemeanor?"

"Yes, I think he did. That's what I was there to ask about. The law."

"Punishable by a term of imprisonment not to exceed sixty days?"

"Yes, he said that."

"Did you express further surprise when he told you this?"

"I guess I was surprised, yes. I didn't think this was such a serious thing, an eyesore. Anyway, I didn't go there to ask about Mary's garden. As I told you, I went there . . ."

"Didn't you tell Detective Sholes that all you were talking about was quote an eyesore in your neighbor's yard unquote?"

"No, I did not."

"Detective Sholes is lying in his report, is that it?"

"I think he must have misunderstood me, is all."

"Did he misunderstand you when you told him to forget the whole thing?"

"I didn't tell him that. There was . . ."

"Doesn't Detective Sholes state in his report, 'Complainant advised me to forget the whole thing. I told her I'd be here if she changed her mind.' Do you see those words?"

"I see them, but I didn't tell him to forget anything. There was nothing to forget. I was there to make an inquiry. I got the information I needed, and I left."

"Without bringing a complaint."

"I wasn't there to bring a complaint."

"What happened, Miss Carmody? Did you decide that throwing a woman in jail for keeping a garden was too much even for your stomach?"

"Objection, Your Honor."

"Sustained."

"Tell me, Miss Carmody, when Detective Sholes described the law to you, didn't you change your mind about what you'd come there to do?"

"No."

"When he informed you that Chapter 823 was all about a *crime?*"

"No."

"When you heard that if you brought complaint, and if the state attorney decided there was a basis for the complaint and filed an information, and if a trial jury determined that a crime *had* in fact been committed, then Mary Barton could go to jail for sixty days . . . when you heard all this, didn't you change your mind and decide not to bring complaint after all?"

"I did not. I wasn't there to bring complaint in the first place."

"Then why did Detective Sholes write in his report, 'Complainant advised me to forget the . . .'?"

"Objection, Your Honor. She has no way of knowing why he wrote whatever he wrote," Atkins said.

"Sustained."

"I have no further questions, Your Honor. May I publish the report to the jury?"

"Certainly."

I went to the jury box and handed in the Detective Division report. Atkins was already on his way to the witness stand, hoping to pick up the pieces.

"Miss Carmody," he said, "did you have any reason to want to put up a fence between your property and Miss Barton's?"

"None."

"You did, in fact, as you've testified, enjoy a neighborly relationship with her?"

"Yes, I did."

"A good relationship, would you say?"

"I would say so."

"Never any trouble between you?"

"Never."

"Never a harsh word?"

"Never."

"You didn't consider her garden a public nuisance, did you?"

"I did not."

"Yet you went to the police to ask if there were any laws pertaining to public nuisances."

"Yes."

"Did you have a *specific* public nuisance in mind?"

"I don't remember now, it was such a long time ago. I think there may have been a refrigerator in someone's yard. An abandoned refrigerator. In a neighbor's yard. Something like that. I really can't remember."

"Would you call an abandoned refrigerator an eyesore?"

"I would."

"Did you tell Detective Sholes about this abandoned refrigerator?"

"I may have."

"This eyesore?"

"I may have."

"In a neighbor's yard?"

"Yes, I may have."

"Do you have many neighbors?"

"All up and down the street."

"So if you told Detective Sholes about an eyesore in a neighbor's yard, this could have been *any* neighbor's yard, isn't that so?"

"Any neighbor's yard."

"Not necessarily Mary Barton's yard."

"Not her yard at all."

"No further questions."

"Miss Carmody," I said, "did you just tell me, a few minutes ago, that you did not tell Detective Sholes about an eyesore in a neighbor's yard?"

"I said I . . ."

"Yes or no, please. Isn't that what you said under oath?"

"Yes."

"And did you not, just now, still under oath, tell the prosecuting attorney that you *did* discuss an eyesore in a neighbor's yard."

"I said I *might* have. I know I went there with the refrigerator in mind . . ."

"Well, we really have no way of knowing what was in your mind, do we, Miss Carmody? All we have is Detective Sholes's report to the effect that you mentioned an eyesore in a neighbor's garden, and then we have your denial under oath that you discussed this, and next we have your confirmation under oath that you did in *fact* discuss it. Now, which is it? *Did* you discuss an eyesore or did you *not*? You're still under oath, Miss Carmody."

"I may have discussed an eyesore. *If* I did . . ."

"Yes or no, please."

"I don't remember. It was a long time ago."

"Was the night of August thirty-first a long time ago?"

"Not as long ago as the first of May."

"On that night, was there a fence separating your property from Mary Barton's?"

"I've already testified that I saw Mary Barton . . ."

"Just answer the question, please."

"There was a fence separating our properties, yes."

"Who put up that fence? You or Mary Barton?"

"I did."

"When?"

"I don't remember exactly."

"Well, it couldn't have been there before June, isn't that right? The No Fences Rule was still in effect before June fifteenth, wasn't it?"

"Which question do you want me to answer?"

"She's right, Mr. Hope."

"I'm sorry, Your Honor. Was the fence there before June fifteenth?"

"No, it was not."

"So when *did* you put up that fence?"

"I didn't put it up personally. I hired a fence company to do it."

"When? Sometime later in June?"

"No, I don't think so."

"July then?"

"I think it was built sometime in July."

"When in July?"

"Around the middle of the month, I guess."

"Miss Carmody, didn't you just tell the prosecutor that you had no reason to put up a fence between your property and Miss Barton's?"

"Yes."

"Yet no more than a month after the rule regarding fences was changed, you *did* in fact cause a fence to be put up."

"Yes."

"Thank you, no further questions."

"Mr. Atkins?"

"The state rests its case, Your Honor."

Rutherford looked up at the wall clock.

"Well," she said, "it's eleven-thirty, so we can either . . . are you ready with your witnesses, Mr. Hope?"

"I am, Your Honor."

"What I think we'll do instead, let's recess for lunch now and be back here by one. That way we won't have to interrupt the witness when he's just getting started. Would that be all right with you, Mr. Atkins?"

"I have no objection to that, Your Honor."

"While we're talking scheduling, I know that Christmas is on everyone's mind, the jury's included, and I thought it might be advisable, so that we can finish our business here a little sooner if possible, I thought we might start a little earlier on Monday morning, eight-thirty rather than nine, and continue on through until five-thirty or thereabouts, unless the attorneys and the jury would find that too tiring. I myself think it's a good idea, or I wouldn't be suggesting it. Anyway, let's think about it over lunch and decide what we want to do when we get back. I want to warn the jury once again about discussing this case among yourselves or with anyone else, no conversations about the credibility of witnesses or anything you've heard or seen in this courtroom. You'll have plenty of time to discuss it later, when you're deliberating, but for now please keep your thoughts to yourselves. So let's all enjoy a pleasant lunch now, and I'll see you back here at one P.M."

The "pleasant" lunch I enjoyed with Mary Barton was in the P.C.R. at the Calusa County Jail, the letters standing for Prisoner's Consultation Room, a euphemism if ever there was one. As cheerless as a cell, lighted by overhead fluorescents, the small square room was sparsely furnished with a Formica-topped metal table and four chairs around it, its single window covered with steel-colored venetian blinds closed tight against the fierce noonday sun. Normally, when you joined your client here, he or she was wearing jailhouse threads. Mary was dressed in what she'd worn to court that morning, a simple beige cotton suit with a pale green blouse that subtly complemented the blue of her eyes and the iron gray of her hair, the color of which had been the cause for much discussion during the past week's testimony.

We ordered sandwiches, which the guard examined as if files or saws were hidden between the slices of bread, and soft drinks, which the guard shook vigorously to make sure nothing rattled inside the cardboard containers. He stood just outside the locked door, the back of his head visible in a diamond-shaped, reinforced-glass panel.

I told Mary who our witnesses would be.

There weren't many of them.

I told her I thought we'd pretty much eliminated Charlotte Carmody as a credible witness since we'd been able to show bias. This left all the people who claimed they'd seen her on that now infamous weekend, whose testimony may or may not have weighed heavily with the jury, there was no way of telling. Our own witnesses would further try to prove misidentification. Toward that end, I hoped they'd be helpful. When she herself testified, of course—

"I'm not sure I want to testify," she said.

We'd been through this before. I had hoped we wouldn't have to go through it yet another time. I had spent hours and hours preparing her for the moment when I would put her on the stand. Now, hearing her tell me, once again, that she wasn't sure she wanted to testify, I sighed in defeat and said, "Then the jury will find against you."

"That's not my understanding of it."

"I know what Rutherford told them . . ."

"She said I have the absolute right to remain silent. She said if I didn't take the stand, the jury wasn't to draw any inference of guilt. She . . ."

"But they always do."

"She told them it shouldn't influence their verdict in any manner what—"

"But it does."

"It shouldn't."

"Mary, it does, believe me. Those men and women want to hear what you have to say about these terrible crimes charged against you. They want to look you in the eye and take your measure. They want to hear you say what you were doing that weekend if you weren't out killing children."

"You know I wasn't."

"Yes, *I* know it," I said, with more conviction than I felt, "but *they* don't."

"Then put someone on who'll tell them what kind of person I am. Put Melissa Lowndes on . . ."

"I plan to."

"Let her tell them what kind of teacher I was . . ."

"I *am* putting her on. I gave you the witness list, Mary, you *know* who I'm putting on."

"You located Fanny Johnstone, did you?" she said, and smiled for the first time since I'd known her.

"She flew in late yesterday," I said. "We've already gone over everything we discussed on the phone."

"Couldn't you get anyone else from the Wagner School?"

"No one who knew you while you were teaching there. I'd like another character witness, believe me. I didn't think Rutherford would let me have *any*. 'Inappropriate in a case of this gravity, Mr. Hope' . . . well, you know her style."

"She would've made a good teacher," Mary said, somewhat wistfully, I thought.

"She finally caved when I cited the Florida and federal rules on a defendant's right to prove good character. 'But three will suffice, Mr. Hope,' " I said, doing Rutherford again. "The point is, Melissa and Mrs. Johnstone can only tell the jury what sort of person you *used* to be. Neither of them can say what you were like on the weekend of August twenty-eighth, when those children were being murdered. Our strongest witness'll be *you*, Mary. You're the only one who can . . ."

"I didn't kill those children," she said.

"Then get up there and tell them you didn't."

"It wasn't me," she said.

"Then testify."

"I have to think about it," she said.

"Think fast," I said.

I called Warren Chambers from a phone booth at ten minutes to one that afternoon.

"Three stops," I said.

"Where?" he said.

"Purcell, New Mexico . . ."

"Is it warm there?"

"Renegade, South Dakota . . ."

"Have a heart, Matthew."

"And Denver, Colorado."

"What am I looking for?"

"A character witness who'll nail the whole thing down."

"Like who, Matthew?"

"Like a kid she saved from drowning."

"Must be millions of those around."

"Or a kid she nursed back to health after a serious illness."

"Those, too."

"Warren, I need someone who'll get up on that stand and tell the jury that Mary Barton once did such an *overwhelmingly* selfless thing . . ."

"I get the point. Tell me what happened."

"She may refuse to testify."

"I'll catch the first plane out," Warren said.

She was the one who burned down the house. I couldn't tell them she'd done it because they died in the fire. They wouldn't have believed me, anyway; they'd already made up their minds about me. Every time I told them she was the one doing all the bad things, they said I was crazy. They said I was making it all up, she was doing this, she was doing that. They took me to see a doctor once. He asked me all sorts of questions about her. Why was I making up such awful things about her? I told him they were always blaming me for what she did. I told him all I was doing was trying to protect myself. Because the things she did kept getting worse and worse. He asked me why I thought she was doing these terrible things. I said it was because she hated me.

I told him about the squashed frog in my bed.

I told him about the time she made me drink my own urine.

I told him about her killing the cat.

I even showed him the scars, he was a doctor. Lifted my skirt and lowered my panties, and showed him where she'd cut me there. He asked me if I was sure I hadn't done that to myself.

He advised me to be a good girl and not to tell so many lies. Otherwise, they'd have to see about me.

The night the house burned down . . .

I was twenty-one years old, visiting home after graduation, sleeping like a babe again in my own bed. I woke up coughing. The room was full of smoke. The first thing I thought was she's back. I ran to the door and threw it open and the hallway outside my bedroom was full of flames, it was as if I'd died and gone to hell, it was as if all the terrible things they said would happen to me if I kept on lying were happening right that minute, flames leaping and coming at me, forcing me back away from the door, go away, I thought, leave me alone, I thought. I slammed the door shut and ran across the room, past the shelves with all my old dolls on them, past the beds and over to the window across the room. The bedroom was on the second story of the house, I struggled with the latch, I couldn't get the latch open, I ran back to the shelves and took Pitty Pat Doakes from the middle shelf, she was the blonde doll with the blue eyes and blonde lashes and a head made of some kind of hard plastic instead of the soft stuff some of the other dolls were made of that made them feel real and cuddly. I hit the window with Pitty Pat's head. Held her by her legs and swung her head at the window, kept smashing the window with her head, thinking leave me alone, leave me alone, leave me alone. There was a rush of air into the room and the scorched door suddenly burst into flame. I was wearing a baby-doll nightgown, no panties, I could hear fire engines coming now, and I knew the firemen would see me, the firemen would see the scars where she'd cut me all those years ago. But the door was on fire and the room was full of smoke and I didn't care who saw me, I had to tell somebody I wasn't the one who'd done this, it was her again. I climbed over the lower frame of the paneless window and grabbed it tight in both hands, cutting my hands, there were still some shards, and hung there for a moment with the wind blowing under my nightgown, and then I let myself fall to the ground, let myself go limp and fell to the ground with my fingers and palms bleeding and all I could think was I have to run far away from here or she'll come back and find me again and again and again no matter how hard I try to get away from her.

13

The first witness I called that afternoon was the man to whom Mary had delivered her red Camry on the morning of August 27, the day before the weekend killing spree started. Joseph Michael Ryan was in his late thirties, dressed for court in what looked like the suit in which he'd received his first holy communion. His hair neatly combed, his face scrubbed clean, his trousers creased, and his shoes shined, he looked more like a traveling salesman than the service manager of Meridian Toyota, but such he was.

He seemed nervous.

I put him through the paces of identifying himself and his occupation and the location of his place of business, and then I said, "Do you know Mary Barton personally?"

"I know her as a customer, yes."

"A customer of Meridian Toyota?"

"Yes. She brings her car in for service there. Well, she *bought* the car there."

"Mr. Ryan, do you keep records of every car brought to you for service?"

"I do."

"Have you had occasion to consult those records recently?"

"I have."

"Did you consult them at my request?"

"I did."

"Mr. Ryan, would you take a look at this, please?" I said, and handed him a sheet of paper. "Your Honor, I would like this marked for identification, please."

"E, the defense," Rutherford said.

"Can you tell me what this is, please?"

"It's a photocopy of a service slip for August twenty-seventh."

"What do you mean by a service slip?"

"What I write up when a customer brings a car in."

"Did you personally write up this slip?"

"I did."

"This is your handwriting, is it?"

"It is."

"Is there a customer's name on this particular slip?"

"There is."

"What is that name?"

"Mary Barton."

"Do you remember Mary Barton bringing her car in for service on August twenty-seventh?"

"I do."

"Is her car identified anyplace on that slip?"

"Yes. It's a red 1992 Camry."

"Is the description of the car also in your handwriting?"

"Yes, it is."

"Anything else on that slip that would identify the car?"

"The license plate number."

"The license plate doesn't begin with the letters Y-A-M, does it?"

"No, sir, it does not."

"What time did Mary Barton bring the car in that morning?"

"Eight o'clock in the morning. We like to get the cars in early."

"Is there anything on that slip that would indicate why the car was brought in?"

"Thirty-thousand-mile service."

"Is that what you wrote on the slip?"

"Yes, at the time. It later turned out . . ."

"But at the time, that's what you wrote."

"Yes. Well, she also wanted the tires rotated and balanced, and she said when she stepped on the brake pedal, it seemed a little soft. She asked me to check that. So I wrote all that down. It's all there on the slip."

"How long does that normally take? A thirty-thousand-mile service?"

"Usually the car's ready that same day. The end of the day."

"At what time did Miss Barton leave Meridian Toyota that morning, would you know?"

"Sometime between eight-fifteen and eight-thirty."

"By what means of transportation?"

"We gave her a lift home."

"By that, you mean . . ."

"Someone drove her home. That's a courtesy we have for people who bought their cars from us."

"Would you know who drove her home?"

"Yes, it was Alex Corman."

"Is Mr. Corman one of your service people?"

"He's this kid we hire for the purpose of doing things like that, a sort of a gofer. Drives people home, goes to get lunch for us, like that."

"Did Miss Barton in fact pick up her car that very same day?"

"No, she did not. I called her after we looked it over, told her she was going to need new brake pads, front and back, and should I go ahead? But I also found a problem she hadn't mentioned, it was with the radio antenna, we discovered it wasn't retracting fully, and when we inspected it, the motor mechanism was shot, and it needed to be replaced. She said I should go ahead and do everything, the brakes and the antenna, too. Problem was, I didn't have a new antenna in stock. I told her I couldn't get one till Monday, did she want me to hold the car here over the weekend or did she want to pick it up and then bring it in again Monday, when I'd have the antenna? She said I should hold it."

"And *did* you hold her car there over the weekend?"

"Yeah. Inside. Like she told me. She didn't want us to leave it outside."

"Did you replace the antenna on Monday?"

"I did. The brake pads, too."

"When did Miss Barton pick up her car again?"

"Tuesday morning, the first of September."

"At what time?"

"She got there around nine-thirty."

"Did you see her arrive?"

"I did."

"How did she get there?"

"She was in a car with a gentleman."

"What kind of car?"

"I didn't notice. Not a Toyota."

"Do you know who the gentleman was?"

"I do not."

"Did you see her when she left?"

"Yes, I personally brought the car around for her. I like Miss Barton, so I try to . . . ."

"Objection."

"Sustained."

"Did you see her drive off?"

"I did."

"What time was that?"

"A little before ten."

"Thank you, I have no further questions. Your Honor, I would like this service slip moved into evidence and published to the jury, please."

"Show it to the jury," Rutherford said to the clerk. "Mr. Atkins?"

"I have no questions," he said, managing to convey to the jury by the tone of his voice and the slight shrug of his shoulders that the witness was totally unimportant one way or the other and it would be a sheer waste of time to ask him anything about a red Camry when the car the killer was driving was a white LeBaron. Which was fine by me. I called my next witness.

Jimmy Di Falco was a man in his early seventies, spry and suntanned, a halo of white hair around an otherwise bald head, wearing a matching white suit that made him look like a Kentucky colonel. I asked him to tell me his name, his address, his occupation . . .

"I'm retired."

. . . and the nature of his relationship with Mary Barton.

"We're good friends," he said.

"Mr. Di Falco," I said, "did you drive Miss Barton to Meridian Toyota on the morning of September first this year?"

"Yes, I did," he said.

"Do you remember why you went there?"

"Her car was in for service. She was going to pick it up."

"What kind of car, do you know?"

"A red Camry. I don't know the year."

"Have you ever seen her driving that car?"

"Of course I saw her driving it."

"You know it to be her car?"

"Yes, I do."

"Would you know the license plate number?"

"No, I'm sorry, I don't."

"Do you know if it begins with the letters Y-A-M?"

"Objection. Witness just said he doesn't know the . . ."

"Sustained."

"Mr. Di Falco, where did you pick up Miss Barton that morning?"

"At her house."

"2716 Gideon Way?"

"Yes."

"What time was this?"

"About nine-thirty."

"Did you go directly to Meridian Toyota?"

"Yes."

"Drove straight there?"

"Yes."

"No stops along the way?"

"None."

"You didn't happen to drop her off at the Templeton Mall, did you?"

"No, that's in the other direction."

"You didn't pick her up *before* nine-thirty, did you?"

"No, it was nine-thirty."

"And you drove directly to Meridian Toyota?"

"Directly."

"What time did you get there?"

"Around a quarter to ten. There was a lot of traffic on the Trail."

"Did you leave as soon as you'd dropped her off?"

"No, I waited to make sure her car was ready."

"Then what?"

"She told me it was okay to go, so I left."

"What time was that?"

"Five to ten? Something like that."

"Did you have occasion to see Miss Barton later that day?"

"No, I didn't."

"Or talk to her?"

"No, I didn't."

"So the last time you saw her was at five to ten that Tuesday morning?"

"Yes. I waved to her as I drove off."

"Thank you, Mr. Di Falco, I have nothing further."

Atkins knew where I'd gone, of course. His earlier witness, the dry cleaner Jerry Callahan, had testified that at eight-thirty A.M. on Tuesday, the first day of September, a woman answering Mary Barton's description had dropped off a bloodstained dress at Dri-Quik Cleaners in the Templeton Mall. Well, at eight-thirty A.M., Mary was without wheels. And if she was home at *nine*-thirty when Di Falco picked her up . . .

"Mr. Di Falco," Atkins said, "are you normally a very fast driver?"

"I drive within the speed limit."

"Do you know what the speed limit is on the Tamiami Trail?"

"Depends which part of the Trail."

"The part you covered while driving the defendant to Meridian Toyota."

"I believe it's forty miles an hour."

"And you say there was heavy traffic on the Trail that morning."

"Very heavy."

"Heading south?"

"Both directions. North and south. Traffic on both sides of the Trail."

"Is it correct to say that driving south, at forty miles an hour, in heavy traffic, it took you fifteen minutes to get from the defendant's house to Meridian Toyota on Meridian Avenue and Jackson Street?"

"Fifteen minutes, more or less, that's right."

"Mr. Di Falco, have you ever driven from the defendant's house to the Templeton Mall?"

"I don't believe I have."

"Have you ever driven from your home to the Templeton Mall?"

"Yes, I have."

"You gave your address as 1172 Barrida Street . . ."

"Yes."

"Can you tell us where that is?"

"On Barrida and Cooper. It's the condominium there. The Dunes."

"How far is that from the defendant's house?"

"It's just up the road from her. Just off Cooper Avenue."

"In minutes, how far would you say it is from your condominium to the defendant's house? Door-to-door?"

"Five minutes?"

"Five minutes. Now Mr. Di Falco, how long does it take from your home to the Templeton Mall?"

"Depending on traffic, it might . . ."

"In heavy traffic. Driving north, at forty miles an hour. How long would it take from your home?"

"Twenty-five minutes, depending."

"Does the defendant live *farther* from the mall than you do, or closer?"

"Closer. She's on the way to the mall."

"Five minutes *closer* to the mall?"

"Yes. Around five minutes."

"Would you agree then . . ."

I really had to admire his perseverance.

". . . that driving north from the defendant's house to the Templeton Mall, in heavy traffic at forty miles an hour, would take no longer than twenty minutes?"

"Well, I don't know about that."

"You said it took twenty-five minutes from where you live . . ."

"Well, yes . . ."

"And the defendant is five minutes *closer,* on the *way* to the mall, isn't that what you said?"

"Well . . . yes."

"Then would you agree that someone driving at forty miles an hour in heavy traffic could make it from the defendant's house to the mall in twenty minutes?"

"Yes, I would agree."

"Or *back* from the mall in that same amount of time?"

"Yes."

"So that on that morning of September first, given the traffic and all, it would have been possible for someone . . ."

"Objection."

"Sustained."

"But you do agree the distance from the defendant's house to the mall can be covered in twenty minutes, even observing the speed limit and even in very heavy traffic."

"Yes, I do."

"No further questions."

I went back to the witness stand and said, "Mr. Di Falco, I don't suppose you saw a white car in Mary's driveway when you picked her up that morning, did you?"

"No, I didn't."

"Or any *other* kind of car, did you?"

"No."

"Did she mention having rented a car to use while her own car was in for service?"

"No, she didn't."

"Didn't say anything about a white Chrysler LeBaron, did she?"

"No."

"Nothing further, thank you."

"Mr. Di Falco," Atkins said, "what was the defendant wearing when you picked her up that morning?"

"I didn't notice."

"Was she wearing a dress?"

"Objection. Witness has already . . ."

"I'll allow it."

"Can I answer?"

"Yes, go ahead."

"It was some kind of dress, yes."

"Not slacks? Or shorts?"

"No, a dress."

"Are you familiar with the name Laura Ashley?"

"No, I'm sorry, I'm not."

"Then you wouldn't know if she was wearing a Laura Ashley dress?"

"No, I wouldn't.

"Was it a long dress?"

"I think it was, yes."

"Something with a flower design?"

"I don't know."

"Was she wearing shoes?"

"Well, she was planning to drive her car home, I'm sure she was wearing shoes."

"What kind of shoes?"

"I really don't know."

"No further questions."

Rutherford looked up at the clock.

"Call Melissa Lowndes, please," I said.

I had deliberately opted not to introduce any evidence regarding the rental car because I was afraid it might backfire. If I opened that door, the state would march right through it, and they might find something harmful to my client. I had no way of knowing whether Atkins had assigned detectives from the State Attorney's Office to locate the renter of the ubiquitous Y-A-M car. If he'd learned anything about it, he had chosen not to bring it up at the trial, probably for a reason directly opposite to mine: if the rented car had been subsequently stolen, he had no way of proving that Mary was the person who'd stolen it. In which case, the gray-haired lady snatching children all over the countryside could have been someone else entirely. Since his entire case hinged on identification, he would not be willing to take that chance—if, in fact, he already knew all the facts. On the other hand, I was unwilling to bring up the car in case he *didn't* know about it, because then I'd be taking the chance that he'd later find something to link the car irrevocably and irretrievably to Mary. However you looked at it, the car was a Mexican standoff.

I had tried to show that Mary had no car at her disposal that weekend. Her own car was in the shop for repairs. A Toyota courtesy car had driven her home, and she had relied upon the good services of a friend to drive her back there on the same Tuesday she was allegedly seen in the Templeton Mall, some thirty-five minutes away in the opposite direction.

I would, of course, summarize all this for the jury during my closing argument, but now it was time to parade my character witnesses. I'd been allowed three, and two of them were in the courthouse this morning. I was praying that Warren would find a third and conclusive one somewhere in the wilds of New Mexico, Colorado, or South Dakota. There were very definite risks in allowing character witnesses to testify—but time was running short, and I did not believe in Santa Claus.

The British normally make very good witnesses. Their speech intimidates most Americans, who feel we sound sloppy in the presence of anyone speaking so impeccably. Granting them the superiority of language, we then take the next tiny step and assume the Brits are superior in other ways as well, especially where it comes to honor and integrity. A Brit under oath would sooner walk naked around the Serpentine in Hyde Park than tell a lie. Or so we believe. Believing this, we listen as if in the presence of royalty. It is a great advantage to have a Brit take the stand.

Nor does it hurt if the Brit in question is an attractive woman in her thirties, beautifully dressed, looking cool and unruffled in a dark blue suit and matching pumps. Sounding like the Queen Mum herself, she took the oath, sat, adjusted the microphone, answered my introductory questions, and waited in polite anticipation for my first real question.

"Miss Lowndes," I said, "when did you first meet Mary Barton?"

And now she told a rapt jury all about the tall woman she'd met on a grassy knoll in England some twenty years ago, Melissa, eleven years old at the time, a shy and stuttering young girl wrapped in a long overcoat and sitting beneath a gnarled oak. On that windy hilltop, she'd known instantly that this woman would become the most important influence in her young life, a teacher who would completely change the way she looked at herself and the world around her, a mentor, a role model, and an inspiration.

And as I questioned her further, she went on to tell the jury all that she had told me earlier, and much more besides, relating anecdote and tale, creating a warm and loving portrait of the vibrant teacher who'd been so cherished by her students all those years ago, and who had left a lasting impression on all of them.

"I have never met a more peaceable, gentle, loving person," she said. "An injured butterfly could bring tears to her eyes."

Her voice almost a whisper.

"She led us gently and carefully through years that were enormously difficult for young girls coming of age . . ."

Her own eyes misting now.

"She was a mother to all of us who were far from our own mothers. She was magnificent and grand, a wonderful teacher and a gentle, kind, and generous woman. None of us who knew her will ever forget her. None of us who knew her will ever stop loving her."

The courtroom was silent.

Melissa took a lace-edged handkerchief from her handbag and dabbed at her eyes with it. I let the moment sink in.

"Had you ever seen her commit an unkind act to a child?" I asked.

"Never."

"A violent act to a child?"

"Never."

"An act to any of her young girl students that was anything but nurturing, caring, and loving?"

"Never."

"Thank you," I said, "no further questions."

Atkins came to the stand quickly, eager to dispel whatever sympathy Melissa's heartfelt testimony had generated.

"You've used the word 'gentle' several times in describing the defendant," he said, "isn't that correct?"

"That's correct."

I knew where he was going, but I didn't know what he had. The risks of bringing on a character witness are manifold. In any criminal trial, the prosecutor cannot attempt to prove the facts of the crime charged by showing a predisposition to that crime through prior bad acts. But if the defense attorney brings on a character witness, the prosecutor can then . . .

"Would it change your opinion if I described the many *un*gentle acts . . ."

There it was.

". . . Mary Barton has committed since the time you knew her?"

"Nothing would change my opinion of Mary Barton."

"Would it change your opinion, for example, if I told you . . ."

"Your Honor, witness has already stated that nothing would change . . ."

"You opened the door, Mr. Hope. I'll allow it."

"Would it change your opinion," Atkins said, "if I told you that last summer, while the defendant was tending her garden, a group of children from the neighborhood strolled by and began chanting 'Mary, Mary, quite contrary,' and she picked up a bottle she was attempting to affix to one of the towers and hurled it at the children, would that change your opinion of her 'gentle' manner with children?"

"No, it would not."

"You've also said you've never seen her commit an unkind act to a child."

"Yes."

"It doesn't change your opinion to know that she threw a bottle at these children?"

"No, it doesn't."

"Would it change your opinion if I told you she once chased a little girl from her doorstep by threatening her with a broom?"

"No, it would not."

"Little girl selling raffle tickets, chased her off her doorstep with a broom—that wouldn't change your opinion?"

"No."

"You said you'd never seen her commit a violent act to a child?"

"That's right."

"But it doesn't change your opinion, now that you know she swung a broom at a child?"

"It does not change my opinion, no."

"Now you also said she was a kind and generous woman . . ."

"Yes."

"Would it change your opinion of her if I told you . . . ?"

"Your Honor," I said, "I really must object to this improper . . ."

"Come on up," Rutherford said.

We went up to the bench.

"Where are you getting all this stuff?" she asked Atkins.

"Your Honor, I'm basing it in good faith on reports from detectives who canvassed the defendant's neighborhood to collect the information."

"Detectives from the State Attorney's Office?"

"Yes, Your Honor."

"Your Honor," I said, "defendant is charged with three counts of first-degree murder. Chasing a kid off the doorstep . . ."

"Well, Mr. Hope, I think you opened the door and now we've got to let the prosecutor in. He's just told me the basis of these questions. They're not fabricated, they're based on a canvass and are being asked in good faith. So I'll continue to allow them. But I warn you, Mr. Atkins, if you veer off into the hypothetical, I'll cut you off."

"Thank you, Your Honor."

"I must again warn the jury," Rutherford said to them, "that questions are not evidence. Only the witness's *answers* are evidence. Proceed, Mr. Atkins."

Whereupon he began running down the rest of his laundry list of the minor neighborhood transgressions Mary had committed since she'd moved to Crescent Cove, harping on the words Melissa had used during my direct examination and turning them to his use during the cross. All of the incidents he'd dredged up had to do with children taunting Mary, and focused on her often violent responses to them, both verbal *and* physical, as with the hurling of the bottle. But as he was relating one incident . . .

". . . the defendant threw a full bucket of water at the child, would that change . . . ?"

. . . Melissa shouted in response, "That's what *you're* telling me!"

. . . and Judge Rutherford jumped in at once.

"Mr. Atkins," she said, "I really think the jury has got the message by now, don't you? I'll permit the witness to answer this one last question and then we'll move on. I'm sure you can go on with this all day . . ."

"I can, Your Honor," Atkins said, and nodded curtly.

"Oh, I'm sure you can, but I don't think that will be necessary. Put your question again, please. And, Miss, no more outbursts, or you'll be held in contempt."

"Miss Lowndes," Atkins said, "would it change your opinion of the defendant's kindness to children if I told you that when a little girl asked for a drink of water while she came upon the defendant tending her garden, the defendant threw a full bucket of water at her?"

"It would not change my opinion of her kindness to children."

"Tell me, Miss Lowndes," Atkins asked confidentially, "are you paying the defendant's legal fees?"

From somewhere at the back of the courtroom, there was a sharp gasp.

Atkins waited.

"Miss Lowndes?" he said. "Would you answer the question, please?"

"Yes."

"Yes, you are paying her legal fees?"

"Yes, I am."

"Thank you," Atkins said with a curt nod. "I have no further questions."

I went to the stand again.

"Miss Lowndes," I said, "why are you paying Miss Barton's legal fees?"

"Because I have every faith in her innocence," Melissa said, and I could have kissed her.

"Nothing further," I said.

"Just one last question," Atkins said, rising, and not bothering to move from the prosecution's table. "Is your unshaken faith in the defendant's kindness and gentleness and grandeur and magnificence and peacefulness and generosity colored by the fact . . . ?"

"Objection, Your Honor!"

"I'll let him finish the question."

"Is this unshaken faith of yours colored by the fact that you have a sizable investment in the outcome of . . . ?"

"Objection, Your Honor!"

"Overruled."

"A sizable investment, as I say, in the outcome of this trial?"

"My faith has nothing whatever to do with that."

Atkins smiled knowingly.

"No further questions," he said.

I had none, either.

I asked the court to call my next witness, Mrs. Fanny Heald Johnstone, and waited while the bailiff went across the hall for her. She came in some five minutes later, wearing a black dress with laced black shoes, a black hat, a black handbag, and a string of pearls that looked pristinely white in contrast. She was carrying a wooden cane, as well she might have: she was eighty-four years old. Bright blue eyes in a powdered white face. No lipstick. White hair to match the pearls. Hands trembling a bit with Parkinson's, head occasionally jerking as well. I had spoken with her last night, after she'd arrived in Calusa, preparing her for her testimony today. I knew her to be bright and articulate and feisty.

The preliminaries over with, I said, "Miss Johnstone, are you familiar with a school called the Elizabeth Wagner School for Girls?"

"I am," she said.

Sharp little nod. Leaning into the microphone when she answered. Blue eyes intent.

"What sort of school is it?"

"It's a private school for girls. Grades six through fourteen."

"What ages would that encompass, Miss Johnstone?"

"Twelve through eighteen years old. The equivalent of middle school through high school."

"Where is the Wagner School located, can you tell me?"

"In Purcell, New Mexico. Foothills of the Sangre de Cristo Mountains."

"Were you once employed at the school?"

"I was."

"When was that?"

"From 1948 to 1973, a total of twenty-five years. I was forty when I joined the staff and sixty-five when I retired."

"In what capacity were you employed?"

"I was headmistress."

"In that capacity, did you have occasion to hire a young woman named Mary Barton?"

"I did."

"Would you know Mary Barton if you saw her today?"

"Well, yes, I think I can recognize that sweet little face over there," she said, and smiled across to where Mary was sitting at the defense table. Mary smiled back. Atkins knew better than to object.

"Even with all that gray hair," Fanny added, and smiled again. Still no objection from Atkins.

"For what position did you hire Miss Barton?"

"As a teacher of English."

"With what credentials did she come to you?"

"Bachelor of arts, English major, from the University of Colorado; master's degree in the teaching of English from New York University. She'd graduated with honors from NYU."

"When did you hire her?"

"She applied for the job in August, I believe it was . . ."

"Of which year, please?"

"1957. I hired her on the spot, and she began work in September."

"Of that same year."

"That same year, yes. September of 1957."

"What kind of teacher was she?"

"Marvelous."

"Can you tell us what you mean by that?"

"I mean marvelous in every way. This was her first teaching job, but it was obvious to me from the very start that Mary had a true calling. Oh, the way she taught those children! The wonderfully inventive ways she found to make learning a joy and a pleasure! No, forgive me, it was much more than that. To be taught by Mary Barton was an honor and a privilege. The children adored her. I can remember . . ."

And she went on to tell the jury how the young Mary Barton . . .

"She was only twenty-three when she came to us, you know, well, almost twenty-four . . ."

. . . once took her class to a Navajo reservation to witness a ritual recital of prayer and song, and later found a way to relate the performance to a mantra written by an Indian of quite another sort, an obscure Hindu poet from the Rajasthan.

The jury listened carefully, students themselves for a moment, caught in the spell of the old lady's voice as she recited from memory the invocation to the sun-god Savitri.

Atkins had a sour look on his face.

Mary was remembering.

I was wondering how much Fanny Heald Johnstone had contributed to making her the teacher she'd become.

"And at other times," she said, and unfurled—like a bolt of golden silk—wave after wave of memories of New Mexico, the parched desert coming to life in a Florida courtroom ablaze with afternoon sunshine, the girls adoringly following Mary as she piped their way through adolescence and into young womanhood, teaching them always to explore, to reach, to grasp . . .

"And to be kind to others," Fanny said. "And gentle. And loving. And caring. This was Mary Barton. I'm sure this is Mary Barton now. She cannot have changed."

"No further questions," I said.

"Just a few questions," Atkins said, and approached the stand. "Miss Johnstone," he said, "can you . . ."

"Mrs. Johnstone," she corrected, like the good headmistress she surely must have been.

"Mrs. Johnstone, yes, forgive me. You say the defendant began teaching at the Wagner School in September of 1957 . . ."

"Yes, that's right."

"When did she leave the school?"

"In June of 1963."

"Was she dismissed?"

"I should say not! She asked to be relieved of her duties."

"Did she give you any reason for wanting to leave?"

"She said she wanted to live abroad for a while. I believe she moved to England."

"Did you hear from her again after she left the school?"

"No, I never did," Fanny said, and there was such a terrible sense of loss in her voice that it threw even Atkins. He hesitated a moment and then said into the stillness of the hushed court-room, "Just left and was never heard from again, is that it?"

"Yes."

"Left her colleagues . . ."

"Yes."

". . . and her beloved little girls . . ."

"Yes."

"And went off to England."

"Yes."

"No further questions," he said.

"Nothing further," I said. "Please call Detective Morris Bloom."

I called Morris Bloom as a witness not because I wanted to hear the details of his arrival at Mary's house on September 1, but because I was hoping to elicit from him, as an experienced detective, information that would eventually prove damaging to the state's case. Atkins knew I would be calling him; his name was on the witness list I'd supplied. He did not know what I would be asking him.

Tall and shambling and wearing a rumpled blue suit, a white shirt and a blue tie, Bloom took the stand, was sworn in, and sat. Heavy-set, some six feet three inches tall, weighing something over two hundred pounds, with shaggy black eyebrows, dark brown eyes that always seemed on the imminent edge of tears, his huge hands folded in his lap now, he sat there calmly, a veteran of many court appearances, waiting for my first question. I knew Bloom well, and liked him a lot. He had not been deposed; he had no idea what questions I would be asking him.

"Detective Bloom," I said, "how long have you been working for the Calusa Police Department?"

"It was eleven years on November twentieth."

"As a detective all that time?"

"Yes."

"Where did you work before then?"

"For the Nassau County Police Department."

"In New York?"

"Yes, on Long Island. In New York, yes."

"Were you a detective there as well?"

"For six years. Before then I was a sergeant of police and before then a patrolman, what used to be called a patrolman in those days, what they call a police officer now. Because there are *women* patrolmen."

"How many years in all have you been a working policeman?"

"Twenty-eight years."

"Have you investigated many homicides during those years?"

"I have."

"How many would you say you've investigated?"

"I worked ninety-three . . . no, wait, ninety-four . . . homicide cases while I was with the Nassau P.D. I've worked fifteen since I came to Calusa."

"A total of a hundred and nine cases."

"Yes."

"Detective Bloom, at what time did you arrive at the Barton house on September first?"

"It was around one o'clock."

"Who summoned you to the scene?"

"Sergeant Thomas Wilkes, Calusa P.D."

"Were you alone?"

"No, I drove over with my partner, Detective Cooper Rawles."

"Had the sergeant told you why he needed you?"

"Yes, he told me on the phone that there were some dead bodies buried in the backyard there."

"This is what brought you to the scene?"

"Yes. That's why the suits were called in. The detectives, that is."

"To investigate what appeared to be a homicide, is that right?"

"Well, *multiple* homicide. There were three bodies."

"Did Sergeant Wilkes show you the bodies?"

"He did."

"Did you then talk to Mary Barton?"

"I did. Well, Coop and I did. My partner. Detective Rawles."

"Questioned her, did you?"

"Yes, we questioned her. It was her house, her garden, we would normally question someone like that."

"You didn't read her her rights at that time, did you?"

"No, this was still a field investigation."

"When did it stop being a field investigation?"

"When we took her into custody."

"When did you do that?"

"After we talked to the lady next door."

"By 'the lady next door,' do you mean Charlotte Carmody?"

"Yes, that was the woman we spoke to."

"And did she positively identify Mary Barton as the person she saw burying a child in the backyard?"

"Positively identified her, yes."

"Was this the *only* identification of her at that time?"

"Yes. The other identifications, the people who saw her here and there, they all came in later."

"So, in effect, you took Miss Barton into custody and charged her on the basis of Charlotte Carmody's . . ."

"Well, there was further questioning before we charged her. Patricia Demming, an assistant state attorney, came in, and there was a lot of questioning before we formally charged her. We didn't charge her till we thought we had real meat here."

"But when she *was* finally charged, it was because of Miss Carmody's positive identification, wasn't it?"

"That and the fact that the bodies were, after all, found in her backyard. The defendant's backyard."

"Which, I'm sure you know, doesn't indicate the defendant *put* them there."

"Well, there are certain things you naturally assume in police work. If, for example, you find a murder weapon under somebody's bed, you've got to reasonably assume the gun belongs to that person and not that it was carried there by someone else and put under that bed."

A faint smile suddenly appeared on Atkins's face. He was thinking Bloom was a terrific witness. He was thinking Bloom had just contradicted everything I'd brought out with Sergeant Wilkes.

"We're not talking police work now, Mr. Bloom, we're talking legal proof of murder . . . proof of murder beyond a reasonable doubt. And surely you know that in a murder trial, the discovery of a victim or victims on a person's property is not clear and positive *proof* that the person *owning* that property is the person who committed the crime. You know that, don't you?"

"Yes, I know that. All I'm saying is that we had reasonable cause to charge Mary Barton with those murders. Is all I'm saying."

"Do you agree that the primary factor in bringing charges was the positive identification by Miss Carmody?"

"I would agree that was one of the main reasons we felt we had a case, yes."

"Now, Mr. Bloom, you've stated that you've been a detective for twenty-eight years."

"I have."

"And during all those years, you must have investigated a great many cases based on identification."

"I have."

"And a great many as well, I'm sure, in which *mis*identification . . ."

"Objection. Leading."

"Sustained."

"Have you ever investigated cases that turned out to have been based on misidentification?"

"I have."

"How many such cases have you investigated?"

"I really can't give you an exact number."

"Would you call identification a *strong* form of evidence?"

"Objection! Irrelevant!"

"Your Honor, this goes *directly* to the quality and quantity of the evidence against my client!"

"I'll allow it," Rutherford said.

But Atkins knew where I was going now, and he was ready to jump in as often as necessary to stop me from bringing out what I was determined to have the jury hear.

"Mr. Bloom," I said, "would you please answer the question? Do you consider identification a *strong* form of evidence?"

"I'd say that depends on the person making the identification and the circumstances under which the identification was made. For example, was the person close by or far away, was the lighting dim or bright, was the witness calm or agitated, and so on. All these things come into play and determine the quality of the identification."

"Do you agree that different people viewing the same event can describe it in . . . ?"

"Objection, Your Honor!"

"Sustained."

"In your experience, have you found *fingerprint* evidence to be strong evidence? Latents on a murder weapon, for example? Or on a windowsill. Would this be strong evidence?"

"Yes, I would consider it strong evidence."

"In your experience, have you found *ballistics* evidence to be strong evidence? Testimony from an expert, for example, stating that such and such a bullet had been fired from such and such a gun?"

"Yes, that would be strong evidence."

"How about *laboratory* evidence? Comparison of blood stains, for example, or hair samples, or fiber samples. In your experience, would this be strong evidence?"

"Yes, it would."

"How about *forensic* evidence? Testimony from a medical examiner as to the course of a bullet inside the victim, for example, or the organs damaged by its trajectory. Would this also be strong evidence?"

"Yes, it would."

"Now, Mr. Bloom, do you consider *identification* as strong a form of evidence as any of these other forms of evi—?"

"Objection!"

"Overruled."

"Mr. Bloom?"

"I would say identification is not as strong a form of evidence."

"Of all these other types of evidence, would you say that identification is often the *weakest?*"

"Well . . . yes, it can be."

"Thank you, no further questions."

Atkins rose and walked to the witness stand.

"Detective Bloom," he said, "have you ever successfully investigated a murder case in which the key evidence was based on identification?"

"I have."

"How many such cases of this nature would you say you've investigated?"

"I really can't give you a number. Identification plays an important role in all sorts of cases. Leading to the perpetrator, I mean. We'll show mug shots, we'll show artists' composites, we'll get a lead on the perpetrator that way."

"In cases where identification was made through a mug shot or a composite, was this later corroborated by any other means of identification?"

"Sometimes yes, sometimes no. A person will identify someone from a mug shot, and then we'll bring in the identified person and run a lineup on him, and there'll be some question about whether or not he was the actual person seen. Other times, there'll be no doubt at all. Identify him from the mug shot or a composite, then identify him all over again when we run the lineup. It all depends."

"Have you ever investigated a case where two or three reliable witnesses have identified the same person as the perpetrator?"

"I have."

"How about three or four?"

"Yes. Even more than that."

"Tell us what you mean."

"Well, in some rape cases, for example, we'll sometimes have half a *dozen* women identifying the same man. That's not at all uncommon."

"And have these multiple identifications proved reliable?"

"Sometimes yes, sometimes no. There *are* look-alikes in this world, you know."

I wanted to kiss him.

Atkins wanted to kill him.

This was evident in the very next question he asked.

"Mr. Bloom," he said, "are you a personal friend of the defense attorney?"

"I'm a friend of his, yes," Bloom said.

"You've worked together before, have you?"

"Usually on opposite sides," Bloom said, and there was laughter in the courtroom. Atkins didn't like the laughter one damn bit. Bloom was altogether too sympathetic a witness and he'd come a long way toward shooting down the invincibility of all that positive identification.

"How long have you known him?"

"Several years now."

"Can you be more exact?"

"Eleven years."

"Have you ever had lunch together?"

"Yes."

"Shared a drink together?"

"Yes."

"Would you say he's a good friend of yours?"

"I would say he's a *very* good friend," Bloom said, and looked him dead in the eye.

"Ever call you as a witness in any other trial?"

"Never."

"Did you discuss this case with him out of court?"

"I did not."

"Did you have prior knowledge of anything he might be asking you today?"

"I did not."

"When he began questioning you today, did you suspect where he might be going?"

"Not always."

"You've testified in court cases before, haven't you?"

"Yes."

"How often?"

"Some fifty or sixty times, I'd say."

"Here in Calusa?"

"Oh, maybe twelve, thirteen times in Calusa."

"So you're pretty familiar with the questions lawyers ask, aren't you?"

"Pretty familiar, yes."

"Weren't you aware that Mr. Hope was asking you to say identification is not a reliable form of evidence?"

"No, I wasn't aware of that."

"But that's what you *did* say, didn't you?"

"I answered his questions honestly."

"Weren't you trying to be helpful to a very good friend of yours?"

"I was trying to answer his questions honestly. And I did."

"Thank you, no further questions."

I went back to Bloom at once.

"Mr. Bloom," I said, "have I ever in our relationship asked you for a favor dependent on your position in the police department?"

"Never."

"Have I ever asked you for information that would compromise your position as a police officer?"

"Never."

"You did not know what I was going to ask you today, did you?"

"I did not."

"Did you slant any of your answers to help my client's case?"

"I did not."

"Did you tell the truth, the whole truth, and nothing but the truth?"

"I did."

"Thank you, no further questions."

"Just a few more, Your Honor," Atkins said, and walked back to the witness stand. "Mr. Bloom," he said, "you *did* know that Mr. Hope would be the defense attorney in this case, did you not?"

"I knew it, yes."

"A very good friend of yours."

"Yes, a very good friend."

"When you were subpoenaed to testify, did you think of informing the court . . . ?"

"Objection, Your Honor! Such action was not incumbent upon . . ."

"Sustained. Leave off this line of questioning, Mr. Atkins."

"I have no further questions."

"Mr. Hope?"

"Witness may be excused."

The courtroom clock read ten minutes to five. Rutherford glanced at it briefly and then said, "Have the attorneys and the jury had a chance to think about the suggestion I made this morning? About starting on Monday at eight-thirty and continuing through to five-thirty?"

"I have, Your Honor," I said.

"Yes, Your Honor," Atkins said.

"Can someone speak for the jury?"

"We would have no objection to that," juror number one said, rising.

"How about the attorneys? Any objections?"

"None, Your Honor."

"None, Your Honor."

"Then perhaps we can do that till we're finished here," Rutherford said, and smiled as if she'd pulled a fast one. "Let's re-cess, shall we?" she said. "I'll see you all at eight-thirty Monday morning."

When I called Patricia that night, she was in tears.

I thought they'd lost the case down there.

But tears?

"What's the matter?" I said.

"It's just my time of the year," she said, and burst into fresh tears.

"I'm driving down there," I said.

"No," she said. "You'll jeopardize . . ."

"We won't budge from that room all weekend. No one'll see us, we won't talk about the case, I won't let you watch anything about it on . . ."

"I haven't been," she said.

Still sobbing, the words coming out between huge gasps for breath.

"What room are you in?" I asked.

"Matthew, you can't . . ."

"What room?"

"Four-eleven."

"I'll be there soon," I said.

I packed a small bag, climbed into the Acura, and went from zero to sixty in ten seconds flat. The distance from Calusa to Fort Myers is roughly seventy-five miles as the crow flies. It took me forty-five minutes to get there, flying low at eighty miles an hour and praying I wouldn't run into any state troopers. At Fort Myers, I hung a louie onto Route 80 and made the remaining thirty-five miles to Pine Crossing in twenty-two minutes.

There was a good Holiday Inn in town, but the state had opted for a cheaper motel closer to the courthouse. The red brick building dominated the downtown area—such as it was—and announced its holiday spirit by decorating its entire face with the outline of a tree, six stories high, done entirely in green lights. I parked the car, hurried into the lobby . . .

"Silent Night" was blaring from a wall speaker.

. . . found an elevator . . .

Music in there, too.

. . . and went up to the fourth floor.

Patricia was still crying.

I took her in my arms the moment she opened the door.

We stood there in the doorway, speakers in the corridor oozing heavenly peace, Patricia in a long white gown and matching robe, her face wet with tears. I kissed her face, I kissed her nose, I kissed her mouth, she broke away and said, "We'll get arrested," and began sobbing in my arms.

We went into the room.

I closed and locked the door behind us.

There are times to make love, and there are times to listen.

I listened.

She sat on the edge of the bed, her hair loose, her hands folded in her lap, looking down at her hands as she recited what had happened on the night of December 11, five years ago, in Rockefeller Plaza in the city of New York. She did not once look up at me. Just kept staring at her hands, tears streaming down her face. I sat in an easy chair upholstered in a fabric printed with giant red peonies. Watching her. Scarcely moving. Listening to her every word. Thinking how much I loved her.

His name was Mark Loeb, he was Jewish.

He was one of the partners in the firm she worked for at the time—Carter, Rifkin, Lieber, and Loeb, he was the Loeb. She was thirty-one years old at the time. He was eleven years her senior at the time.

Those words were the litany.

At the time.

He was forty-two years old at the time.

They had celebrated his birthday not two months earlier.

October the fifteenth.

"Birth date of great men," she said now, and began sobbing again.

I waited.

She kept looking at her hands, folded in her lap.

Tears rolling down her face.

At the time . . .

They'd been living together for almost two years, in a little apartment on Bleecker Street in the Village. It was his apartment, she'd moved in with him. Her own apartment had been uptown on Eighty-ninth near Lex, which was a longer subway ride to the office on Pine Street. His apartment was nicer, and closer to the office. It had seemed the right thing to do at the time. Everything had seemed so right at the time, they were so very much in love.

He was Jewish . . . had she mentioned that he was Jewish?

It always seemed so ironic that he was the one who wanted to go uptown to see the tree in Rockefeller Plaza.

He'd never had a tree in his own home while he was growing up, never had a tree during his marriage to a Jewish girl, who'd divorced him after five years of what she called turmoil and anguish—just before Christmas, incidentally, but that was a coincidence. He'd always thought of Christmas as a time to escape, get down to St. Barts or Caneel, get away from the insistent Christian barrage that made him feel excluded in his own city, made him feel somehow . . . un-American.

Because this was his city, you know, he'd been born here and raised here, had only once in his life lived outside of it, and then not too distant—in Larchmont, with his ex, whose name was Monica. Patricia had met her at a party once. This was three years after the divorce, Mark hadn't expected to see her there, he seemed flustered when he introduced them, three years after the divorce. She was a tall and gorgeous brunette who made Patricia feel like a frump. He'd apologized afterward. Never would have gone there if he'd known, and so on. In Patricia's apartment later—they hadn't yet started living together—it was as if . . .

"I'm sorry," she said, and shook her head, and tried to hold back the tears.

"No, tell me," I said.

"It was as if . . . seeing her again . . . seeing Monica . . . he knew he . . . truly loved me."

She's going to tell me it's over between us, I thought.

I waited.

Her shoulders were heaving.

"I loved him so much," she said.

I'm going to lose her, I thought.

"At the time," she said . . .

. . . at the time, the firm had been litigating an important case, a mere matter of tax evasion that could have sent their client to prison for the next fifty years and cost him millions in fines. December 11 fell on a Friday that year, which also happened to be the day the trial ended in an acquittal for their client. So they'd gone out to celebrate with the other partners and their wives, and afterward Mark suggested that they all go uptown to look at the tree in Rockefeller Plaza. None of them wanted to go except Lee Carter, who wasn't Jewish, but his wife said she had a headache, which Mark thought was a euphemism for Let's go home and fuck, Lee. So they . . . they all went home and . . . just the . . . just the two of them . . .

"Just Mark and me . . ."

. . . got into a taxi and headed uptown. This was pretty late. Neither of them knew what time they turned the lights out on the tree. She guessed they both had some vague idea that the tree couldn't stay lit all night long, but they didn't know exactly what time the plug was pulled. Neither of them was paying any attention to the time, anyway. It had been a wonderful victory today, and a great party, and they'd each had too much champagne to drink, this was now maybe eleven-thirty, maybe later, when they climbed into a taxi and told the driver to take them uptown to Rockefeller Plaza.

There were still people skating on the ice.

The tree was still lighted.

They got out of the cab and stood on the sidewalk on the almost deserted street, holding hands, looking up at the tree. If you're familiar with New York . . .

"I'm not, really."

"Well, Rockefeller Plaza is this little street that runs for three blocks, I think it is, between Forty-eighth and Fifty-first . . . well, that's four blocks, whatever. Anyway, if you're standing on Rockefeller Plaza, you're standing behind the tree . . . I'm sure you've seen it on television, they make such a big thing of lighting it each year. The tree faces this sunken ice-skating rink . . ."

. . . where girls in short skirts were cutting fancy figures on the ice, and old men with their hands behind their backs were plodding along like ocean liners, and the giant tree with its multicolored lights dazzled the night air above them. And suddenly, all the lights went out. On the tree. The rink below was still illuminated, a glowing rectangle in an otherwise suddenly black landscape. Well, there were lights on the street corners, and some lights on in the windows of 30 Rockefeller Plaza, across the street, but everything suddenly felt dark in comparison to what it had been not a moment before. There was a collective disappointed *ohhhhh* as the lights on the tree went out, but the skaters below went about their determined circling of the rink, and the few people on the street above began dispersing, some heading into the plaza itself, where some of the store windows were still lighted, others walking down toward Forty-ninth, Patricia and Mark walking—well, strolling really, still hand in hand—toward Fiftieth.

The two men who attacked them seemed to materialize out of nowhere. They were both black, but they could just as easily have been white; this was the Christmas season in New York, and muggers at that time of the year came in every stripe and persuasion. The mink coat was what they were after. That and Patricia's handbag, which happened to be a Judith Leiber with a jeweled clasp that looked like money. One of them hit her on the back of the head while the other one grabbed her handbag. As she started to fall forward, the first one circled around her and yanked open the flaps of the coat, popping the buttons. He was starting to pull it down off her shoulders when Mark punched him.

The punch rolled right off him. The man was an experienced street fighter and Mark was merely a downtown lawyer who'd taken his girl uptown to see a Christmas tree. Jewish, no less. The irony. The man hit him twice in the face, very hard, and as Mark fell to the pavement, he turned toward Patricia again, determined to get that fucking coat. The other man kicked Mark in the head. Patricia screamed and took off one of her high-heeled shoes and went at the man who was kicking Mark, wielding the shoe like a hammer, striking at his face and his shoulders with the stiletto-like heel, but the man kept kicking Mark, kicking him over and over again, his head lurching with each sharp kick. There was blood all over the sidewalk now, he was bleeding from the head, she almost slipped in the blood as she went at the man again. "Stop it!" she yelled, "stop it, stop it, stop it," but he kept kicking Mark, kicking him, until finally the man trying to get her coat off yelled "Let it be!" and on signal they vanished into the night as suddenly as they'd appeared.

She was still wearing the mink.

One of the sleeves had been torn loose at the shoulder.

They'd got the Judith Leiber bag.

Mark Loeb was dead.

A month later, she joined the D.A.'s Office.

"I never did find them," she said. "If I'd found them . . ."

She let the sentence trail.

Her eyes were dry now.

There was only anger in them.

I waited for her to tell me she could never love another man again.

In the corridor outside, I could hear yet another Christmas carol.

"Hold me," she said, and began crying again.

I held her close to me all night long.

We lay side by side in a bed too narrow for both of us, the windows tinted green from the tree of lights that was outlined on the face of the building, the Christmas carols muted now but still playing incessantly in the corridor outside.

She fell asleep at last.

She trembled in her sleep.

I held her close.

I did not want to lose her.

I got back to Calusa at close to midnight on Sunday. There was an urgent message from Warren, asking me to call him back at once, and leaving the number of his hotel in Purcell, New Mexico. I figured it was a little before ten out there. The phone rang twelve times before someone picked up.

"Harley Hotel," a man's voice said. He sounded as if I'd just awakened him.

"Yes, please," I said, "would you connect me with Mr. Chambers in room seven-oh-one?"

"Checked out," the man said.

"Did he leave any messages?"

"Who's this?"

"Mr. Hope. Matthew Hope. Did he leave a message for me?"

"Hope, Hope, Hope," he said, "lemmee see now." There was a silence on the line. I assumed he was leafing through a sheaf of messages "Yep," he said at last. "Said to tell you he was on his way to South Dakota, he'll call soon as he has anything."

"When was this?" I asked. "When did he check out?"

"Yesterday afternoon."

"Thank you," I said.

I had Mary to worry about, I had Patricia to worry about, and now I had Warren to worry about.

I was due in court at eight-thirty tomorrow morning.

I went to bed.

14

I was in the shower when the phone rang, at seven-thirty the next morning. I wrapped a towel around my waist—God knows why, since I was alone in the house—and rushed into what I laughingly call a study, hoping to catch the phone before it went into its outgoing message mode. I caught it on the fourth ring. It was Warren.

"Where are you?" I said.

"Denver," he said. "The Mile-High City. Guys in cowboy hats and boots and—you won't believe this, Matthew—Crips and Bloods fighting over drug territory not four blocks from my hotel."

"I thought those were L.A. gangs."

"When you're in love," Warren said, "the whole world's L.A."

"What've you got for me?"

"I've been working all weekend," he said. "It's not easy to get information on the weekend."

I waited.

"Matthew," he said, "there's no record of a Barton family in Renegade, South Dakota."

"Robert Barton?" I said. "Judy Barton?"

"No one by those names. No birth certificate for a Mary Barton, either."

"How about Borgen?" I said. "Or Bargen."

"Nothing."

"That's impossible. She was born there. Her parents died in a car crash there."

"Nothing on a family named Barton," Warren insisted.

"Did you go through all the B's?"

"There're only three hundred and eight people in the whole damn town. I talked with the town clerk for an hour and a half. There is not now, nor has there ever been, a Barton family in that town. No Bartons, period. Or anything like Barton."

"Warren, are you sure we're talking about the same town?"

"Renegade, South Dakota. Lyman County. There's a Renegade in Polk County, Tennessee, and another one in Sweetwater County, Wyoming, but I checked both of those . . ."

"You did?"

"By phone, and there's no record of her in either of those places, either. The trail starts when she's twenty-three years . . ."

"Starts?"

"Starts," Warren said. "Mary Barton did indeed teach English at a private school in Purcell, New Mexico . . ."

"I returned your call there, by the way."

"Lovely town, do you adore cactus as much as I do? Private school named the Elizabeth Wagner School for Girls has her teaching there from September of 1957 to June of 1963. They had to go through records filed in cartons in the basement of the old gymnasium building, they were much put out, believe me. Going through all that shit on a Saturday? Anyway, her original application listed a B.A. from the University of Colorado at Denver . . ."

"That's right."

"Which is why I'm here, and a master's in the teaching of English from NYU in New York. I called NYU, Mary Barton did, in fact, get her master's there when she was twenty-three years old, in June of 1957. Graduated with honors a month before she applied for the job in New Mexico. But . . . and this is funny, I think . . ."

I held my breath.

"There's no record of her having graduated from the University of Colorado."

"What are you saying?"

"Nothing here, Matthew. No Mary Bartons. She'd have graduated at least two years before she got out of NYU, but I went back five years, just in case, and there's nothing."

"Warren, that's . . ."

"I'm not saying a Mary Barton never graduated from Colorado. But none of them graduated when our Mary Barton should have."

"Well, wouldn't the Wagner School have checked that before hiring her?"

"Not necessarily. If she showed them a transcript from NYU, that might've been enough."

"How do you figure that?"

"The NYU files list a B.A. from Colorado."

"You checked?"

"I checked. Her index, by the way . . ."

"At NYU?"

"Yes, was a three-point-eight. Very close to a perfect four-oh."

"So what happened to Denver?"

"I have no idea."

"Or Renegade?"

"Who knows? It's as if she started life when she was twenty-three."

"Right after her parents died in that car crash."

"What car crash? What parents?"

"Check Social Security. Find out . . ."

"I did. The job in New Mexico was the first time she ever worked. Social Security has a Mary Barton registering in Purcell, New Mexico, on the fifth of September, 1957."

"Never worked before then?"

"No contributions listed before that teaching job."

"Twenty-three years old . . ."

"Closing fast on twenty-four."

". . . and never in her life worked?"

"Apparently not."

"I had a part-time job when I was sixteen."

"I was fourteen," Warren said.

"She would've had to show proof of citizenship, wouldn't she?"

"What do you mean?"

"When she applied for a Social Security card?"

"Sure, a birth certificate. If she was born here."

"Well, we know she was born here."

"Do we?"

The line went silent.

"Why would she be lying, Warren?"

"I don't know. All I know is the lady has no past before she started teaching in New Mexico."

"Keep digging," I said.

"Where, Matthew?"

"I don't know where. Go back to Renegade . . ."

"Matthew, it was even colder in Renegade than it is here."

"She says her parents died right after she graduated from college. That would've made it 1955 or thereabouts. Go through every newspaper for that year and the two years flanking it. Find that car crash, Warren. And find out why there's no record of a Barton family in that town."

"I'll check the flight schedules," he said. "It isn't easy getting to these shitty little towns, Matthew."

"Charter a plane if you have to."

"Charter a plane?"

"I'm putting her on the stand this morning, Warren."

"Charter a plane, right," he said.

I personally carried to the Calusa County Jail the clothing I wanted Mary to wear when she testified today. A simple blue suit with a straight skirt and a narrow-lapeled jacket. A plain white blouse with a stock tie. Low-heeled blue pumps—in the infamous size seven of the bloodstained sneakers. She looked exactly like a schoolteacher. Which is what I wanted her to look like.

She told me she couldn't possibly imagine what had happened to all her records.

It began raining just as I was leaving for the courthouse.

"Do you, Mary Barton, swear to tell the truth, the whole truth, and nothing but the truth, so help you God?"

"I do," she said.

"Please be seated," the clerk said.

Mary sat. Every eye in the jury box was on her. Every eye in the entire courtroom was on her. I rose and walked to the witness stand. I was about to begin the direct examination of a woman I did not know at all.

"Miss Barton," I said, "can you please tell me where you live?"

"2716 Gideon Way. Here in Calusa."

"How long have you been living at that address?"

"For five years now."

"Miss Barton, were you living at that address on the weekend of August twenty-eighth this year?"

"I was."

"Were you at home that weekend?"

"All weekend."

"When you say 'all weekend' . . ."

"Friday, Saturday, and Sunday. I didn't budge from the house once that weekend."

"You were home on Friday the twenty-eighth . . ."

"I was."

"And Saturday the twenty-ninth . . ."

"Yes."

"And Sunday the thirtieth, as well."

"Yes."

"Is it customary for you to stay home all weekend?"

"Not usually. But my car was in for service. I didn't have a car that weekend. So I stayed home."

"When did you take your car in for service, Miss Barton?"

"On Thursday the twenty-seventh of August."

"And when was it returned to you?"

"I picked it up on Tuesday morning."

"The first of September?"

"The first of September."

"So, in effect, you were essentially immobilized that week—"

"Objection. Leading the . . ."

"Sustained."

"You didn't have the use of any other automobile that weekend, did you?"

"I did not."

"Where'd you take the car in for service?"

"Meridian Toyota."

"Did Meridian Toyota lend you a car to use that weekend?"

"They did not."

"Did you yourself rent a car to use that weekend?"

"I did not."

"You didn't rent a white Chrysler LeBaron that weekend, did you?"

"I did not."

"Or any other kind of car, did you?"

"I did not rent a car that weekend, period."

"You were without transportation, isn't that so?"

"I had no means of transportation that weekend. Which is why I stayed home."

"Have you ever in your life driven a white Chrysler LeBaron?"

"Never."

"Miss Barton, you weren't in the town of Somerset, Florida, at any time that weekend, were you?"

"I was not."

"Were you in Alietam, Florida, at any time that weekend?"

"I was not."

"Were you anywhere near Palm Island that weekend? I'm referring to Palm Island here in Calusa."

"I was at home all that weekend. I didn't go anyplace that weekend."

"Not to Somerset, not to Alietam, not to Palm Island."

"Not to anyplace."

"Do you recall what you were doing that weekend?"

"I do."

"Miss Barton, did you hear the testimony of Gertrude Fowler here in this courtroom?"

"I did."

"Did you hear her say that on Friday afternoon, the twenty-eighth day of August, at approximately ten or fifteen minutes past three, she saw you at her checkout counter in the G&S Supermarket in Somerset, Florida?"

"Absurd," Mary said.

"Your Honor . . ."

"Just answer the question, please."

"Yes, I heard her testify to that effect."

"Where were you, in fact, at that time, on that day?"

"I was in my garden."

"At 2716 Gideon Way?"

"Yes."

"What were you doing in your garden that day?"

"Working on one of the towers."

"Can you explain that more fully?"

"I'd found some shells on the beach the day before, and I wanted to add them to one of the towers. That's what I was doing that afternoon. I usually save any construction work for the afternoons."

"Your Honor, I would like this marked for identification, please."

"Mark it Exhibit F for the defense."

"Miss Barton, I show you this photograph, and ask if it's a picture of your garden."

Mary took the picture, an eight-by-ten color enlargement of a Polaroid Andrew had taken of the garden a week before the trial started. A startled little gasp escaped her lips.

"Miss Barton?" I said.

"It . . . it looks so . . . uncared for," she said.

"But is it your garden?"

"When was this taken?" she asked.

"Your Honor . . ."

"Sustained. Please answer the question, Miss Barton."

"It's my garden, yes, but in a state of extreme neglect."

"Your Honor, I would like the picture moved into evidence, please."

"For what purpose?" Atkins asked.

"Merely to illustrate what the garden looks like. So that the jury will be able to identify reference points."

"I'll admit it," Rutherford said.

I carried the enlargement to the foreman, handed it to him, and went back to the witness stand. Mary still seemed a bit stunned by what the photograph had revealed. She'd been in custody since the beginning of September. This was now December. No one had been caring for her precious garden in all this time.

"Miss Barton," I said, "when you say you were working on one of the towers that afternoon, which tower do you mean?"

"I have a system of identification," she said. "There are the A towers, the B towers, and the C towers, and I number them by rows from front to back and left to right. Front to back is in

Roman numerals, one to six; there are six front-to-back rows in my garden. Arabic numerals are from left to right; there are ten left-to-right rows. So that, for example, the tallest tower in the upper row on the extreme left-hand side of the garden is A-VI-1—A is for the tall towers, B for the medium-sized towers, and C for the small ones."

"How many towers are there in all?"

"Thirty-one."

"Identified by height and left-to-right position, is that correct?"

"Left to right and front to back."

"Yes."

"Exactly."

"Why is it necessary to identify them?"

"Well, so that there'll be a record of the work. I started the garden three years ago—well, that's not quite accurate. First there was the garden, and I began adding the towers to it three years ago. I keep a record of new towers, for example, or what's been added to existing towers. That way, I'm able to . . ."

"Your Honor, where are we going with all this?"

"Is that an objection, Mr. Atkins?"

"Your Honor," I said, "may the witness *please* finish her answer?"

"Go ahead, please," Rutherford said, and scowled at Atkins.

"I was merely trying to explain that the towers and the plants are what together form the garden. By keeping a record of what bits and pieces of color and texture I add to the towers, I can then determine what colors and textures I want in the plants. Or vice versa. Even in Florida, different plants bloom at different times of the year. It's essential for me to know which colors in the towers . . ."

"Your Honor, I must object," Atkins said. "I find all of this endlessly fascinating . . ."

A roll of his eyes to accompany the sarcasm.

". . . but nonetheless irrelevant."

"Sustained. Let's move along, Mr. Hope."

I went back to the defense table, picked up a book there, and carried it with me to the witness stand.

"Your Honor," I said, "I would like this marked for identification, please."

"Mark it Exhibit G."

"Miss Barton," I said, "I show you this and ask if you recognize it."

"I do."

"Can you tell me what it is?"

"It's a diary."

"A personal diary?"

"No, it's my garden diary."

"Can you define that for me?"

"It's a record of whatever work I do in the garden."

"Does it indicate the dates on which this work was done?"

"Yes, the work is listed on the calendar page it was done. But that's not the important thing, the date. The important thing is what was done. So that I can go back over it, check exact colors, textures, materials . . ."

"Materials like what?"

"Ceramic, tin, silver . . . there are all sorts of materials embedded in the towers."

"Well, couldn't you just look at them to see what you've done?"

"Well, yes, I suppose I could. But the A towers are quite high, you know, and it's not always easy to determine from the ground exactly what some shiny little object is. Is it a bronze earring or an Indian penny? By keeping a record, I know exactly what the composition of each tower is."

"Is there a record of planting in the diary as well?"

"Yes."

"Also by date?"

"Well, yes. As I explained, it's a regular diary with dates on its pages. I simply indicate on any given date what was done in the garden on that date."

"Everything that was done?"

"Well, I'm not sure I'd indicate that I pruned the azaleas on such and such a date, that wouldn't be necessary. But I would note when I'd fertilized, or when I'd planted a border of Blue Daze, for example, anything like that. To have a record, you see. A garden has to be cared for, you see. And it's easier to care for it if there are records."

"Your Honor," I said, "I would like the diary moved into evidence."

"Objection!" Atkins said at once, and got to his feet. "Your Honor, this diary constitutes nothing but hearsay, a statement out of court, introduced as to the truth of the matter asserted."

"Your Honor," I said, "the diary is an exception to the hearsay rule because the declarant is testifying at the trial and the document is consistent with her testimony. Counsel's objection should go to the weight, not the admissibility of the document."

"I'll allow it in evidence," Rutherford said. "You'll have ample opportunity, Mr. Atkins, to argue on the reliability or trustworthiness of the document. Let's proceed."

"Miss Barton," I said, "would you please open the diary to the page for Friday, August twenty-eighth?"

Mary opened the book.

"Can you read what's written on that page, please?"

Mary cleared her throat.

The courtroom was as still as a mausoleum.

" 'Insert shells in B-IV-5,' " she read.

"Is that exactly what it says on that page?"

"Exactly."

"What does B-IV-5 mean?"

"It's one of the medium-sized towers in the fourth row back, fifth row from the left of the garden. Not quite the center of the garden. More to the left."

"And did you, in fact, insert those shells into B-IV-5 on that day?"

"I did."

"On August twenty-eighth, as indicated in the diary?"

"On August twenty-eighth."

"At what time?"

"I began work after lunch, and worked all afternoon."

"From what time to what time?"

"I'd say from one o'clock to four o'clock."

"So you couldn't possibly have been in . . ."

"Objection."

"Yes, yes, sustained."

"How about August twenty-ninth, Miss Barton? Is there anything listed in your garden diary for that day?"

"Yes, there is."

"Can you read what it says on that page, please?"

"Well, it's a sort of code."

"What does it say, exactly?"

"It says, 'Move BP to II-9.' "

"Does that mean something to you?"

"Yes. It means that I planned to move my bird of paradise to the second row from the front, ninth row from the left. There's only one bird of paradise in my garden, so I didn't have to indicate the position I planned to move it from."

"How about Sunday, August thirtieth? Any garden work listed for that day?"

"No."

"Any reason for that?"

"Sunday," she said, and shrugged. "Day of rest."

"What did you do on that Sunday?"

"I don't remember. I probably sat around reading."

"But you didn't work in the garden?"

"No, I didn't."

"And you didn't go to Palm Island, either, did you?"

"I certainly did not."

"Do you keep any other sort of diary?"

"No."

"Just the one for the garden."

"Yes."

"Do you keep an appointment calendar?"

"Yes, I do."

"Have you looked at that calendar recently?"

"I have."

"At my request?"

"At your request."

"Your Honor, I would like this marked for identification, please."

"Objection!" Atkins said. "Self-serving hearsay."

"Your Honor, we've already argued this with the garden diary. The declarant is here testifying . . ."

"I'll allow it. We'll let the jury decide its worth, Mr. Atkins. Mark it H for the defense."

"Miss Barton, is this the appointment calendar you kept for this year?"

"It is."

"Could you look at the page for August, please?"

She began leafing pages. She looked up.

"August twenty-seventh, do you see that date?"

"I do."

"Can you tell me what's written in the box for that date?"

"The words 'Car in.' "

"Anything in the boxes for the weekend of the twenty-eighth?"

"Nothing."

"Nothing for the twenty-eighth, twenty-ninth, or thirtieth, is there?"

"Nothing."

"How about Tuesday, September first? What does it say in that calendar box?"

"It says 'Pick up car.' "

"Your Honor, I would like the calendar moved into evidence."

"Mark it."

"Did you, in fact, pick up your car that day?"

"I did."

"How'd you get to Meridian Toyota?"

"Jimmy Di Falco drove me."

"What time did you get there?"

"Around nine-thirty, a quarter to ten."

"Was your car ready?"

"It was."

"What kind of car is it, by the way?"

"A Camry."

"The year?"

"1992."

"It isn't white, is it?"

"No, it's red."

"A red 1992 Camry."

"Yes."

"What time did you leave Meridian Toyota?"

"A little before ten."

"Where'd you go from there?"

"Straight home."

"Stop anyplace?"

"No place."

"You didn't happen to drop a dress off at the Templeton Mall, did you?"

"I did not."

"Place called Dri-Quik Cleaners? You didn't drop off a blood-stained dress there, did you?"

"No, I didn't."

"Miss Barton, what were you wearing that morning? The morning you picked up your car?"

"A simple dress and loafers."

"What sort of dress?"

"A long dress."

"What material?"

"Cotton."

"And the color?"

"Pink."

"Was there a flower design on it?"

"No."

"Was there any design on it?"

"No."

"How about the loafers? What color were they?"

"Brown."

"Were you wearing socks?"

"No. I was planning to work in the garden when I got home. The dress was an old one, the loafers were what I usually wore in the garden."

"Was the dress a Laura Ashley dress?"

"No, it was just an old dress I've had for years."

"A pink cotton dress, you said."

"Yes."

"Have you ever owned a Laura Ashley dress?"

"I may have. I don't now."

"Had you worn this pink dress in the garden before? Working in your garden?"

"Oh, yes, many times."

"Any stains on it?"

"Earth stains. It's a work dress, you see. I'd wipe my hands on it, throw it in the washer at the end of the day. But stains linger. It's not the sort of dress one would wear to the governor's ball."

"Miss Barton, you were in the courtroom, were you not, when a dry cleaner named Jerome Callahan testified that a woman answering your description had dropped off a bloodstained, size eight, blue denim dress in his shop on the morning of September first?"

"I was here, yes."

"And you were here in this courtroom, were you not, when a young girl named Marabelle Hawkes testified that she'd found a pair of bloody size seven sneakers in a drainage ditch four blocks away from the Templeton Mall?"

"I was here, yes."

"Were you also here when Detective Lewis of the State Attorney's Office testified?"

"I was here, yes."

"You heard him say, did you not, that he'd gone to your house looking for evidence in the crime of murder and that he had not found any blue denim dresses or any sneakers?"

"I heard him say that, yes."

"I ask you now, Miss Barton, have you ever owned a size eight, blue denim dress?"

"I have not."

"Never in your lifetime?"

"Never."

"Have you ever owned a blue denim dress in any size?"

"I have never owned a blue denim dress, period."

"What is your normal dress size, Miss Barton?"

"It varies according to my weight."

"Varies from what to what?"

"From a size seven to a size nine. I normally put on weight during the winter months, I don't know why."

"Would there be dresses in sizes seven, eight, and nine in your closet?"

"Yes, there would. There are."

"Are there any sneakers in your closet?"

"No. I don't own any sneakers."

"Have you ever owned sneakers?"

"I have. But I don't own any now."

"Did you own sneakers on the weekend of August twenty-eighth."

"I did not."

"How can you be so certain?"

"I used to wear sneakers working in my garden. But they really got terribly soiled, and they were very hard to clean. I threw away my last pair of sneakers, oh, it must've been at least three years ago."

"Never bought another pair after that?"

"Never."

"Miss Barton, you heard Charlotte Carmody testifying in this courtroom, did you not, that on the night of August thirty-first she saw a woman in your garden . . ."

"That woman was not me."

"Objection, Your Honor. Unresponsive."

"Sustained."

"She saw a woman in your garden, who she is certain was you. I ask you now, were you in your garden at a little after ten on the night of August thirty-first?"

"I was not."

"Where were you at that time?"

"In bed. Asleep."

"How can you be so sure of that?"

"I go to sleep every night at nine-thirty. That night was no exception."

"Did you set an alarm clock before you went to bed?"

"I did. Well, all I do is click the switch to the 'On' position. I wake up at the same time every morning."

"The alarm is set for the same wake-up time each morning, is that correct?"

"That's correct."

"And what is that time?"

"Seven A.M."

"You wake up at seven o'clock every morning, is that right?"

"Seven o'clock, yes."

"Objection, Your Honor. May we approach?"

"Please," Rutherford said.

"Your Honor," Atkins said, "this is habit testimony, and doesn't say anything about the night in question."

"I'll sustain it. Narrow your scope to the night in question, Mr. Hope."

"I thought I had, Your Honor. I asked if she'd set the clock that night and she responded that she had."

"I don't believe he brought out that she'd set it for seven o'clock, Your Honor."

"Well, it's sustained, so bring it out now."

I went back to the witness stand.

"Miss Barton," I said, "on the night of August thirty-first, did you set your alarm clock for seven A.M., as you've testified you always do?"

"I did."

"Do you ever deviate from setting it for seven A.M.?"

"Never."

"Would you know if it's set for seven at this very moment?"

"It was set for that time when I left the house in September. I haven't been back there since."

"Would you know if anyone else has been in your house since your arrest?"

"Aside from the police . . ."

"Yes, aside from the various policemen who've been in there, would you know of anyone else who's had access to the house?"

"No one."

"Anyone who'd have had access to your alarm clock?"

"No one that I know of."

I walked to the defense table, picked up a small box sitting there, walked to the witness stand with it, took off the lid, and removed from the box an alarm clock.

"Your Honor," I said, "I would like this marked for identification, please."

"Mark it I for the defense."

"Miss Barton," I said, "do you recognize this clock?"

"It looks like my alarm clock," she said.

"By looking at it more closely, can you tell me for what time the clock is set?"

I handed the clock to her. It was an old-fashioned windup clock, round, with a big white dial. She looked at the dial. A narrow metal strip resembling a sweep hand was pointed to the numeral 7.

"It's set for seven o'clock," she said.

"Your Honor," I said, "I would like the clock moved into evidence."

"I must object to that, Your Honor."

"Come on up."

There was impatience in her voice. It showed on her face, too.

At the bench, Atkins said, "Your Honor, I have no way of knowing when the time was set on this clock now offered in evidence. It could have been last September, it could have been last week, it could have been yesterday. I don't even know how the clock came into defense's possession. Or whether or not it was tampered with before it left the defendant's house—if indeed that's where it was located—or tampered with after it came into defense's possession, for that matter."

"Mr. Hope?"

"It was removed from Miss Barton's house last week, with her permission, and by my assistant, Andrew Holmes."

"That still doesn't tell me what may have been done to the clock since the last time the defendant saw it."

"Well, I think you'll have ample opportunity to argue that to the jury, if you so choose, Mr. Atkins. Meanwhile, I'll admit the clock as evidence."

"Thank you, Your Honor."

"Mark it I in evidence," Rutherford said to the clerk.

We stepped back. Atkins to his table, I to the witness stand again.

"Miss Barton," I said, "would you describe yourself as a creature of habit?"

"Leading," Atkins said.

"Sustained."

"Do you go to bed every night at the same time?"

"Asked and answered."

"Sustained."

"On the night of August thirty-first, what time did you go to bed?"

"Asked and answered."

"Sustained."

"You say you were in bed asleep at a little after ten that night. Did you hear anything that awakened you?"

"Nothing."

"Heard nothing in the house?"

"Nothing."

"Nothing in the garden outside?"

"Not a thing. I was asleep."

"Slept peacefully all night long, did you?"

"I did."

"And woke up at what time?"

"Seven o'clock. When the alarm rang."

"Miss Barton, did you know a little girl named Jenny Lou Williams?"

"I did not."

"Did you know a girl named Kimberly Holt?"

"I did not."

"Or Felicity Hammer?"

"No."

"Never knew any of these girls?"

"Never."

"Never saw any of these girls?"

"Never."

"When did you first hear of these girls?"

"When I was charged with their murders."

"Which was when?"

"The first day of September."

"Who first mentioned these girls to you?"

"Detective Morris Bloom."

"Is he the detective who arrested you?"

"He and his partner, Cooper Rawles."

"Before then, you had never heard of these girls, isn't that so?"

"Asked and answered."

"Sustained."

"Thank you, Miss Barton, I have no further questions."

"Let's take a ten-minute recess," Rutherford said.

My partner Frank was waiting in the corridor outside. He looked somewhat agitated.

"I just got a call from Warren," he said. "He's in South Dakota, freezing his ass off. He checked the town records again, found nothing relating to Barton, Borgen, Bargen, Bergen, Batten, or anything remotely similar. Did you ask him to go to the town newspaper?"

"I did."

Warren had sought out the editor of a weekly called the *Renegade Reporter,* who was thrilled to have a private detective in their morgue. He checked through back issues of the paper for the years 1954, 1955, and 1956. There'd been car accidents in those years, yes, even fatal car accidents, but in none of them had the parents of a then-recent graduate of Colorado U been killed. Nor had anyone been left orphaned by a crash during any of those years. Warren had gone further, conducting a whirlwind door-to-door canvass, only to confirm what he already knew: no one in that town could remember a Robert, a Judy, a Mary, or any other kind of Barton ever having lived there. In Renegade, South Dakota, the family simply did not exist.

"So what the hell is going on?" Frank asked.

"I wish I knew," I said. "Did he leave a number where we can reach him?"

"Yes."

"Call him back. Tell him to run the same drill on a woman named Mary Jones."

The courtroom was silent as Atkins approached the witness stand. Mary looked up into his face. He seemed trying, earnestly but unsuccessfully, to hide his contempt for her. Without preamble, he said, "How do you know that clock is yours?"

"It's my clock," she said. "I ought to know my own clock."

"Couldn't it be a clock just *like* your clock?"

"If so, it's a remarkable double."

"You haven't seen this clock since the second day of September, is that right?"

"That's right."

"But you recognize it in this courtroom today."

"I recognize it, yes. It's my alarm clock. I set it every night of my life. Of course I recog—"

"I thought you didn't have to set it every night. I thought it was *already* set for seven A.M."

"The *time* was set. I *still* had to set the alarm."

"And you did that on the night of August thirty-first, did you?"

"Yes."

"Do you know for a fact that no one has tampered with that clock since last you saw it?"

"I do not know that for a fact, no."

"Do you know for a fact that no one but your defense attorneys have had that clock in their possession since last you saw it?"

"No, I don't."

"Do you know what time that clock was set for when your defense attorneys went to pick it up at your house?"

"I'm assuming it was set for . . ."

"Yes or no, do you know for a fact that it was still set for seven A.M.?"

"No, I don't."

"All you really know for a fact is that you yourself set the clock on the night of August thirty-first."

"Yes."

"You don't know if anyone else has touched that clock since. Except for your defense attorneys."

"No, I don't know."

"And what you did that night was turn on the alarm switch before you went to bed."

"Yes."

"Pushed it up? Moved it sideways? How do you set the alarm switch?"

"I push up the little lever on the back of the clock."

"And that's what you did that night."

"Yes."

"What time was it when you pushed up the little lever on the back of the clock?"

"Nine-thirty."

"You looked at the time?"

"Not right that minute, perhaps, but . . ."

"Then how do you know it was nine-thirty?"

"I started getting ready for bed around nine-fifteen. By the time I'd washed my face and brushed my teeth and got into my nightgown . . ."

"What I asked you, please, was how you knew it was nine-thirty when you pushed up the little alarm lever on the back of the clock?"

"I always go to bed at nine-thirty."

"Exactly nine-thirty?"

"Within a few minutes either way."

"So you knew it was nine-thirty because you always go to bed within a few minutes of nine-thirty either way, is that correct?"

"Yes. Besides, I'd looked at the clock before I started getting ready for . . ."

"How do you know it wasn't nine-forty when you went to bed?"

"I know it was nine-thirty, give or take a few minutes."

"Even though you didn't look at the clock?"

"I know how long it takes to get ready for bed."

"Does it always take fifteen minutes exactly?"

"Well, not exactly. But . . ."

"Could it take twenty minutes? Or thirty minutes? Or an hour? Or . . ."

"Your Honor, he's asked three questions."

"Choose one, Mr. Atkins."

"Might it sometimes take twenty minutes to get ready for bed?"

"Sometimes."

"How about thirty minutes?"

"Rarely."

"But sometimes?"

"Once in a blue moon."

"Does that mean it sometimes takes you half an hour to get ready for bed?"

"Occasionally. But not very often."

"How about an hour?"

"Never."

"Isn't it true that you might very well have been awake at a little after ten that night?"

"No, it is *not* true. I was in bed at nine-thirty."

"Even though you didn't look at the clock."

"Is that a question?"

"Tell me, Miss Barton, did you sleep the whole night through?"

"I already said I did."

"Didn't get out of bed for any reason, did you?"

"No."

"Visit the bathroom at any time during the night?"

"No."

"Take a little stroll in the garden?"

"No."

"Went straight to bed at nine-thirty and didn't wake up until seven the next morning?"

"That's right."

"You knew you got up at seven because that's what your clock is always set for, correct?"

"Correct."

"Did you look at the clock when you woke up?"

"I turned off the alarm when it went off."

"But did you look at the clock to see that it was, in fact, seven A.M.?"

"I knew what time it was. The alarm always goes off at seven."

"So, in much the same way that you knew it was seven without looking at the clock, you also knew it was nine-thirty the night before—without looking at the clock."

"Yes."

"Ever have any heated words with Charlotte Carmody?"

"No."

"Any arguments with her?"

"No."

"Ever throw a pail of water at her?"

"Of course not."

"Well, you've thrown a pail of water at someone *else*, haven't you?"

"I may have, but . . ."

"Well, you *did*, didn't you?"

"Yes, but I was being bothered."

"Ah. Charlotte Carmody ever bother you?"

"No."

"Did you ever have any reason to believe Charlotte Carmody might wish you any harm?"

"No."

"You heard her testify that she saw you burying a body in your backyard, didn't you?"

"I did."

"What do you make of that?"

"I don't understand the question."

"If she had no reason to wish you any *harm*, why would she say such a thing about . . . ?"

"Objection, Your Honor. Witness has no way of . . ."

"Overruled."

"How do you explain her saying she saw you in your garden burying the body of a child?"

"Maybe she was still carrying a grudge. She went to the *police* about my garden, you *heard* her say that. Maybe she . . ."

"And *you* heard her say that she saw you in your garden at ten that night . . . a little after ten . . . under the light of a full moon.

Yet you say you were in bed asleep at that time. How do you explain that?"

"I can't explain what Miss Carmody saw or didn't see. I can only tell you where *I* was. I was in bed. Asleep."

"Not in your garden burying a body?"

"Certainly not."

"So, in much the same way that you were in bed asleep while Charlotte Carmody was seeing you in your garden, you were also inserting seashells into one of your towers while two other witnesses were seeing you with Jenny Lou Williams in the town of Somerset, Florida. Isn't that so?"

"Isn't what so?"

"That you claim to have been in your garden on August twenty-eighth, rather than in Somerset, Florida?"

"That's where I was, yes. In my garden."

"And in much the same way, the very next day, the twenty-ninth day of August, you claim to have been transplanting a bird of paradise in that very same garden while yet another witness was seeing you dragging a little girl into a car in Alietam, Florida, isn't that so?"

"I was in my garden that day, yes."

"And in much the same way, on the day after that, the Sunday, you claim you were home all day while still another witness was watching you drive a little girl bleeding from the mouth out of the parking lot on Palm Island, isn't that so?"

"Yes, I was home that Sunday."

"Doing what?"

"Relaxing."

"No work in the garden that day?"

"No."

"Little vacation from the garden that day?"

"I don't work on the Lord's day."

"Do you get up at seven on the Lord's day?"

"I sometimes sleep a little later on Sunday."

"Oh. How late?"

"It varies."

"Do you set the alarm on Saturday nights?"

"Not usually. I just sleep through till . . ."

"Then you don't *always* set your alarm for seven A.M., is that right?"

"Not on Saturdays."

"Just the rest of the week."

"Yes."

"I was sure you said you *always* set the alarm for seven A.M."

"What I said was that the *alarm* is always set for seven A.M., but . . ."

"Exactly."

"But I don't normally switch *on* the alarm when I go to bed on Saturday night."

"Thank you for clarifying that. But how do you explain all these people identifying you?"

"Your Honor, witness can't possibly . . ."

"Sustained."

"Do you *know* any of these people who've testified against you?"

"I do not."

"Do you have any reason to believe they would wish you harm?"

"I don't know why they're saying . . ."

"Please answer the question."

"No reason."

"Yet all of them have identified you. You heard each of them identifying you, didn't you?"

"I did."

"Do you remember my asking you about your alarm clock?"

"Yes?"

"Do you remember my asking you if the clock here in court couldn't be a clock just *like* your clock?"

"Yes?"

"Do you remember what you answered?"

"Not exactly."

"You said, 'If so, it's a remarkable double.' Do you remember saying that?"

"Yes."

"Do you think you have a remarkable double out there, Miss Barton?"

"No."

"Do you think Charlotte Carmody saw a remarkable double in your garden on the night of August thirty-first?"

"No. I don't know who she saw. It wasn't me."

"Do you think Gertrude Fowler saw a remarkable double in the G&S Supermarket on the afternoon of . . ."

"I don't know who any of these people saw. The woman they saw wasn't me."

"She merely looked exactly like you."

"I don't know what she looked like."

"All of these witnesses have testified that she looked exactly like you, this remarkable double of yours. Yet . . ."

"Objection, Your Honor. Witness cannot testify as to what others claim to have seen. If the prosecutor insists on continuing this line of . . ."

"Sustained. Please move on, Mr. Atkins."

"The truth is you don't have a remarkable double, isn't that the truth?"

"If there's someone doing terrible things . . ."

"Please answer . . ."

". . . and she looks like . . ."

"Please answer my question."

"I'm not the one doing bad things," Mary said.

"You do realize, do you not, that *someone* did these bad things, don't you?"

"Yes, I realize that."

"But not you."

"Not me."

"Someone who looks remarkably like you."

"Apparently."

"Mary Jones perhaps."

"I don't know any . . . anyone named Mary Jones."

"Didn't you use that name when you . . . ?"

"I've never used that name in my life."

"Let me finish my question, please. Didn't you use that name when you took a dress to the Dri-Quik Cleaners?"

"I told you. I never used that name in my life."

"But you *did* take a dress to the Dri-Quik Cleaners, didn't you?"

"No, I didn't."

"And gave your name there as Mary Jones . . ."

"No."

". . . and your address as 2716 Gideon Way, which *is* in fact your address, is it not?"

"That's my address, yes, but I'm not the person who . . ."

"Mr. Callahan must have seen this remarkable *double* of yours, is that right?"

"Your Honor . . ."

"I withdraw the question. You keep a garden diary, do you?"

"Yes."

"But not a personal diary."

"I have no need for a personal diary."

"Keep a garden diary and an appointment calendar . . ."

"Yes."

"But no personal diary."

"No."

"Ever keep a personal diary?"

"Perhaps when I was a girl."

"How about this year? Ever keep a personal diary this year?"

"No."

"So there wouldn't be any record of what you did personally on the weekend of August twenty-eighth, would there?"

"The work I do in my garden is very personal to me."

"So it would seem. And on Friday the twenty-eighth, according to your garden diary, you remodeled one of your towers, inserted some seashells into it, as you say, and this occupied you all day long."

"Not all day long. Most of the day."

"To insert a few seashells into an existing . . ."

"Not a few seashells. There were at least a dozen of them. And they had to be placed very carefully. So as not to disturb the balance."

"Oh? Would the tower topple over if a few seashells were put in the wrong place?"

"I'm talking about esthetic balance."

"Ah. So you very carefully plastered these . . ."

"Cemented them."

"Cemented them, excuse me, cemented these seashells into the tower in the—what did you say it was?—QB VII?"

"I think you know that's the title of a novel," Mary said.

"Is it? Thank you for informing me. But what was the location of the tower?"

"B-IV-5."

"You inserted these shells into B-IV-5."

"Yes."

"Began work after lunch . . . around one o'clock, you said . . ."

"Yes."

"And quit at about four."

"Yes."

"And on the twenty-ninth, your garden diary indicated that you moved a bird of paradise plant to a more prominent spot in your garden."

"Yes."

"How long did this take?"

"It was a difficult job. It's a big plant, and I was a woman working alone."

"I asked how long it took."

"A good part of the day."

"From what time to what time?"

"I started in the morning, and then I broke for . . ."

"What time in the morning?"

"Around ten."

"Yes, go on."

"I broke for lunch at around noon . . . I'd dug the hole at the new location by then, and had balled the plant for moving . . . and I got back to work again at around one, one-thirty. I believe I was finished with the job at three, a little after three."

"And on Sunday, you did nothing."

"On Sunday, I read."

"That's the thirtieth of August, the day little Felicity Hammer was abducted, on that day you sat around the house reading."

"Sat in the back*yard* reading, as a matter of fact. It was a lovely day."

"You didn't go to Palm Island that day, did you?"

"No, I didn't."

"What were you reading?"

"I don't remember. The newspaper, I suppose. And then a novel. But I don't remember in detail."

"But all of this . . . all you've remembered about that weekend, is premised on the entries you made in your so-called garden diary, is that correct?"

"That's correct."

"Tell me, Miss Barton, when were those entries made?"

"On the dates indicated."

"You're sure, for example, that the entry for the twenty-eighth of August was made on that day?"

"Yes, it was."

"Before the seashells were cemented into the tower or after?"

"After. The diary is a record of what was done, not a plan of what was about to be done."

"So you sat down after you'd done the work . . ."

"Yes."

"And made your entry."

"Yes."

"The entry for the twenty-eighth on the twenty-eighth . . ."

"Yes."

"And the entry for the twenty-ninth . . ."

"On the twenty-ninth, yes."

"And so on."

"Yes."

"Anyone there with you while you were making these various entries?"

"No."

"You were alone."

"I was alone, yes."

"So no one saw you making the entries on those particular dates."

"No one saw me."

"In fact, was anyone there with you in the house, or in the garden, at any time during that weekend?"

"No."

"You were alone all weekend."

"Yes, I was alone."

"You didn't write those entries at some later date, did you?"

"No, I didn't."

"Since they're a record of work actually done, they could have been written into the diary at any time, isn't that so?"

"Objection, Your Honor."

"Overruled."

"There's no *urgency* about making these diary entries, is there?"

"Well, yes. If I delayed too long, I might forget what was done on any given day."

"Have you ever delayed in making a diary entry?"

"Not for very long periods of time."

"You normally make the entry after the work is performed, is that right?"

"Yes."

"An hour after the work is performed?"

"Sometimes. It depends on how tired I am."

"Two hours?"

"Sometimes."

"How about six hours?"

"Occasionally."

"How about a day later?"

"Very rarely."

"Ever make an entry a *week* after you've performed the work?"

"I may have done that. But it's very difficult to keep track of things if you don't . . ."

"How about a *month* after the work?"

"No, I don't think I've ever been that tardy."

"Isn't it true, Miss Barton, that you made those diary entries only after you'd been seen by Charlotte Car—"

"No, it is *not* true!"

"Only after you realized you'd better have an alibi for . . ."

"No!"

". . . the weekend of August twenty-eighth, isn't that true?"

"No! I made those entries on the dates indicated! I was home all that weekend! I wasn't anywhere those people say I was!"

"It was Mary Jones, right? Your remarkable . . ."

"Objection, Your Honor."

"Sustained."

"Let me understand this clearly," Atkins said. "You're telling us that all these witnesses who've identified you all over the state of Florida that weekend must be wrong because you—Mary Barton and *not* Mary Jones—were home in your backyard as proven by a *clock* that could have been *set* at any time and a *diary* that could have been *written* at any . . ."

"Objection, Your Honor!"

"Sustained."

"I have no further questions," Atkins said.

"Witness is excused," I said. "Defense rests its case."

Rutherford looked at her watch.

"Well," she said, "it's almost one-thirty. If we take a brief recess now, will you be ready to present your closing arguments when we come back?"

"I'm ready now, Your Honor," I said.

"So am I," Atkins said.

"All right, then, let's break for lunch, and then we'll resume."

The armed attendant outside the locked door recognized me at once and unlocked the door for me. The room was comfortable but not commodious. It was furnished with a pair of leather easy chairs undoubtedly salvaged from a judge's chambers, a wooden conference table with four wooden straight-backed chairs around it, a bookcase containing last year's edition of the Florida Statutes, and several floor lamps. Venetian blinds on the two windows at the far end of the room stood open to the afternoon rain, revealing that the windows were barred. Mary sat on one side of the conference table, her hands folded in front of her, her head bent as if in prayer. She did not look up when I entered the room. The bolt behind me turned with a small oiled click.

"You did very well," I said.

"Sure," she said.

"Really."

I thought, in fact, she'd handled herself with dignity, pride, and a good deal of calm. Except for her explosion just before Atkins ended his cross . . .

No! I made those entries on the dates indicated! I was home all that weekend! I wasn't anywhere those people say I was!

. . . and her odd hesitation while he was harassing her about her "remarkable double" . . .

I don't know any . . . anyone named Mary Jones.

. . . she'd been a good witness, and I felt she'd made a highly favorable impression on the jury.

She didn't think so.

"Everything I said only confirmed what they already believed," she said. "They thought I was guilty even before I opened my mouth, and they *still* think so. Nothing will ever convince them otherwise."

"I don't think so. You came across as an honest, straightfor-ward . . ."

"Murderer," she supplied.

"No, Mary, I don't think that's the impression you gave."

"Too bad you don't get a vote," she said.

"I *do* get a chance to sum up, though."

"Well, you'd better make it good," she said. "Because if that jury comes in with a guilty verdict, I'm disappearing. I'm not waiting till they . . ."

"Mary . . ."

". . . transport me to some goddamn impregnable fortress . . ."

"Mary, please . . ."

". . . where I won't have a chance in *hell* of breaking out! If you think I'll let them . . ."

"Nobody's going to . . ."

". . . put me in the electric chair, you've got another thing coming! If they find me guilty, I'm out of here in a minute! I promise you."

"I didn't hear any of this," I said.

"I promise you," she said again.

In your opening statement at the beginning of a trial, you tell the jury what you *hope* to prove. In your closing argument, you repeat for the jury everything you believe you *did* prove. In the state of Florida—as opposed to New York, for example—the prosecution normally closes first; the defense attorney closes next, and then the state has an opportunity to conclude in rebuttal. Atkins chose to waive his opening argument. This was a shrewd maneuver; it denied me the opportunity of rebuttal while leaving him the advantage of the last word.

I started by telling the jury that the state attorney's entire case was based on identification and that since the burden of proof was upon him, if there was even the *slightest* doubt in their minds as to the accuracy or reliability of these identifications, then in the name of truth and justice they must find Mary Barton innocent of the charges against her. I reminded them that they had heard an experienced detective telling them that identification was the *least* reliable sort of evidence, and I asked them to remember that if they could not believe beyond reasonable doubt that Mary Barton was indeed the woman these various people *thought* they had seen, they must bring in a verdict of not guilty.

I told them that they'd heard testimony to the effect that Mary was without an automobile on the weekend those little girls were abducted and killed, and that she could not possibly have been in those sections of the state where she had been identified in error. I told the jury that, in fact, her diary clearly showed where she had been and exactly what she'd been doing on that weekend.

Going back to the unreliability of eyewitnesses, I told them that Gertrude Fowler was wearing reading glasses when she mistakenly identified the woman standing three feet away from her at her cash register, and that she wasn't wearing any glasses at all when she subsequently identified her at a police lineup.

Following this same line of attack, I told the jury that whereas Edward Farrow claimed to have overheard a conversation taking place fifteen feet from where he was sitting, in this very courtroom he could not hear me at all when I was speaking to him from fifteen feet away, or from six feet away with my back turned.

As for yet another "reliable" witness, Martha Williams, mother of one of the victims, it was understandable that in her grief she may have thought she'd seen a white Chrysler LeBaron with the defendant at the wheel, but it turned out later that without the state attorney's careful preparation, she would not have known what such a car even looked like.

And while we were on that vaunted Chrysler LeBaron, the state attorney himself had shown that it was a rented car, but had he produced any evidence at all to show that Mary *Barton* was the person who'd rented that car? Because . . .

". . . I can tell you, ladies and gentlemen of the jury, if he possessed such evidence, he would have brought it to your attention, it would have clinched his case for him, there would have been no need for anything further. *If.* But you heard no such evidence in this courtroom, and that's because the state attorney could *find* no such evidence, could *find* no way to link Mary Barton to this car that was rented by the gray-haired woman who abducted and killed those children."

Getting back to Martha Williams, I went on to explain that she had never seen Mary Barton anywhere in the vicinity of her child, and had no reason to believe that her child was being watched or followed or observed or in any danger whatever from a person who had spent virtually all of her life teaching and nurturing young girls.

As for Harold Dancy, the man who claimed to have seen a gray-haired woman dragging a little girl into a car—a girl he identified the same day as Kimberly Holt—his perception was certainly dimmed by the teeming rain, and his initial identification of Mary Barton was made through photographs, five full days after he had seen the gray-haired woman in the rain, and after he had also seen pictures of Mary Barton on television.

"A sixty-eight-year-old man," I told the jury, "who saw a woman and a child in a blinding rainstorm and who later mistakenly and understandably assumed the woman who'd been arrested for the serial killing of three little girls was the same woman he'd seen five days earlier. And identified her at first from mug shots taken after her arrest and questioning. Made initial positive identification from *mug* shots! Never mind that they later held a lineup for him, he'd already made up his mind by then, the woman on television and in the mug shots was *certainly* the gray-haired woman he'd seen in that horrendous rainstorm, the woman who should be on trial in this courtroom today, and not Mary Barton, who did not kill those children!"

I went after all of the identifying witnesses in much the same manner, pointing out whatever inconsistencies there'd been in their separate testimonies, landing hard on all the circumstances that would have made true identification difficult if not impossible.

I saved my particular bile for Charlotte Carmody, whom I attacked not on misidentification but on bias, reminding the jury that they had heard her testifying in her own words that she had gone to the president of the neighborhood association to inquire about a so-called eyesore law, and had then actually gone to the police to try to have Mary Barton *arrested* for the unspeakable crime of having created a unique and wonderful garden. Failing in that, and for reasons known only to herself . . .

". . . she identified her neighbor as the woman she'd seen burying those bodies on the night of August thirty-first. But are we to believe the testimony of a woman who previously tried to have this same neighbor *jailed?*"

In conclusion, I reminded the jury that Mary Barton had not been *obliged* to testify, but that she had taken the stand of her own *volition*. Nor was it incumbent upon Mary Barton or her attorneys to identify or apprehend the gray-haired woman responsible for these terrible crimes; it was our task to show only that Mary Barton could not have committed them.

"I think you know she's innocent," I said. "You've seen the picture of the garden she worked on tirelessly, the garden in which she was working on the weekend that someone other than she was voraciously roaming the Florida countryside in search of victims. Even in its untended state, you surely must have recognized the garden's great beauty and the loving care that went into its creation and maintenance. That garden reflects the sort of woman Mary Barton is, a woman who all her life has taught others to grow and to find in themselves potentials they could not have imagined without her guidance. I ask that you find this woman innocent of the crimes with which she's been charged. I ask that you return Mary Barton to her garden . . . and to her life. Thank you."

It had taken me an hour and forty minutes.

It took Atkins almost two hours, by the end of which time he almost had me convinced that the Remarkable Double ravaging the countryside on the weekend of August twenty-eighth, the gray-haired beast who'd lured three children into her rented automobile and murdered them and buried them in a garden bristling with towers and plants, the so-called Mary Jones responsible for the brutal murders of three young innocents, was none other than my client, Mary Barton.

I left the courtroom at twenty to seven that night.

By that time, Judge Rutherford had charged the jury, and they'd been escorted to the Hyatt Regency, where they would spend the night before beginning their deliberation the next morning.

It was still raining.

Up the street, the lights on the big Christmas tree blinked on and off in the rain. Red. Green. Red. Green. My daughter would be arriving from Boston at eleven thirty-nine tomorrow morning. I hoped it wouldn't still be raining.

I drove home, tried Patricia, and got no answer. I put a macaroni dinner in the microwave, but didn't turn it on till I'd drunk two martinis. I tried Patricia again when I finished eating. Still no answer. I went to bed at nine-thirty and was asleep in ten minutes.

15

I have never been able to get used to the big metropolitan airport they've built in Calusa to serve the tri-city area. In the old days, when you were meeting a plane, you simply wandered over to the only baggage area there was and waited there for the passengers to stream in from the field. Now we were big-time. Five major airlines serviced the Calusa/Bradenton/Sarasota airport, familiarly called Calbrasa, which made it sound vaguely Italian, and codified on baggage tags as CBS, which made it sound like a television network. Whatever else it may have been, it was huge.

Where once there had been a seedy little restaurant with Formica-topped tables and waitresses in assorted cotton sweaters and polyester slacks, there was now a two-level eating establishment with tablecloths on the tables, waitresses in spanking-clean matching uniforms, and a fountain that shot multicolored water jets two stories into the air. Where once there had been a lone newsstand selling newspapers and the latest paperback hits—

have you ever noticed that there's never anything you'd care to read in an airport bookshop?—there were now a dozen or more shops selling everything from swimwear (including the infamous thong banned from Calusa beaches by the town's ever alert conservative minority) to tacky souvenirs of the lovely state of Florida, not so lovely on this Tuesday morning, the fifteenth day of December: it was still raining.

A Christmas tree well suited to the new size and stature of Calbrasa Airport dominated the main terminal, vying for attention with the rainbow fountain that sprayed water to the musical accompaniment of a medley of favorite Christmas carols. Most times of the year, the musical background was summery and frivolous, as suited the notion of a carefree tropical resort, but now the strains of "God Rest Ye Merry, Gentlemen" flooded the bustling premises, vainly hoping to evoke visions of snow-covered fields and sleighs jingling along country byways. This was Florida, however. And it was raining. And if it never really felt like *winter* down here, how could it even *hope* to feel like Christmas on this dreary, flat, and dismal morning?

An announcement advised me that USAir's flight number 1875 out of Boston had been delayed by bad weather—*there* not *here*—and would not be arriving till twelve thirty-seven. How they had pinpointed it to the minute was beyond me. I debated having a hot dog. I looked at my watch. I called the courthouse again and asked the clerk who answered how the jury on the Barton case was doing. She said she didn't know. I asked her to find Andrew Holmes for me, and when he came to the phone, I asked him how close they were. He told me that the senior court officer—usually a reliable source for what was happening in the jury room, legend picturing him standing guard outside with his ear to the door—figured it would probably be hours yet.

"Is that good or bad?" Andrew asked.

I told him it was neither good nor bad. A jury could sometimes take half an hour to reach a verdict, and it could sometimes take three weeks. Many lawyers believed that the shorter the deliberation, the more likely a conviction. Conversely, the *longer* a deliberation, the greater the possibility of a hung jury. But they could find Mary guilty in ten minutes or *not* guilty in ten weeks, or vice versa. As one of my law school professors had been fond of putting it, "It all depends on the level of sugar in the bile."

There were now three separate and distinct snack bars in the Calbrasa Airport—pizza, tacos, and all-around junk food—but I chose the sumptuous new restaurant instead, from which I could watch the dancing fountain and see the glittering, blinking, artificially frosted Christmas tree. In Florida, the people frost their trees more than they do anywhere else in the world. Perhaps, recognizing the dearth of *real* frost, they overcompensate. The trees down here all look falsely snow-laden and, if truth be told, somewhat anemic. They also use a lot of bows on the trees down here, either replacing more conventional ornaments or augmenting them. Pink bows or white bows or green bows or blue bows or multicolored bows, the choice depending on the artistic bent of the tree's decorator and the overall color scheme in his or her mind. The airport's tree, in keeping with the theme of airborne things, was done all in blue and white. Blue skies and white clouds. White bows and blue lights and green branches sprayed with foam that made them look like snowy Vermont, fat chance.

On the assumption that Joanna would not have eaten on the plane, I ordered only a cup of coffee, suffered the disdainful look of the waitress in her spanking-clean pink uniform, and sat back to wait. The fountain sprayed water into the air, pink and green and blue. The Christmas tree blinked its blue lights. When the coffee finally came, it was cold. I looked at my watch again. Twenty minutes past twelve. Seventeen minutes until the plane arrived. I wondered where Patricia was. I finished my coffee, found a phone booth, and dialed a credit-card call to the motel down there in Pine Crossing. The man at the front desk told me that Miss Demming had checked out. I asked him why someone hadn't told me that the last hundred times I'd called. He said he was sorry but he'd just got back from lunch. It was twenty-seven minutes past twelve. I called the courthouse again. No word from the jury yet.

At Calbrasa Airport, people meeting arriving passengers are supposed to wait for them in the baggage area. This is presumably the rule in airports all over the United States. You're not supposed to go through security to the gates unless you've got an airline ticket in your hand. In America, however, you're not supposed to blow your automobile horn incessantly, and you're not supposed to scrawl graffiti on the faces of buildings, and you're not supposed to drive through red lights or full stop signs, and you're not supposed to verbally abuse passersby, and you're not supposed to commit any one of a thousand acts that violate minor laws designed to make mass living a bit more comfortable.

But when law enforcement officers are busy dealing with murder, armed robbery, rape, burglary, assault, and a thousand other crimes spawned by the proliferation of guns and the easy availability of drugs, why then the rest becomes merely civilization. Here in our new and luxurious airport, families and friends breezily marched through security to see passengers off or to greet them upon arrival. I am an officer of the court, sworn to uphold the laws of nation, state, and city; however eager I was to see my daughter again—I hadn't seen her since this past summer, and then only fleetingly—I went to the baggage area to meet her.

She came striding into the area like a fresh northern wind, all suntanned from weekend skiing on the slopes of Vermont, long blonde hair cascading from beneath a red woolen watch cap, which she snatched from her head the moment she saw me. Loping toward where I was waiting beside the USAir carousel, she threw herself into my arms and shouted, "Dad! There's a *blizzard* in Boston!" and I hugged her close and she said, "I'm lucky I got here at *all!*" and I said, "So am I."

The deal I'd made with Susan was that Joanna would spend her first night home at my house, after which I'd drop her off at

Susan's in the morning. She'd spend Christmas Eve with me—only nine days away and I *still* hadn't done any shopping—get dropped off at Susan's again late that night, and then spend Christmas Day and most of her school vacation with her. Joanna was almost fifteen; she'd made her own plans for New Year's Eve. I was hoping I'd get to see her on New Year's Day and perhaps once again after that, before she left for school again on the third of January.

Divorce is a kind of killing, you know. The principal parties murder whatever they had known together, effectively reducing memory and desire to ashes. But the homicidal fallout extends to everyone around them—especially the children. And when a divorced couple tries to make another go of it—as Susan and I had—only to fail the second time around, the ensuing confusion can be disastrous for an innocent kid watching from the wings. I think Joanna had by now abandoned all hope of her mother and me ever getting together again, and yet—

I had chosen for lunch a small Italian restaurant on Calusa's Main Street, a successful spin-off of the owner's larger restaurant out on Whisper Key. Richard Cantieri's first location was called Piazza della Republica, an ill-chosen name in that Calusa's globe-trotting citizens immediately began calling it "The Pizza Republic," a misleading Americanization that caused fast-food snow-birds to expect anything but the fine Northern Italian cuisine Richard served. The firm of Summerville and Hope had handled the closing for Richard when he bought the new property down-town. He'd been hell-bent on calling the place Piazza Garibaldi, which in Calusa would have been translated immediately to "Baldy's Pizza." Frank and I begged him to reconsider. He had come up with "Cantieri's," straight from the shoulder, take it or leave it. This didn't stop the local intelligentsia from calling it "The Canteen"; some things remain ever and always the same. But at least they didn't expect pizza.

Joanna was starving. She ordered the bruschetta *and* the pro-sciutto con melone *and* a small order of spaghetti con basilico e pomodoro *and* the veal Milanese. I ordered the minestrone to start and then the linguini with white clam sauce. I asked Joanna if she'd like some wine. She asked if they'd card her. I told her I didn't think so and ordered a half bottle of the Pinot Grigio. Some sworn officer of the court.

It was while she was gobbling down the spaghetti that Joanna looked up suddenly and asked, "Remember what Christmas used to be like?"

I didn't say anything for a moment.

Then I said, "Yes, I remember."

"It was fun," she said, and looked down at her plate, and gave a slight shrug, and began twirling spaghetti strands around her fork. I could remember when she used to call it "pascetti." I think every kid in America calls it pascetti at one time or another. But not every kid in America knows how to twirl it around a fork like an expert. I credit myself for that.

"It was," I said. "Fun."

She nodded. Working the spaghetti, twirling it around the fork, head bent.

"Do you ever see Mom anymore?"

Twirling the spaghetti.

"I run into her every now and then."

"But you're not *seeing* each other, huh?"

"No, we're not, darling. Not anymore."

"Well," she said, and shrugged again, and lifted the fork to her mouth. Shoveling the bulk of the spaghetti inside, she deftly caught the hanging strands on the tines of the fork. I had taught her well. "Maybe I can talk her into inviting you over," she said.

"I'd rather you didn't."

"Okay."

Working the spaghetti into her mouth, chewing, faint shrug of the shoulders yet again, as if to say Well, I tried.

I debated mentioning Patricia.

I decided not to.

Before we left the restaurant, I called the courthouse again. It was almost two-thirty, and there was still no verdict. I was about to tell Andrew that I'd call him as soon as I got back to the house, when he said, "Hold it, Matthew."

I waited.

"You'd better get down here," he said. "The word is they'll be coming in soon."

Once upon a time, when Joanna was a little girl, I took her to my office as part of a school project. See Daddy at Work. That sort of thing. My Daddy Is a Lawyer. I took her to work again that Tuesday afternoon. I don't think she'd ever seen me in a courtroom situation before. Truth be known, before I began specializing in criminal law, I'd rarely done any litigation.

She sat on the first row of spectators, alongside Melissa Lowndes, who—now that she had already testified—was allowed inside the courtroom.

I sat at the defense table with Mary and Andrew.

Atkins sat at the prosecution's table with two assistants from the State Attorney's Office.

The jury filed in at five minutes to three.

Rain drilled the windows facing the street outside.

"I understand the jury has reached a verdict, is that so?" Rutherford asked.

The man who'd been elected foreman got to his feet.

"Yes, Your Honor, we have," he said.

"Before we hear the verdict," Rutherford said, "I want it understood that in my courtroom, there will be no public expression upon the pronouncement of the verdict. Family, friends, reporters, any other spectators who feel they will be unable to control themselves may please leave now. When the verdict is announced, I don't want to hear any applause, any cheering, any booing, any hissing, any catcalls, any expressions whatever of approval or disapproval of the verdict. No one—and I direct this particularly but not exclusively to the various reporters present—*no* one will enter the well or approach the jurors, and no one will leave this courtroom until I say that they may. If all that is understood, may I please see the verdict?"

The foreman handed a slip of paper to the clerk of the court, who carried it to Rutherford and handed it up to her. She looked at it, nodded, said, "The verdict is in order," and then said, "The clerk may publish the verdict."

The clerk stepped up to the microphone on the witness stand.

"In the case of the State of Florida versus Mary Barton, the verdicts are as follows. On the first count of murder in the first degree, the verdict is guilty. On the second count of murder in the first degree, the verdict is guilty. On the third count of murder in the first degree, the verdict is guilty."

"Thank you," Rutherford said.

"Your Honor," I said, "I would like the jury polled, please."

"Clerk will please poll the jury," Rutherford said.

I looked at Mary. Her face was expressionless.

"Ladies and gentlemen of the jury," the clerk said, "you have heard the verdict of guilty on all three counts of first degree murder. Juror number one, is that your verdict?"

"Yes, it is."

"Juror number two, is that your verdict?"

"Yes, sir."

"Juror number three . . ."

And on and on, eight good men and true, four good women equally true, each in turn rising to confirm that he or she had found Mary Barton guilty of all three charges of first-degree murder. Mary sat as still as any stone. On the first row of spectators my daughter, Joanna, looked pained. Melissa Lowndes was scowling.

"The officers of the court will remand the prisoner for sentencing," Rutherford said.

They snapped handcuffs onto her wrists. They virtually lifted her from where she was sitting at the defense table. She glanced back at me once as they led her out of the courtroom. On the front row, Melissa was still scowling.

"I want to thank the jurors for their participation in this democratic process," Rutherford said, "and I want to thank the opposing attorneys for their professional behavior during the course of the trial. In just a moment, I'll be adjourning this court, and you will be free to leave at that time. Mr. Hope, Mr. Atkins, we will reconvene for sentencing in two to three weeks; you and the jury will be informed of the exact date. Thank you, ladies and gentlemen."

"All rise!" the clerk shouted.

Melissa Lowndes came to me at once.

"I'm not paying your bill," she shouted, and stormed out of the courtroom.

Joanna came to me and took my hand.

"Let's go home, Daddy," she said.

This was not the house in which my daughter had been raised. Then again, neither had she been raised in the luxurious new Whisper Key condo Susan had just purchased. I liked to think she preferred my home to Susan's, if only because it was a *house* and not an apartment.

I had deliberately purchased a three-bedroom house, the master bedroom for me, the largest guest room for Joanna whenever she visited, and the second guest room—what I called the "spare" room—for whoever might drop in from time to time; northern drop-ins are to be expected if a person chooses to live in Florida. The house had a large living room with a fireplace—yes, we often need fireplaces in Florida—a good kitchen, a fair-sized dining room, a room that was called a maid's room in the real estate flier, two full-sized bathrooms (in the master bedroom and Joanna's room), and two so-called powder rooms, one in the spare room and the other just off the entrance foyer. There was also a pool and a small garden. It was a nice house.

Joanna immediately carried her duffel to the laundry room opposite the foyer bathroom; I sometimes think she comes home only to do her laundry; I *also* sometimes think she brings home all her *friends'* laundry as well. Talking a mile a minute, reeling off the names of schoolmates I'd never met but was expected to remember, relating about each of them either horror stories or amusing anecdotes or school secrets or personal idiosyncrasies, she methodically and incessantly transferred laundry to washer, added detergent and softener, set the dials in an instant—she's the only one in the family who can program a VCR—and then led me into the kitchen, where she snapped on the lights, went to the refrigerator, took out a bottle of milk, cut a slab from the chocolate cake I'd bought especially for her visit, poured herself a tumbler full of milk, scooped a ball of vanilla ice cream onto the cake, and, despite all she'd eaten at Cantieri's, sat at the kitchen counter and began eating all over again.

There was a sudden flash of lightning.

"Wow," Joanna said.

Thunder now, loud and close and shaking the house.

It had been raining for the past two days, and one would have thought enough was enough. But weather changes are sudden and dramatic in Florida, and now the rain was accompanied by a violent electrical and acoustic display, another flash of lightning following almost instantly on the heels of the booming thunder, and then new thunder even before the first boom had rolled away.

The telephone rang.

I pulled the receiver from the wall mount.

"Hello?"

"Matthew?"

Another flash of lightning. I blinked my eyes against it, instinctively hunched my shoulders when the thunder came.

"Warren?" I said. "Where are you?"

"Back in Renegade. It's snowing to beat the band here. I may *never* get home."

"What do you mean, *back* in Renegade?"

"I drove over to the county seat, figured I'd check out the records there."

"Will I need a pencil and paper?"

"Maybe."

"Let me take this in the study," I said. "Honey, will you hang up when I yell?"

"Give him my love," Joanna said.

There was more lightning and thunder as I walked through the house to the study. One wall of the room was fashioned entirely of glass, with sliding doors opening onto the garden and pool outside. I hit the light switch just as new lightning flashed outside, a coincidence that created the momentary impression that I'd controlled both the interior lighting *and* the storm raging beyond the glass doors. I picked up the phone receiver.

"Hello?" I said, and thunder rattled the house.

"Still with you," Warren said.

Another flash of lightning, *very* close this time.

"Jesus!" I heard Joanna shout.

Over the following crash of thunder, I yelled, "I've got it, honey," and heard a click on the line as Joanna replaced the receiver in the kitchen.

"We're in the middle of a thunderstorm here," I explained into the mouthpiece, and to prove I wasn't lying there was another flash of lightning that illuminated the pool and the garden, and a blast of thunder that sounded just as all the lights went out.

"Shit," I said.

"What is it?"

"We just lost power."

"Dad!"

"Yes, honey!"

"Are you all right?"

"Yes!"

"Shall I light some candles?"

"Please. They're in the . . ."

"I know where," she shouted.

"What's happening?" Warren asked.

"Joanna's here. She sends her love."

"Give her mine, too. You ready for this?"

"What've you got?"

"Well, it may be nothing," he said. "But I was working on the computer in the county courthouse . . ."

"Yes?"

"Looking for a Mary Jones anywhere in the county . . . or a Robert or a Judy . . . I assume you wanted me to check for the whole family . . ."

"Yes?"

"And something interesting popped up."

Lightning in the backyard again, the sliding glass doors suddenly alive with an eerie blue light. A quick glimpse of palm fronds dancing wildly in the wind and then darkness again and the boom of thunder.

"Man, that sounded close," Warren said.

"It was. Tell me what popped up."

"Well, I typed 'Mary Jones' into the computer and got nothing. So I narrowed the field a bit, typed in a 'Mary J,' and began searching for any surname beginning with a 'J.' I found plenty of those, all right, from Jackson to Jekyll to Johannson to you name it."

I stood listening in the darkness. Somewhere in the house, I heard Joanna crash into a piece of furniture and yell, "Shit!"

"You okay?" I shouted.

"Yeah, yeah," she mumbled.

"Go on, Warren."

"So I widened it a bit. Figured I'd land somewhere between Mary J and Mary Jones if I typed in a 'Mary Jo,' which is just what I did."

"What'd you find?"

"*Lots* of Mary Jo's, Matthew. But only one of them the daughter of a Robert and Judy Bjorvatten. That's a B-J, Matthew— Bjorvatten, I don't know if I'm pronouncing it correctly, B-J-O-R, I guess it's Swedish or something."

"Norwegian," I said.

"Whatever," he said. "And *not* in Renegade. The family lived in a town named Fallon, some twenty, thirty miles away. Anyway, there was a big fire in the Bjorvatten house in August of 1955, both parents killed, the . . ."

"Not a car crash," I said into the darkness.

"A *fire*, Matthew. The police suspected arson, but no one could prove it. The two . . ."

There was another lightning flash.

I looked up.

A woman was standing in the rain just outside the sliding glass doors.

"Mary," I whispered.

Darkness again. A crash of thunder. And then a rapping on the glass panel. Mary rapping to be let in.

"I'll call you back," I said.

"There's a lot more, Matthew."

"I'll call you back," I shouted, and slammed the phone down on the receiver, and only then realized I didn't know where the hell he was *staying* in Renegade.

More rapping at the window.

Blackness in the study, blackness outside.

I groped my way across the room. Found the latch on the sliding door. Clicked it to the unlocked position. Slid open the door. Another flash of lightning. Mary standing there in the torrential rain. Thunder boomed again.

"Get in here," I said.

She stepped into the room.

Blackness again.

The lights came on as suddenly as they'd gone off. There was a sudden explosion of brilliance, another flash of lightning outside, more distant now, a rolling peal of thunder. I slid the door shut. It banged to in the stillness of the room. I locked it. Mary was standing here in her lawyer's house. Mary had broken *jail*.

Her gray hair was plastered to her forehead. Her dress, long and brown, was soaked through to the skin, appearing even darker than it was—but it wasn't jailhouse clothing, where'd the dress come from? White sneakers on her feet, mud-covered from the sodden earth outside—these weren't standard jailhouse issue, either. Nor was the canvas bag hanging from her shoulder on a long canvas strap. Where'd she pick up all this stuff? How'd she . . . ?

"What'd you do, Mary?" I said. "What the hell did you *do?*"

"Everything," she said.

There was an odd look in her eyes, something . . . crafty. No, not crafty. Cunning. No. Something . . .

"Mary, *why?*" I said. "For God's sake, *why?* You *knew* I'd be requesting an appeal! The IDs were tainted, the whole damn identification procedure was . . ."

She grinned at me.

"Dad!"

Joanna. Yelling from the living room.

"Yes, honey!"

"Is somebody here?"

"No."

"Who's that?" Mary asked.

"My daughter."

"The little blonde girl in the restaurant?"

"Yes," I said. "Mary, I'm taking you back. Before this goes any further . . ."

"No," she said.

"Yes. I'll file an appeal, I'll request a new trial . . ."

"I don't *want* a new trial," she said.

"Mary, you . . ."

"I'm happy with *this* trial," she said.

Still grinning.

"Mary, what's wrong with you? Don't you under—?"

"Mary *Jean,*" she said, and reached into the canvas bag.

"What? What do you . . . ?"

"Mary *Jean*," she repeated.

"Dad?"

Joanna. Standing in the doorway to the study. Eyes wide.

A knife came out of the canvas bag.

16

She went for Joanna, not me.

The weapon in her hand was a chef's knife with a wooden handle and a blade some twelve to fourteen inches long. She wielded the knife with a frightening, almost casual ease, its tip dancing lightly on the air as she went for Joanna swiftly and smoothly, a dancer on ice, a maniacal glint in her eyes, gliding toward my daughter where she stood transfixed in the doorway to the room.

"Daddy!" she shouted, and this was suddenly no longer a teenage girl standing there, this was a terrified nine-year-old instead. *Daddy* not Dad, and the primeval scream shattered the air, ricocheted off the bound volumes of the Florida Statutes on the bookshelves behind me, spiraled back like a boomerang, *"Daddy!"* from her lips again as Mary brought the knife in low for a thrust.

"Yes, doll," she said, "come taste it," and I hurled myself at her back.

Her strength surprised me. She flung me off easily and then

whirled to face me, the knife coming up defensively. A boxer might have used his hands, but Mary had used this knife before, Mary knew how to use this knife, the knife was an extension of her hands, and she brought it up with almost gleeful anticipation, holding it between us as if I were Dracula and she was defying my power by flashing a crucifix. I brought up my own hands, fingers and thumbs spread as if I were holding a basketball between them, waiting for her move, hoping to catch a wrist or an arm and not the slicing edge of a kitchen knife.

The look on her face said it all, the terrifying grin on her mouth, the vacant look in her blue eyes, as if they were blindly seeing, knowledgeably unaware, casually determined. The look said it all, she was crazy, she was crazy, the knife said it all, she had killed before, she had mutilated before, she would do it again, how could I have been so *wrong*?

Joanna is on her school's soccer team, but I didn't know until that moment how strong she was. She hit Mary at the base of her neck with her clenched right fist, using the fist like a hammer, hitting her once, and then hitting her again as she staggered forward toward me. I dodged the flailing knife, swung a roundhouse blow at the left side of her head, and then hit her again. Blood spurted from her nose. The blue eyes wandered, rolled, and went blank an instant before she collapsed to the floor.

Joanna was breathing very hard.

So was I.

There was thunder outside again, far in the distance.

Skye Bannister himself handled the Q&A.

Her recitation was sometimes lucid, sometimes ranting, a remarkable blend of rambling disorientation and rational understanding. She seemed to know she was here in the State Attorney's Office, hearing questions put to her by persons in authority, but she was someplace else as well, some dark and secret place in the tortured reaches of her mind.

"Can you tell me your name, please?" Skye asked.

"Mary Jean Bjorvatten," she said, and smiled. "It's a difficult name, hard to pronounce. We both hated it."

"Where do you live, can you tell me, please?"

"I live in Fallon, South Dakota."

"Miss Bjorvatten, your driver's license . . ."

"Call me Mary Jean," she said, and smiled again. "It's so much easier."

The lens of the video camera was pointed directly at her. A backup cassette recorder was going. And there was a woman operating a stenotab machine, taking it all down in case everything else failed.

Q: This *is* your driver's license, isn't it, Mary Jean?

A: Yes, it is.

Q: This is a Florida driver's license, isn't it?

A: Oh yes.

Q: Then you don't live in South Dakota, do you?

A: Well, Fallon is nice, too. I've lived a lot of places, you know. She moves around so much, it's hard to keep up. I only found out she was in Florida a little while ago. Which is why I moved down here. I thought she was still in England, someone told me she was in England, never could find out where. She tries to hide from me, you know. Because I'm the prettier one. Never lets me play with her dolls, either, so selfish. She thinks her shit doesn't smell, you know.

Q: Miss Bjor—

A: Mary Jean. Please.

Q: Mary Jean, this person you're referring to . . .

A: Miss Goody-Two-Shoes, shit doesn't smell. I showed her.

Q: What did you show her?

A: That they loved me better.

Q: Who?

A: Mommy and Daddy. Never took *her* side, did they? I showed her with the dolls, too. Fixed the dolls good, all right. The cat, too. I showed her.

Q: Which dolls do you mean, Mary Jean?

A: Oh, the dolls in our room. The other dolls, too.

Q: What did you do to the dolls?

A: Cut them up. Under their dresses. Where nobody could see. She showed them to Mommy and Daddy, told them look what Mary Jean done. They didn't believe her. I'll give you Mary Jean. Always blamed everything on me, but they wouldn't believe her. Cut the dolls under their dresses, right where they wee. Oh boy was she mad!

Q: Mary Jean, do you know why you're here?

A: Oh sure. 'Cause of the dolls. What I did to the dolls. Did she tell you about the cat? She told them about the cat, too, wouldn't believe her. I'll give you Mary Jean. They loved me more than her, you see. I fucked myself with a banana once, did you know that? Made her watch.

Q: Why do you think you're here, Mary Jean?

A: The dolls, I told you.

Q: The dolls you cut under their dresses?

A: Oh, let's quit playing games, shall we? You *know* why I'm here. I'm here because you think I killed those three little girls.

Q: *Did* you kill those little girls?

A: *She'll* blame it on me, that's for sure. But no one'll believe her. Cry wolf, you know. Keep saying *I'm* the bad one, no one'll believe her.

Q: Tell me about the little girls.

A: Took the first one right after school.

Q: Where?

A: Somerset. Not too far from my house. Did it to

her in my house. I have a nice little house, there was money when they died, you know, Mommy and Daddy left both of us money. Well, how do you think she could afford to go gallivanting all over the place, trying to get away from me? I did it to her in the bathtub. Washed the blood down the drain afterward, did you ever see the movie *Psycho*?

Q: When was this, Mary Jean? When you did it to her in the bathtub?

A: In August sometime. I don't remember the exact date.

Q: Could it have been August twenty-eighth?

A: Could've been, who knows?

Q: A Friday? August twenty-eighth?

A: Sounds okay to me, sweetie.

Q: And you say you took the girl right after school?

A: Coming out of school. Told her I'd buy her some candy. Drove her to the supermarket downtown.

Q: The G&S Supermarket?

A: Sounds right to me, honey.

Q: And then took her to your house?

A: Drove her in the car, right.

Q: What car?

A: Car I picked up. Didn't want people seeing me in my *own* little car, did I?

Q: Where'd you get the car?

A: Found it.

Q: Where?

A: Outside a motel on the Trail. Star-Way Motel, nice white car.

Q: A Chrysler LeBaron?

A: I don't know cars.

Q: When you say you picked it up . . .

A: Found it there, picked it up.

Q: Do you mean you stole it?
A: Whatever you say, honey.
Q: What was the girl's name, do you know?
A: Oh sure, she told me.
Q: What was it?
A: Jenny Lou.
Q: Jenny Lou Williams?
A: She had a doll named Pitty Pat, can you imagine such pretentious shit? That was her favorite. Hid that one away from me, never could find what she'd done with it. Did she tell you where she put it? I wish I could find that doll, I'd do her like all the others.
Q: Tell me about the others.
A: What others?
Q: That weekend.
A: What weekend?
Q: The weekend you took Jenny Lou.
A: Kimberly Holt, too. And Felicity Hammer. She was my favorite. Because of her name. One of her dolls was named Felicity, she had all these utterly stupid names for her dolls, Pitty Pat Doakes and Felicity Pissity, whatever, I *hated* her fucking dolls! Oh I enjoyed doing Felicity, I really did, the screaming little brat, woke up the dead when I was driving her out of that park, smacked her across the face, made her bleed, the little cunt.
Q: Where did you find Kimberly Holt?
A: Little town.
Q: Where?
A: Oh I don't know. It was raining.
Q: Was this the day after you took Jenny Lou?
A: If you say so, honey.
Q: Saturday the twenty-ninth?
A: Your guess is as good as mine.

Q: Where'd you find her?

A: Wandering the main street. Told me she'd walked outside the beauty parlor where her mother was getting a haircut, wanted to look at the rain, and then couldn't find the beauty parlor again, could I help her find the beauty parlor? I said Oh *yes,* my darling little doll, I'll help you find the beauty parlor, just come with me, sweetheart.

Q: What'd you do then?

A: Took her to my car, drove her back to the house.

Q: Did you kill her?

A: That's for me to know and you to find out, smartie.

Q: Did you put her in the bathtub, the way you did with Jenny Lou?

A: Jenny Lou was all wrapped up, thank you.

Q: What do you mean?

A: In a blanket. All wrapped up and ready to go, thank you.

Q: Go where?

A: Why to the garden.

Q: Did you wrap Kimberly up, too?

A: After I was done with her. She bled more than the first one had, I don't know why. Is there something that makes some people bleed more than others? I wonder. Took me an hour to clean up the tub. Wrapped her up and put her in the spare room with the first one. It was raining so hard that day. I hate it when it rains, don't you? I cut her all over, she had no hair down there.

Q: What'd you do the next day?

A: Went for a drive again.

Q: Where?

A: See my better half. That's a joke, son.

Q: What'd you do with the little girls?

A: Oh, they were back in the house, waiting for company. Three little pigs went to market, right?

Q: Did you go out to Palm Island that day? This would've been Sunday the thirtieth of August.

A: You know I'm no good on dates, honey.

Q: Did you go to Palm Island the day after it was raining?

A: I don't know where Palm Island is.

Q: Picnic area, lots of tables, lots of boats . . .

A: Oh yes, little Pissity Felicity with her big yelly mouth, I smacked her good and hard. Walking around with an ice cream cone, I asked her did she want something to wipe her hands with, she said, Yes, ma'am, thank you, ma'am, little Pissypants Pitty Pat Goody-Two-Shoes Felicity Shit. Got her in the car where I keep the tissues in the glove box, locked the doors, she started screaming, oh I smacked her good all right.

Q: What'd you do then?

A: Why, drove her back home and put her in the tub to wash off all that sticky ice cream, hmm? Washed her good and clean, marked her down there like all the others, wrapped her up good, too.

Q: Marked her how?

A: Little crisscrossy marks all over her sweet little pussy, did I tell you about the cat? Do you know about the cat? Oh there was a little cat, his name was Spidey, she was the one who'd named the cat, can you imagine a more ridiculous name for a cat, Spidey? I hated that cat, an all-white cat, Spidey the spider cat, skinny and scrawny, I slit his throat. She told them I'd done it. They didn't believe her, why should they, she was *always* saying I'd done it.

Q: So you had the three little girls wrapped in blankets . . .

A: All tucked in nicely.

Q: What'd you do then?

A: Put them in the garden. Mary, Mary, quite contrary, how does your garden grow? Have you ever
seen that ridiculous garden? Looks like cement
cocks sticking up all over the place, she's so full of
shit, I mean it. Buried them in the garden. Pretty
maids all in a row, am I right? Planted them by
the light of the silvery moon. Danced off into the
night, wanna dance, sweetheart?

Q: Are you familiar with a store called Dri-Quik
Cleaners?

A: Oh yes. Dri-Quik, yes indeed.

Q: Did you take a dress there to be cleaned?

A: Yes, I did. Favorite dress of mine. Got blood on
it from the three little dolls.

Q: When did you take the dress there?

A: Now that's where you get me, handsome, on the
dates.

Q: Would it have been on Tuesday morning, the first
of September?

A: Dates, dates, dates.

Q: Do you remember giving the man your name?

A: Oh yes.

Q: Why'd you use the name Mary Jones?

A: I didn't.

Q: He asked you your name . . .

A: He asked me whose *dress* it was.

Q: And you told him . . .

A: Mary Jo's. I told him it was Mary *Jo's* dress. *Her*
dress. He wrote down Mary *Jones,* who was I to
correct him, a poor, uneducated merchant? I'm a
college graduate, you know, look it up, we graduated college together, the University of Colorado,
look it up, June of 1955. So you see . . .

Such a lovely graduation ceremony.
We stood in the summer sunshine . . .

A: . . . although she'd have it otherwise, I'm not quite
as ignorant as she'd make me.

We were so proud of ourselves. Ready to step out and
conquer the world. How young. How foolish.

A: That's what bothered me most about her . . . well,
it *still* does, her fucking air of superiority, as if
she's the smart one. *She's* the one with the fucking
gorgeous garden! After the house burned down
. . . oh, of *course* she blamed me, by the way, how
could she *not* have blamed me, even though I was
a million miles away at the time, would I have set
fire to my own *parents*? Was she crazy? Is she *crazy*?

We buried them in the blistering August heat. We
stood in the sunshine and wept bitter tears . . .

A: This was in August, two months after graduation,
she disappeared almost immediately afterward, I
couldn't find her for years. Finally tracked her
down at a posh school in New Mexico, sur-
rounded by little dolls again, her precious little
dolls she wouldn't let me touch. She told me to
leave her alone, get away from her, she wanted
nothing more to do with me, I was crazy, she
wanted nothing more to . . . *I* was the crazy one,
can you believe it? She was calling *me* the crazy
one. I told her I *liked* New Mexico, how about
that? Told her I was thinking of settling *down* in
New Mexico, you little prissy pisspants, how does
that sit with you? She disappeared again.

So if I've got this right, you lived in Lockbourne . . .

Yes.

. . . and taught there for . . . well . . . twenty years, it
would seem.

Yes. A bit more than twenty years.

A: But now I've found her, haven't I? And now I'll
      put as many fucking dolls in her garden as I like.

The room went silent. I could hear the stenographer's nails
clicking on the keys as she caught up with the last words spoken.
Then silence again.

"Mary Jean," Skye said, "do you know how to sign your
name?"

"Of *course* I know how to sign my name. I'm a college graduate."

"Because I'd like you to read this transcript when it's typed up,
and if it's okay . . . or if you'd like to make any changes or
additions, we'll do that for you . . . but once you're satisfied with
it, I'd like you to sign it."

"I'll be happy to."

"You won't sign it Mary *Jones*, now will you?"

"Of course not. I *told* you, what I said to him was Mary *Jo*, it
was Mary *Jo's* dress, *her* dress. Not mine. *Hers*. It belonged to
her, Mary Jo, not me. Mary Jo. My sister. My twin."

"I changed my name the moment I got to New York," Mary
said. "I'd already been accepted at NYU—as Mary Jo Bjorvatten,
that was the name on my diploma from Colorado U. But I got
the court order and entered school as Mary Barton. That was in
September of 1955. I started classes as Mary Barton, and graduated as Mary Barton, and went to New Mexico under that name,
went to England under that name . . . I *am* Mary Barton, you
see."

We were sitting in the cheerless Prisoner's Consultation Room
at the Calusa County Jail. This was early Wednesday morning,
the sixteenth day of December. It had stopped raining. Sunshine
streamed through the open, steel-colored venetian blinds. I had
asked her why she hadn't told me about her sister's existence. She
still hadn't answered me.

"You knew all along, didn't you?" I said.

"I was hoping she wasn't the one."

"But surely, when all those identifications were made . . ."

"Yes, I suspected."

"Mary, you *knew*."

"Yes, I knew. I knew she was back again. I knew she was doing terrible things again."

"Why didn't you tell me?"

"I thought you'd exonerate me, anyway."

"That *still* would've left your sister out there . . ."

"Yes."

". . . doing *terrible* things, as you put it . . ."

"Yes."

"Then why didn't you . . . ?"

"I guess I was hoping you could really persuade a jury that I was inno—"

"Mary, that has nothing to do with it! Your sister is a murderer! You were protecting someone who'd killed *three* . . ."

"Yes, but . . . if they'd found me innocent, you see . . ."

"Mary, for God's sake . . ."

". . . then maybe I could have *talked* to her, *convinced* her to change . . ."

"Mary, you can't be ser—"

"She was different in college, you know."

"I don't care *how* diff—"

"She wasn't quite as close to me then, you see. She had her own room, her own roommate, her own friends. There wasn't that constant *proximity*, you see. I think it was our closeness that forced her to do those terrible things. Being together all the time. I think that was it."

"Mary, that's *not* what it was. Your sister is insane. They'll judge her incompetent, and she'll be sent to a hospital for the . . ."

"Oh, no, I hope *not*," Mary said. "I was hoping, in fact, that *you* might represent her. That you . . ."

"No," I said.

". . . might try to help her."

"I don't represent people I know are guilty."

"Perhaps just this once . . ."

"No."

"Because she's not truly a *bad* person, you see. She's just had a very difficult life. She didn't *ask* to be born a twin, you know. She didn't *ask* to be subjected to the constant comparisons, the constant little competitions, she didn't ask for *any* of that, Mr. Hope."

"Neither did you," I said.

The room went silent.

She folded her hands on the table before her, looked down at them.

"I've filed a motion for judgment of acquittal," I said. "My office is already preparing affidavits to bolster the motion in court. I'm sure that in light of everything that's happened, Judge Rutherford will grant bail until the hearing. My guess is you'll be out of here by lunchtime."

"Thank you," she said.

"So I guess that's it," I said.

"I appreciate all you've done for me."

I nodded.

There seemed to be nothing more to say.

I was starting for the door when she whispered, "I hate her, you know."

I turned to look at her.

She was still sitting at the table with her hands folded, her head bent, seemingly unaware of my presence.

"But I love her, too," she said.

We were eating pizza in Frank's corner office. Warren had just told us that he now knew what Hell was. Frank interrupted him in his charming New Yorker way to say that Hell was driving through the Holland Tunnel for eternity.

"Hell," Warren went on, undaunted, "is flying on commuter

airlines from New Mexico to South Dakota to Colorado and back again in the dead of winter, that's what Hell is."

"I don't get it," Toots said to Frank. "How can there be *tunnels* in Holland? The whole country's at *sea* level, isn't it?"

Frank gave her a shrug and a look. I picked up another slice of pizza. I was wondering where Patricia was. I'd been trying her at home ever since I'd got back to the office.

"What I was trying to tell you on the phone," Warren said, "before I was so rudely interrupted . . ."

"Only by a lady with a knife," Frank said.

Toots picked up a slice of pizza, snapped at a string of cheese about to fall into her lap, and began chewing her way along it till she got to the wide end of the wedge.

". . . was that I'd found birth certificates for a pair of twins named Mary Jean and Mary Jo Bjorvatten. This was when I was still looking for a Mary Jones and trolling merrily along."

"I still don't see how there could be any tunnels in Holland," Toots said.

"How's your hand?" Warren asked.

"Fine, thanks."

"Parents' names were Robert and Judy, which jibed," Warren said. "Please don't eat it all while I'm still on my first slice, huh? But they didn't live in Renegade . . . did I tell you this?"

"Yes."

". . . they lived in a town named Fallon. Kids went to elementary school there, and then to high school in Hedmark, and then off to Colorado U."

"All this was in the courthouse records?" I said.

"No, no. But once I zeroed in on the names, I was able to get the rest from the locals. By the way," he said to Toots, "I'm sorry for what I said."

"What'd you say?"

"Well, maybe I *didn't* say it, maybe I only *thought* it. Either way, I'm sorry."

"What was it you thought?"

"That you were back on."

"Bite your tongue," she said.

"I know it. I'm sorry."

"And don't even *think* it again," she said.

"I won't."

"You better not. You'll jinx me."

"You two married or something?" Frank asked.

"Bite your tongue," Toots said again.

The buzzer on Frank's desk sounded. He clicked on. "Yes?"

Cynthia Huellen's voice came from the speaker.

"Patricia Demming's on six," she said. "For Matthew."

"I'll take it in my office," I said.

"Transfer it to Matthew's office," he told her.

I was already on my way out.

"Don't get lost," Frank said.

"Hi," she said.

"It's all over," I said. "You can come home."

"I *am* home," she said. "We finished down here on Friday. We lost."

"I've been trying to reach you."

"I've been wandering the countryside. Things I had to work out, Matthew."

I said nothing.

"I think I've found some answers," she said. "At last."

I waited.

"I want to see you as soon as possible," she said. "We have a lot of catching up to do."

"When did you have in mind?"

"Now?" she said.

"I'm on the way," I said.

"What's taking you so long?" she said.